The Scum Villain's Self-Saving System

REN ZHA FANPAI ZIJIU XITONG

墨香铜臭

The Scum Villain's Self-Saving System

REN ZHA FANPAI
ZIJIU XITONG

4

WRITTEN BY
Mo Xiang Tong Xiu

TRANSLATED BY
Faelicy & Lily

ILLUSTRATED BY
Xiao Tong Kong (Velinxi)

Seven Seas Entertainment

THE SCUM VILLAIN'S SELF-SAVING SYSTEM:
REN ZHA FANPAI ZIJIU XITONG VOL. 4

Published originally under the title of 《人渣反派自救系统》
(Ren Zha Fan Pai Zi Jiu Xi Tong/The Scum Villain's Self-saving System)
Author ©墨香铜臭(Mo Xiang Tong Xiu)
English edition rights under license granted by 北京晋江原创网络科技有限公司
(Beijing Jinjiang Original Network Technology Co., Ltd.)

Arranged through JS Agency Co., Ltd

Illustrations by Xiao Tong Kong (Velinxi)
Special Thanks to Kamille Areopagita

Seven Seas press and purchase enquiries can be sent to Marketing Manager Lianne Sentar at press@gomanga.com. Information regarding the distribution and purchase of digital editions is available from Digital Manager CK Russell at digital@gomanga.com.

Follow Seven Seas Entertainment online at sevenseasentertainment.com.

TRANSLATION: Faelicy, Lily
INTERIOR DESIGN: Clay Gardner
INTERIOR LAYOUT: Karis Page
PROOFREADER: Meg van Huygen
COPY EDITOR: Jade Gardner
IN-HOUSE EDITOR: M. Suyenaga
BRAND MANAGER: Lissa Pattillo
PRINT MANAGER: Rhiannon Rasmussen-Silverstein
EDITOR-IN-CHIEF: Julie Davis
ASSOCIATE PUBLISHER: Adam Arnold
PUBLISHER: Jason DeAngelis

ISBN Standard Edition: 978-1-63858-554-1
ISBN Barnes & Noble Exclusive: 978-1-68579-713-3
ISBN Special Edition: 978-1-68579-718-8
Printed in Canada
First Printing: November 2022
10 9 8 7 6 5 4 3 2 1

THE SCUM VILLAIN'S SELF-SAVING SYSTEM

CONTENTS

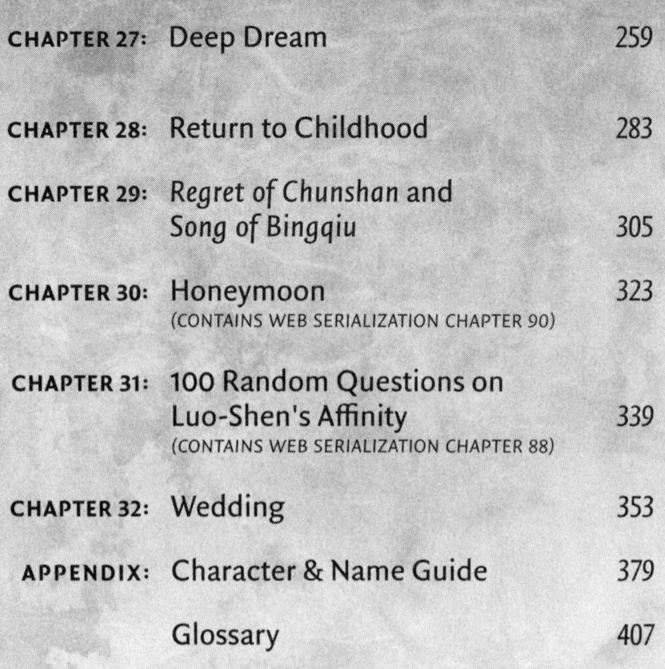

Contents based on the Pinsin Publishing print edition originally released 2017

22

Bing-mei and Bing-ge's Ultimate Showdown

THE FIRST STOP after leaving Cang Qiong Mountain (having been chased out by everyone else) was, of course, Luo Binghe's demon headquarters at the northern border of the Demon Realm.

Shen Qingqiu had stayed in the underground palace for a while previously during his "house arrest." At that time, the soil outside the perfect replica of the Bamboo House had been overturned and strewn with fertilizer, while the bamboo, both tall and short, had died and been replanted, only for the new bamboo to die as well. But when they visited that old location now, he found that Luo Binghe's demonic lackeys must have employed some mysterious technique, for the bamboo had actually flourished to form a canopy of rustling green.

The first ten or so days after their arrival, as was to be expected, Luo Binghe had clung to Shen Qingqiu such that he couldn't be swatted off no matter what Shen Qingqiu tried. But these last few days, he'd started to show some restraint and suddenly become courteous. Citing his many pressing duties—due to the unending conflict in which the northern and southern borders had lately been embroiled—the amount of time he spent orbiting Shen Qingqiu greatly decreased.

Naturally, this was an excuse. Shen Qingqiu was pretty sure that the true reason for Luo Binghe's absence was that he'd gracefully declined Luo Binghe's request to sleep in the same bed, thus yet again hurting Maiden Luo's glass heart. Goodbye!

Look, he'd only refused out of habit. If Luo Binghe had just pestered him a little more, he would have agreed! Who could have guessed that after a mere wave of his hand, Luo Binghe would rush out the door to go find a corner to sulkily grow mushrooms in...?

Shen Qingqiu suspected that over these few days, Luo Binghe had probably gone to hide in the inner hall. So, he decided he might as well head over there himself to soothe him.

All were forbidden from entering the inner hall, except for Luo Binghe. Needless to say, "all" didn't include Shen Qingqiu. Luo Binghe had said before that Shen Qingqiu was free to wander anywhere in the underground palace, and that he could even do so with his eyes shut. This order had been passed down to everyone, so obviously there were no utter fools who would dare stop him.

Shen Qingqiu boldly slipped into the hall, but to his surprise, he didn't see Luo Binghe. Thus, instead, he gave this private little space of Luo Binghe's, which had been kept tightly under wraps in the past, a deep and thorough look.

Just as he was preparing to also give the room a deep and thorough probe, the stone gates were flung open and a silhouette barreled in, stumbling and tripping.

At first, Shen Qingqiu's expression sharpened, but after taking a good look at this person, he blurted out, "Luo Binghe?"

It seemed that Luo Binghe hadn't anticipated that another person would be within the inner hall. His dazed pupils contracted, leaving Shen Qingqiu's face reflected in his jet-black irises, and what had originally been overflowing murderous intent abruptly transformed into ten thousand points of stupefaction.

But Shen Qingqiu failed to notice this. All he could see at that moment was the fresh blood drenching Luo Binghe's face and body. Luo Binghe took several steps forward, then his legs went weak. Shen Qingqiu went to meet him, just in time to catch Luo Binghe as he fell forward into his embrace. His arm automatically and easily wrapped around Luo Binghe's blood-soaked back. "What happened? Who did this?"

To think there would come a day when Luo Binghe could be beaten up to this extent, and in his own territory! All right, to be honest, this couldn't be considered a bug in the code. If the male lead of a stallion novel had turned gay, what type of plot development could qualify as a bug?

Luo Binghe's throat bobbed, and his teeth were clenched so tightly that they seemed about to break, but he still furiously spat out a word from between them: "Leave!"

Leave? Meaning...he wanted Shen Qingqiu to escape?

"All right, let's leave," Shen Qingqiu said quickly. As he spoke, he moved to support Luo Binghe's waist.

Unexpectedly, Luo Binghe's lips thinned, and he violently shoved him away.

It was the first time Shen Qingqiu had ever been shoved away by this particular person, and he froze on the spot. Did the kid want him to leave by himself first? Was he afraid he'd drag him down?

That seemed like the only reasonable explanation. So, he immediately said, "Don't fuss. This master will take you back to Cang Qiong Mountain."

The veins on Luo Binghe's forehead bulged. "No!" he snarled.

Shen Qingqiu thought he was throwing another tantrum. "How

can you fuss when you're already in such a state? We'll hide there for a bit first."

As Shen Qingqiu spoke, his palm pressed against Luo Binghe's back. Luo Binghe's face went rigid. From behind him flowed a warm, ceaseless stream of spiritual energy; wave after wave of it was sent into his body.

After a while of this, Shen Qingqiu decided he'd done about enough and withdrew his hand to unsheathe Xiu Ya. He pulled up Luo Binghe and lifted off, soaring into the skies.

Xiu Ya was from Wan Jian Peak, so regardless of the time, riding Xiu Ya through Cang Qiong Mountain's aerial defense barrier didn't trip any alarms. Therefore, Shen Qingqiu could bring another person back to Qing Jing Peak completely undetected.

It was just that while concealing this from the other peaks was possible, concealing it from his own disciples was not. When he crept into the Bamboo House dragging Luo Binghe beside him, people were already waiting inside.

Ming Fan was holding a broom, sweeping the floor while chattering away. Ning Yingying stood on her toes on a little bamboo stool with her sleeves rolled up, using a horsetail whisk to clear off the dust on the bookcase's topmost shelf.

Shen Qingqiu kicked the door open, giving them both quite a scare. After a proper second look, right away, they let out a cry of "Shi—"

Shen Qingqiu made a zipping motion before his lips, instantly stopping them from making another sound. "Don't yell," he whispered. "Do you want to summon that Bai Zhan Peak crowd too?"

If Liu Qingge knew of their return, he'd definitely come over, and if he came over, there would be no way to hide Luo Binghe while he was in this state.

One must understand that whenever there was a glimpse of Luo Binghe on Cang Qiong Mountain, the ones most raring to deliver a beatdown unto him were those terrorists from Bai Zhan Peak. Because of Shen Qingqiu, Luo Binghe dared not strike back, so every time he ended up being a sitting duck as they chased and pummeled him. Even if they couldn't beat him to death, it was incredibly troublesome.

Ning Yingying's apricot eyes went wider and she covered her mouth with both hands while automatically nodding, the image not unlike that of a little chick pecking for grain. As she gave the blood-soaked Luo Binghe another look, she removed her hands and gasped, "Shizun, what happened to A-Luo?"

Luo Binghe sent Ming Fan a sideways glance, and an expression of extreme loathing mixed with disbelief flashed in the depths of Luo Binghe's eyes. The look was bone-piercingly cold. Ming Fan couldn't help but clutch his broom tighter and shrink into himself, almost falling to the ground right there.

But Shen Qingqiu didn't catch this little exchange and helped Luo Binghe to sit on the side of the bed. "He's suffered some injuries. You two head out first. Is the medicine chest from Qian Cao Peak still where it used to be?"

"Nothing inside the Bamboo House has been moved," said Ning Yingying. "Everything's in its place. Does Shizun need his disciples to help?"

"No need. This master can do it himself."

After chasing off both disciples, Shen Qingqiu helped Luo Binghe sit up, then placed a pillow behind his back for him to lean on. Only after this did he crouch to remove Luo Binghe's shoes.

Luo Binghe remained silent, his lips pressed tightly together.

Once Shen Qingqiu lowered his head, Luo Binghe's line of sight focused on his pale nape, his gaze unfathomable as a frigid wariness circulated within him.

Shen Qingqiu assumed that he was grievously injured and lacked the strength to speak. Noticing how his forehead trickled with cold sweat, he brought over some clean water and soft towels to help him wipe his face. Then he picked out a selection of bottles from the medicine chest Mu Qingfang had issued to him before turning around, reaching out to undo Luo Binghe's clothes.

Luo Binghe abruptly caught his hand.

The force of this grip was tremendous. Shen Qingqiu frowned, but he couldn't use his other hand to smack Luo Binghe's forehead. He lowered his voice to say, "Stop being difficult. Let me see your wound."

Still Luo Binghe refused to release his hand. Shen Qingqiu's left hand was clutching an assortment of medicinal pills, and he'd long since lost his patience. At this moment, he decided to just cram them all into Luo Binghe's mouth.

Now that a few dozen medicinal pills, all of various sizes, had been stuffed into his mouth, Luo Binghe's face was dark. He finally withdrew his hand. Shen Qingqiu took this chance to tear open his clothes. After a couple of glances, he was at a bit of a loss as to where to start. In the end, he only risked using a soft towel to dab at a large bloodstain.

Threads of black qi oozed from curling flesh. It didn't look like a regular wound; otherwise, with Luo Binghe's regeneration abilities, it would have flawlessly healed long ago. Shen Qingqiu carefully cleaned it for him while saying, "Where have you been hiding these past few days? Who did you fight who could leave you like this?"

From beginning to end, Luo Binghe remained silent. Once Shen Qingqiu finished wiping his chest, he followed Mu Qingfang's teachings and took Luo Binghe's wrist to examine his pulse. If the situation really was bad, he'd call Mu Qingfang over first and figure out the rest later.

As he studied Luo Binghe's pulse, Shen Qingqiu gave his hand and chest another couple of glances.

A strange uneasiness crept over his heart. He had a vague feeling that something was wrong. As if...something was missing.

But when he looked at Luo Binghe's paling lips and cold eyes, Shen Qingqiu couldn't spare it too much thought. He sat on the edge of the bed and continued to send spiritual energy into him.

As that energy slowly flowed into Luo Binghe's meridians, Shen Qingqiu felt his stiff muscles gradually relax. He quietly sighed with relief, then reached out, intending to pull Luo Binghe into his arms.

Once again, Luo Binghe struggled free.

Now that Shen Qingqiu had been shoved away a second time, he tossed aside the towel in his right hand and said helplessly, "What's wrong with you now?"

Luo Binghe's eyes overflowed with a wary guardedness.

Shen Qingqiu internally rolled his eyes. "We've already reached this point, and you're still throwing a tantrum?" he chided him. "The simple fact that I wouldn't sleep with you two days ago was enough to make you this angry for this long?"

At these words, the corner of Luo Binghe's mouth seemed to twitch.

Upset, Shen Qingqiu changed the direction of his outstretched hand to touch Luo Binghe's forehead instead. "It's a bit hot," he muttered. "Do you...feel dizzy?"

Suddenly, Ning Yingying's voice drifted in from outside. "Liu-shishu, you can't go in—it's a bad time for Shizun right now!"

The usual Ning Yingying was soft-spoken, her manner coquettish, sometimes to the point that she was impossible to understand if you weren't right next to her. So if she was acting so out of character as to yell, she was obviously sending a message to Shen Qingqiu where he was inside. He leapt headlong off the bed. Right as he closed the curtains behind him, the Bamboo House's door slammed open with a thud.

Liu Qingge burst into the room, sword on his back. Shen Qingqiu had one arm behind his own back as he turned around, eyebrow raised. "I trust Liu-shidi has been well."

Liu Qingge opened fire right away. "Cang Qiong Mountain has a rule forbidding entrance to Luo Binghe."

"How come I've never heard of this rule?"

"It's new."

Ming Fan stretched out his head to interject. "That's right, Shizun. Cang Qiong Mountain really does have that rule now. It's just that Zhangmen-shibo hasn't yet engraved it upon the rule slab. Everyone knows—"

"You shut up!" Shen Qingqiu scolded him. *Don't think I don't know that you're the one who called Liu Qingge here, you rascal!*

That kid had admired Bai Zan Peak for forever. Anytime something slightly noteworthy happened, he reported it to Liu Qingge; he'd practically become their personal spy on Qing Jing Peak.

Though one could say that the widespread admiration of Bai Zhan Peak among the youths was understandable, this kind of little maneuver—even going so far as to secretly tattle—was simply shameful!

I'll teach you a lesson later!

Having been scolded, Ming Fan wilted and withdrew in dismay. Ning Yingying had been apprehensively standing at the door, but needing to vent her anger, she viciously stomped on his foot, all while muttering that he'd ruined things.

The moment the two of them retreated, Liu Qingge threw open the bed curtain.

Luo Binghe was half sitting on the bed, his eyes flashing with a savage light, not unlike a young, wounded leopard. His murderous intent roiled as he glared at Liu Qingge, his gaze like unto both icy knives and poisonous flames. A spiritual blast was clasped within his hand, ready to fire at any moment.

Shen Qingqiu rushed to put himself between them, bracing one leg on the bed board as he shielded Luo Binghe behind him. "Shidi, stop this."

Liu Qingge was surprised. "He's injured?"

Shen Qingqiu wanted dearly to bow to him. He sighed. "If he wasn't injured, I wouldn't have brought him back. Just pretend you didn't see anything, Liu-shidi. Don't chase him off."

"If he's injured, why not remain in the Demon Realm?"

It was because he'd remained in the Demon Realm that he'd gotten injured!

"Something happened..."

"Did those demonic monsters stage a revolt?"

"Uh." Shen Qingqiu sent Luo Binghe a brief sideways glance. He didn't actually know if this was the outcome of demonic internal affairs or whether it was appropriate to say if so, and thus he gave a vague answer: "They might have."

"He should clean up his own mess. Cang Qiong Mountain will always be here to support you, but not him."

Luo Binghe suddenly let out a cold laugh. This aggravated the wounds on his chest, and he gritted his teeth, silently braving the pain.

Watching him endure and suffer, a sudden rush of courage bloomed within Shen Qingqiu and he said sternly, "Liu-shidi, don't forget that this is Qing Jing Peak."

Whether Qing Jing Peak gave someone safe harbor was, it went without saying, a decision to be made by the Qing Jing Peak Lord!

Liu Qingge's expression became cold with anger and disappointment. "Then continue protecting him!"

After throwing down these words, he stomped out the door. It hadn't been two seconds before he came stomping back, and he threw something into Shen Qingqiu's arms.

Shen Qingqiu caught it and looked: it was that fan of his, again.

The fan that had fallen out of his grasp sometime during that chaotic battle on the Luo River. Every time, it was Liu Qingge who picked it up. It seemed like his fate and the fan's were quite intertwined. *Maybe I should just straight-up give it to him as a present!*

He coughed dryly, then said genially, "I'm forever troubling Liu-shidi."

Liu Qingge left with a flick of his sleeves.

Luo Binghe's voice rang out from behind Shen Qingqiu, the sound a little raspy: "Liu Qingge?"

It was said as a genuine, doubt-filled inquiry.

"Don't worry about him," said Shen Qingqiu. "He's just like this, all bark and no bite. After barking, he leaves."

Luo Binghe narrowed his eyes, his face gradually taking on a thoughtful expression.

Shen Qingqiu placed the fan on the table. "Have no fear," he consoled him. "Since this master has spoken his piece, he won't come bothering you for some time. If the Bai Zhan Peak disciples come to gang up on you again, you can hit back. As long as you don't kill them, it'll be fine; there's no need to accommodate them. This would also save Qing Jing Peak some face."

The more Luo Binghe listened, the odder the expression in his eyes became. As if testing the waters, he said the word: "Shizun?"

"Mm?" Shen Qingqiu cocked his head. Both his tone and expression brimmed with one hundred and twenty percent warm indulgence—a promise to grant whatever request Luo Binghe might have.

Luo Binghe withdrew his gaze, the corner of his mouth twitching. "Nothing. I just wanted to try...saying it."

No matter the situation, this child would unfailingly call out to him, "Shizun, Shizun"; none of this was news to Shen Qingqiu. He stroked the back of Luo Binghe's head. "Why don't you sleep? Whatever is happening over there with the demons can be left until you've finished recovering."

Luo Binghe gave him an almost imperceptible nod.

At this, Shen Qingqiu bent down and removed the pillow at his back, then helped him lie down. Before Luo Binghe met the bed, Shen Qingqiu carefully unfastened his hair tie, in case his skull pressed on it in his sleep and he hurt his head.

Only after doing this did Shen Qingqiu blow out the lamps, remove his own outer robes with a rustle, and get into bed as well. He held Luo Binghe and said, "Sleep. This master will regulate your breathing."

Now he'd both hugged and slept with Luo Binghe; that ought to dispel that little tantrum from before, right?

Shen Qingqiu closed his eyes, adjusting his spiritual circulation to its calmest possible state, as placid as evening dew, and used it to gently flush Luo Binghe's meridians.

In the darkness, a pair of clear, glittering eyes flashed with cold light. Even after a long time, they did not close but remained fixed on the peacefully sleeping Shen Qingqiu.

Shen Qingqiu's long hair lay draped over his arm and between his fingers. Luo Binghe took hold of one of those black locks, his grip slowly clenching, and soundlessly mouthed a name over and over again.

Shen Qingqiu.

Shen Qingqiu.

A dark and sinister curve tugged his lips upward.

The silent smile on "Luo Binghe's" face grew wider and wider.

As if he'd discovered some amusing plaything, his eyes began to shine with an excitement, one that seemed to hold the slightest hint of cruelty.

That night, Shen Qingqiu's dreams were both tortuous and unending.

When the dawn of the second day came, the first to open his eyes was Luo Binghe.

Some color had returned to his snow-pale face, and his complexion was much improved over how it had been the previous night. On the contrary, the one who'd been bursting with energy the evening prior before they retired, who'd held Luo Binghe all the way until they woke, was now dazed, drowsy, and seemed a bit fatigued.

Shen Qingqiu had in fact passed an entire night's worth of spiritual energy into Luo Binghe, not stopping even after he'd dozed off.

Luo Binghe slowly fluttered his eyelashes. For a while, he gazed at Shen Qingqiu with a complicated expression, then reached out to move Shen Qingqiu's arms.

The moment Shen Qingqiu was moved, he startled up, jolted even further awake. Luo Binghe took this chance to sit up and leave the bed.

Shen Qingqiu was profoundly bewildered. Usually, it was impossible to dislodge Luo Binghe even when he kicked, yet this morning, Luo Binghe had voluntarily detached himself. He pinched the bridge of his nose and wrinkled his brow. "What are you doing up so early? Making breakfast? You don't have to today."

Then he saw that Luo Binghe was wearing only a thin inner robe, the collar left undone. His vast, crisscrossing wounds had already closed, leaving nothing more than faint marks. They would probably be done healing by the end of the day. However, this left almost half his chest wholly exposed to the elements. That outer robe from the night prior could no longer be worn, so Shen Qingqiu reminded him, "Your old clothes are still in the side room. Yingying and the others haven't touched them."

Luo Binghe slipped around and behind the screen, heading to the side room.

A spotless little world of its own met his eyes: there was a furniture set constructed from green bamboo, complete with a table, chair, bed, and cabinet. At the head of the bed there was even a small stand, upon which lay neatly shelved scrolls and all manner of brushes, the latter arranged according to length. Upon opening the cabinet doors, he found folded white robes, all stowed away in a tidy fashion. Above them there even hung high-quality jade accessories in various styles.

In the time Luo Binghe was in the side room, Shen Qingqiu slowly rose from the bed. He scanned for where he'd left his shoes while rubbing his temples.

What a terrible fucking sleep he'd had. He was about to lose it! It'd been dream after dream! Dream after dream after dream after dream! Even his shameful dark memory of fighting the Skinner Demon in Shuang Hu City had been dredged up! And even dreams within dreams!

The Immortal Alliance Conference, Jin Lan City, Hua Yue City, the Holy Mausoleum...he'd gone through everything like a merry-go-round, including the times he'd been beaten, the times he'd coughed up blood, the times his body had sprouted all over with foliage...

Having had so many dreams crammed into his head in one night, it was about to explode. It was abso-fucking-lutely because he'd passed all that spiritual energy into Luo Binghe while sleeping. Whenever Luo Binghe's psyche was unstable, anyone who slept near him would suffer.

At that moment, Luo Binghe finished dressing and emerged from the side room with a turn. Shen Qingqiu had yet to find his shoes, but he stopped looking. Instead, he waved at Luo Binghe to beckon him over to the bed, then pulled him down.

However, Luo Binghe failed to be pulled. He raised an eyebrow. "What are you doing?"

Shen Qingqiu felt around beneath the pillow and pulled out a hair tie alongside a wooden brush. "What do you think?"

Only then did Luo Binghe obediently sit down in front of him while glancing all around the Bamboo House.

As Shen Qingqiu brushed his hair, he asked on a whim, "What are you looking at?"

Luo Binghe's gaze remained sharp and cold, but his voice warmed and softened. "These past few years, every time I returned to Qing Jing Peak, it was in a rush. I never could give it a proper look."

Shen Qingqiu held the hair tie between his teeth and impishly braided him a tiny plait in secret. "Then these days, you can look your fill. I'll pay Bai Zhan Peak a visit later and get Liu Qingge to properly discipline the lot of them. There's absolutely no rationale to justify Qing Jing Peak disciples being chased around by Bai Zhan Peak's."

Luo Binghe stilled for a while. Then he slowly turned his head and smiled at him before saying sweetly, "Shizun?"

"Mm?"

"Shizun."

"Mm."

It was as if this was Luo Binghe's very first time using such a novel term of address; he repeated it again and again without pause. Every time he did, he received an answer, and he grew increasingly addicted to it until Shen Qingqiu couldn't take it anymore. He picked up his fan and swatted the back of Luo Binghe's head. "Enough with the 'Shizun.' Once is sufficient. Say what you mean properly."

Now that he'd been struck on the back of his head, Luo Binghe's expression darkened, but he swiftly rectified it and smiled ambiguously. His gaze swept to the side. "Did Shizun sleep well last night?"

Could I sleep well while holding you? Shen Qingqiu thought. But he said mildly, "I dreamed of a number of old affairs, that's all."

"Then next time, should I hold Shizun while we sleep instead?"

Of course he could say such words so casually. Having accomplished his task, Shen Qingqiu patted his head and pushed him off the bed. "Go, go. Go, go."

Then Shen Qingqiu did as he'd promised and paid Bai Zhan Peak a visit.

Heading over there was familiar and easy; he didn't even need to deliver a visitor's notice. After swallowing two mouthfuls of the light congee Ming Fan sent him, he adjusted his clothes and sauntered off. He left Luo Binghe behind in the Bamboo House, admonishing him to "be good and wait until this master comes back"—

But as if Luo Binghe would be willing to just "be good and wait."

Luo Binghe had just opened the door when he saw a delicate, orange-colored figure bound toward him. He took a good look, then said, full of smiles, "Yingying."

Unexpectedly, Ning Yingying shuddered and paled in shock. "What's wrong with you, A-Luo?! Did you hit your head?! Why did you address me like that?! What the hell is with this 'Yingying'—that's terrifying!"

Luo Binghe fell silent.

Ning Yingying's expression of pure horror had yet to fade. "Why didn't you call me Ning-shijie?!"

A pause. "Ning-shijie."

That "shijie" was uttered with a fair amount of internally gnashed teeth.

Ning-shijie sighed in relief and patted her chest as she chided him. "Now that's better. Changing terms of address like that out of the blue—it didn't sound like you at all. Shizun may dote on you, but you must always respect seniority. That way we dishonor neither our status as Qing Jing Peak's disciples nor Shizun's teachings."

Upon hearing this, veins bulged in Luo Binghe's forehead and he lost his patience. "I have something to ask you."

Understanding shortly dawned on Ning Yingying's face. With a wave, she solemnly placed a whisk and broom into Luo Binghe's hands. "Shijie understands. Here."

Silence.

"Don't take offense, A-Luo," Ning Yingying said sincerely. "You invariably want to clean Shizun's Bamboo House by yourself, I know that. But the two of you were gone for a long time, so Da-shixiong and I could only get started on it ourselves. However, since you've returned, I'll leave it to you. Shijie won't compete with you for chores. When it comes to this, Shijie still understands."

Like fuck you do!

Luo Binghe turned and left for Xian Shu Peak.

Xian Shu Peak's disciples had always welcomed him very warmly—no matter where he went, it was the same.

In the past, Shen Qingqiu had given Luo Binghe quite a few miscellaneous errands. Thus, one could often have found him on Xian Shu Peak. From time to time he'd gone there to deliver a letter, distribute a notice, invite someone over, or borrow something.

When male disciples from other peaks came, they would at least sneak a couple of peeps, peering around and around until they ended up looking inside the maidens' quarters or bathhouse. Naturally, they'd be r-【beep–】-ed to death by the maidens' swords long before they made it to the bathhouse. Only Luo Binghe had treated the peak's disciples with respect and consciously maintained a strict distance every time he came; his reputation at Xian Shu Peak was correspondingly high. Therefore, everyone on Xian Shu Peak had given him tacit permission to enter the inner halls to wait.

With her face veiled, Liu Mingyan politely bowed in greeting. "Luo-shixiong." Luo Binghe had yet to speak when she nodded at him and continued, "Did Luo-shixiong come to invite Shizun on Shen-shibo's orders? Please wait here for a while; I will first make arrangements for my Taoist friends from Tian Yi Temple, then I will return."

The three Taoist friends she spoke of were those three beautiful nuns.

Their lovely, delicate figures were enveloped in aquamarine Taoist robes as they orbited her. Six liquid eyes stared at Luo Binghe as they spent a moment whispering into each other's ears, then spent another moment stamping their feet coquettishly, their cheeks flushed red. They were like three radiant blue blooms circled around a slender lotus, playful and giggling, before they all headed out as a group.

As promised, Luo Binghe waited patiently for Liu Mingyan to return.

After standing there for only a short while, he realized that the corner of a small book was peeking out from amidst the mess of scrolls upon her desk. It was obvious that it had been shoved beneath them in a hurry.

So, Liu Mingyan also had things she wanted to hide.

He casually pulled out the booklet she'd hidden and gave it a rough glance over. Finding the cover gaudy, with each of the title's three words written in a more ridiculous cursive than the last, he wrinkled his brow. He smiled at the signature of "Sleeping Willow Flower" and flipped it open.

And was struck silent.

When Shen Qingqiu returned from Bai Zhan Peak after drinking tea and having a heart-to-heart, Luo Binghe was waiting for him within the Bamboo House. The moment he entered, he felt a gaze shoot over him, boiling and burning.

Shen Qingqiu made an internal face. *Well, now I'm a bit afraid to close the door. What's going on?!*

Atop the bed, Luo Binghe reclined on his side and smiled. "What's wrong? Why won't Shizun come here?"

While it was said in that same soft tone, touched by a little bit of hurt, his eyes told a different story. He was looking Shen Qingqiu up and down as if he'd never seen him before; it was like he was trying to scrape off a layer of Shen Qingqiu's skin with his eyes.

Shen Qingqiu's appearance was stellar: his shoulders were neither too broad nor too bulky, while his waist was thin and his legs long. Enveloped in Qing Jing Peak's many-layered teal uniform, he was immaculate and slender, with a great deal of graceful beauty.

Yes... It was his graceful beauty.

Shen Qingqiu pushed the door shut behind him. He had yet to get within five steps of Luo Binghe when he was yanked forward, and he fell into Luo Binghe's embrace as those arms tightened around his waist.

Luo Binghe's fingers trailed down his side, occasionally squeezing and kneading.

Hand. Hand. Thank you—hand! Your hand!

When Shen Qingqiu went to grab Luo Binghe's paw in a back-handed grip, he twisted. Somehow Shen Qingqiu found himself pressed down on top of Luo Binghe's thigh with his legs apart, trapped in place. In the next moment, Luo Binghe caressed his nape before pulling him down, and his lips were captured again.

He dared not move. Fuck, in this position, he really didn't dare move!

Though they'd engaged in activities far surpassing this a while back, the previous time had been a special situation—plus there'd been an impending disaster, so there had been no time to worry about shyness or reservations. And while they'd been fairly intimate during their near half month in the Demon Realm, for some reason, whether out of bashfulness or something else, Luo Binghe had never done anything too forward.

Yet at this time, and at this location, the situation was completely different. The sun hadn't even set yet. Was sex in broad daylight really okay?! Had he sheltered this child so much it'd broken him?

Shen Qingqiu was highly unaccustomed to being so close to someone while wide awake, but Luo Binghe was a porcelain doll who shattered at the slightest touch, and he would never survive another careless drop. So, Shen Qingqiu reciprocated Luo Binghe's actions and opened his mouth a little.

Speaking of, something was strange. Shen Qingqiu had been in this body for ages now, and it had always felt like so: cold and unfeeling from head to toe, no matter where he was touched. Nothing tickled him regardless of where he was poked, and he seemed to have no sensitive spots. But as Luo Binghe kneaded him, the pressure gentle yet varied, he felt a nigh unbearable prickling itch.

Why is he so proficient? Why?! Even though he's a virgin! Why?! An instant expert after only one time? Why?! How is this fair? I'm going to sue! I'm going to yell! Why?!

Luo Binghe nibbled on Shen Qingqiu's lip while his tongue probed and prodded within Shen Qingqiu's mouth; having difficulties keeping up with the pace, Shen Qingqiu began to pant faintly.

However, whenever he moved his head away even a little, Luo Binghe pulled him back and kissed him even more deeply.

Unable to catch his breath, his eyes squeezed shut in a frown, Shen Qingqiu was naturally unable to see the malice flashing within Luo Binghe's gaze.

As his perch on Luo Binghe's thigh was unsteady, he involuntarily reached out and grabbed at Luo Binghe's collar. But he missed the cloth, instead landing on the skin of Luo Binghe's chest.

The smooth, unblemished skin of his chest.

In that moment, Shen Qingqiu's mind went as blank and white as snow.

Then his palm suddenly exerted great force, and he fired a spiritual blast at "Luo Binghe's" heart.

"Luo Binghe" took this powerful surge of spiritual energy head-on, but he remained utterly unaffected. With a cold laugh, he encircled Shen Qingqiu's right wrist with one hand while continuing to press down on his nape with the other. Then he skillfully flipped them over, rolling them onto the bed together. Looking down at Shen Qingqiu from overhead, he smiled brightly. "What's wrong, Shizun? Don't you love me very much? So why aren't you willing to give in to me?"

Go fuck yourself!

"Beat it!" spat Shen Qingqiu.

"Luo Binghe's" lips and teeth went from gentle worrying to vicious biting, instantly filling Shen Qingqiu's mouth with the taste of blood. Shen Qingqiu formed a seal with his left hand, summoning Xiu Ya from where it lay on the table. When "Luo Binghe's" movements slightly slowed, Shen Qingqiu took the chance to kick upward and plant his foot against the impostor's chest.

But he hadn't managed to get all the way up when something clamped down on his ankle. He looked back to see "Luo Binghe's" hand grasped there, at which point it abruptly yanked, dragging Shen Qingqiu back beneath him a second time. Right after, he forced Shen Qingqiu to straighten, then with a hand still clasped around Shen Qingqiu's calf, folding Shen Qingqiu's leg against his chest with a downward press.

He accomplished this entire set of movements in a single breath.

"Where is he?!" yelled Shen Qingqiu.

"Luo Binghe" cocked his head. "Who are you asking about? If it's me, aren't I right here?"

Now able to catch his breath, Shen Qingqiu asked, "How did you end up here?"

"Luo Binghe" toyed with his hair. "For my part, I'm more curious as to how Shizun found me out."

Motherfucker. There were sword scars on both Luo Binghe's palm and chest—once given to him by Shen Qingqiu himself!

"Do you really want to find out?" asked Shen Qingqiu.

"Luo Binghe" lowered his body further and said, his voice chilly yet colored by a hint of provocation, "It's fine if you don't want to say. We have plenty of time—enough for me to slowly 'find out.'"

"Then why not take a look behind you?"

The curve on "Luo Binghe's" lips froze. Startled, he abruptly swiveled his head back, guard raised.

A face exactly like his, partly illuminated and partly in shadow, rushed forward. That face was like snow, like frost, frigid down to the core, yet its eyes burned like ghost fire, the color a searing, bloody crimson.

Within the Bamboo House were two identical people with the same exact face. Other than one being dressed in white, the other in black, there was not a single discernible difference between them.

At the black-robed Luo Binghe's waist hung a sword sealed tightly within layers upon layers of paper talismans.

To think that the once-kingly Xin Mo, overflowing with power and tyrannical energy, would end up bound in such a rough and unseemly manner, unable to release a single wisp of demonic energy.

Luo Binghe's voice came in a hoarse but forceful whisper: "Unhand him!"

A spiritual blast accompanied this quiet, enraged snarl.

The white-robed "Luo Binghe" locked firmly between Shen Qingqiu's legs promptly and decisively returned it. The two attacks met in midair with a harsh sound, scattering dust and smoke throughout the room.

"Luo Binghe" wore an expression of incredible disappointment. "You couldn't have returned a little earlier or a little later?" he asked contemptuously. "You just *had* to choose a time like this—"

He had yet to finish speaking when Shen Qingqiu curled his pointer and middle finger. Xiu Ya's hilt trembled slightly where the sword had stabbed into the wall, then flew into his hand. His grip clenched into a fist, and he immediately swung his arm, chopping downward.

Sandwiched between two attacks, "Luo Binghe" finally couldn't maintain that provocative posture any longer. He flipped off the bed, not forgetting to give Shen Qingqiu's waist another squeeze before leaving, then gracefully landed at the other end of the Bamboo House. "Shizun is so merciless with his attacks," he said, adopting a sad expression. "Doesn't his heart hurt for his disciple even a little?"

Get the fuck out! Who's your shizun?!

This guy was the male lead of the Zhongdian stallion novel *Proud Immortal Demon Way*—the original flavor Luo Binghe! Previously, the System's punishment protocol had set him loose, this godly man who was admired by Zhongdian readers everywhere. On those forums, anyone who brought him up reverently uttered the same name: Bing-ge!

Shen Qingqiu could never have anticipated that this guy would show up not only within the punishment protocol, but within the standard world as a real, solid entity. All this given, it seemed like the System's so-called punishment hadn't just been setting a character simulation loose—it had directly pulled Bing-ge over from a parallel universe, one that belonged to the original novel.

Ever since the day before, Shen Qingqiu had nursed the vague feeling that something was off, but Maiden Luo had always been the type to kick up a fuss or act spoiled at the drop of a hat. Plus, because he'd been anxious and concerned, Shen Qingqiu had only paid attention to treating his injuries and failed to give Luo Binghe's behavior careful thought.

On the real Luo Binghe's palm and chest were sword scars that had been left by Shen Qingqiu himself. That child treasured even that kind of thing, and he refused to heal them, instead preserving them on his body. How, therefore, could Shen Qingqiu ever get to touch "smooth, unblemished skin"?

In the end, he and Luo Binghe were too unfamiliar with each other's bodies That was why it had taken him so long to figure out what was wrong here. A thousand fortunes that he'd reined it in right at the edge of the cliff. So close, so close—he'd almost lost all integrity (cough) there.

At this point, that "Leave!" Luo Binghe had directed at him the day before on their first encounter within the underground palace became much easier to understand. The word hadn't meant, "Hurry and run, I don't want to drag you down," but rather, "Get the fuck away from me, you scumbag piece of shit!"

The sword-carrying, black-robed Luo Binghe threw himself forward and said in a rush, "Shizun, did that bastard do anything to you?"

Uh, isn't calling him a bastard basically calling yourself one?

It was only a roast for the sake of roasting. Shen Qingqiu looked at Luo Binghe's face, at its brimming urgency as he clung to him, unwilling to let go, and felt deeply relieved. Now *this* was how Luo Binghe should be.

Shen Qingqiu cleared his throat, confirming that his clothes were neither torn nor crooked and that his appearance was all in place, before saying, "This master is fine."

He suddenly recalled how, the day before, the other Luo Binghe's body had been covered in wounds, his skin split and bleeding. He feared that this one might not have been left unscathed either and quickly asked, "What about you? Are you injured?"

Luo Binghe nodded. "It's all healed already."

Shen Qingqiu grabbed his wrist and flipped it over. Upon his palm was a white scar that could be called neither faint nor clear; Shen Qingqiu's heart stirred at the sight. "What happened, exactly? Where have you been these last two days? Why is he here?"

Luo Binghe shook his head. "This disciple doesn't know. The day before yesterday, I'd secluded myself within the underground palace's inner halls when Xin Mo's fragments unexpectedly glowed purple. Then this...person appeared, and in his hand was another

Xin Mo. I exchanged blows with him, but in a moment of carelessness, I entered one of Xin Mo's rifts, which sealed closed behind me. I only had enough time to swipe the sword from him. When I returned, I couldn't find Shizun, so I could only head to Cang Qiong Mountain."

So for these past two days, Luo Binghe had been in *Proud Immortal Demon Way*'s original world? And Xin Mo's space-severing slash were already at that heaven-defying level of OP? Its slashes could slice apart even the space between parallel universes...

That was no longer something you could explain away by calling it a mere bug!

And now a homegrown Green JJ gay had found himself in one of Zhongdian's uncountable harems of beauties. The child must have been frightened out of his wits. Shen Qingqiu couldn't help the tender fondness (ahem) that welled up within his heart.

But he suddenly heard a voice say coldly, "Excuse me. I'm still here. Could you not leave me hanging?"

The original Luo Binghe was used to forever being at the center of everyone's attention. Watching this duo jump on each other at first sight, thoroughly ignoring his existence and being all cloying and disgusting, filled him with an unspeakable irritation. With a subtle burst of force from his foot, he soundlessly smashed several of the stones beneath it into a fine powder.

Luo Binghe shielded Shen Qingqiu behind him, his tone ominous. "What were you doing just now?"

"Just playing around," the other Luo Binghe said mildly.

Shen Qingqiu was stunned silent. *Playing around with who? Playing around with* me*? Bing-ge, you...you'd accept all comers?! Welcoming both men and women! Is this something like "both meat and fish are fine—I'm not picky, I'll eat whatever I'm given"?*

Or was it because this Luo Binghe had failed to collect even a single member of the original harem, leaving the other Luo Binghe deprived until he couldn't take it any longer?

Bing-ge humphed. "Who made you so useless?" he asked disdainfully. "To think you have not a single woman."

His standard for "uselessness" was practically a drunkard's. But Luo Binghe's focus wasn't on this at all. In his fury, scarlet blood seemed about to drip from his eyes, and he said sharply, "You dare to humiliate Shizun like this..."

The other Luo Binghe's eyes also flooded with crimson as he met that gaze and sneered. "How was I humiliating him? Look at that worthless appearance of yours! To think you'd be so unsightly when you're also 'Luo Binghe.' You even spend all day messing around with Shen Qingqiu, that depraved degenerate—"

He had yet to finish his sentence when Luo Binghe exploded.

Dark qi suffused the interior of the Bamboo House, to the point that one couldn't have seen their hand in front of their face. Neither protagonist was willing to yield an inch—but then a ray of white light lanced in from above. It appeared that while throwing spiritual blasts around haphazardly, the poor rafters in the Bamboo House's ceiling had suffered undue collateral damage: a large hole had been blown open.

Luo Binghe raised his head and gazed upward, his face darker than even the demonic energy he'd been firing off.

Shen Qingqiu had approximately the same expression. *Motherfucker, how are we supposed to explain when An Ding Peak comes to make repairs?*

Luo Binghe was unwilling to destroy the Bamboo House; he jumped out the door and yelled, "Come out here!"

The original flavor humphed. "Perfect—I wasn't able to let loose inside that run-down little house!"

The two silhouettes, one black and one white, vanished in an instant. Meanwhile, Shen Qingqiu pondered whether calling Bai Zhan Peak would result in them trying to kill both Luo Binghes indiscriminately.

At this moment, Ming Fan and Ning Yingying rushed in with a group of disciples behind them. By Shen Qingqiu's guess, they'd been doing their evening reading when they heard the strange noises and hurried over. Some of them were carrying guqin while others held books.

"Halt!" said Shen Qingqiu.

The entire group of disciples quickly stood at attention.

Ming Fan opened his mouth to ask, "Shizun, what's going on here—"

"Line up," Shen Qingqiu interrupted.

The Qing Jing Peak disciples lined up promptly, as if by reflex.

"Go down and run laps around Qing Jing Peak. Thirty of them!"

If Shen Qingqiu tried to shoo them away after letting them know what was going on, these kids would unquestionably refuse—they'd even insist on staying to help (read: to make a mess). Better, then, to just shoo them off before it reached that point.

As he had issued such a direct command, the disciples all looked at one another. If their shizun wanted them to run, they would run. A group of teal-robed boys and girls ran down Qing Jing Peak in a trailing conga line, one after another.

Now that he'd directed them away, Shen Qingqiu let out a sigh of relief. Then he turned around, taking off toward the bamboo forests at the back of the mountain.

While the original flavor Luo Binghe had complete control over Xin Mo, the Luo Binghe who Shen Qingqiu had raised—whether due to an unstable psyche or a surplus of distracting thoughts—was prone to suffering its recoil and psychic assaults. Therefore, the latter was probably leery of carelessly handling Xin Mo, meaning his hands were somewhat tied. It was likely for this exact reason that he'd taken the initiative to bind and seal the blade with paper talismans. Holding a golden finger while being too afraid to use it was like holding a golden bowl but being unable to ask for rice.

With the sword still in its sheath, they seemed to have engaged in a brawl. But this brawl was packing way too much destructive power!

Dozens of yawning ditches had already been gouged into the ground. Bamboo toppled and sent fallen leaves scattering, while roosting birds soared into the sky with frightened cries. If this continued, the "clear and tranquil" Qing Jing Peak was going to end up shaved into a "bald-headed" Tu Ding Peak. The second he spied a gap between the two, Shen Qingqiu prompted Xiu Ya to lunge at the original flavor with a shriek.

Silvery light sparked back and forth as the blade streaked toward narrowed eyes. The other Luo Binghe abruptly moved his head and flicked the sword away, then asked with head still cocked, "We're clearly the same person, so why does Shizun help him but hurt me?"

Like fuck you're the same person!

The Luo Binghe he'd raised was eccentric Maiden Luo, a.k.a. Bing-*mei*, whose story, following Shen Qingqiu's plot interference, had by the System's grace been reshuffled onto the Green JJ's danmei page. He wasn't a Zhongdian stallion novel male lead like this guy, with his "cool badassery" oozing out of every pore and his head full of vulgar thoughts, who'd farmed and leveled-up on low-IQ villains and side characters.

No, he's nothing like you at all!

Shen Qingqiu kept his mouth shut and didn't answer. He met gazes with Luo Binghe, and without needing any further words, they attacked the original as one.

From the beginning, there hadn't been much difference in power between the two Luo Binghes—the original's injuries had mostly been due to Luo Binghe hacking at him. With the addition of Shen Qingqiu, the balance slowly tipped.

Amidst sword glares as snow-white and airy as soaring dragons, spiritual energy and black qi roiled and intertwined, working seamlessly in concert. The original Luo Binghe narrowly avoided several waves of attacks and squinted a little. He seemed angry, but not enough to express his emotions further, only pursing his mouth.

Suddenly, he said, "With technique that bad, what's so good about him anyway?"

When this line came out of nowhere, Shen Qingqiu's hand trembled a little. But he forced it down and continued attacking.

Unfortunately, Bing-ge refused to restrain himself. "Shizun, you've already experienced my prowess. Since we're the same person, why not come with me? I'll definitely give you more pleasure than he could."

"Shut up!" snapped Shen Qingqiu.

"Already experienced?" muttered Luo Binghe.

"Concentrate on the fight," said Shen Qingqiu.

"What does he mean by 'already experienced'? What does he mean by 'more pleasure than he could'?"

"Or perhaps," the original said ambiguously, "Shizun actually likes it when it hurts? Even if that's the case, this disciple guarantees that he could satisfy you."

In that instant, Luo Binghe's face twisted. In what seemed an unconscious action, he placed his hand on Xin Mo.

"Don't draw it!" Shen Qingqiu urgently yelled.

Only then did Luo Binghe come back to himself. He removed his hand right away, but the crimson of his eyes became even more intense, and his breathing quickened as well. He gritted his teeth and threw himself forward, taking the initiative to shift to close-quarters combat.

In a direct, brute-force confrontation, as their power levels and techniques were identical, the consequences they suffered were twinned as well. Shen Qingqiu heard a muffled crack.

One Luo Binghe had broken his left arm, the other his right, and both limbs now dangled limply. Their reactions were also the same: with their arms broken, they kicked. And so another cracking noise sounded. This time it was their legs.

Shen Qingqiu couldn't take it anymore. "Enough!"

If they went on fighting like this—did they intend to perish together?!

The original's expression suddenly gentled as he looked at Shen Qingqiu. "Shizun, do you blame me for making things too painful last time?"

Luo Binghe went wide-eyed. "Shizun, you've met him before?"

If an encounter in the System counted as a meeting, then that was a yes. Not wanting to give a half-hearted answer, Shen Qingqiu said, "It was only a chance meeting."

Bing-ge really knew how to push someone's buttons. "It was my fault last time," he said mournfully. "This disciple admits his

wrongdoings, but just now, didn't Shizun find my touch most pleasurable? We're both your disciples, so how can you bear to treat me like this?"

Fake. You faker. You're still faking! As expected of Bing-ge, that two-faced backstabber, with his honeyed tongue and a belly full of knives, who could smile and agree with you while stabbing you a thousand times in his heart!

The male leads in Zhongdian's grimdark works were truly sinister. By taking this tack, he was obviously trying to disrupt Luo Binghe's focus.

Of course Shen Qingqiu couldn't let him succeed. He snapped back, his words unambiguous and full of righteousness, "It wasn't pleasurable in the slightest!"

The second after he spat these words, a powerful, numbing wave of heat surged within his belly. It was impossible to ignore and impossible to suppress—as if thousands of ants were sluggishly crawling about inside his body.

The corner of "Luo Binghe's" lips twitched upward as he said, cheerful and ominous, "You still insist on lying about your feelings?"

Heavenly demon blood. How could he forget? As long as it was *a* Luo Binghe, he could control the blood mites within Shen Qingqiu's body!

Two Luo Binghes openly competed with each other: one agitating the blood mites, the other suppressing them, and the result was that numbing weakness and prickling heat ebbed and flowed through Shen Qingqiu, coming in waves as they rapidly spread from his abdomen to his entire body, even to his fingertips. Shen Qingqiu gulped a couple of painful breaths; his vision blurred, and the hand holding his sword began to tremble.

The moment Luo Binghe was distracted, the Xin Mo at his waist was snatched away.

The original flavor gave them a gleeful smile, a hint of bloodthirsty excitement within it. Right as he grasped the hilt, ready to draw the sword from its sheath, Shen Qingqiu suddenly said coldly, "Don't celebrate too early. Look above you."

At this moment, the only things above their heads were rustling twigs and leaves of bamboo, swaying and undulating in the wind. The original didn't need to raise his head to tell that no threat awaited him above, and he smiled slightly. "Shizun, that sort of ploy is for dealing with little children. Trying to trick your disciple that way is a bit too condescending."

You won't look? All right, you brought this upon yourself! Shen Qingqiu formed a seal with his left hand and crisply snapped his fingers, his expression hardening.

The original was about to say something when a fluttering leaf streaked across his vision. The smile on his face froze. A fine trickle of blood slowly dripped down his cheek.

All around him, bamboo leaves fell more and more thickly, until the leisurely drifting foliage suddenly sped up, each one slicing toward where he stood in the center like the frigid, cutting wind from the east.

Plucking Leaves, Flying Flowers: Ultimate Version—Hundred Leaves, Thousand Flowers!

The original Luo Binghe flung out his palm, routing the dense assault of leafy razors, but for Shen Qingqiu, the entire forest was full of ammunition—thick with leaves that rained down like confetti, homing in on their target in hot pursuit. Though they appeared unassuming, with a single touch, they could carve flesh from bone.

A leaf or two could be dodged, but hundreds upon thousands blotting out the sky as they enveloped a target was inevitably enough to fluster anyone.

On top of that, the original had broken both an arm and a leg during his crude duel earlier, hampering his mobility. Shen Qingqiu was about to take his bullying further when a black shadow stole in front of him. With his remaining good hand, that figure struck the original Luo Binghe square in the chest.

A look of disbelief flashed over that impossibly familiar face, and in that instant, Shen Qingqiu actually found it all somewhat unbearable.

The original backed up two steps, his throat bobbing as if he'd swallowed a mouthful of blood. "How harmonious," he sneered. "Not bad, hm?"

His words were mocking, but his good hand had already clenched into a fist, his veins faintly bulging.

Since he'd come of age, no one had ever managed to push him this far. Being at such a disadvantage reminded him of the days when he'd been persecuted and humiliated, trampled over in all kinds of ways.

The hot tea spilled upon his head, the cold and drafty woodshed, the relentless beating fists, the verbal abuse, the kneeling that lasted from the blazing afternoon into the dead of the night, the paucity of his meals.

And connected to those days via a thousand inseparable threads was the face before him.

But right now, that face's owner stood beside a person identical to him, cradling his double's broken arm, too afraid to touch it but also too worried to let go. As if he himself could feel the pain,

Shen Qingqiu frowned. "Why did you fight him head-on? And you kept fighting even though you knew your arm was broken. Don't be so reckless next time."

It was a scolding, but the tone wasn't just urgent and upset, it was anguished and full of heartache. Even an idiot could hear that.

A chill wind blew through the forest, rustling the foliage. Leaves drifted down one by one.

It was so infuriating.

And so *unfair*.

The image of the two of them standing together was so glaring that his eyes began to hurt, the rims prickling with heat.

Even though they were both Luo Binghe... For what reason had that one been able to meet *this* sort of Shen Qingqiu, while he had only met a rotten bastard—vindictive, petty, and jealous to the core?

For what reason?!

The carefully preserved clothes and belongings, the pristine and tidy side room, the gentle whispers, the boundless doting and indulgence.

He'd only wanted to humiliate them, because that disgusting relationship of theirs elicited nothing but his contempt, and yet—

And yet the, "Come with me," that left his mouth in that instant was involuntary, and it was addressed to Shen Qingqiu.

Luo Binghe heard those three words and sneered. "What did you say? Huh?" His knuckles cracked; from the looks of it, they had triggered a killing rage.

It was true that Shen Qingqiu approved of finishing people off—he was a big fan of finishing things off!—but...if he had Luo Binghe kill the other Luo Binghe, exactly what would they be doing here?

Then again, if Shen Qingqiu were to land the killing blow himself… That was even more unthinkable. Furthermore, what if the law that "the male lead has plot armor," was still in effect with regard to the original Bing-ge?

Shen Qingqiu pressed down on his Luo Binghe's shoulder with two fingers, telling him to calm down. As he was racking his brains as to how to deal with this, the original Luo Binghe moved first.

He slapped away Xin Mo's paper seals. Dark qi and purple light surged forth, and with the other two still on full alert, he cut a dimension-severing slash, opened a spatial rift, and leapt inside.

As he looked back, he viciously bit his lip.

So *infuriating*.

Then the rift vanished, together with his figure.

Just like that…he was gone?

He had been that easy to defeat?!

Though he was frozen for a while, Shen Qingqiu finally recovered. "Head back and destroy Xin Mo's fragments this instant. You can't keep something like that around."

The bugs in that thing's code were way too serious. If they held on to it, who knew what kind of ridiculous development it'd stir up next?

Luo Binghe silently nodded. Though he probably didn't need anyone's support, Shen Qingqiu continued to lend him one of his arms to lean on.

They'd barely walked a single step when Luo Binghe said mournfully, "Shizun, is my technique really that awful?"

Ah.

To be honest, it was indeed awful. *Really* awful. Regardless of whether it was a matter of kissing, touching, stripping, or rolling around, the difference was far more than a few levels.

And when it came to thrusting...he hadn't had the chance to compare, but if one followed this line of logic, it would also be... a fail.

Obviously Shen Qingqiu wouldn't say these words; instead, he skirted around it with a, "Not really."

The gloom on Luo Binghe's face grew heavier and heavier.

"After all, you don't have much experience." Shen Qingqiu consoled him.

Bing-ge's skills had been honed through fighting hundreds of battles and having trysts with hundreds of women!

Luo Binghe's head drooped. From the look of it, he was probably contemplating squatting in some corner to grow mushrooms again.

More than anything, Shen Qingqiu couldn't stand just watching Luo Binghe in one of these moods. "This master will treat your arm and leg first, and once they're healed, we can...do some exploring together," he said in a coaxing tone. "How about that?"

Luo Binghe abruptly jerked his head up. "Really?!"

Shen Qingqiu had known that he would react like this and calmly patted his head. "Treatment first."

Luo Binghe nodded, then with two cracks, he slotted his arm and leg back into place. He instantly straightened, using his perfectly whole hands to grasp Shen Qingqiu's arms, a soft flush rising to his cheeks as his eyes sparkled. "I'm healed! Shizun, let's...let's do some exploring?"

A hole yawned overhead in the Bamboo House, and the whistling wind funneled in through it.

Shen Qingqiu lay on his back facing the sky. Luo Binghe's weight was on top of him; like a puppy, he licked and kissed down the line of his throat.

He stared at the gaping hole above them, which had been blasted open by one of the Luo Binghes during their battle. Finally unable to pretend he couldn't see it any longer, he said, "How about we change locations."

Luo Binghe raised his head. "No," he said obstinately.

Leaving the mountain and booking a room or whatever would be better than this!

Shen Qingqiu had yet to comment when Luo Binghe repeated himself. "No changing. Let's do it here. In the Bamboo House."

He said this very firmly. In all likelihood, the Bamboo House was a very special place to Luo Binghe.

Shen Qingqiu capitulated and went to remove his clothes himself. At this point, he could say he had *some* experience. He couldn't wait for Luo Binghe to remove them; if he did, those clothes would no longer be in a wearable state. So, it was better to fully strip himself first.

After a spate of rustling, their outer robes, inner robes, and waist sashes all fell to the floor one by one, the teal and black overlapping.

Now that they were exposed to each other, a chill wind blew past, and Shen Qingqiu felt very keenly that he was both a bit cold as well as a bit embarrassed. Yet Luo Binghe didn't seem to feel the same in the least.

He knelt between Shen Qingqiu's legs, his Adam's apple bobbing and expression terribly nervous.

The last time they'd done this on Mai Gu Ridge, he'd been in a daze. He didn't remember it very well, but he'd seen the disastrous, bloody aftermath and knew just how dreadfully he'd done. On top of that, he'd just suffered a massive blow to his ego, so he sorely wanted to put on a good performance. But he had no idea how to go about doing so.

Watching him hesitate, Shen Qingqiu found him pitiful. He sighed and took the initiative, reaching out to undo the belt of Luo Binghe's pants. Luo Binghe's pale face flushed red, and Shen Qingqiu couldn't resist using a hand to scratch at his chin. This child really was quite adorable when it came to these things.

But after undoing his belt and looking down, he saw that *thing*, already alert and erect, and all thoughts of adorability instantaneously flew off beyond the nine heavens.

Fuck. The *size*!

"Absolutely not!" Shen Qingqiu said resolutely.

Those words struck Luo Binghe like lightning. "Shizun, you promised..."

What he meant by "absolutely not" was: *We can't just go to town like this—I'll die!*

Just how had he managed to survive last time? How had this thing gotten inside his body without killing him? How had he not been *annihilated*?!

Shen Qingqiu struggled for a moment, then said, "Let this master...let me take care of you once with my hands."

At least he could jerk him off to deflate it a bit first!

Shen Qingqiu's five digits had never serviced another person before, so this was a groundbreaking first for him. He prodded the purple-red head of that fleshy pillar, with its ridiculous construction and bulging veins, then steeled himself and grabbed it.

Luo Binghe yelped in pain, his expression a little aggrieved.

Shen Qingqiu focused on hypnotizing himself, his grip neither tight nor loose as his hand slowly began to move.

The more he jerked Luo Binghe off, the more alarmed he became.

Whether it was a question of girth, hardness, or temperature, this definitely wasn't something that belonged on a living organism, right? It'd be more correct to call it a weapon, right?!

After the rough start, where Shen Qingqiu hadn't yet figured out the right level of force, leading his grip to be a little painful, Luo Binghe visibly got into the mood with a quickness. He stared at Shen Qingqiu, squinting a bit through limpid, quavering eyes, and his breath too became slightly unsteady.

Shen Qingqiu's face was blank, but his actions were fervent. The more he rubbed, the sorer his hand became, but other than a tiny trickle of white fluid released from that flared head, this infernal object demonstrated absolutely no intentions of further release. It wouldn't go down, it wouldn't surrender—if anything, it stiffened further. No matter how calm Shen Qingqiu kept himself, he couldn't stop his expression from twisting.

Luo Binghe had secretly been paying attention to his face the entire time. At this moment, he carefully said, "Then, Shizun, how about...you do it?"

What? Shen Qingqiu thought he'd heard wrong. Luo Binghe was going to let him top?

"I'm afraid of hurting Shizun again," said Luo Binghe. "So it'd be better if Shizun did it."

He spoke very earnestly, his expression sincere. He was seconds away from lying down before Shen Qingqiu hastily said, "No. It will be best if you do it."

If Shen Qingqiu took charge—he didn't have any experience, okay? If he wasn't careful and made Luo Binghe bleed everywhere—even though he knew Luo Binghe would still be overjoyed, he wouldn't be able to sleep at night!

There would be more opportunities in the future anyway; there was nothing wrong with going along with him a bit more, or letting him taste a little sweetness first.

In short, it unequivocally wasn't on account of being a little moved that Shen Qingqiu was offering to give up the lead himself! Goodbye! As if to encourage Luo Binghe, Shen Qingqiu patted his head and turned himself over, lying face-down over the pillow. His elbows were propped on the bed, his shoulder blades raised high, and the line of his waist dipped in a soft arc, practically presenting his backside to Luo Binghe.

Shen Qingqiu was so ashamed that his face was burning, but unexpectedly, Luo Binghe grabbed his waist and flipped him back around.

"What's wrong with you now?" he asked helplessly.

"Shizun," Luo Binghe said, "I want to do it from the front..."

You want to do me face-to-face?!

Shen Qingqiu's expression was dark. "Don't be greedy." He tried again to lie on his front while mumbling in his heart. *This child is so fucking fussy! He's lucky enough that I'm letting him do it at all!*

But lo and behold, Luo Binghe again flipped him over like a pancake, his expression mournful. "Shizun, do you really hate looking at my face that much?"

Fine beads of sweat dotted his forehead, his nose was dusted red, and tears seemed to be shivering on the rims of his lids. Shen Qingqiu had absolutely zero doubts that if he refused again, Luo Binghe would burst into tears on the spot.

Faced with this scene, he felt both embarrassed and tender; his heart melted. He couldn't help but say, "That's not it."

Luo Binghe was on the verge of weeping. Heartbroken, he whined, "Then why does Shizun insist on having his back to me every time?"

You're really thinking about it too much... Where do all these little moods and ideas come from, exactly?!

Whatever! He didn't need his face; it would be better for Luo Binghe not to read into things so much. "All right, all right," Shen Qingqiu said recklessly. "From the front is fine. Cease this weeping. Aren't you ashamed?"

Luo Binghe's following actions proved that his tears held no value whatsoever.

"Oh," he said, and the moisture vanished as swiftly as it had arrived. He shamelessly pressed his head closer, his hand caressing Shen Qingqiu's skin.

Shen Qingqiu possessed both a slim waist and delicate limbs; his bare legs were long and slender as well. As they were face-to-face, those legs were forced to bend and fold. Luo Binghe looked down: he had a clear view of everything between them, of the deep gully separating the two round buttocks.

Luo Binghe's hand shook slightly as he skimmed up a smooth, silky inner thigh. Shen Qingqiu couldn't help but shrink back. As if afraid that he'd renege, Luo Binghe held one of his thighs down, then pressed a finger right inside.

The digit was slick and greasy, as if already slathered in oil. It had little problem popping into him, where it was quickly received and enveloped by Shen Qingqiu's scalding-hot inner walls.

The sensation of that nimble finger prodding and crooking against his tight passage was incredibly bizarre, and a shudder traveled up Shen Qingqiu's spine as his scalp went numb. Thus he didn't have the mind to wonder where Luo Binghe had acquired such ample tools for preparation.

Luo Binghe held his breath, totally focused on his task. When he pressed in a third finger, there came the slight sensation of something tearing. Shen Qingqiu gasped and grabbed Luo Binghe's forearm, gritting his teeth. "Slow down."

Like a toddler learning to walk, Luo Binghe did indeed slow down and followed Shen Qingqiu's instructions, proceeding step-by-step as he tried to press and rub. When he found a tender spot along those walls, Shen Qingqiu shuddered, suddenly finding it all less unbearable. Enduring his shame, he said, "Mm, there...that's fine..."

Why did he need to teach another person how to fuck him? Having to act the master even in this situation! Shen Qingqiu truly wanted to light an entire Cang Qiong Mountain's worth of candles for himself.

Luo Binghe stretched him out carefully while studying his expression. The corners of his eyes, which had been dyed a faint red; the tightly pressed lips that stifled all sound; the brows that at times wrinkled, at times relaxed. Luo Binghe's eyes captured each and every minute change. The sensation of having nowhere to hide made Shen Qingqiu feel even more excruciatingly ashamed, and he was about to turn his head to the side in embarrassment.

Suddenly, he detected something out of the corner of his eye. Close to Luo Binghe's heart was a hideous scar that cut right across his chest. It was from when Shen Qingqiu had pushed him into the Endless Abyss, where Shen Qingqiu had stabbed him right by his heart.

He'd never once intended to hurt Luo Binghe, but time after time, he had been the one to do so. That was the truth. Falling into a brief trance, Shen Qingqiu unconsciously reached out to touch that scar.

At this same instant, Luo Binghe finished his preliminary preparations. He withdrew his fingers, and the hole immediately clenched shut. Then Luo Binghe's blazing chest came forward and pressed against his.

That flared tip, hot and blunt, prodded against his soft, moist entrance. Shen Qingqiu wrapped his arms tightly around Luo Binghe's neck and gasped deeply like a dying man as his body was slowly split open by that length.

It still hurt. The entrance was too small. He was too full, and it hurt.

Even with that lubricating oil sourced from heavens knew where, the girth of the intruding object was simply too large. As it continued to aggravate the pain in his lower half, Shen Qingqiu couldn't help but squeeze Luo Binghe harder and harder, his legs involuntarily rubbing along his waist.

"Shizun...is this all right?" Luo Binghe asked, the sound reverberating in his eardrums. Luo Binghe's voice was tight with restraint. It was obvious that it was taking everything he had not to just drive himself in all the way.

Shen Qingqiu defied his own thoughts to say, "It's...fine."

Having received confirmation, Luo Binghe's hands on his waist tightened a little, and he thrust himself in with increasing eagerness.

Shen Qingqiu's insides were crammed full, his entrance stretched into a strained ring. It felt like his bottom half no longer belonged to him. Luo Binghe pulled out a little, then thrust inside again, burying most of himself within. As he advanced and retreated in this manner, moist squelches came one after the next, and the torment left Shen Qingqiu both itching and in pain. He almost wanted to slam his head into the wall, and tears streamed down his face without his knowledge.

At the same time, Luo Binghe turned Shen Qingqiu's face forward, preparing to kiss him, only to see him overwhelmed with pain. He froze for a moment and, having taken another blow to the heart, his own tears followed, spilling down.

The teardrops pitter-pattered onto Shen Qingqiu's cheek, pattering until he was left speechless. *What are* you *crying for?!*

"I'm sorry...I hurt Shizun again..." Luo Binghe said in a trembling voice.

Shen Qingqiu didn't reply.

"It's because this disciple is too stupid..."

Two people crying at each other. What the hell kind of situation was this?!

Enduring the discomfort in his lower body, Shen Qingqiu pecked Luo Binghe's eyes and cheeks, kissing away his tears. "I'm fine. It doesn't hurt that much. Everyone experiences moments in which they're less capable. Go on."

"I'll pull out," Luo Binghe said sadly.

Fuck! Don't joke around—if we leave things like this, we'll both end up with psychological trauma! What if we get ED?!

A brief pain was better than a drawn-out one! They'd come this far; at least one person had to feel good, right?!

Shen Qingqiu made his decision and abruptly sat up, pushing Luo Binghe beneath him.

The strength he'd been building for so long was exhausted in one go: he had none left to brace his legs. His bottom plunged down, swallowing Luo Binghe within himself to the fullest extent. The tip seemed to press all the way up into his stomach, bringing with it a sudden urge to retch before he forced himself to swallow.

Luo Binghe hadn't come the last time, so it probably hadn't

counted as fully losing his virginity. Then this time, he had to at least help Luo Binghe get that far!

As he thought this, he propped his arm against Luo Binghe's abdomen and managed to sit up a little. Suddenly, the thick, hard object inside him rubbed against something, and a burst of tingling numbness swept through him, exploding within his stomach and flooding his entire body. Taken by surprise, Shen Qingqiu's back went weak and he collapsed forward. Luo Binghe sat up just in time to catch him and folded him into his arms.

Luo Binghe's senses were incredibly sharp. "Shizun, does it stop hurting when I touch there?" he asked doggedly.

Not only had it stopped hurting, it had even...felt a little good!

In this position, Shen Qingqiu's legs were spread wide open as he sat atop Luo Binghe, face-to-face, their lower halves pressed seamlessly together.

In order to keep his balance, Shen Qingqiu was forced to circle his limp arms around Luo Binghe's neck. Even Luo Binghe's gentlest movements shifted their snugly joined lower bodies, and Shen Qingqiu couldn't stop a couple of close-mouthed whines from slipping out. Delighted and rejuvenated, Luo Binghe fully embraced Shen Qingqiu's hips and lifted them a little, then dropped him down while aiming for that spot.

This time, Shen Qingqiu could no longer hold it in. He let out a gasp, his trembling legs no longer obeying him as they clamped down on Luo Binghe. His entrance too clenched in a death-grip. Having found the key, Luo Binghe officially went on the offensive.

He had no technique at all; he only knew to thrust fervently. But it was precisely this that could strip a person of their last defenses. Shen Qingqiu didn't know whether he was in pain or taken by bliss.

The jostling disrupted his faint groans and disordered gasps, turning them choppy and intermittent, while the sounds of sticky squelches and slapping flesh came from below. A milky white fluid exuded from his tip, and the trickles grew as they dribbled down. The more fervent the thrusts, the more difficult it was to relieve the prickling heat and numbing tingles within him.

Suddenly, scattered footsteps drifted in from outside the Bamboo House.

"I'm so tired..."

"Shixiong, wait for us... I can't...run any farther..."

If Shen Qingqiu had been drunk on lust moments before, now his soul was about to flee his body. It was the disciples he'd sent to run laps around Qing Jing Peak!

Shen Qingqiu abruptly grabbed Luo Binghe's shoulder, wanting to get off him. But to his chagrin, Luo Binghe clamped onto his waist, viciously pressing him downward.

This thrust was suddenly too deep, the fullness stretching him too far, the stimulation too powerful. Shen Qingqiu opened his mouth, but Luo Binghe instantly blocked it with his own. Unable to do more than grunt, Shen Qingqiu could only choke down his sobs, squeezing his eyes shut as reflexive tears streamed down his face.

Having tasted that sweetness, how could Luo Binghe let him go so easily? He gently worried at him with lips and teeth while his lower half forcefully drove in and out.

"Eh? Why do I feel like something is missing on top of the Bamboo House?" Ming Fan asked outside. "Is that a hole?"

"You're right, Da-shixiong, it really does look like a hole."

"When did that happen? Should we go tell An Ding Peak? Get them to come and fix it right away."

Shen Qingqiu was terribly afraid of them coming in now, or of them telling someone else to do so. His fingers clenched, digging hard into Luo Binghe's back while his entrance tensed, making the slide increasingly difficult.

Then Ning Yingying seemed to stomp her foot as she snapped, "What are we going to fix? After running for so long, we're exhausted! If you want to fix it, do it tomorrow!"

All the disciples quickly chimed in.

"All right. Let's listen to Shimei."

"If Shimei says to fix it tomorrow, we'll fix it tomorrow."

"Besides, Shizun doesn't like it when people even casually enter and clean A-Luo's side room," Ning Yingying said. "He definitely wouldn't be happy if we did anything without his permission. Haven't you gotten that into your heads yet?!"

At these words, Luo Binghe's eyes flashed, and he abruptly pushed Shen Qingqiu onto the bed.

As the disciples all headed toward the dining hall while muttering, Luo Binghe finally stopped covering Shen Qingqiu's mouth. Instead, he moved his head to Shen Qingqiu's chest, where he nibbled on a nipple while his lower half's thrusts became increasingly ferocious. Shen Qingqiu didn't even need to look to feel the delicate flesh of his walls being dragged in and out, the sensations alternating between cool and hot. After so many thrusts, his insides had grown used to the size of Luo Binghe's cock: it slid in and out easily, the accommodation perfect.

"Shizun," murmured Luo Binghe.

"Don't...say that!" Shen Qingqiu couldn't help but plead.

To address him properly as a disciple to his master at a time like this! He was going to explode with shame a hundred times over.

No matter how thick his face, how shameless he was, he couldn't take it.

But Luo Binghe suddenly murmured by his ear, "Shizun, I couldn't find you on the other side."

His voice was trembling slightly. Shen Qingqiu dragged himself back to attention.

"The 'me' over there had so many people at his side, but he didn't have you. Shizun, I searched for a long time, but I still couldn't find you. The reason 'I' became like that...was it because 'I' didn't have you?"

A pause.

"I...I don't want to become like that."

Shen Qingqiu took a deep breath and pulled Luo Binghe's head toward his chest, where he stroked it. "Don't worry. You won't become like him."

A moment.

"And your shizun will never throw you away, ever again."

Demons had incredible stamina; this Shen Qingqiu knew.

Male leads also had incredible stamina; Shen Qingqiu knew this as well.

But that someone who shared both the demonic blood and male lead traits could last this long, that he had such profound stamina—Shen Qingqiu absolutely hadn't been mentally prepared for that.

By the time Luo Binghe finally came, Shen Qingqiu was in a daze. It was the searing flood of hot fluids spilling inside him that finally brought him back to his senses.

At this moment, he no longer wanted to fuss over condoms or the lack thereof, or whether or not it was fine to come inside him. He just wanted to sleep!

His walls felt swollen. Even a gentle rubbing made them prickle with pain. Luo Binghe reluctantly pulled out, then put his all into relieving Shen Qingqiu's desire in front.

Yet even after being jerked off twice, Shen Qingqiu was still singing the same tune: he just wanted to sleep!

"Shizun..." said Luo Binghe.

Shen Qingqiu knew what he wanted to ask and mercilessly spoke first. "Awful."

However, this time, even after receiving criticism, Luo Binghe wasn't depressed. Rather, he exuberantly declared, "Yes, it was awful. Unacceptably awful."

"What are you saying...?"

"Because it was simply awful, this disciple requests that his shizun assist him with further exploration."

Well.

23

Recalling an Experience of Fighting Succubi with Great Master Liu

THIS STORY TOOK PLACE during the period of time after Shen-laoshi kicked Luo Binghe into the Abyss.

"I still think it would be better if you didn't come," said Shen Qingqiu. "Really."

Liu Qingge acted as if he'd heard nothing and continued walking. He stalked with large strides and an arrogant gaze, Cheng Luan's tassel swaying behind him. It was as if he was walking not on a narrow, thicket-ridden mountain path full of uneven shrubs and hanging vines but on Bai Zhan Peak's training grounds underneath a blazing sun.

"Shidi, don't force yourself," Shen Qingqiu sincerely admonished him.

"Are you heading back or not?" Liu Qingge interrupted.

"After I take care of this support ticket—ah, I mean, after I take care of those succubi, I'll head back."

"You said that last time too."

"Mm."

"And then you vanished for a month!"

"Shixiong won't die out here. Every time Without a Cure acts up, don't I always return to Cang Qiong Mountain to look for you? Shidi doesn't need to go out of his way to chase after me..."

"I'm not chasing you," Liu Qingge said emphatically. "Zhangmen-shixiong ordered me to come."

Yes, yes, yes. Shen Qingqiu said sorrowfully, "Zhangmen-shixiong really is too kind..." After a pause, he added, "In truth, Shixiong's only looking out for you. The rumors at the foot of the mountain say these succubi adore beautiful men who are full of vigor, so if Liu-shidi insists on coming, they'll undoubtedly target him."

Liu Qingge humphed and was about to reply when a stream of gorgeous, enchanting song began to languidly echo down the valley. The singing was beautiful, filled with an invitation that lingered after the melody, and any who heard it felt a feathery touch brush their heart.

The two of them turned off the path and arrived at the entrance to a cave. Some ten young servant girls emerged from the surrounding grass and flowers. Every single one was radiant, their hair combed into twin buns, their appearance young and tender. In fact, they *were* young and tender, so much so that they didn't know to restrain their fey aura.

"Who are you, newcomers?" they called out crisply.

At the sight of this bevy of young girls blocking their way, Shen Qingqiu said pleasantly, "We are—"

But before he could finish greeting them, Liu Qingge reached back for Cheng Luan and slid the blade two inches from its sheath. Sword glares swept through the area. This simple motion carved the boulder covering the cave in two, and the girls immediately shrieked, retreating into the foliage.

Because of the advantages of their race, succubi often had a pleasing appearance, and they rarely had a chance to encounter such violent treatment. On top of that, these ones were young and had little real-world experience. They promptly started to cry.

The mountainside was filled with the sniffling and sobbing of young girls as they wailed and wept.

Shen Qingqiu rubbed his ears. "Shidi, you have absolutely no idea how to treat women gently."

Liu Qingge was irritated, and his words were clipped and forceful, spoken without hesitation. "There's no need to be gentle with monsters. Hurry up and fight, then we can go back!"

Suddenly, someone from within the cave said, "These two immortal masters are so rude. Exactly how have my girls wronged you to warrant such an awful scare?"

With these soft and gentle words, a willowy woman in deep green sashayed outside. Sunlight illuminated her at the entrance to her cave, revealing her dewy white skin and coquettish face, and how within every single one of her movements their lay an overwhelming charm.

"Madam Meiyin, this cultivator's scary!" cried the succubi who Liu Qingge had frightened to tears. "He's bullying us!"

This Madam Meiyin was not only a succubus but also stunningly beautiful. Therefore, as was the way of harem novels, she and Luo Binghe had necessarily enjoyed an affair.

Normally, Shen Qingqiu was very self-conscious around any woman who Luo Binghe had touched. Forget voluntarily approaching them to cause them trouble, he avoided them like the plague. As for why he'd steeled himself and joined in on the fun this time, he had two reasons.

The first was that the crying of the old couple at the foot of the mountain had been too heartbreaking to ignore as they bemoaned the plight of their only son, whose soul had practically been stolen away. The second was Madam Meiyin's promiscuity. Outside of Luo Binghe, she had an uncountable number of husbands and lovers. Her affair with Luo Binghe was only a one-night stand; she never actually entered his harem. The purpose of her episode had mainly been to give readers the vicarious pleasure of cucking a whole bunch of people.

So, to be precise, Madam Meiyin didn't count as one of Luo Binghe's wives!

Liu Qingge clearly had no intention of chatting with this member of the opposite sex; he showed no remorse for destroying the madam's gate as he turned his head away.

Shen Qingqiu coughed. "My shidi isn't used to engaging with outsiders."

Madam Meiyin looked serenely at Shen Qingqiu. "My girls here are young and ignorant; I apologize if they offended you. But we only just finished building this place, and what a greeting you've given us, collapsing the door so terribly."

Don't look at me, look that way! He collapsed it! That's Cang Qiong Mountain's Director of Demolitions! Want to learn how to blow things up? Bai Zhan Peak is the place to go!

On principle, Shen Qingqiu always tried diplomacy first. "We didn't mean to damage your place of residence," he said apologetically while waving his fan. "Please excuse our rudeness. But we've come on behalf of the Huang family at the foot of the mountain; they wish for you to release Young Master Huang."

"Oh? A Young Master Huang?" said Madam Meiyin. "I've met many young masters named Huang. If not ten, then at least eight or so. Which Young Master Huang could these immortal masters be asking after?"

Liu Qingge sneered. "Release them all—that will suffice!"

Madam Meiyin put on a troubled face. "It's not that I don't want to release him, but he himself insists on staying and won't go home. There's nothing I can do about that."

Liu Qingge snorted.

Shen Qingqiu had no wish to continue dragging this out either. "Even so, could you at least bring him here? We'll figure out the rest ourselves."

"If that's the case, then please, I ask the two immortal masters to come inside," Madam Meiyin said sweetly. She turned and headed into the cave, walking leisurely before them.

Shen Qingqiu made sure to keep a couple of steps back as he followed, then lowered his voice so only Liu Qingge could hear. "She doesn't intend to bring him out, nor will she let us go."

"She won't succeed," said Liu Qingge.

Different situations called for different strategies. Instead of prematurely dropping their facade, it seemed wiser to play along and use discretion.

They were guided into a wide cavern carpeted with sweet-smelling herbs and damask. Twelve elegant, full-figured maids stood in two groups on either side, oval fans in hand, all gentle smiles.

Madam Meiyin sat them before a stone table. "I've already sent a servant to invite Young Master Huang to join us," she said. "While you're waiting, shall I serve you something to drink?"

Shen Qingqiu knew that whatever she tried, it'd all be from the same bag of tricks anyway. Thus, he was unworried and smiled slightly. "Sorry to trouble you."

Madam Meiyin hospitably poured them both some wine, all while seductively eyeing the deeply frowning Liu Qingge. The longer she looked, the sultrier her expression became, until Liu Qingge simply dismissed her with a roll of his eyes. Despite this, Shen Qingqiu was bubbling over with excitement.

Madam Meiyin had a strong preference for pretty boy faces—like those of Luo Binghe and Liu Qingge! Now that she had her sights set on Liu Qingge, would he be able to escape her demonic clutches?

Once she sighted this kind of man, with his delicate facial features and skin as pale as snow, she'd be willing to pull out all the stops. She'd harass him remorselessly and without end until she could latch on to him, pin him down, and have her way with him until she was (ahem) satisfied.

In no time at all, Liu Qingge's expression would without a doubt be *spectacular*. Shen Qingqiu was actually (criminally) kind of looking forward to it.

Indeed, before they'd sat for long, Madam Meiyin covered her mouth with a sleeve and glanced at Liu Qingge with affected bashfulness. "Does this one have a cultivation partner?"

How direct.

No human—or other fey—had ever dared to ask Liu Qingge such a question. It was as if he'd been struck by lightning. For a moment, he seemed to be questioning whether he'd misheard her, his lips and brows twitching, his gaze a little dumbfounded; he involuntarily turned to look at Shen Qingqiu.

Shen Qingqiu had never seen this sort of expression on Liu Qingge's face before—it was almost outraged in disbelief. It was as if a thousand-year-old iceberg had come crashing down. The hysterical laughter within Shen Qingqiu's heart surged into a terrifying wave. He managed to keep a straight face, enduring it until even his fan hand was trembling as he struggled to cover his spasming mouth. "No," he said solemnly. "He doesn't."

"Why not?" asked Madam Meiyin. "With such a striking appearance, how can it be that no woman has fallen for him? I don't believe it."

Shen Qingqiu expressed his agreement. "Mm. I'm curious too."

Otherwise, why would one of the ten great mysteries of Cang Qiong Mountain Sect be "Is Great Master Liu asexual?"

Liu Qingge stuffily sucked in a breath, then icily said, "Why hasn't the boy arrived yet?"

"Please don't be impatient, Immortal Master," said Madam Meiyin. "Perhaps Young Master Huang isn't willing to come. If you're frustrated, how about I entertain you for a bit to help lift your spirits?"

Shen Qingqiu cheerily agreed.

"I have no other skills, but at the very least my meager divinations and fortune-telling on the matter of love have always been accurate," she said. "Which of these immortal masters is willing to let me read him?"

Shen Qingqiu asked to his side, "Shidi, are you interested?"

"I am not!" Liu Qingge said stiffly.

Shen Qingqiu shrugged. "Since he's not interested, it will have to be me."

Indeed, in accordance with the canon of the original work, Madam Meiyin's fortunes and divinations regarding predestined love and foretellings pertaining to marriage were one hundred-percent accurate.

If she said Luo Binghe would have six-hundred and thirteen wives, there was no question that he would have more than six-hundred and twelve. If she said that one of his wives liked the cow- 【beep–】 girl position, then the wife in question definitely wouldn't enjoy doggy- 【beep–】 style!

How could Shen Qingqiu, being a bachelor with an uncertain future, help feeling anxious?

Madam Meiyin smiled pleasantly, then turned over her porcelain wrist to produce a delicate flower bud, which she presented to Shen Qingqiu. "Please breathe upon it."

Shen Qingqiu was familiar with the process. He lowered his head and blew gently.

When Madam Meiyin withdrew her hand, the originally closed bud had already slowly begun to blossom. She picked it up by the stem and held it before her eyes, lips quirked in a smile, before glancing at the flower's center and freezing.

Liu Qingge had been sitting up straight, alert. At this, he bent slightly toward them, like he wanted to listen in.

Shen Qingqiu nudged his shoulder with his fan. "Shidi, weren't you 'not interested'?"

Liu Qingge swiftly straightened again.

The longer Madam Meiyin looked at the petals, the more solemn her expression became. Finally, she said, distressed, "Sir, about the red thread from your past—my skill is insufficient, so I can't...see it clearly. At first glance, it seemed like you were alone, but if I look carefully, I can catch a faint glimpse of another thread." She concluded regretfully, "This thread has been cut... Such a pity."

Shen Jiu had once had a fiancée, but Shen Yuan was a single dog! Their two threads were tangled together, so it was no surprise that the madam couldn't see it all clearly. Shen Qingqiu expressed his understanding. "Don't worry about the past. If the madam doesn't mind, please look into my future."

He desperately wanted to know if he'd ever find a woman over here. She didn't have to be a peerless beauty, as long as she wasn't a tranny!

Yet who could have guessed that Madam Meiyin's face would become even stranger, like she couldn't find the words to explain.

This expression made Shen Qingqiu's heart thump heavily. Shit, could it be...he'd be single for life?!

At last, Madam Meiyin began to speak. "Ah...the other party...is younger than you," she stammered. "And their seniority, or perhaps their status...isn't as high as yours."

Well, if he only considered the older, more senior women he knew, as of now, Shen Qingqiu had only met a handful of elderly female nuns from Tian Yi Temple a couple of times, and they really weren't to his taste. By his guess, even if you took into account the entire cultivation world, there wouldn't be many women who were both older and senior to him; thus, Madam Meiyin's two points were each incredibly rational, to the point that they were pretty much garbage.

"Your first meeting was unhappy, and there might even have been loathing involved," said Madam Meiyin. "But after a critical moment, that all began to change, and thoroughly so."

Now this criterion seemed meaningful, and Shen Qingqiu's heart couldn't help but flip.

Liu Qingge unconsciously turned toward them again. This time, Shen Qingqiu didn't bother teasing him and simply listened closely to the explanation.

Madam Meiyin raised an eyebrow. "The two of you are often together. You have both saved each other's lives."

Upon hearing this, Shen Qingqiu was again confused. Why did it feel like not a single woman in his vicinity seemed to qualify? Ning Yingying? Liu Mingyan? No need to wonder if it was them; they were in Luo Binghe's harem. Cross them out!

Qi Qingqi? She was indeed slightly junior to him, and their first meeting...he'd long forgotten how it went. "Often together" wasn't quite right, though. Perhaps he at times dared to think about going to Xian Shu Peak so they could be "often together," but while he had the wicked intentions, he lacked the courage required to follow through—and he could never commit an act as depraved as stalking. In the end, he couldn't imagine any romance between himself and Qi Qingqi.

"Is there more?" Liu Qingge suddenly asked.

Shen Qingqiu startled. Only then did he realize that Liu Qingge was no longer listening in secret—he'd moved over to face them completely. Since when had Great Master Liu had so much interest in gossip?

"Your fated person has very little interest in others," Madam Meiyin went on. "But once they find someone, their devotion is absolute."

Liu Qingge thought for a while, his expression solemn. Then he asked, "What about appearance-wise?"

Shen Qingqiu stared at him, speechless. *Even I haven't asked that! Why are you asking?! And you're even getting to the important bits straight-on!*

"A first-class beauty, peerless among all humans." Madam Meiyin said with certainty.

Uncharacteristically, Liu Qingge pressed on in hot pursuit. "What about spiritual energy? Talent?"

"Outstanding talent, incredible spiritual energy, and of illustrious status and noble blood."

Liu Qingge seemed to be shaking his head in disbelief. "You just said that—him and this person, they're often together?"

Madam Meiyin nodded. "Perhaps they may endure short periods of separation, but they quickly reunite. And each time, the other party takes the initiative to chase him."

The corner of Liu Qingge's eyes kept twitching, then he would violently suppress it, like something had greatly disturbed him. Or perhaps it would have been more correct to say that he'd stepped on a great big landmine.

Then Madam Meiyin spoke a final line, which dealt him a fatal blow. "I'm very jealous," she said to Shen Qingqiu. "Do you know, Immortal Master? This person is deeply in love with you."

Liu Qingge stiffly swiveled his head toward Shen Qingqiu; he wore a complicated expression that was impossible to describe. It was clearly neither joy nor anger, yet it was intensely tormented.

Shen Qingqiu was confused. "Shidi, what's wrong?"

Liu Qingge struggled to speak. "Inaccurate."

"Hm?"

Liu Qingge jerked his head up and insisted, "Her fortune is inaccurate!"

"On what grounds do you claim my fortune is inaccurate?" Madam Meiyin asked defiantly.

Honestly, Shen Qingqiu also thought it was inaccurate.

Often at his side, young and beautiful and honorable, even clinging to him... It reeked of some kind of Zhongdian reader male sexual fantasy. No, even sexual fantasies don't go that far into blatant Gary Stu Land, okay? A dream girl who met all these criteria—there was definitely no one like that in his circles. Even if there were, she'd be a member of Luo Binghe's harem. Augh!

"Nonsense," Liu Qingge said firmly. "'Deeply in love'? Absolutely not!"

With her specialty and exclusive ability having been called into question, Madam Meiyin became furious. "You're not his fated partner, so how would you know if it's inaccurate?"

Wait, Young Master Huang hasn't even arrived yet, so could you two stop clashing over something so trivial? And the person this matter concerns is me, isn't it?

Liu Qingge had long since run out of patience. The moment Madam Meiyin snapped, he exploded, slamming his palm down. The stone table split cleanly in two, and Cheng Luan unsheathed itself in answer, unleashing razor-sharp sword glares.

Enraged, Madam Meiyin clapped. "Everyone, come out!"

Wait... Why fight now*? What was the catalyst?! I still don't know what the turning point was...*

Naturally, everyone ignored Shen Qingqiu's outstretched hand. At the sight of Madam Meiyin and her several dozen succubi servants surrounding them, he adjusted his expression and hurriedly readied himself for battle. Cheng Luan wove back and forth with a chaotic flurry of spiritual blasts, after which Madam Meiyin whistled shrilly.

Shit, not so fast! I haven't psychologically prepared myself!

At their mistress's whistle, all of the succubi servants' clothes exploded off of their bodies.

White, white, no matter where he looked, it was all a great sea of nude white bodies...

Though Shen Qingqiu knew that succubi loved playing this trump card—destroying their clothes en masse in a fiendish and frenzied dance—that didn't mean he could witness such a shocking scene firsthand and withstand the impact!

He subconsciously closed his eyes and backed up two steps, slamming into Liu Qingge.

The cavern reverberated unendingly with the succubi's charming, incessant cries. A normal man would have been mesmerized and thrown down his sword, gladly succumbing to a blissful paradise of tender women's warmth. But Shen Qingqiu was stunned to see that not only did Liu Qingge act like he had seen nothing, he was utterly expressionless as his sword swept in wide arcs, the blade flashing and trailing blood, slaughtering his foes in a frenzy.

The nude succubi revealed their true forms and moved on all fours, their sharp nails digging into the mud and stone, spittle dripping from their mouths. They flung themselves at the two people they had surrounded only to be knocked back by spiritual energy.

Shen Qingqiu wanted to fight seriously too. Really, he did. But he couldn't bring himself to look at them head-on!

Even an experienced, well-guarded elder like himself, faced with such a fresh and lively flood of nude bodies, had a hard time maintaining his composure. How could Liu Qingge fight like it was nothing?!

Madam Meiyin's lovely face had gone pale; she hadn't predicted that she would fail to mesmerize them even with all her subordinates. She picked up her skirts and ran. Shen Qingqiu had originally wanted to give chase, but when he thought about it, their current task was only to rescue the old Huang couple's son and the other captured men who the succubi were keeping as pets. "There's no need to fight anymore," he said to Liu Qingge. "There isn't much they can do, anyway. It's more important to rescue everyone."

Out of the blue, Liu Qingge said, "Don't believe her."

Shen Qingqiu was baffled. "Huh?"

"That thing before! She was just messing around!"

"Don't be so agitated. I never believed her."

Great Master Liu's behavior was awfully strange; Shen Qingqiu couldn't help glancing at him.

He'd barely done so when Liu Qingge met his eyes and snapped, "Don't look at me!"

The more insistent he became, the more Shen Qingqiu wanted to look at him. Only then did he realize that—whether because of anger or for some other reason—Liu Qingge's face, from the corners of his eyes to his cheeks, was now dusted pink. His always indifferent gaze seemed like a frozen lake that had been shattered into a thousand fragments, and the fragments now surged about in his eyes.

Shen Qingqiu kept staring at him, then suddenly reached over to feel his pulse.

As soon as he grasped Liu Qingge's wrist, he realized that Liu Qingge's temperature seemed slightly high. He counted his pulse for a while, then said sternly, "Liu-shidi, tell Shixiong the truth. Have you dual-cultivated with someone before?"

"Why are you asking this."

"Just asking. You know how dual cultivation works, right?"

Liu Qingge exhaled, then said through gritted teeth, "Shen. Qing. Qiu."

"All right, I'll ask something else. Liu-shidi, right now...how do you feel?"

Could he endure until they got back...?

"Not good," said Liu Qingge.

Of course not.

Even if he *was* Great Master Liu, being poisoned by the succubi's natural, innate Mesmerizing Fragrance—or in other words, their aphrodisiac, was profoundly...not good!

Shen Qingqiu sprang to action. "Liu-shidi, do your best. Shixiong has things to do and will be going on ahead!"

Liu Qingge grabbed the back of his collar. "What do you mean 'my best'?!" he snapped. "What do you mean 'things'?!"

Shen Qingqiu looked back and jerked in shock. If Liu Qingge's face had only been a soft red a moment ago, like the clouds at sunrise, now it was like the clouds above a fiery blaze, flooded with a terrifying crimson as the veins in his neck began to bulge.

"Don't be rash!" he said hurriedly. "Liu-shidi, calm down! You sit here. Shixiong will go free the young masters, then return and find you. Rest easy, I absolutely won't be back for a while, so you can do whatever you want. No one else will know."

With that, he turned on his heel and tried to leave, but Liu Qingge clasped his shoulder with a hand that felt more like a fine iron claw. "Why are you running?!"

Motherfucker, he's still at it! Liu-shidi, Peak Lord Liu, blood brother! I'm giving you the time and space you need to resolve your problem! Don't tell me you can't even take this kind of hint? Have you lived all your years doing nothing*? Did your core consume your brain?!*

"Even if Shixiong stayed, he would be useless," said Shen Qingqiu.

Liu Qingge laughed coldly. "Let me beat you up. Help me vent. That'll be plenty useful!"

This wasn't a problem that beating him up would solve. "Shidi, why are you so irritable? If you go on like this, the succubus poison will take over your mind."

Liu Qingge's handsome face was splotched with red and white; it seemed like he'd been worked up into true distress, but he had no idea what to do with it. He clung helplessly to Shen Qingqiu, simply unwilling to let go.

At the sight of him being so pitiful, Shen Qingqiu couldn't help but think of how Bai Zhan Peak was a gang of thugs who knew only violence, and about how everyone there was obsessed with cultivating and fighting. Perhaps Liu Qingge, who'd grown up with such traditions, really was mentally deficient with regard to this sort of thing and didn't even know how to jerk off. A deep pang of sympathy struck him.

When it came to coaxing others, Shen Qingqiu was an expert. Unfazed, he said, "Liu-shidi, come, come. Do you remember how we first met?"

As was to be expected, the original novel had never explained in detail how these two cannon fodder characters had become nemeses; Shen Qingqiu was only rambling as he tried to distract him.

Normally, you could never have so easily messed with Liu Qingge, but now he let himself be pulled along, barely managing to keep his focus in his confused daze. As they walked, he ground out, "I remember. I hit you at the Twelve Peaks' sword trials terrace!"

Silence.

So that's how it was. It takes a good fight to forge a true friendship. Could it be that, at the time, Liu Qingge had found hitting Shen Qingqiu so enjoyable that he had asked for another round moments ago so he could vent?

Shen Qingqiu replied, "Oh," and led him deeper into the cave before asking, "Did I manage to hit you back after?"

Even while running a high fever, Liu Qingge remembered to let out a conceited humph. "Of course not."

Excellent. Shen Qingqiu placed a hand on his shoulder and patted it. "Then today, Liu-shidi, Shixiong shall get his due."

And then—

He kicked Liu Qingge into Madam Meiyin's rose petal-filled bathing pool.

Water splashed nearly six feet up. Even though Shen Qingqiu had the foresight to cover his face with his fan, icy coldness managed to splash all over his head.

A soak at this temperature would assuredly cure Liu Qingge. Shen Qingqiu got down on one knee, half-kneeling at the poolside, and said gingerly, "Liu-shidi, how are you now? How do you feel?"

A long time passed without any response. Ever since Liu Qingge had sunk beneath the surface, not even a string of air bubbles had appeared.

Does he not know how to swim? Shen Qingqiu wondered. That didn't seem right. Then had he passed out from the fever? Had Shen Qingqiu managed not to kill Liu Qingge back in the Ling Xi Caves only to drown him here instead?

The more he thought about it, the more likely this seemed. Shen Qingqiu hurried closer. "Liu-shidi? Liu-shidi!"

Red rose petals covered the entirety of the water's surface; he couldn't see beneath them clearly and could only continue to approach. Suddenly, something seized his ankle and a hand dragged him into the pool.

Abruptly submerged and slammed in all directions by the icy churn of water, Shen Qingqiu's face almost turned blue from the cold. With great difficulty, he managed to grab onto the poolside before turning his head to see Liu Qingge, soaking wet and floating behind him with a deadpan expression. There were even a couple of rose petals in his hair.

"Liu-shidi, that was wrong of you," said Shen Qingqiu. "Shixiong submerged you to remove the Mesmerizing Fragrance; how could you retaliate like that?"

"You asked me how I felt, didn't you?" asked Liu Qingge. "However you feel right now, that's how I felt."

His thinking was clear; his counterattack had strength. Seemed like he was fine now.

24

Yue Qingyuan and Shen Qingqiu

— PART 1 —

A CLATTER RANG OUT as Shen Jiu sent the little black dish flying with a kick.

He crossed his arms and said nothing. The youth, who was either Shisi or Shiwu,[1] shrank back, while the young boys around him couldn't help but send him encouragement with their eyes. So, he steeled himself and put on a brave face to say, "Shen Jiu, don't think you can just throw your weight around. You don't own this street. What gives you the right to tell us we can't stay?!"

This main street was wide and even, and many people came and went upon it. If one wanted to beg, it was the best and prime location. Some of the passersby watched this group of children fight, but even more hurried on their way.

And this new brat had the gall to challenge *him*. Shen Jiu looked down and around, preparing to find a brick with which to teach him a lesson, when a tall youth happened to walk over. He saw Shen Jiu rolling up his sleeves, head lowered, and hastily went to stop him. "Xiao-Jiu, let's go somewhere else."

"No," said Shen Jiu. "I'm staying here."

---

1 *Shisi means "fourteen," and Shiwu means "fifteen."*

That first youth took the opportunity to tattle. "Qi-ge, he's bullying me."

"That wasn't bullying, Shiwu," said Yue Qi. "Xiao-Jiu was just joking around."

"Who's joking?" said Shen Jiu. "I'm telling him to get lost. This is my territory. I'll kill anyone who tries to steal it."

With Yue Qi standing in front of him, Shiwu grew bold. He leaned forward and yelled, "Every time we go to a new place, you always hog the best spot! Everyone's been sick of you for ages! You think you're all that? That everyone's afraid of you?"

"Shiwu," Yue Qi scolded. Amidst the struggle, Shen Jiu kicked Shiwu in the shin. "If you want a fight, I'll give you one. Only losers would blame their spot for their incompetence. You bastard—who's your Qi-ge? I dare you to say that again!"

"You're the bastard! I bet you'll get sold off soon and end up a pimp!"

Yue Qi didn't know whether to laugh or to cry. "Where did you learn that kind of nonsense language?!" Then he dragged Shen Jiu off to the side of the road while coaxing him. "All right, you're the most competent one here. Even if you didn't pick and choose your spot, you'd be the best. So let's change streets."

Shen Jiu stepped on his foot. "Get off me! Like I'm scared! Come on, fight me! Wanna gang up on me? Go ahead!"

Of course Yue Qi knew he wasn't scared. If he really let Shen Jiu brawl with the other kids, he would fight dirty. He'd gouge at their eyes and kick them in the belly or crotch or shin. He was terribly vicious, and the other party would be the one to end up suffering and bawling in terror. Yue Qi forced down a smile. "Are you done stepping on my foot yet? If you are, stop it. Qi-ge will take you somewhere fun."

"What shitty 'fun'?" Shen Jiu asked savagely. "The most fun I'll have is if they're all dead."

Yue Qi looked at him helplessly and shook his head.

With a Qi for "seven" and a Jiu for "nine," naturally there had also been a "one" through "six." But of the previous batch of children, everyone "six" and under had either been sold off or was long dead. Of the children left, these two were the closest.

When Shen Jiu had been a little younger, he'd been small and skinny. Yue Qi had held his head while they sat on the ground, a "letter of blood"[2] before them. Written on it was the tale of how all their siblings and parents had died, how they'd stumbled upon hardship while searching for other relatives, and how now they were penniless and alone, drifters without anyone to depend on, etc.

According to the orders given to them, Yue Qi should have wailed and wept, but no matter what, he never could manage to cry. Therefore, this task had instead fallen to Shen Jiu, even though he was faking an illness that supposedly left him too feeble to weep. But he was small and his face wasn't too unsightly to look at, so whenever he sobbed and bawled, the passersby found him pitiful and generously opened their wallets. It would have been no exaggeration to call him a money tree.

Eventually, as Yue Qi gradually grew older, he had become less and less willing to do this kind of thing, and so he'd been relegated to patrolling and keeping a lookout. Shen Jiu had wanted to go with him but had been forbidden to do so. Therefore he continued to terrorize the streets, a scourge to everyone in his path.

---

2 *A piece of text written using one's own blood as ink. Commonly for expressing one's grudges, hatreds, mourning, or determination.*

As the pair were about to head away from the most prosperous street in town, there suddenly came the sound of thundering hooves.

Stall owners on both sides of the street paled in a panic. Those with carts pushed them away while others ran as if their mortal enemy approached. Yue Qi didn't understand the reason for this, but Shen Jiu had just dragged him to the roadside when a gigantic horse turned onto the street.

The horse's bit was forged from pure gold: heavy and solid, gleaming and bright. Haughtily riding astride the beast was a spirited and youthful young master. His face was fair and striking, his brows and eyes slender. Where the light struck his dark irises, two brilliant pinpoints shone, the effect blindingly piercing. His purple hem fluttered against both sides of his saddle, his narrow sleeves sat snug around his wrists, and in his pale hand, he gripped a jet-black whip.

Dazzled by the gold, Shen Jiu couldn't help but lean out to look, but Yue Qi quickly pulled him backward, and the two of them retreated.

They hadn't walked for long when they heard a scream and the sound of people scattering. A group of young boys sprinted toward them and pounced on Yue Qi one after another, practically smearing him with their terrified snot and tears. Shen Jiu flew into a rage, but Yue Qi hurriedly said, "What's wrong? Why are you crying?"

"Shiwu's gone!" someone wailed.

Yue Qi halted in his tracks. "He didn't follow you?"

"There was too much going on," the child bawled. "I couldn't see clearly..."

"Don't panic. Slow down and tell me everything."

As it turned out, when that young master on horseback had taken his guards past the street entrance, he'd glanced sideways and spotted Shiwu and the other children on the street corner.

"Where are they from?" he'd asked, wrinkling his nose.

"They're beggar children, Young Master Qiu," said a guard. "We don't know where they come from."

"What are you doing, allowing such filthy things to hang about?"

The guards needed no further instruction from their master. They brazenly stalked over to chase the children away. But Shiwu had been unwilling to leave so easily, not after he'd finally managed to snatch away Shen Jiu's territory. He yelled angrily, "What gives you the right to kick us out—"

He'd wanted to finish with, "You don't own this street," but then that youthful young master waved his hand. A dark shadow descended, slashing a bloody whip mark onto Shiwu's face.

The wound was barely a hair's breadth from his eye. Shiwu had yet to register the pain; he was scared stiff.

That youthful young master smiled brightly. "What right? Not much of one. It's just that my family built this street."

Whether from pain or fright, Shiwu collapsed to the ground with a thud.

Shen Jiu hadn't finished listening to this tale before he burst into loud laughter, but he soon found himself unable to laugh anymore. Yue Qi did a headcount and discovered that some other children were missing as well. He looked back and said, "You should go. I'll come soon."

Shen Jiu was full of schadenfreude. "Leave it—don't go poking your nose into this. That Qiu guy doesn't actually have the guts to kill them."

Yue Qi shook his head. "You head back. I'm the oldest; I can't leave this alone."

"He won't die," Shen Jiu insisted. "At most he'll just get beaten up. That'll teach him a lesson."

"Go back," said Yue Qi.

Unable to restrain him, Shen Jiu spat, "You meddle too much!" After yelling this, he ran after him.

— PART 2 —

QIU JIANLUO thought that Shen Jiu was incredibly fun.

It was like hitting a dog. If you hit a dog, it would duck its head and cringe, cowering away as it whimpered. Though this reaction posed no threat, it also wasn't very interesting. However, if you stepped on this dog, it would growl low in its throat while staring at you fearfully. But it'd be too afraid to fight back, and *that* was interesting.

He gave Shen Jiu a slap. By now, Shen Jiu had doubtless mentally sworn to fuck the Qiu family's graves a hundred and eighteen times, but he could only obediently take these kicks; he even exposed his face for Qiu Jianluo to hit.

How incredibly fun.

As Qiu Jianluo thought this, he couldn't help but laugh out loud.

Shen Jiu had just taken a good beating and was currently cowering off to the side. Qiu Jianluo practically rolled with laughter as he eyed him.

After he'd purchased Shen Jiu, he'd locked him up for a few days, leaving him covered in grime and filth. When Qiu Jianluo looked at him again, he had been utterly disgusted, so he'd picked him up, dangling him like a kitten as he walked him over to several heavyset guards, and then told them to "scrub him clean."

Thereafter, Shen Jiu had been given a thorough scrubbing and cleaning, to the point that they'd almost scoured off a layer of his skin. Then they'd lugged him back to the study. Now that years of grime and dust had been boiled off of him, and because they'd pressed too hard when washing his face and arms, his pale skin glowed with a soft flush, while his wet hair still steamed from the bath. Standing off to the side, neatly dressed, he really did cut a rather pitiful figure.

Qiu Jianluo studied him for a long time, head cocked. A strange feeling rose in his heart, alongside a dash of fondness. He even held back the kick he'd planned on giving him.

"Can you read?" he asked.

"I know a couple characters," Shen Jiu said quietly.

Qiu Jianluo laid out a sheet of snow-white paper, then rapped on the desk. "Try to write them."

Shen Jiu reluctantly picked up a wolf-hair brush and held it, his grip surprisingly correct. He dipped it in some ink and thought for a moment, then first wrote a "seven." After another pause, he wrote a "nine."

Though the direction of his strokes was all wrong, the results were neither crooked nor slanted. Indeed, they were uniform and impeccable.

"Where did you learn these?" asked Qiu Jianluo.

"I watched someone write."

This brat knew absolutely fuck all—he only understood how to copy patterns. Yet he'd been able to fool Qiu Jianluo, which left him incredibly surprised. Thus, feeling increasingly amiable, he copied the tone of his family's old tutor and praised the boy. "You have some talent. If you put some effort into studying, you too might be able to go places."

Qiu Jianluo was sixteen, four years older than Shen Jiu, and he bore the weight of all of his parents' expectations. Having been raised in a house of golden bricks, he thought everyone beneath him; the only person he adored, the apple of his eye, was his little sister Haitang. She was the darling of the entire Qiu family. Whenever Qiu Jianluo was in front of Haitang, he always played the good older brother. In the past, he'd wished his sister would never marry, and now that Shen Jiu was here, he began to hatch an alternative plan.

Qiu Haitang loved Shen Jiu very much. If Shen Jiu were properly educated, Qiu Jianluo could turn him into a brother-in-law on the cheap. That didn't seem bad at all. Then his sister would remain by his side, and he could continue using Shen Jiu for his own amusement. As long as the boy remained honest and obedient, there would be no issues.

If Haitang married Shen Jiu, she wouldn't need to leave, and she'd still rely on their family for food, clothes, and money. It would be as good as not marrying her off in the first place. The plan had no flaws, other than the fact that matching her with Shen Jiu was a bit like letting a toad get a taste of some sumptuous swan meat.

Having calculated his plans to perfection, Qiu Jianluo would often give Shen Jiu warnings like:

"If you dare to make Haitang unhappy, I'll make sure to end your sorry life."

"If not for Haitang, I would have beaten you to death long ago."

"Humans must understand and repay kindness. Our family gave you the chance to play human, so even if it means repaying us with your life, that's just how it should be."

The older Shen Jiu grew, the more he understood that this person wouldn't tolerate even the slightest bit of disobedience. His every request was to be obeyed—even if what he heard filled him with indescribable disgust—he knew he must not express it. Only in this way could he avoid a vicious beating.

But within his heart, he still thought back on the first time he'd met Qiu Jianluo. That day had been the one and only time he'd driven the young master mad with rage.

Yue Qi had insisted on retrieving Shiwu and the other children. Right away, he'd almost collided with the hooves of Qiu Jianluo's horse. In that instant, Shen Jiu forgot Yue Qi's warnings—that it would be best not to reveal their rudimentary immortal arts to others. He transformed metal into a sharp blade and stabbed it into the horse, straight to the bone.

Qiu Jianluo and his horse spun around in place on the street, the animal rearing and bucking wildly. Shen Jiu silently cursed him to fall off with all his might, to fall and break his neck, but as it happened, Qiu Jianluo had outstanding horse-riding skills. Even with the horse's forelegs in midair, he remained firmly in the saddle. "Who did that?!" he roared. "Who did it?!"

Of course Shen Jiu had done it.

But even afterward, when Qiu Jianluo came knocking, if Shiwu hadn't taken the initiative to say so, no one would ever have known of Shen Jiu's interference.

If they hadn't saved Shiwu, he would have been trampled to death beneath the Qiu family's hooves. He'd kept his sorry life only to betray them. Shiwu should have been trampled to death, trampled into minced meat for thousands to spit upon. Qi-ge should never have gone back to save him. Even if Shiwu had died, it would have served him right.

As Shen Jiu suffered through day after day of torment, he turned those sweet yet futile thoughts over and over again in his mind, drawing strength and comfort from them.

And he waited for a certain someone to keep his promise to rescue him from this sea of suffering.

— PART 3 —

SHEN JIU THOUGHT a lot about why Yue Qi never returned to look for him.

Perhaps he'd been discovered while making his escape, and the human traffickers had broken his legs. Perhaps he had been unable to find any food on his journey and, being unwilling to beg, he'd starved to death. Perhaps his potential had been too meager, so none of the immortal mountains had been willing to take him in. Shen Jiu even imagined walking to the ends of the earth looking for Yue Qi's remains, and how, after finding them, he would dig him a grave with his own two hands. Perhaps he would even do his best to shed a tear.

Or, if Yue Qi was fortunate enough to still be alive, Shen Jiu imagined how he himself would cast away everything to rescue Yue Qi from whatever hellish straits he'd fallen into—even though Shen Jiu himself had only gone from the wolf's den to a tiger's lair, and so was in dire straits himself.

But no matter what, he could never have imagined this kind of reunion.

He raised and lowered his sword again and again, sending blood splattering everywhere in a horrifying tableau. Flecks of blood splashed into his eyes, but he only blinked a few times and otherwise wore no expression. One could have described his movements as deft and composed.

After taking him from Qiu Manor, the most Wu Yanzi had taught this "disciple" of his were things like murder and arson, stealth and robbery, and how to profit from chaos. For example, what he was doing now: using the Immortal Alliance Conference to loot the bodies of some foolish, immature, and rich children who had thought themselves elite cultivators, divesting them of their storage pouches, and then disposing of their corpses.

When Yue Qi discovered him, he must have been stunned frozen by Shen Jiu's ghastly appearance, for he didn't even register the disciples' bodies on the ground and instead took two steps toward him.

Shen Jiu shivered and abruptly looked up.

The moment Yue Qi got a clear look at his face, both of them paled into a bloodless white.

"Stay away!" Shen Jiu yelled.

Unexpectedly, his first reaction was to throw himself to the ground, snatch an emergency firework from one of the bodies, and release it into the sky.

Yue Qi was shaken but still confused. He walked toward Shen Jiu while extending his hand, opening his mouth to say—

At which point a disturbing chortle emerged from the dense forest beside them.

"My dear disciple, who is he? He's scared you so terribly. So you do know what it is to be afraid."

Shen Jiu released his grip, and the firework casing fell soundlessly to the ground. He hastily turned around. "Shifu, I'm not afraid of him. I made a mistake just now; I wasn't paying proper attention, which gave this lot on the ground the chance to release a firework. What I'm afraid of is that someone will show up soon!"

Yue Qi had realized that this situation was incredibly dangerous. Without batting an eyelid, he began to gather spiritual energy.

Wu Yanzi humphed. "When I saw that firework, I guessed that was the case. You've always been quick and nimble. What happened this time?! If they were going to set off fireworks, why didn't you chop off their hands?"

Shen Jiu lowered his head. "It's all this disciple's fault. We should go at once. If those old men get here, we won't be able to leave even if we try."

But Yue Qi moved to block them, raising the sword in his hand. He glanced at Shen Jiu with faintly reddened eyes, his voice hoarse but unusually resolute. "I can't let you leave."

Furious, Shen Jiu glared at him.

Wu Yanzi looked him up and down, then gave his sword the same once over. He scoffed. "From Cang Qiong Mountain—and even Qiong Ding Peak. The Xuan Su Sword, Yue Qingyuan?"

At this, Shen Jiu startled, then swiftly returned to his urging. "Shifu, since he's from Cang Qiong Mountain, we won't be able to kill him swiftly. It will be better for us to escape, and fast. Once everyone arrives, we'll be finished!"

Wu Yanzi sneered. "Cang Qiong Mountain may possess grand

prestige, but I need not stoop so far as to fear a junior cultivator. Besides, he came seeking death himself!"

As he and Yue Qi truly came to blows, Shen Jiu realized that his worry for Yue Qi, together with the various clumsy tricks he'd used because of it, were rather laughable. He was terrified of that "master" of his, Wu Yanzi. Terrified to death, even. But as Yue Qi—or Yue Qingyuan—met him in combat, he proved to be more than Wu Yanzi's equal even without drawing his sword.

Nevertheless, Shen Jiu couldn't relax completely; he was all too familiar with Wu Yanzi's fighting style and last-resort trump cards.

Wu Yanzi had a set of Cursed Black Light talismans. Countless times, Shen Jiu had witnessed Wu Yanzi toss out one of these paper talismans when at a disadvantage and score a kill by catching his opponent off guard. More than one famous cultivator had failed to escape this sinister maneuver. Moreover, it was easy to see that as he was now, Yue Qi had little experience fighting enemies: his movements were by the book, and he methodically attacked and parried in turns.

Therefore, right when Wu Yanzi was about to throw a talisman, Shen Jiu stabbed a sword through his back.

Yue Qi grabbed his hand and frantically sprinted away.

Having gone through a fierce battle, both youths were in shock. They leaned against a tree, panting heavily.

Once he'd calmed down, Shen Jiu finally gave Yue Qi a long, thorough look. His cultivation was extraordinary, and his bearing poised and steady. His clothes weren't of the common make either, and his demeanor was exactly like that of the great masters themselves. He couldn't have been further from the hellish straits Shen Jiu had imagined.

This was not Yue Qi but Yue Qingyuan.

Yue Qingyuan looked excited, his face flushed as he prepared to speak. But Shen Jiu opened fire first.

"You joined Cang Qiong Mountain?"

Shen Jiu couldn't tell what Yue Qingyuan was thinking, but the excitement on his face faded a little. Indeed, his complexion paled.

"You've become Qiong Ding Peak's head disciple? Not bad," said Shen Jiu. "Why didn't you come back to look for me?"

"I..."

Shen Jiu waited for some time, but the next words never came. So he said, "Why aren't you saying anything? I'm still waiting. I've already waited so many years, after all. Waiting a little longer will be nothing."

But how could Yue Qingyuan say anything?

Shen Jiu crossed his arms.

Finally, his waiting was rewarded with Yue Qingyuan's quiet words: "Sorry. It's Qi-ge who let you down."

Ice-cold fury crawled up inside Shen Jiu, engulfing his entire heart. His mouth and nose seemed to fill with the taste of his frenzied, raging blood.

First, he'd been a rat forced to swallow its anger, cringing while awaiting more beatings. Then he'd become a gutter rat, scurrying back and forth as everyone chased and hit it. No matter how he changed, he was a rat; cowering with its tail tucked between its legs, unable to see the light; letting years slip by in vain, squandering its time and life.

Meanwhile, Yue Qingyuan was a true phoenix that had flown to the summit, a carp that had leapt over the dragon's gate.

"Sorry, sorry, sorry... All you've ever known to do is say sorry." Shen Jiu sneered, then delivered the final, ringing blow: "It's utterly useless."

Some people were rotten from birth. Shen Jiu thought of himself in exactly this way—someone vile and poisonous from the start. Because, at that instant, he came to a crystal-clear realization:

That he'd rather have met a Yue Qi who'd died in some unknown corner, his remains unsightly and forgotten, than a Yue Qingyuan who was elegant and powerful, his prospects and future boundless.

— PART 4 —

SHEN JIU HATED far too many people and far too many things.

Obviously, people found it hard to say anything good about the character of someone who hated everything. So fortunately, by the time he became Shen Qingqiu, he understood he ought to at least keep that hatred from bubbling to the surface.

Within Cang Qiong Mountain, the one he undoubtedly hated most was Liu Qingge.

Liu Qingge had achieved success in his youth; his talents were extraordinary, his spiritual energy vast, and his swordplay awe-inspiring. His family background was excellent, and both his parents were alive. Any one of these things would have been enough to make Shen Qingqiu gnash his teeth and toss and turn for three days and three nights, let alone all of them together in one person.

During Cang Qiong Mountain's annual martial arts tournament, Shen Qingqiu's opponent had been Liu Qingge. Naturally, the conclusion had been an overwhelming loss on his part.

There was no shame in losing to the future Bai Zhan Peak Lord, or perhaps one should say that this was how it should be. That it was normal.

But Shen Qingqiu would absolutely never think such things. What he saw wasn't the bystanders' amazement at how he'd valiantly held out for so long but Liu Qingge's matter-of-fact arrogance as he held the point of Cheng Luan's blade inches from his throat.

Qing Jing Peak prided itself on being the gentleman's peak, and Shen Qingqiu took to playing a gentleman like a fish to water. Yet Liu Qingge was always able to make his rage boil to the surface, to the point that he didn't bother wasting energy playing nice with his sect sibling.

The thing Shen Qingqiu most often said to Liu Qingge was: "Liu Qingge, I'll definitely kill you one day!"

In this particular instance, the tender young lady carrying the pipa had long since thrown on her thin robes and dashed out in terror.

Liu Qingge sent him a glance. "You? Kill me?"

It was only three words, but Shen Qingqiu heard boundless venom within them. His wrist turned.

Yue Qingyuan saw that the situation didn't look good and pressed Shen Qingqiu's elbow downward, preventing him from drawing his sword. He looked back and yelled, "Liu-shidi! You should head back."

Liu Qingge looked like he couldn't be bothered to deal with this further. With a cold laugh, his figure instantly vanished.

This left only the two of them inside the Warm Red Pavilion. One person's clothes were mussed and disheveled, while the other's had not a thread out of place. The contrast couldn't have been clearer.

Yue Qingyuan yanked Shen Qingqiu off the bed. He was in a rare fit of anger. "Why are you like this?"

"How can I do what?" asked Shen Qingqiu.

"Two of Cang Qiong Mountain's head disciples getting into a huge brawl inside a brothel—does that sound good to you?"

"If you don't tell them and I don't either, who'd know which sect we're from?" Shen Qingqiu countered. "Cang Qiong Mountain is Cang Qiong Mountain. Tell me, which of Cang Qiong Mountain's rules decrees that its disciples can't visit this place? Cang Qiong Mountain isn't a Buddhist monastery or Daoist temple. They might be able to control everything else, but they can't stop me from looking for women! If Shixiong finds it shameful, he should watch that mouth of Liu Qingge's."

Indeed, Cang Qiong Mountain had never expressly ordained such a rule. But cultivators were supposed to naturally understand the concept of preserving a pure heart and nature, of exercising self-discipline—especially those of Qing Jing Peak, where the peak lords and disciples had invariably remained virtuous and unsullied. Instead, this unwritten consensus had become Shen Qingqiu's justification for sophistry.

Rendered speechless, Yue Qingyuan spent some time swallowing his words before giving a muted response: "I won't say anything. Liu-shidi and the others won't say anything either. No one will know."

"Then I must thank you both," said Shen Qingqiu as he put on his shoes.

"Lusting after women damages one's cultivation," said Yue Qingyuan.

Shen Qingqiu sneered. "Didn't you hear your Liu-shidi's tone with those words of his? 'You? Kill me?' 'With your abilities?' Damaged or not, they are as they are."

Yue Qingyuan was silent for a moment. "Liu-shidi isn't really such a bad person. He's like that with everyone, not just to you."

Shen Qingqiu scoffed. "'Like that with everyone'? Don't try to deceive me, Zhangmen-shixiong. Is he like that with you?"

"If you extend him a single share of kindness, he'll return it two-fold," Yue Qingyuan said patiently.

"Zhangmen-shixiong is truly considerate and understanding. It's just, why doesn't he extend kindness to me first? Why not have pity on me—show me some compassion? Why must *I* accommodate *him*?"

As Shen Qingqiu had turned a deaf ear to his every plea, Yue Qingyuan found it difficult to speak further. After all, he couldn't straight-up tell him something like: *If you hadn't used every means to ambush Liu Qingge after the meet in order to teach him a lesson, the two of you wouldn't fly into a rage at the slightest contact now, nor would you loathe the mere sight of each other.*

Shen Qingqiu yanked his clothes over his shoulder with a jerk of his hand, then slid Xiu Ya into its sheath. After taking two steps, he thought of something and turned around to inquire, "How did you know to find me here? Who reported it to you?"

"I went to Qing Jing Peak but didn't see you," said Yue Qingyuan. "Then I saw a few shidi from Bai Zhan Peak preparing to head there."

"Preparing to head there for what?"

Yue Qingyuan fell silent.

Shen Qingqiu sneered. "Preparing to gang up on me, is that right?"

Though conflict often erupted between Shen Qingqiu and Bai

Zhan Peak, the conflict this time was truly overblown. A Bai Zhan Peak disciple had gone to this small, remote town for a task, where he had just happened to see a familiar person enter the largest brothel in the area, the Warm Red Pavilion. From top to bottom, Bai Zhan Peak felt the same as Liu Qingge: none of them harbored any goodwill toward Shen Qingqiu. Therefore the disciple had obviously refused to let this chance pass by; he'd directly followed Shen Qingqiu into the brothel, then mocked him for being a hypocrite and actually entering this sort of place, saying that he'd lost face for their entire sect.

After a couple of undiplomatic words, Shen Qingqiu had beaten him severely, leaving him with serious injuries. When this disciple returned to Bai Zhan Peak, he'd run into Liu Qingge. After questioning him, Liu Qingge had been steaming with rage, he had promptly rushed over on his sword for payback, ready to hit Shen Qingqiu back for every blow.

If Yue Qingyuan hadn't caught Bai Zhan Peak's junior disciples in their preparations to head to Qing Jing Peak and dismantle Shen Qingqiu's bamboo lodgings, there was no telling what wreckage this little town would have suffered.

Noting how Yue Qingyuan refused to speak, Shen Qingqiu could guess the situation. As if Bai Zhan Peak ever had any good intentions. So, he changed the topic. "Why did you go to Qing Jing Peak? Didn't I tell you to not come looking for me?"

"I just wanted to see how you were doing," said Yue Qingyuan.

"I've troubled Yue-shixiong," said Shen Qingqiu. "I'm doing very well. I might be a hateful thing to most people, but luckily the Qing Jing Peak Lord doesn't despise me."

"If you truly are doing well, why do you never spend the night on Qing Jing Peak?" Yue Qingyuan asked, following on his heels.

Shen Qingqiu gave him a dark look. He knew that Yue Qingyuan must be thinking that he was being excluded by the rest of Qing Jing Peak.

Yue Qingyuan's guess wasn't unreasonable, but he was genuinely wrong this time. Though Shen Qingqiu was unpopular among his peers, it wasn't to the extent of being kicked out of the communal sleeping quarters.

He just loathed being in close quarters with those of the same sex.

All those years, whenever one of his beatings from Qiu Jianluo was over, or whenever he had a premonition of another beating, he had crawled to Qiu Haitang's room and remained there, quivering. As Qiu Jianluo was unwilling to let his sister see the side of him that was perverse and lunatic, that had been the only place where Shen Jiu could hide.

And even longer ago, there had been some girl in their group, their big sis. But after she reached a certain age, that big sis had been sold to a withered old man to be his second wife. Afterward, they'd left that city, so they'd never seen her again.

Liking women wasn't the least bit shameful, but treating women like saviors, cowering within their embrace and seeking courage from them...even without anyone saying it, Shen Qingqiu knew that was *horrendously* shameful. So even if it meant his death, he would never tell anyone, least of all Yue Qingyuan.

"If I said that I wasn't doing well at Qing Jing Peak, what would you do?" Shen Qingqiu asked, slow and measured. "Would you help me enter Qiong Ding Peak, just as you recommended me for Qing Jing?"

Yue Qingyuan gave it some thought, then said solemnly, "If that's what you wanted."

"Clearly I don't want that," Shen Qingqiu said with a resolute humph. "I want to be head disciple. Would you be willing to give me your position? Let me become the sect leader?" he asked, forceful and lofty. "For better or worse, Qing Jing Peak ranks second among the Twelve Peaks. I'd rather wait to succeed this one."

Yue Qingyuan sighed. "Xiao-Jiu, why must you always act like this?"

When he heard that name, Shen Qingqiu's entire back shuddered with incomparable irritation. "Don't call me that!"

Among his "Qing" generation peers, Shen Jiu stood out as sharp and resourceful, so the peak lord was quite fond of him. He hadn't been around for long, nor was his foundation up to par with his peers, yet he'd been designated the successor. Once the peak lord gave their head disciple new names, their original ones would be discarded.

In the past, Qiu Jianluo had forced Shen Jiu to learn how to read and write. Shen Jiu had been unwilling to learn, had detested it to the point of madness, yet now it was only through his abilities in reading and studying—through being smarter than his peers—that he'd been able to earn the Qing Jing Peak Lord's favor. To make it even more laughable, of the thousands of possible names in this world, the peak lord had just happened to name him "Qing*qiu*."

But no matter how laughable, no matter how it made him gnash his teeth, Shen Qingqiu still wanted that name, for this name represented that from now onward, a shining new life was his.

Shen Qingqiu gathered his thoughts and smiled happily. "That name irritates me whenever I hear it. I've long forgotten it. So please, Zhangmen-shixiong, you should also discard it."

Yue Qingyuan said, "Then the day you respond to it would be the day it no longer irritates you?"

A pause. Shen Qingqiu sneered. "That will never happen. Yue Qingyuan, allow me to say it once more: never let me hear that name, ever again."

— PART 5 —

SHEN QINGQIU FINALLY couldn't take it any longer. He headed to Qiong Ding Peak.

When it came to Qiong Ding Peak, Shen Qingqiu always tried to visit as little as possible. And when it came to Yue Qingyuan, he always tried to see him as little as possible too.

Therefore, the Twelve Peaks' annual martial arts tournament was terribly troublesome for him.

Cang Qiong Mountain's Twelve Peaks had a fixed ranking. This ranking was unrelated to the strength of each peak. Instead, it had been designated back when Cang Qiong Mountain's first generation of peak lords had established themselves. All successive peak lords had addressed each other in accordance with this ranking rather than by their order of entry into the sect. Therefore, even though he'd entered the sect quite some time after Liu Qingge, because Qing Jing Peak was ranked second—only below Qiong Ding Peak—while Bai Zhan Peak was ranked seventh, Liu Qingge still had to address Shen Qingqiu as "Shixiong," if through gritted teeth.

At the same time, because of this ranking, Qiong Ding Peak and Qing Jing Peak disciples were customarily positioned such that their squadrons neighbored each other's. On top of that, their head disciples had to stand side by side.

Yue Qingyuan was unable to catch Shen Qingqiu at other times, so he would latch on to these opportunities to ask him all sorts of questions. He chattered nonstop as he inquired after important things like how his cultivation and studies were going, as well as trivial matters like whether he had ample food or clothing, or whether he was cold or warm. Though Shen Qingqiu found this unbearably annoying, he wasn't stupid enough to embarrass the sect leader's head disciple before such a large audience. For every twenty questions Yue Qingyuan asked, he replied once, maintaining his distance and courtesy both, while ruminating over the techniques from his studies the night prior and contemplating other things.

This was the martial arts tournament's most comical scene every year. Perhaps the two of them didn't realize it, but for many disciples, watching these two head disciples was the only fun to be had during the peak lords' tedious pre-meet speeches. They'd watch one party act unlike himself, ignoring the silence as he murmured and whispered, while the other party absentmindedly stared straight ahead, hemming and hawing.

Therefore, Shen Qingqiu's decision to voluntarily come to Qiong Ding Peak not only surprised and pleased Yue Qingyuan, but practically all the disciples at the scene were jumping over themselves, banging gongs and drums as they yelled for everyone to come watch.

Shen Qingqiu didn't have much to say; he had no interest in playing the part of circus monkey for others. He applied for permission to cultivate in the Ling Xi Caves, then left immediately afterward.

Isolated from the outside world, the Ling Xi Caves overflowed with abundant spiritual energy. As Shen Qingqiu moved through the caverns, his expression grew increasingly grim.

Those days he'd squandered under Qiu Jianluo and Wu Yanzi had been of no small consequence.

Within the new generation of peak lords, Yue Qingyuan had naturally attained Core Formation first. Qi Qingqi and Liu Qingge had followed practically on his heels, breaking through at the same time. An Ding Peak's Shang Qinghua, with his mediocre background, had barely managed to keep up—but even he had achieved official ascension.

However, the more anxious Shen Qingqiu grew, the more stuck he became, until he was suspended in place and unable to progress. He was racked with stress and anxiety. It was like he was swallowing a hundred kilos of tobacco every day; it smoldered within his head and stomach, stoking his flames of rage and irritation until they erupted. With Shen Qingqiu like this, no one dared to get on his bad side. But even if they didn't dare, Shen Qingqiu didn't let them go.

Luo Binghe was using the incorrect cultivation manual that Shen Qingqiu had handed him; he should have long since died bleeding from the seven apertures, his body rupturing down to his bones, skin, meridians, tendons, and flesh. But not only had this failed to come to pass, Luo Binghe's cultivation was steadily improving.

Furthermore, Shen Qingqiu had told Ning Yingying thousands of times to stay far away from Luo Binghe and that she wasn't allowed to get involved with him. So why did he see them every day, whispering together before his eyes?

Shen Qingqiu was filled with paranoia; he forever felt like everyone was secretly talking behind his back, discussing how he'd been unable to attain Core Formation even after this long. That it was unbecoming for one in his position. That they hoped to secretly finish him off and replace him.

So now, he secluded himself within the Ling Xi Caves. If he still couldn't make a breakthrough...

Shen Qingqiu sat upon the stone platform, but his thoughts continued to spiral everywhere until he'd worked himself into a cold sweat. His breaths and circulation choked, stars flashing in his vision. Suddenly, he felt a burst of spiritual energy raging rampant throughout his meridians.

This was no small matter. Panicking, he quickly went still, sitting tight as he attempted to rein in his mind—when a person suddenly approached him from behind.

Shen Qingqiu's hair stood on end, and he snatched up Xiu Ya, drawing it halfway as he yelled, "Who's there?!"

A palm gently pressed against his shoulder.

"It's me," said Yue Qingyuan.

Shen Qingqiu said nothing.

Yue Qingyuan continued to send him spiritual energy, pacifying his wild spiritual fluctuations in their violent stampede. "My apologies. Your mind and spirit are currently disturbed. I've frightened you."

Shen Qingqiu had been frightened by his own spiraling thoughts. For this reason, he was even less amenable to listening to others point it out. "Who's frightened?" he snapped angrily. "Zhangmen-shixiong never enters the Ling Xi Caves for secluded cultivation, no? So why must you fight me for a spot the moment I do!"

"It's not true that I've never entered them," said Yue Qingyuan. "I've come here before."

Shen Qingqiu was baffled by this tangent. "Who cares whether your esteemed self has come here?"

Yue Qingyuan sighed. "Shidi, can you not just stay quiet for a while and concentrate on regulating your breathing?"

Upon a stone candlestick's dried wax, a faint flame flickered to life. Shen Qingqiu hadn't planned to retort, but when he took in the full sight of the cave he'd chosen, he was stunned. "Did someone duel to the death in here?" he blurted out.

Countless slashes from either blade or axe gouged the cavern walls, leaving the impression of a disfigured face covered with layer upon layer of scars. The effect was both sinister and terrifying.

Behind him, Yue Qingyuan said, "No. Duels are forbidden in the Ling Xi Caves."

Other than the sword gashes, there were also swathes upon swathes of dark-red bloodstains. Some looked like blood spray, as though splattered there after someone had been pierced through by a sharp blade. Others appeared to be from someone slamming their forehead into the wall, as if they were begging for something, leaving behind smear after smear with each impact.

Shen Qingqiu stared at those almost blackened stains. "Then... did someone die here?"

Whenever they interacted, it was usually Yue Qingyuan who talked tirelessly. Never had there been a situation like this, where Yue Qingyuan refused to utter a single word.

Shen Qingqiu found this alien and strange, to the point that goosebumps broke out over his body. "Yue Qingyuan?"

"I'm here."

"If you're here, why won't you say something?"

"Isn't it because the moment I do, you'll find it annoying?"

Shen Qingqiu snorted and laughed. "That's right. You're very annoying. So you know it too!" But he didn't want to fall into a silence within this darkness either, so he could only reluctantly continue on this thread. "I heard that sometimes, they'll shut disciples and other sect members inside the Ling Xi Caves—like those who are experiencing a qi deviation or those who have resorted to unnatural paths. Do you think this might have been one of those situations?"

After a long time, Yue Qingyuan made a noncommittal noise: "Oh."

Shen Qingqiu had received the cold shoulder, but he still squinted at a stretch of wall. "It seems that whoever this was wanted very much to leave," he concluded. "They struggled for a long time before dying."

If all this blood had come from the same person, even if they had survived, they would have had one foot in the grave.

Shen Qingqiu suddenly felt that something was off about the hand Yue Qingyuan had on his back. Alarmed, he said, "What's wrong?"

It was a long moment before Yue Qingyuan replied. "Nothing."

Shen Qingqiu shut up.

He couldn't see Yue Qingyuan's expression where he stood behind him, but he could feel the hand passing him spiritual energy, and how it trembled slightly.

— PART 6 —

When Shen Qingqiu stirred, he felt a coolness trickling from the wounds on his body. The burning, hellish pain had been alleviated by quite a bit.

He struggled to open his eyes. On one knee beside him was a figure, currently looking down as he examined Shen Qingqiu's condition.

Upon the white stone platform, a black hem was evenly laid, a plain and rustic longsword held firmly beneath it. Several empty, upended medicine bottles lay scattered about.

The sword was Xuan Su. The person was, as one would expect, Yue Qingyuan. It was the same gentle and handsome face, just a good deal paler than usual, the exhaustion evident. At this sort of time, only Yue Qingyuan would still come to see him.

"How did you get in?" Shen Qingqiu asked, his voice hoarse. Luo Binghe was determined to make him suffer. There was no way he'd have been willing to let Yue Qingyuan enter the Water Prison to help him keep holding on by a thread.

Seeing that Shen Qingqiu could speak, Yue Qingyuan sighed in relief. He held his hand while whispering, "Stop talking. Focus."

He wanted to pass Shen Qingqiu spiritual energy and help those wounds heal faster. This time, at last, Shen Qingqiu didn't brush him aside, because right now he was thinking, *That's right, no matter what, he's still a sect leader.*

As harsh as Luo Binghe and that old geezer from Huan Hua Palace wanted to be, they had to at least show some superficial courtesy.

But it must have taken a lot of trouble for Yue Qingyuan to gain entrance.

Spiritual energy coursed through Shen Qingqiu's wounds, and the pain in his twisting flesh felt like dense clusters of iron needles stabbing into him. Shen Qingqiu clenched his teeth, his hatred surging to the point that he laughed instead. "That little bastard Luo Binghe sure has plenty of tricks up his sleeve."

At the sound of the bone-deep venom within his tone, Yue Qingyuan sighed again. In truth, Yue Qingyuan wasn't the type to sigh much, but Shen Qingqiu was inevitably capable of wearing him to the bone. "Shidi," he said, exhausted, "we've already come this far, so why do you still refuse to consider your wrongdoings?"

Even if someone had knocked out his teeth, even if he was left swallowing his own blood, Shen Qingqiu had always stubbornly refused to admit his transgressions—especially in front of Yue Qingyuan, in front of whom you could absolutely forget about any confessions.

"What 'wrongdoings'?" Shen Qingqiu asked bitterly. "Zhangmen-shixiong, please tell me, what is Luo Binghe if not a bastard? You just wait. He won't be satisfied only taking it out on me. If, in the future, some tumultuous storm upsets the cultivation world, then the only thing I will have done wrong was fail to cut him down at the start."

Yue Qingyuan shook his head. It seemed like he'd anticipated this answer and that he had no desire to advise or admonish him. The situation had already gone past the point of no return. Any further admonishment was pointless. Suddenly, he asked, "Did you really kill Liu-shidi?"

Shen Qingqiu didn't want to look at his face at all while he answered. But he couldn't help but lift his eyes, giving Yue Qingyuan's expression a quick glance. He froze for a moment, then abruptly yanked his hand out of Yue Qingyuan's grip and sat up.

"You repeatedly said that you'd kill him one day," said Yue Qingyuan. "But I never thought that you would actually do it."

"Aren't you thinking it now?" Shen Qingqiu asked coldly. "He's already been killed. Does Zhangmen-shixiong not think it too late to rebuke this humble Shen at this point? Or do you wish to cleanse the sect?"

"I have no right to rebuke you," said Yue Qingyuan.

Both his eyes and expression were exceedingly serene, so much so that Shen Qingqiu inexplicably became furious with shame. "Then what are you trying to do?!"

"Has Shidi ever considered that, if you hadn't treated Luo Binghe like that in the beginning, everything that unfolded today never would have happened?"

Shen Qingqiu burst into laughter. "Why does Zhangmen-shixiong say such ludicrous things? What's happened has happened! I've already 'considered' it hundreds and thousands of times! There is no 'if,' no 'in the beginning'—there was never any chance of redemption!"

Yue Qingyuan slowly raised his face.

Shen Qingqiu knew that saying those words was as good as taking a knife and stabbing it into Yue Qingyuan's chest. At first he was gleeful, but then he looked at Yue Qingyuan, woodenly kneeling as he stared blankly at Shen Qingqiu. All of Yue Qingyuan's composure, poise, and demeanor had disappeared, as if he'd aged many years in an instant. And when Shen Qingqiu saw this, a strange sensation suddenly welled inside his heart.

It was probably pity.

The stalwart mountain that never changed, the eternally calm and collected Sect Leader Yue of Cang Qiong Mountain, was at this moment so wretched, so browbeaten, that Shen Qingqiu couldn't help but feel pity.

And with this pity, something inside Shen Qingqiu's chest, a knot that had resided within him for many years, finally came undone.

With that, he came to the cheerful conclusion that Yue Qingyuan had truly done everything he could; he'd gone above and beyond to fulfill the calls of both kindness and duty. Regardless of how much guilt weighed down his heart, his debt had long since been repaid in full.

"You should go," said Shen Qingqiu. "I'll tell you this: Even if all of this could be redone from the beginning, in the end, the conclusion would remain the same. My heart is full of malice, my insides hatred and resentment. Today, Luo Binghe wishes for me to die horribly, and I only have myself to blame."

"Do you still hold such hatred within yourself?" asked Yue Qingyuan.

Shen Qingqiu laughed uproariously. "Only when I see other people unhappy can I be happy myself. What do you think?"

Holding Xuan Su across both hands, Yue Qingyuan offered it to Shen Qingqiu. "If you still hold such hatred, draw Xuan Su and take my life."

Shen Qingqiu scoffed. "You ask me to kill you here, Sect Leader Yue? Are you unsatisfied with the crimes Luo Binghe's already charged me with? You think them too few? Besides, who do you think you are? My hatred will be resolved as long as I kill you? I'm far beyond cure; I hate *everything*. Don't blame this humble Shen for any disrespect or mockery, but if Sect Leader Yue considers himself that very cure, he thinks too highly of himself!"

He was devastatingly straightforward with his humiliation of Yue Qingyuan, but the latter didn't withdraw his hands; it was like he hadn't understood. Instead, he seemed to summon his courage. "Xiao-Jiu, I—"

"Don't call me that!" Shen Qingqiu snarled.

Slowly, Yue Qingyuan's hands slumped, the sword lowering with them. A long moment passed, and then he went to hold Shen

Qingqiu's hand again. He sent him an unceasing flow of spiritual energy, helping to alleviate those injuries.

It was like his courage had been shattered, for all through the following moments, Yue Qingyuan never again opened his mouth to speak.

Finally, Shen Qingqiu said, "I thank Zhangmen-shixiong for his generosity. Now get lost. Never appear before me ever again."

Yue Qingyuan put Xuan Su back on his waist, then complied with Shen Qingqiu's wish and slowly walked out.

If you can escape this, Sect Leader Yue, get far away, as far as you can. From now on, never again involve yourself with a thing like Shen Qingqiu.

— PART 7 —

WITH HIS REMAINING EYE, Shen Qingqiu stared at the cellar entrance. After staring at it for an unknown number of days, Luo Binghe finally returned.

Even when inside a damp and gloomy underground prison, Luo Binghe was as graceful and elegant as ever, unsoiled and pristine. As he stepped over the hardened, blackened bloodstains on the ground, he spoke charmingly. "Sect Leader Yue kept the appointment, as expected. I am truly grateful to that tactful yet sorrowful letter of blood Shizun wrote. Otherwise this disciple could never have succeeded so easily. Originally, this disciple wanted to bring Sect Leader Yue's body back to show Shizun, but the arrows had been drenched in a rare poison. When he got close and touched them, even slightly, Sect Leader Yue just... Alas, I could only retrieve his sword; let's call it a memento for Shizun."

Luo Binghe was lying.

Luo Binghe was a shameless, treacherous little liar who spoke only falsehoods. His flagrant lies were uncountable. So this time, too, he had to be conniving away with some plot or scheme with which to deceive others.

Luo Binghe sat down on a chair off to the side. Whenever he watched Shen Qingqiu scream and wail, he always used this seat. He scraped at the leaves drifting within his steaming cup of tea and commented, "Heroes and famed swords come in pairs. Xuan Su is indeed an excellent blade, worthy of Sect Leader Yue. However, there's something even more wondrous about that sword. Sect Leader Yue's cultivation has truly opened my eyes. While Shizun is enjoying his remaining days here, if you're bored with nothing to do, you can thoroughly ponder it. It is truly very interesting."

Shen Qingqiu didn't understand.

In Huan Hua Palace's Water Prison, upon their last meeting with each other, he'd done his utmost to be callous, cruel, and sarcastic. He'd told Yue Qingyuan to get lost, and Yue Qingyuan had done so. Shen Qingqiu had been uncertain if that letter of blood would call him here. But no normal person, if they were of sound thought, would step into such a blatant, undisguised trap.

He still didn't understand.

I thought you weren't coming.

Luo Binghe found his results yet unsatisfactory. He smiled brightly. "Ah, right. Though Shizun's letter of blood was awfully heart-wrenching, it was a bit sloppy and half-hearted. After all, it had been perfunctorily written for this disciple while under great duress. This disciple understands. Therefore, in order to express your sincerity, I had two other things specially sent with it."

Shen Qingqiu understood. Those "other things," were the two legs that had once been attached to his body.

This was far too comical.

Once, he'd waited days and nights for that person, and he hadn't come. And now, when he'd never thought that person would, he just had to.

On the corner of Shen Qingqiu's lips hung a cold smile. "Ha. Ha ha. Yue Qingyuan, ah, Yue Qingyuan."

Originally, Luo Binghe's mood could have been considered cheerful, but when he saw that bizarre smile, he inexplicably became upset. "What are you smiling about?" he asked gently.

Shen Qingqiu ignored him but continued to sneer.

Luo Binghe shed his gleeful expression. "Shen Qingqiu," he said attentively, "do you think that pretending to be insane will work on me?"

"Luo Binghe," said Shen Qingqiu, enunciating every syllable, "you're a bastard, you know that?"

A sudden silence descended around them.

Luo Binghe stared at him, and Shen Qingqiu stared unswervingly back.

Suddenly, Luo Binghe's lips twitched. His right hand gently caressed Shen Qingqiu's left shoulder, then squeezed.

A terrifying scream pierced the air.

Blood sprayed from the fresh stump that had been Shen Qingqiu's left arm, and he howled while roaring with laughter, his breaths broken and stilted. "Luo Binghe, ha ha ha ha… Luo Binghe, you…"

For Luo Binghe, torturing Shen Qingqiu was an incredibly satisfying pastime. Shen Qingqiu's screams made him feel like he was floating in paradise. But this time, for some reason, Luo Binghe didn't feel the same joy.

His chest heaved, its rise and fall growing increasingly violent. With a kick, he knocked Shen Qingqiu over, making him spin in place on the ground, smearing blood all over the floor.

Previously, Luo Binghe had ripped off his two legs in the same manner, as if plucking limbs from an insect. Pain tore through Shen Qingqiu, the kind that made him feel like he was in hell, yet the sensation no longer seemed real.

On the contrary, he became lucid—clear and rational. "Luo Binghe, everything you have today you owe to taking me as your master, so shouldn't you thank me? Instead, you're wholly unable to tell what's good for yourself. As expected, you're an ungrateful bastard, ha ha ha ha..."

Luo Binghe's rage passed in an instant, and he suddenly calmed down. His smile was sinister as he said softly, "Do you want to die? How can something like death come so cheaply? Shizun, you've committed many evils in your life. You hurt those with whom you had grievances and also those against whom you bore no grudges. Even when half in your grave, you managed to drag down a sect leader. If your death isn't drawn out, if you don't simultaneously endure everyone's else's suffering at least once, how can you do right by them?"

With a wave of his hand, he cast Xuan Su's fragments onto the ground.

When Shen Qingqiu heard the resulting clatter, it was as if his throat had been slashed with an invisible knife—his laughter instantly stopped.

Amidst disheveled hair and a face drenched in blood, a single eye shone brightly, a white fire glowing in the dark night. He shakily dragged himself toward those broken sword fragments.

There was nothing left.

Only a single blade.

He had singlehandedly created the Luo Binghe of today, but who had singlehandedly wrought this ending of Shen Qingqiu's?

Yue Qingyuan shouldn't have met this kind of fate.

For the purpose of attending a decades-late appointment, in order to fulfill a futile, meritless promise.

The sword broken, the man dead.

It shouldn't have been like this.

Threads of blood unfurled, extending outward. Right before they should have converged into one, they passed each other by.

25
Bamboo Branch Poem

ZHUZHI-LANG HAD KNOWN for a long, long time that it was a disgusting monster.

Even on the southern border, where monsters flourished, it was considered a monster among monsters.

Back then it hadn't been called Zhuzhi-Lang, for it had possessed no name. Generally speaking, upon sighting a half-man, half-snake thing slithering about on the ground, no one would be bored enough to think of giving it a name. Even if they *were* bored enough, the southern border demons preferred to give it a couple of kicks, stab its tail, or study this weird little thing for a weak spot to see if you even could beat it to death.

Its daily schedule was very simple: slither, look for water, slither, look for food, slither, bite and scrimmage with other beast-shaped demons.

Though it lacked an impressive appearance, when it came to fighting, it wasn't at too much of a disadvantage. On the contrary, not only was its body flexible and agile, its disgusting appearance often disturbed and distracted its opponent during battle.

Therefore, this weird little thing, being both ugly and a pain, was extremely unpopular on the southern border.

Upon seeing it for the first time, even an educated noble like Tianlang-Jun stared it up and down for a while before he said with all sincerity, "It's so ugly."

As was to be expected, the black-armored generals standing apathetically behind him said nothing.

"*Far* too ugly," Tianlang-Jun repeated. It was uncertain who he was complaining to.

There was too much emphasis in that sentence. The weird little thing shrank away.

Then again, it felt, somehow, that this esteemed noble's criticism held no true disgust. It had seen gazes rife with disgust many, many times, and they hadn't been like this.

Tianlang-Jun gracefully shifted into a half crouch, staring at it. "Do you remember your mother?"

It shook its head.

"Oh," said Tianlang-Jun. "That's good too. If I had that kind of mother, I too would prefer not to remember her."

It didn't know what to say. Of course, even if it had known, it wouldn't have been able to say it. All it could do was release a raspy hiss.

Tianlang-Jun gave it a smile. "However, there are some things you should be told. Your mother is dead. I'm her older brother. To fulfill her dying wish, I've come to see you."

Demons were cold-blooded. When it came to the death of a blood relative, any one of them could speak of the event cavalierly, glossing over it with a single line. The weird little thing didn't feel anything in particular; it only stiffly nodded out of habit.

Tianlang-Jun seemed to find this dull. "All right," he said dryly. "I've seen to her last request. All of these are your subordinates. From here on out, this plot of land will be yours."

The subordinates he referred to were those hundreds of black-armored generals. Although these things had no mind and couldn't think, they feared neither pain nor death, and would never stop nor feel fatigue. They formed an invincible, all-conquering army, and Tianlang-Jun had indeed handed them off to a half-man, half-snake monster on a whim.

Tianlang-Jun stood up and patted the nonexistent dust from his hem, then turned and left. In an unexpected development, the weird little thing wavered in place before wriggling its way after him.

Tianlang-Jun looked back, bewildered. "What are you following me for?"

The snake-man dared not move. At the sight of this, Tianlang-Jun took another step forward, and it once again began to slither behind him, squirming.

Tianlang-Jun stopped in place and asked in confusion, "Can you not understand me?"

This scene repeated once, twice, then three times. In the end, Tianlang-Jun simply ignored the thing, going on his way with his hands clasped behind his back. The snake-man clumsily tagged along after him.

Tianlang-Jun's was a special existence: his blood was noble and his status extraordinary, so naturally he had no shortage of enemies. As the snake-man followed, countless rabble came to make trouble for him. Despite Tianlang-Jun clearly having no need for outside help, the snake-man always stepped up to fight with all its might, offering its meager martial ability.

This happened numerous times, until Tianlang-Jun finally couldn't ignore the thing's existence.

He sent the battered and bruised snake-man two glances and delivered his assessment: "Still so ugly."

Wounded, the snake-man shrank back.

Tianlang-Jun smiled again. "And also stubborn. That's not very personable."

Even after following him all this time, the snake-man had never once flinched back from the many difficulties and obstacles. But when met with this unkind evaluation, it was filled with the impulse to turn and run—no, slither—away.

It never would have guessed that in the next moment, Tianlang-Jun would place a bare hand on its head and sigh. "Both ugly and stubborn; I can't stand to watch this any longer."

A strange and gentle flow, both warm and cold, coursed through all its limbs and bones.

But how could it have limbs?

The snake-man realized very quickly that, without its knowledge, four perfectly whole limbs had sprouted from its once-deformed torso. On top of that, ten fingers, things he had found exquisite yet unattainable, had appeared upon his new palms.

It was the body of a youth. The body's age was around fifteen to sixteen, its complexion fair and figure slender, healthy and whole.

Tianlang-Jun moved his hand away, his pitch-black irises reflecting a white silhouette. While holding the youth's chin, he said, "I think this looks a bit better. Any thoughts?"

The other opened his mouth, wanting to speak. He'd finally managed to obtain a man's form, yet no matter how he tried, his mouth and tongue failed to obey his commands. The moment he opened his mouth and a slightly sluggish sound escaped, a warm liquid slipped out of his eyes.

Though Zhuzhi-Lang firmly believed that his lord could do no wrong, he secretly thought that his lord's brain actually wasn't too sharp.

Even after receiving tacit permission to stay at Tianlang-Jun's side, for a long period of time, Zhuzhi-Lang had no name.

Tianlang-Jun didn't often command the people around him, so he didn't need to call the youth by name; hence, they passed many months in a muddle.

Then one day, Tianlang-Jun wanted to find a certain poetry collection from the Human Realm. He overturned boxes and cabinets but couldn't find it, and it wasn't until he was forced to call someone for help that he suddenly remembered he had a nephew whose presence was about equivalent to that of a patch of empty air, and who was currently sitting in the corner of his study.

But after calling out, "Hey," he couldn't think of what to say next. Tianlang-Jun frowned and thought for a while, then said, "Have I never asked for your name?"

"My lord, this subordinate has no name," his nephew honestly replied.

"How can you have no name?" Tianlang-Jun asked, bewildered. "That's so strange. Then what am I supposed to call you?"

"Whatever my lord wishes to call me will do." After saying this, the youth walked to the bookcase and pulled out the poetry collection from where Tianlang-Jun had randomly stuffed it after finishing his read. Then he presented it to his lord with both hands.

Tianlang-Jun was most satisfied. As he took the collection, he said, "Not having a name isn't much of a problem. We can simply give you one." After flipping through a couple of pages at random with his head lowered, he chose a phrase on a whim. "Let's call you Zhuzhi-Jun."

With his sharp eyes, he'd given the text a skim or two.

"By tender green willows over placid river waters / I listen to my lover sing his song on the shore. / The sun rises from the east as rain dims the west / Here clear skies and dark mingle in concord."

Bamboo Branch Song, Zhuzhi-Ci.[3]

His nephew shook his head.

"You don't like it?" asked Tianlang-Jun. He handed him the book. "So picky. Then choose one yourself."

His nephew didn't know whether to laugh or to cry. "My lord, only nobles can use such a title."

"So particular even at your tender age," said Tianlang-Jun. "Fine, then we'll call you Zhuzhi-Lang."

Everything Tianlang-Jun did was done flippantly. He'd flippantly given his nephew a life, and he flippantly gave him a name. And at this moment and this place, due to him, "Zhuzhi-Lang" was flippantly born.

But no matter how careless, how childish his behavior, he was still Tianlang-Jun, the person for whom Zhuzhi-Lang would brave both fire and flood, for whom he would sacrifice ten thousand lives.

One could scarcely imagine that Tianlang-Jun was also pondering whether his nephew had spent too many years as a snake and had therefore become a little foolish.

Said nephew refused to call him "Uncle," and insisted on calling him "my lord." He refused to go be a carefree lordling on the

---

3 *A poem written by Liu Yuxi expressing the conflicted feelings of a maiden in love. The original makes use of hard-to-translate wordplay, as "clear" and "love" are homonyms in Chinese.*

southern border and instead insisted on following Tianlang-Jun to be an errand boy. He even refused a good-quality name, insisting on demoting himself.

He truly was a bit foolish. But a brain that wasn't sharp was a lifelong problem, so it couldn't be helped.

Let him do as he wishes.

Tianlang-Jun truly loved any and everything to do with humans.

He probably felt that demons were a cold and boring lot. Yet when it came to humans, he nursed a strange passion for and a beautiful mental image of that foreign race, almost to an exaggerated extent.

Any time he went anywhere, his most common destination was the borderlands. He'd pass the boundary markers, and on his short stays, he'd drink some wine while listening to stories. But on his long stays, it wasn't out of the question for him to spend a whole year—or even more—touring the Human Realm.

Tianlang-Jun probably wasn't the type who enjoyed being followed. He often dismissed his black-armored generals in the hundreds or thousands. But as far as Zhuzhi-Lang was concerned, first off, he didn't talk too much, and second, he didn't get in the way. He only silently followed after Tianlang-Jun, so it wouldn't have been very different if he hadn't existed at all. Sometimes he helped out by paying the bill or running an errand, and he was both convenient and considerate, so he didn't particularly annoy his uncle.

Even when he was meeting with that Maiden Su, neither of them minded Zhuzhi-Lang tagging along. As if of one mind, they both pretended Zhuzhi-Lang was a real snake who could understand neither normal conversation nor more intimate exchanges; they focused on each other and acted like he wasn't there.

Only once did Tianlang-Jun try to drive Zhuzhi-Lang away, even telling him to, "Get lost." As someone who'd always pursued grace and refinement, it had been some of the crudest language he'd ever used.

Bai Lu Mountain.

As for what Tianlang-Jun and Su Xiyan's first meeting was like, Zhuzhi-Lang didn't witness it himself; at the time he had, at Tianlang-Jun's request, been standing in line for a famous author's newest work.

Initially, he felt no curiosity about their meeting. But after it happened, Tianlang-Jun fell into an odd state for a long time.

While Zhuzhi-Lang was acting as a snake-shaped transportation device, Tianlang-Jun said from his seat on his head, "In the plays I've read, maidens from the Human Realm are unanimously gentle as water, considerate and charming; hence, I thought that all maidens would be like this. So. I've been lied to. Zhuzhi-Lang, one can't read too many plays."

Then another time, his lord—who'd conclusively forgotten about not reading too many plays—was enjoying another one with relish as he said, "Do I look like someone who can't carry things? Or someone who's so poor they can't even afford the trip home?"

Then, when Zhuzhi-Lang was doing his laundry, Tianlang-Jun crouched gracefully beside him while saying, "Zhuzhi-Lang, what do you think of my face? Is it not handsome? Typically speaking, shouldn't anyone who beholds my face immediately transform into a young woman tenderly budding into love?"

Zhuzhi-Lang shook out the clothes he'd wrung and hung them on a bamboo pole, respectfully agreeing. At the same time, he was thinking of how he'd read quite a few of his lord's nonsensical plays together with him. He didn't know what other people were like, but the way his lord was acting now was really rather akin to the lovestruck teenage girls in those books.

Therefore, he inevitably became curious.

In Zhuzhi-Lang's imagination, a maiden who entered an abandoned town filled with troublemaking demons all by herself, who while dispatching evil spirits had told Tianlang-Jun to sing and play his music farther away so he wouldn't get in the way, and who after dispatching them had handed Tianlang-Jun three silvers, saying that it was money for his trip home, well… Even if she wasn't burly and heavyset, she should at least look like a martial arts master with fierce and ferocious eyes.

For all that, when he finally met the culprit behind Tianlang-Jun's bout of philosophical soul-searching, which had tormented Zhuzhi-Lang for many days, he realized that the culprit in question was not quite like what he'd envisioned.

Tianlang-Jun loved wandering the Human Realm, and wandering the Human Realm required spending money. Yet he never remembered to bring any. So, Zhuzhi-Lang could only remember for him. However, Tianlang-Jun had no concept of money's value, and therefore he knew no restraint. Whenever he felt gallant, he slapped down thousands at once, and it was impossible for Zhuzhi-Lang to stop him. With these spending habits, things would have been difficult even if they'd had a mountain of gold or a sea of silver. Thus, in the end, they consistently ended up broke.

Just as these two tourists were standing penniless in the street, a tall woman dressed in black strolled by, sword on her back.

"Halt," said Tianlang-Jun.

As their shoulders brushed, that woman slightly raised her eyebrow, a mocking smile curling a corner of her lips, and she did indeed halt.

"If one sights an injustice while on the road," said Tianlang-Jun, "should they not draw their sword to give aid?"

"If it's a matter of drawing her sword, this humble one will consider it," said the woman. "Conversely, if it's a matter of opening her purse, this humble one refuses—for you have yet to return the three silvers I lent you last time."

"Is that so?" said Tianlang-Jun. "It's only three silvers. All right, if you lend me three more, you can purchase me for three days."

The woman flatly refused. "Your distinguished self doesn't look strong enough to carry any burdens; rather he looks like someone who has never toiled, who can't distinguish wheat from rice. What's the point of buying you?"

Zhuzhi-Lang watched this for a long time, then said frankly, "My lord, I fear that this one...is disparaging you for being too expensive."

Tianlang-Jun was indeed being disparaged. This wasn't new; sometimes the servants and guards who served him secretly disparaged him too, especially when he was performing his passionate and dramatic recitations. But being told he was worth less than a mere three silvers? That was a bit much.

"Let's put all that aside for now," said Tianlang-Jun. "Surely my face can't be worth *less* than three silvers!"

The woman choked a little, then studied his face for a while and smiled. "Mm, true, it's worth that much."

Then she tossed him a heavy ingot of gold.

From then on, it was as if a dam had broken, and Tianlang-Jun's expenditures in the Human Realm burst out like a flood. He became even more unrestrained, even more unfettered, to the point that it was terrifying to watch. He'd found a rich patron, a mountain of gold. Whenever Zhuzhi-Lang pulled out an empty purse with a slightly embarrassed expression, Tianlang-Jun would happily and thoughtlessly go to that mountain and knock on her gates.

Zhuzhi-Lang couldn't shake the feeling that something about this was wrong—that something was backward.

Why was Su Xiyan acting like one of those wealthy young masters in plays, with their distinguished statuses and heaps of money?

Why was Tianlang-Jun acting like one of those pampered young ladies, who had run away from home and was ignorant of the world?

And why was Zhuzhi-Lang acting like the prudent servant girl accompanying that lady, running errands and doing odd jobs?

Zhuzhi-Lang had attempted to alert his lord to this reversal of roles, to tell him that he needed to retrieve his dignity as the highest ruler of the demon realm, but Tianlang-Jun seemed to find pleasure in this sugar daddy, sugar baby relationship. The blind passion that he had in the past directed to the entire human race was now poured entirely upon a single person.

Su Xiyan was truly a cold and ruthless, yet wholly extraordinary person.

When they met up, she took them to see various rare and wonderful things, and to all manner of interesting and intriguing places. Forbidden codices Zhuzhi-Lang couldn't find no matter how he tried, a wondrous spirit mushroom within a certain hidden cave, a dew lake with waters that shone like crystal, an obscure, yet marvelously skilled, pipa-playing prostitute. When they weren't together, they'd see no trace of her for ten of fifteen days and would be unable to find her no matter how they tried.

She never batted an eyelid, nor expressed a hint of infatuation, nor spoke of pining. She had her own plots and calculations, and she looked coldly on from the sidelines.

Because half his blood came from the serpent race, Zhuzhi-Lang possessed a kind of natural animal instinct. He faintly sensed that this person who kept approaching them was an exceedingly dangerous entity.

She wasn't like demon women, with their enchanting, by the book charm. Instead, she was solemn and driven, though she gave off the impression of being refined and courteous. Yet it was indeed only the *impression* of being refined and courteous. Zhuzhi-Lang dared not assume he would in fact get off easy at her hands if it ever came to a true, brutal fight.

Beneath the refined surface lay arrogance and indifference, along with an ambition that further concealed her scheming. As Huan Hua Palace's second-in-command, Su Xiyan enjoyed a high and lofty status, and commanded thousands at every turn. On top of that, the cultivation world that Huan Hua Palace led alongside the other major sects had been the demon race's nemesis since ancient times. Su Xiyan was indeed someone incredibly dangerous as far as they were concerned.

Zhuzhi-Lang reported all the information he'd found in full detail. Yet Tianlang-Jun wasn't remotely concerned. Once he became infatuated with something, he disregarded even life and death as he threw all his eggs into that one basket. It wasn't like he didn't know the truth, he just nonetheless never showed any doubt.

The price of never doubting her was to be sealed beneath the sunless, skyless darkness of Bai Lu Mountain for more than ten years, with no chance of return.

"I want to kill humans."

During those more than ten years, that was the line Tianlang-Jun repeated most often. In the past, he had loved humans more than anything, so he'd never done such things.

Without his vast demonic energy to sustain Zhuzhi-Lang's man-shaped form, Zhuzhi-Lang once again reverted to his half-snake appearance. Every time Tianlang-Jun saw him arduously slithering back and forth, he would lash out with a, "Get lost."

Or he'd say, "Your slithering is far too ugly."

Zhuzhi-Lang would then silently squirm away and search the outside for a place untouched by the sun and moon. There, he would continue to practice his slithering, now rusted from years of disuse.

His lord's temper became unimaginably terrible, but Zhuzhi-Lang couldn't summon even the slightest bit of strength to feel hurt or angry.

Tianlang-Jun's "get lost" was telling him to "get lost" to the Demon Realm, or to "get lost" to the southern border, or to "get lost" to his old home, or to "get lost" to anywhere, so long as he didn't remain in front of Tianlang-Jun.

Tianlang-Jun couldn't stand for others to see him so wretched and downtrodden, in a state where he could beg for neither life nor death. From the moment of his birth, he'd been the demon race's most respected crown prince. He'd never tasted suffering, had always been composed and elegant, and had rejected all crude and vulgar things that would ruin his reputation. He'd even had some slight mysophobia. He'd hated anything ugly, but now, as he was, he was uglier than anyone.

Covered in blood, he'd been sealed beneath seventy-two metal chains and forty-nine potent paper talismans, forced to watch every day as his body slowly rotted and began to stink, all while his mind remained perfectly clear, unable to lose consciousness even if he wished to. That gang from the cultivation world had lacked the ability to kill him outright, so they'd thought up every possible method to torment him instead. Even Zhuzhi-Lang's ugly half-snake form looked slightly better than Tianlang-Jun did in this state.

Having reverted to his old form, Zhuzhi-Lang was unable to speak, so Tianlang-Jun began talking to himself. For almost half the hours in every day, he would recite the songs and dialogues from those plays. Sometimes, as Tianlang-Jun was singing, he would abruptly cease, as if his throat had been slit. Zhuzhi-Lang would then know that it must have been a play Su Xiyan had taken them to watch.

But after pausing for a time, Tianlang-Jun would start again just as abruptly, continuing in a louder voice. Between his hoarse throat and the deserted valley, the lingering melodies drifted, long and drawn out. Drawn out and heartrending.

Zhuzhi-Lang was unable to speak; he couldn't tell him to "stop singing"; he couldn't raise his arms, couldn't cover his ears, couldn't prevent himself from hearing the notes. More and more, he understood what it meant to be "utterly powerless."

When something makes you sad, when something brings you pain, why continue to force yourself to do it?

The only thing he could do was to persistently, day after day, use leaves to carry the Dew Lake's water and bring it drop by drop to clean Tianlang-Jun's eternally unhealing wounds.

In all those years, they never learned of Luo Binghe's existence. Furthermore, Su Xiyan didn't succeed to her position of power as expected. Instead, she silently vanished to somewhere unknown. Even long after they'd once more greeted the sun and sky, they still hadn't learned.

Therefore, when Zhuzhi-Lang saw that face for the first time at the southern border, he was so shocked that he forgot to complete the business he'd been tasked with. After a bout of fighting, he went straight back and reported it to Tianlang-Jun.

Hence, there had been the battle at the Holy Mausoleum.

After Shen Qingqiu had been spat out and settled with proper arrangements, Tianlang-Jun had stared at Zhuzhi-Lang as his nephew single-mindedly fanned burning coals with a cattail leaf fan. "Do you think he's like me, or like her?"

Zhuzhi-Lang knew very well who this "he" and "her" referred to. "Didn't my lord say it himself? He's like his mother."

Tianlang-Jun shook his head and smiled. "The way they pretend to be callous..."

In truth, both of them knew that Luo Binghe's tendency to be attached to and dependent on others, and his utter lack of reservations in his obstinate infatuation, were more like Tianlang-Jun.

Tianlang-Jun leaned his cheek on one hand as he watched the closed-eyed Shen Qingqiu and sighed. "But he's far more fortunate than I am."

The person who Luo Binghe refused to let go of was someone like Shen Qingqiu. That was indeed a fortunate thing. At least Shen Qingqiu wouldn't summon the entire cultivation world to seal Luo Binghe beneath Cang Qiong Mountain.

On top of that, there had only ever been two people in this world who hadn't looked at Zhuzhi-Lang's ugly appearance with disgust. One was Tianlang-Jun, and the other was Shen Qingqiu.

"How about it?" asked Tianlang-Jun. "Do you want to steal that fortune for yourself?"

Zhuzhi-Lang stared at Tianlang-Jun for a long time before understanding what he meant. Then he blushed a bright red. "My lord!"

"Steal it, steal it," said Tianlang-Jun. "We're all demons—why fuss about something like this? Besides, he's only your younger cousin. What are you afraid of? The last lord of the Mobei clan even openly stole his younger brother's official wife."

"I don't have any such wishes!"

Tianlang-Jun was confused. "Then why is your face red?"

Zhuzhi-Lang patiently bore with him. "My lord...if you hadn't asked me to find all those books, or told me to read them with you, or recited them aloud to force me to review them, this subordinate's face definitely wouldn't have turned red."

Because of this exchange, some strange things echoed in his ears from time to time, which made him unable to look at Immortal Master Shen with a clear conscience.

Zhuzhi-Lang understood why Tianlang-Jun habitually teased him this way. Beneath all the ribbing was a desire to probe and provoke.

From the day he emerged from beneath Bai Lu Mountain to the sun and sky, Tianlang-Jun hadn't planned to use his new body for long, nor had he had any plans regarding the future.

But when he saw Shen Qingqiu, Tianlang-Jun had actually felt a kind of relief. He'd thought, *Finally, someone to whom I can entrust my foolish nephew.*

Zhuzhi-Lang's stupid brain could only revolve around other people. He never thought of himself. If he could find a new person to follow, then even after Tianlang-Jun got himself killed, he wouldn't end up lost with nowhere to go. Tianlang-Jun thought that Shen Qingqiu wasn't a bad target to follow, regardless of what kind of "follow" it was.

Having achieved this mysterious peace of mind, Tianlang-Jun became increasingly reckless with throwing about his demonic energy, and his body's deterioration and decline hastened, day by day, to the point that his arm or fingers often fell off. Zhuzhi-Lang was overwhelmed to the point of exhaustion trying to find means by which to repair him.

One time, he was trying to use a needle and thread to mend his lord's limbs. Tianlang-Jun held out his arm for Zhuzhi-Lang to prick however he wished and said, "Your instincts have always been very accurate."

Zhuzhi-Lang gave a confirmation.

"Between me and Luo Binghe. Who will win and who will lose?" After a long silence, he said languidly, "Even if you don't say it, I know. I'm plainly going to lose."

Zhuzhi-Lang bit off the thread and tied a knot.

"After today, how about you follow Peak Lord Shen?" Tianlang-Jun asked, sincere yet not. "He's already taking care of Luo Binghe; taking care of you as well shouldn't be too different."

"My lord should sleep," said Zhuzhi-Lang.

But Tianlang-Jun continued to talk nonsense. "Aren't you heading to Immortal Master Shen's tent tonight to help him remove the Ties That Bind? You were listening when I asked if he and Luo Binghe had dual-cultivated before. His reaction made it obvious that they haven't. The early bird catches the worm. Do you understand what I'm saying?"

Zhuzhi-Lang acted like he couldn't hear and bowed down to remove Tianlang-Jun's shoes. But then Zhuzhi-Lang's hands went empty: Tianlang-Jun had crooked his legs so his shoes were firmly upon the beast skin cover. "What must I do to crush your self-esteem?" he asked in all seriousness. "To make you lose heart and give up on me—so that you'll leave?"

"My lord has read too many scripts and plays," said Zhuzhi-Lang. "That trope is old hat. You could never crush this subordinate's self-esteem. That's why my lord should sleep."

"I don't want to go to sleep so early. Quickly, go to Peak Lord Shen's tent. I'll come to see you two after a bit."

"My Lord, you're so willful," Zhuzhi-Lang said helplessly. Pestering others endlessly, full of wild fantasies, forever coming up with these stupid suggestions.

"Haven't I been 'so willful' this whole time?" asked Tianlang-Jun. "So how about it? Why not consider leaving me?"

His lord was acting like a drunk today. The number of things he said that left people unable to laugh or cry had multiplied by ten. Zhuzhi-Lang shook his head and reached out several more times before he finally caught hold of Tianlang-Jun's shoes. He yanked them off by force and repeated, "My lord should sleep."

Tianlang-Jun was pushed onto the bed and forcefully covered with a blanket. "You're becoming more and more like a mother," he said. Then he sighed. "Do you think your uncle is only poking fun at you? You don't urge me to stop, nor do you seek a way out for yourself. If you're always like this, Zhuzhi-Lang, what are you going to do in the future?"

"As expected, I can't bring myself to hate humans."

Tianlang-Jun had said this to Shen Qingqiu.

When Zhuzhi-lang heard these words, he was actually a little happy for his lord.

Tianlang-Jun had finally admitted that his true heart had never changed. Finally, he would no longer need to force himself.

Amidst the rolling dust and falling rubble, Tianlang-Jun sighed and muttered, "Zhuzhi-Lang, that appearance of yours truly doesn't look good."

This time, Zhuzhi-Lang had no need to complain. Its only thought was that it still had a tiny bit of strength left—enough to hold on for a little longer, so that its lord wouldn't die with it. There was no need for him to worry that dying alongside it would be unsightly.

As Mai Gu Ridge transformed into smoke and dust with a thunderous roar, an enormous snake plummeted down toward the heart of the Luo River, which glittered like silver scales.

In truth, Shen Qingqiu hadn't finished listening to what Tianlang-Jun had been saying, for after that first sentence there had been another, quiet, heard only by Zhuzhi-Lang.

Tianlang-Jun had said, "But why is loving a person such a difficult thing?"

At the time, Zhuzhi-Lang had been unable to squeeze out a smile, nor had it been able to speak. As if lost in thought, it had flicked out its tongue, spraying Tianlang-Jun with a face full of snake saliva.

It truly is difficult, it thought. *But no matter how difficult, it's less difficult than making one's heart stop loving.*

26

Airplane's Fortuitous Encounter

— PART 1 —

AIRPLANE SHOOTING TOWARDS THE SKY was an author of stallion novels.

A somewhat well-known author of stallion novels.

An author of stallion novels who, even on a site like Zhongdian Literature, where great gods ran all over the place and lesser gods sprouted up like grass on prime soil, was mentioned with some frequency.

That extreme speed and perseverance as he updated ten thousand words a day, every day, for three years straight! Those periodic burst releases of eight whole chapters! A daring so bold it could engulf the whole country! To the authors following the same road up from the streets where they had openly prostrated themselves, he was a legend. But he was a legend only to be glimpsed, not obtained, a myth one could search for endlessly but only meet by chance.

Those harem plotlines whose integrity had been fed to the dogs, as well as those story lines whose intellectual depth had also been fed to the dogs—they were the defining characteristics of his style, and they were enthusiastically discussed by his thousands of readers.

The most common assessment of his work was: "A popcorn novel. It's indisputably a popcorn novel! But what a satisfying read!"

That's right, Airplane Shooting Towards the Sky's newest masterpiece, *Proud Immortal Demon Way*, was the perfect example of a novel with many haters but even more fans. It was the sort of work everyone called "a popular novel with a terrible reputation."

Those who liked it loved it, while those who hated it could have stomped it into dog shit and spit on it multiple times without satisfying their hatred. This sort of controversial work was, inevitably, a prime breeding ground for fan-on-hater fights.

For example, at this very moment, while Airplane Shooting Towards the Sky was mindlessly hammering out the day's new update, he opened a certain famous webnovel forum, where he intended to spout some nonsense to gain site XP. He briefly scanned the page, and the first glance made him shudder. His gaze had landed on a trending post that bobbed fiercely up and down on the home page. It had an extremely aggressive subject line, which included both his pen name and the title of his book.

This was not the first time Airplane Shooting Toward the Sky had stumbled onto the scene of a fight. As always, he didn't hesitate to jump into the fray, and he gleefully clicked the link.

Sure enough, it was a familiar recipe with a familiar taste.

#1 Ten Years of Reading Sharpens One Sword [OP]:
After reading novels online for close to ten years, I've never read a cultivation novel shittier than *Proud Immortal Demon Way*. Wait, the MC just spends all day eating, sleeping, and collecting girls, and you have the fucking gall to tell me that this is a cultivation novel? Fuck the logic, fuck the writing, and fuck the author's integrity. I bought these emojis last year People who liked this novel, come in here and tell me: What part of it did you

even enjoy? What sort of mindset do you need to read it? How much do you have to hate someone to recommend this novel? I really can't take it—I'm done!

#2 Your Infatuated Pupil:

I've wanted to roast it for a long time 💦... Is there even any meaning to the levels system? There's no difference between being at Core Formation or Nascent Soul, or even just being an ordinary person, but it's just padding and fluff. Every time I see another paragraph about eating or sleeping, I can't bear to continue. And one or two big moments of revenge is all right, but if you throw in a thousand revenge fantasy episodes, they lose all meaning. In short, it's simply not as satisfying as they say. There's a bit of a pyramid scheme feeling to the whole thing...

But the novel's fans are both swift and fierce; I'm guessing they're going to come gang up on you soon. Best of luck, OP, I'll give you a saucepan lid to shield you. I'm out.

#3 Swordsman Must Say:

The writing is shit. All the readers are idiots.

#4 Your Sin Cannot Be Forgiven:

Who are you calling an idiot up there? What a loser.

#5 Overtaken by Longing, Mistaking Red for Green:[4]

Before I opened this post, I knew it would go in this direction. Every time people discuss this novel, they start arguing ╮(￣▽￣)╭ I've never seen a single exception. Pulling up a chair to watch the fun.

4 *The first line from a love poem written by Tang Empress Wu Zetian.*

#6 Your Sin Cannot Be Forgiven:

I'm sick of arguing every time. What's there to argue about? Just because you don't like it doesn't mean other people won't like it. It's really very simple. If you like it, then read it; if not, then get lost. Write your own story if you can—YOU CAN YOU UP, you understand? OP started spewing BS before they even finished reading. What's the point of spewing BS just for the sake of spewing?

#7 Ten Years of Reading Sharpens One Sword:

Everyone, gather around: here's an elementary schooler in the flesh. We've even gotten a U CAN U UP—I'm laughing at this wank. Kid, keep reading for a few more years. Is it really wise to waste your time on forums outside of breaks? Watch out, if you can't finish your homework, your teacher's going to tell your parents. "Just because you like it doesn't mean other people will like it." See, I'm quoting your own words back at you. Also, I don't need to finish eating a pile of shit before I realize it's a pile of shit, OK?

#8 Sha Hualing's Little Bell:

💕🤤🤤 I don't think it's as shitty as OP claims. I like reading this novel. I like Sha-meizi, huehuehue~~~

#9 Peerless Cucumber 【Expert】:

I understand what OP is feeling. I've been reading this novel lately, and it's so damn long—long and pumped full of filler.

I've never seen villains with a lower IQ than the ones in this book; they're a prime example of "cannon fodder with an IQ of 40 and a protagonist with an IQ of 60." It's like the author went on a

24-hour revenge orgasm without once going soft. Most of the female protagonists are stupid sexy lamps, and the male lead doesn't even bed Liu Mingyan, the only breath of fresh air? He doesn't bed the *rightful empress*? Are you fucking kidding me?

All my fellow readers have already roasted the setting for the last three hundred thousand words, so I won't say more on that. The most interesting things in *PIDW* are actually the monsters of the Demon Realm; it'd be better if those got more focus. The rest is just taking in all fifty girls from a given clan in one go, and not a single distinct personality in the lot. And the writing is incomparably atrocious; every time a woman appears, it's all "soft bosoms trembling." Trembling my ass. You could at least try a different phrase—even a different word would be fine, you know? Serious question: Who taught Airplane this elementary school-level writing?

At least the portrayal of the male lead was all right. The transformation from innocent and upstanding to hateful and sinister was detailed and natural; debts of kindness and grudges were both repaid, and those who should have been killed were mercilessly cut down. Every time I see a useless male lead, I just want to slap him in the face. Bing-ge deserves that "ge"—he's cool enough *and* darkened enough. I like him!

Shen Qingqiu, though, that bastard needs no explanation.

#10 Cang Qiong Mountain Stair-Cleaning Manager:
whispering, silently floating by Does anyone here like Sect Leader Yue? I like the gentle top type the most.

#11 Warrior's Hammer:

Boring. It's not as well written as *Immortal XX Battle*—the difference is huge. That one's a real cultivation novel. The worldbuilding is rigorous and the plotline is grand; the author put a lot of thought into it and was very serious with the writing.

#12 Your Sin Cannot Be Forgiven:

Upthread, shitting on one while praising the other feels good, doesn't it? Ha ha.

#13 Refusing to be a Plotholer:

Cucumber-bro up there wrote how many words just to hate on it? Must be true love.

#14 Ten Years of Reading Sharpens One Sword:

To answer #12: Heh heh, still at it? I'll turn your own words on you. Aren't there also a ton of *Proud Immortal* fans who leap at the chance to shit on other novels? Do you want me to flip through the receipts for some screenshots to fling in your face?

#15 Cang Qiong Mountain Gate Guard Platoon:

> >>>To answer #10: **whispering, silently passing by** Does anyone here like Sect Leader Yue? I like the gentle top type the most.

Grabbing the sister up there! You're a sister, right?! I like Zhangmen-shixiong too! I like him a lot! ☆\\(￣▽￣)/★ Is there anything more moe than pampering and indulging, etc. with no bottom line?! (´இ皿இ`) It's a pity the target was such a disastrous shidi; the bad end was so complete, I couldn't even sell people on the ship...

#16: Qingge's Blood Brother:

That bastard Shen Qingqiu needs no explanation +10,086! My god, to think #15 can feel moe over anything involving that scum. Just thinking about him makes me want to throw up. He killed my fave—unforgivable!

I always felt it was such a waste that the Bai Zhan Peak Lord died so early. "Great Master" Airplane just refused to write him, or else there would be more ships to choose from.

#17 Occasionally Filling Holes:

There sure is a lot of info in the last few posts. Did this forum get invaded by weirdos…?

#18 Peerless Cucumber [Expert] :

Upthread, keep cool. This forum has a lot of Green JJ sisters 

#19 A Stately Waiter:

Of course it's true love for Cucumber-bro, but the stuff he spews here isn't as vicious as what he puts in the comments. Not malicious enough, thumbs down.

#20: Hoeing Wheat is My Noontime Occupation:[5]

The *Proud Immortal* fans are here to argue again; I see this novel everywhere. The novel's quality doesn't live up to its popularity; no way Airplane didn't pay for shills. Sit back and wait for the next time the forum data guru makes a post. Their analysis will show whether he spam-voted.

---

5 *A reference to a line in a poem by Tang poet Li Shen, one of a pair of poems written to depict agricultural life in the feudal era. This line is used to make dirty jokes because "sun" (noontime sun) is also used as "to fuck," though this particular username is an indirect allusion.*

#21 Hoeing Wheat is My Noontime Occupation:

To answer #4: Who are you calling an idiot up there? What a loser. What a joke, the schoolkids who like to read shit books like *Proud Immortal* have the nerve to call people losers. No one's a bigger loser than you.

#22 Qingge's Blood Brother:

To start firing into the crowd because of one or two people, you must be drunk. The way #20 is shit-stirring—is that just the OP's alt…? Airplane gets a lot of upvotes because he's got no bottom line when begging for clicks; he'd even grovel naked on the ground… And not to pass judgment on anything else, but look at Airplane's update rate. He posts 10k every day and 25k bursts on the weekends—how many people can do that? Put the question of quality aside for now.

#23 Looking for Friends at the North Pole Every Day:

I wrote some Bing-ge x scum!Shen slash _(:3)∠)_ Don't know if anyone wants to see. Signing up for a rarepair is like going to the North Pole, so painful. Looking for ships in a Zhongdian novel is also seeking death.

#24 Cang Qiong Mountain Stair-Cleaning Manager:

Slash-writing sister, don't go! Does it have smutty content?! Please, sobsobsob!

#25 Occasionally Filling Holes:

Airplane really doesn't know how to write romance plotlines; it'd be better if he just didn't. I feel like Luo Binghe doesn't have feelings for a single one of his wives—he just wants to use them. And I can't see how any of these women have really fallen in love with him.

#26 Warrior's Hammer:
As long as he collects all the girls, it's fine. Who cares if there's romance or not?

#27 Peerless Cucumber [Expert]
Filling Holes-bro: You're joking—you want Airplane not to write the harem? Four-fifths of the book would be gone.

#28 Overtaken by Longing, Mistaking Red for Green:
But I feel like I can see which peak lord has really fallen in love with which other peak lord (delusional)... But speaking seriously, the same-sex interactions he wrote between brothers and comrades were all much more detailed and natural than Bing-ge's scenes with his wives. That deep emotion was practically visible to the naked eye. Airplane really is a natural fudanshi.

PS: To the sister at #24: Guess you'll eat anything when you're starving, huh...

#29 Hoeing Wheat is My Noontime Occupation:
[This post has been hidden due to a personal attack. Currently waiting for the poster to edit.]

With his legs propped up, "Great Master" Airplane Shooting Towards the Sky stirred his instant noodles as he nonchalantly rolled the scroll wheel on his mouse, skimming over the forum posts. His eyes automatically highlighted that familiar ID "Peerless Cucumber."

Vicious sniping that flowed like a running stream; a cucumber forged of iron. Even though this famous Lord Cucumber spewed criticism constantly and without end in "Great Master" Airplane's comments sections, his subscription payments and demands for updates never waned. Because of this, "Great Master" Airplane had come to suspect that this person was a masochist.

"Very good, you have successfully attracted my attention." Like some sort of domineering billionaire CEO, "Great Master" Airplane began to coolly review Cucumber-bro's howling in the comments sections.

In the end, he concluded: This guy was just like a woman married to a disappointing husband; she itched to jump on his back to grab and shake him by the neck, filled with love and hate as she simultaneously kissed and spat on him. Peerless Cucumber was locked in precisely this type of conundrum, unable to extricate himself from following this novel while he cursed, "Why can't I control this damn hand that just keeps clicking on the **READ** button?!"

"Your mouth says no, but your body says yes!" As "Great Master" Airplane delivered his final verdict, he smacked his computer table, howling with laughter.

This one smack was disastrous. His instant noodles toppled over, splashing all over his beloved, hardworking, and invaluable keyboard, drenching it in a thousand kilometers' worth of spicy broth. Airplane turned pale with fright, quickly leaping up to rescue it. But he jumped too high and his foot caught on the power strip. With a crackle, his laptop screen went dark.

After this chain reaction wherein extreme joy turned to profound sorrow, Airplane's face went deathly white.

WTFFFFF!

He had just been scrolling through the forums while downloading movies and typing away—his file had still been open! Fuck!

He couldn't have lost today's update just like that! He'd gotten to eight thousand words! Augh!

He subconsciously threw himself down next to the power strip, picking up the plug to shove it back in the socket—

Only to experience firsthand what could have been called "full-body electrocution, like lightning from the ninth heaven."

— PART 2 —

"WHAT ARE YOU DAYDREAMING about, you moron?! Get to work!"

"Great Master" Airplane Shooting Towards the Sky spat out the green foxtail hanging from his lips with a "pah."

Internally, he waved a thousand middle fingers and yelled a thousand words beginning with F at this fiendish An Ding Peak shixiong, but when he turned around, he wore a flowery smile. He plastered on the expression and flounced up to him, calling, "I'm coming!"

"All you do is slack off!" X-shixiong spat.

The older-than-average outer disciple Shang Qinghua, who currently occupied a seventeen-year-old body, looked around in all directions as he trailed behind the main team, who were unloading goods from the ship onto the docks.

Indeed, "Great Master" Airplane could now be referred to as Shang Qinghua.

That wretched reprobate from the stallion novel he had written with his own two hands, that treacherous spy who toiled assiduously for Mobei-Jun all his life, only to be thrown aside by his coldhearted and unfeeling boss as soon as he lived out his use. That cannon fodder, that logistics guy—*that* Shang Qinghua.

Although, at this time, he was still an outer disciple who could be pushed around by everyone on An Ding Peak. He wasn't yet head disciple, and he hadn't changed his name to join the Qing generation.

An Ding Peak was, in itself, a very stifling sort of peak.

The peak lord was like the director of a housekeeping-services department: stifling. Even when leading disciples, he was like an unpaid hourly worker: also stifling. The outer disciples didn't even bear mentioning. They were at the very lowest end of the food chain, the most stifling of the stifling. Everyone had huge reserves of pent-up anger. Those with more seniority bullied those with less; that was simply the routine state of things.

Shang Qinghua would occasionally utter a silent curse: *Just you wait until I take the position of peak lord, just see if I don't... Heh heh heh.*

However, he swiftly extinguished these flights of vain fancy.

Think about it! Taking the position of peak lord meant enjoying assistance from the Demon Realm, which meant acquiring Mobei-Jun as boss, which would lead to the end result: getting thrown away by said boss as soon as he'd lived out his use. He wouldn't even get a clean death.

It went without saying: not worth it.

If Shang Qinghua could have done as he wished, he would have stripped off his sect robes and rolled up his bedding, rushed down Cang Qiong Mountain, escaped the cultivation world, and fled toward a free life as a poor commoner. If he relied on all the research he had done to write a transmigration stallion novel in his past life—such as how to create soap, glass, the abacus, etc.—he believed he could live freely and easily, ha ha ha ha ha!

But as soon as this sort of thought appeared in his head—

[Rule violation, point deduction.]

So, he'd transmigrated into his own stallion novel. Why hadn't he been assigned to the protagonist? And okay, so what if he wasn't the protagonist. What was up with this damned System?!

It was all that OP's fault. If he hadn't started that fight, Shang Qinghua wouldn't have suffered the brunt of it. And then there was that Peerless Cucumber! *Curse him! May he never get a chance to use that cucumber for the rest of his life!*

Shang Qinghua moved box after box of heavy books from the ship onto a flatbed cart. As he hitched up the horse, he continued to endlessly stew over his grudges.

Cultivation novels usually handwaved inconsequential things like how goods were shipped. In the end, Shang Qinghua had only himself to blame. Damn it—why had he written a low-fantasy setting where all the hard labor had to be done by hand? He'd only managed to screw himself over.

Okay, in fact, what he really wanted to say was: *Qing Jing Peak really fucking knows how to use people for all they're worth!*

They were the ones who made all the trouble! If you were helping Xian Shu Peak's female immortals and fairy maidens transport cosmetics, hair pins, new clothes, and whatnot, even if it was tiring, at least you felt light in your heart. Though it was hard for the body, it was sweet to the soul.

But when you had to act as a porter for Qing Jing Peak—what was up with that? Every time they made a purchase, it was hundreds and hundreds of kilograms of books. Then they would make An Ding Peak's people huff and puff their way down the mountain to fetch them, then huff and puff their way back up to the peak. Meanwhile, they'd be living the high life—their butts stuck to their seats and their fingers stuck to their instruments. They'd just sit and wait for the goods to be delivered to their door.

To hell with that aloof demeanor! If you have the legs, then come down and get your stuff yourself!

The other outer disciples were also complaining.

"It's obvious those Qing Jing Peak disciples look down on our An Ding Peak, but time and again we have to work like beasts of burden for them."

"Especially that Shen Qingqiu," one person said indignantly. "He's way too full of himself. His nose is stuck straight up into the air."

"So what if that Xiu Ya has a bit of a name for itself—*he's* far too arrogant."

"Hah, he even dares to provoke Bai Zhan Peak's head disciple, Liu Qingge. How would he ever care about nameless foot soldiers like us?"

"Given Bai Zhan Peak's temper—given *Liu Qingge's* temper—how has he not gotten himself killed yet?"

"How could he? You think Yue-shixiong would just stand by and watch? So long as he's around, Liu Qingge can't kill Shen Qingqiu no matter what."

"What I don't know is how Shen Qingqiu got chosen as head disciple after starting cultivation so late," said another outer disciple who'd joined Cang Qiong Mountain at an older age, his expression sour. "They say he had a good relationship with Yue-shixiong, but I've never seen him go to Qiong Ding Peak. And even when he does see Yue-shixiong, he keeps up that damn fake expression, all aloof and whatever. But if you said they weren't friendly, that wouldn't seem right either."

Shang Qinghua kept his silence, choking down his words.

Ay! How I long to gossip—how I yearn to take up the backstory I outlined but ended up killing in the cradle to toss it in your face! No one's got a clearer sense of those old affairs of years long past than this great master, your omnipotent creator!

Shrouded in resentment, the whole party muttered their grievances like a broken record, getting angrier and angrier, their envy and hatred mixing together. But who could say who they were trying to argue with?

Shang Qinghua drove the cart, shoulders hunched. Whenever someone addressed him, he brushed them aside with a laugh, being very careful not to add anything. Sure, they were enthusiastically proclaiming their sufferings now, but you never knew when, some day in the future, they'd covertly go and tattle on the very people who'd complained today. Running your mouth was fun in the moment, but once someone reported you and you caught the attention of the other peaks' disciples, you'd be in serious hot water. Human hearts were treacherous. You couldn't forget to guard against them, ah!

The road after rain was full of potholes. As the wheels rolled over them, the cart pitched left and right. During one such pitch, the System sent Shang Qinghua a notification with a ding.

【 Upcoming mission; be prepared. 】

When Shang Qinghua heard this, his face creased like a chrysanthemum. He smiled obsequiously. "System-dage, aren't you skimping a bit, being so brief with these messages? Couldn't you tell me what mission this is? What preparations? Prepare for what? At least give me a tip, okay?"

【 You will see. 】 the System said vaguely.

Shang Qinghua was silent. *No, this esteemed one sees nothing!*

Then, with a crack, the flatbed cart suddenly stopped moving, seemingly stuck on something on the ground.

The outer disciple shixiong, whether on the cart or following along behind, jolted along with it and fell all over the place. They were already steaming with anger, and they summarily began to smack the rails and curse with rage.

"You moron, can't even properly drive a cart! Go already. What are you stopping for?!"

Shang Qinghua didn't know why the cart had suddenly gotten stuck either. Puzzled, he jumped off. After a single look, his soul flew off in a fright.

The reason why the wheels couldn't move was because the water in the hole they were stuck in had iced over, freezing the wooden wheels solid.

All around them, a formless cold in the air weighed oppressively down. Winter was cold, but Shang Qinghua's heart was even colder. Shaking uncontrollably, he lifted his gaze.

A shadow draped in a black cloak slowly walked toward them, straight and tall. One could vaguely make out the figure of a youth.

For once, the System said a few more words:

【 Current opponent's anger points: 1,000. 】

【 Mission objective: Survive. 】

[Tip complete. We wish you the best of luck.]

"Great Master" Airplane Shooting Towards the Sky had a bad habit. That was, he cut plot points.

Before he officially set pen to paper on future chapters, he would first plant little sprouts in his novel. Then he would watch how the winds were blowing in the comments section. Using this information, he would decide which plotlines to follow from his overall outline.

For instance, the Shen Qingqiu who had been called a "cheap villain with no justification" ten thousand times was a tragic product of plot cuts.

Oh, and then there was Bing-ge's dad. His plot had been cut even more viciously, to the point that in the end, he hadn't even appeared.

The benefit of this method was that he could cater to the readers. It at least guaranteed that his subscription count wouldn't take a huge dive and crash to its death in the pool at rock bottom.

The consequence was that buried foreshadowing went to waste and there were gaps all over the ground, leaving it bumpy and full of p(l)otholes. Any readers who had some standards, or who had a bit more taste and weren't as easy to fool, would rain curses on the author without restraint.

Airplane Shooting Towards the Sky had often been depressed about it too. The thing was, he actually didn't like repeatedly writing all the crazy revenge stuff either, especially when it was getting revenge on a crowd of villains with IQs lower than a bar on the ground. Once in a while, he wanted to craft a three-dimensional villain—still cannon fodder, but with multiple sides—to show that he had also done some basic research on human nature, that he had some literary standards too.

But the readers never bought in. So he couldn't guarantee he'd make a living.

So, what did human nature and literary ideals count for against readers and making a living? Ha ha ha ha ha ha ha ha ha ha!

Back on topic. Precisely because of this bad plot-cutting habit, many of the original particulars of the story had been lost, doomed to suffocate in the womb. For example...

When had Mobei-Jun captured Shang Qinghua?!

Naturally, the main text had never brought it up. The main text's plotline was just Bing-ge oozing badassery, slaughtering and massacring people all over the place—who gave a fuck how that one cannon fodder became a spy?

However, this world automatically filled in the parts that had been cut. Therefore, "Great Master" Airplane had categorically lost the authorial advantage of foreknowledge. Therefore, whenever the plot began to develop, he was always a good few beats late before he caught on to what was going on.

X-shixiong drew his sword (which, as an An Ding disciple, had never had the chance to be unsheathed even after eight hundred years), and let out a vigorous yell. "What sort of evildoer dares to cross us?!"

One after another, the disciples all became agitated, and they subsequently unsheathed their swords as well.

"You dare to appear in front of Cang Qiong Mountain Sect disciples!"

Mobei-Jun was clearly in an extraordinarily bad mood. He didn't even let the cannon fodder finish their traditional opening monologues before his knuckles cracked.

A storm of icy arrows swept through the air, and heads slammed to the ground one by one.

One side of Shang Qinghua's mind shrieked while the other howled: So scary! But also so cool! Really fucking cool!

But regardless of whether he was cool enough to shake the heavens and earth, and to make devils and deities cry, if that guy was destined to kill Shang Qinghua in the future, he was absolutely not friend material!

Suddenly, X-shixiong shoved his shoulder. "Get down there!"

Shang Qinghua felt like his heart was being fried in oil and roasted over a fire, but his mind was wholly sober. He stuck his hands and feet to the cart as securely as chewing gum. "Get down and do what?"

"Defeat the demon and defend the righteous way! Execute the will of the heavens!"

Why don't you go first? thought Shang Qinghua. "After you, Shixiong!"

X-shixiong flew into a rage. "I told you to go, so go! What's with your nonsense?!"

More hands and feet joined X-shixiong in kicking and prying Shang Qinghua off. Obviously he understood what was going on—these outer disciples just wanted him to stall Mobei-Jun to give them time to escape. His mind was as clear as a mirror, and his current stance couldn't have been any more fixed.

Shang Qinghua clung firmly to his base of operations and refused to be moved. "Shixiong, I don't wanna!" he sobbed. "Our comrades will remember how you made me go be cannon fodder at a time like this!"

X-shixiong began to ramble incoherently in terror. "What cannon fodder? If you can defeat this monster of the demon race, you'll definitely earn great merit—you'll soar like the divine steed, Feihuang.

This is the only way out for us outer disciples. The opportunity is right in front of your eyes at this very moment!"

Shang Qinghua couldn't hold on to the cart much longer. He whimpered like his organs were being ripped apart. "I'm going, then. I'm really going!"

Just as he finished speaking, he was firmly pried out of the cart and thrown to the ground.

His body: fallen right in front of Mobei-Jun's boots. His sword: still halfway in its sheath. His heart: not quite decided as to whether he should draw his sword.

Mobei-Jun sneered, an ice-cold glint of blue flashing through his eyes. No sooner said than done, Shang Qinghua threw himself forward to cling to his thighs with a plop.

Every one of his shixiong made an aggrieved face.

Mobei-Jun made a blank one.

Shang Qinghua fell to one knee. "My king, please let me follow you for the rest of my life!"

Mobei-Jun tried to throw Shang Qinghua off with a kick, but to no avail—his adhesive ability was just too strong. Mobei-Jun then tried to kill him and be done with it, but that proved even more difficult. Just like a gecko clinging to the wall, Shang Qinghua nimbly crawled back and forth but managed to stay stuck firmly to his thighs.

Mobei-Jun couldn't help but steam with rage.

As the An Ding Peak outer disciples bore witness to this incredible feat, they were overjoyed. They threw down their goods and fled. Just as Shang Qinghua was silently cursing them out, not three seconds later, a wave of screams came from down the road.

Dozens of ice strands as thin as silk threads had pierced their chests. In a mad dance of silver light, droplets of blood flew in all directions.

Upon seeing this, Shang Qinghua's grip on Mobei-Jun's thighs became as strong as steel. He started to chatter incessantly, "My king, please accept me. I'm very useful!"

Mobei-Jun seemed to cant his body. "Oh? What use are you?"

"I can serve tea, carry water, wash clothes, fold blankets...wait, no." Shang Qinghua considerately gave him an analysis: "You see, my king, I can serve you as an undercover agent in Cang Qiong Mountain, pass on intelligence, and help the demon race accomplish the magnificent feat of conquering the Human Realm."

Mobei-Jun laughed. "An outer disciple, and an An Ding Peak outer disciple at that. With you as a spy, how long would it take to accomplish this feat?"

"Don't discriminate against my peak," Shang Qinghua said awkwardly. "That isn't very nice."

Why does even the demon race look down on us? And the disdain for "An Ding Peak" even surpasses that for an "outer disciple"... That's too much, that's really too much!

As Shang Qinghua overflowed with snot and tears, clinging on for dear life, begging to pledge fealty to Mobei-Jun—wholly without warning, the demon collapsed.

Shang Qinghua was still hugging his thighs, and when Mobei-Jun fell, he was almost squashed right under him. He hurriedly let go. He crouched there for a while in a daze until he suddenly came to his senses. Had Mobei-Jun come here already injured?

No wonder his expression had been so ugly and his temper so high, and no wonder he had been so easy to push over! Had

Shang Qinghua accidentally poked one of his wounds when his hand slipped? Sometimes a slip of the hand is advantageous!

Shang Qinghua cautiously moved over to examine him carefully. Just as expected, there was a thin wound the length of a finger on the back of Mobei-Jun's lower waist, roughly over his right kidney. A sharp corner of something gold protruded from inside the wound. He could vaguely make out that it was the petal-shaped edge of an intricate piece of handicraft that had been forged from gold threads.

So coquettish and cultured. It was Huan Hua Palace's Ling Hua Dart, all right!

This weapon was one of the nonsense details "Great Master" Airplane had cooked up on the fly while writing. The body of the dart was light and thin and coated with a bit of anesthetic, so it was very difficult for its targets to discover the object once it breached their body. If they moved too much, the dart would magnificently "blossom," growing six sharp flower petals to slice up the victim's internal organs.

Does this perhaps sound a bit familiar? Doesn't this device overlap with a certain Demon Realm organism? No problem; it's easy enough to justify. Just explain it away by saying this Ling Hua Dart was created by some Huan Hua Palace senior who'd escaped from the Demon Realm by the skin of their teeth, then based this design on a strange organism called Ties That Bind. In short, don't make a fuss over this sort of tiny detail!

Background narration complete, let's jerk ourselves back over to the main topic. That is to say, this pure-blooded demonic second-gen who, in the future, would very likely beat Shang Qinghua to death with a single strike; not only had his kidney been punctured through by Huan Hua Palace, he was also severely anesthetized.

It seemed like Mobei-Jun had just killed his way out of a Huan Hua Palace ambush. The Demon Race held their grudges for a long time, and the Mobei clan had held a long-standing animosity toward Huan Hua Palace. That sect would suffer the greatest number of deaths and injuries at the ill-fated Immortal Alliance Conference precisely because Mobei-Jun wished to retaliate against them. This event had connected seamlessly with Airplane Shooting Toward the Sky's master plan.

Shang Qinghua muttered to himself back and forth, a mischievous cast to his face. He looked around on the ground for a while before finding a stone about half the size of a skull and hefted it up; it was quite heavy.

One, two, three—he got in position above Mobei-Jun's head, the demon's eyes still closed.

The System offered neither warning hints nor prohibiting alerts.

Shang Qinghua relaxed. There was no warning, which meant, in other words: Go ahead and kill him!

"My king, ah, my king, this is the will of the heavens—don't blame me." With a thoroughly insincere prayer, Shang Qinghua's hand rose and the stone fell.

And braked to a halt, right above the tip of Mobei-Jun's arguably perfect nose.

To tell the truth, this Mobei-Jun character held an unusual significance to him. It could have been said that Mobei-Jun was the type of man "Great Master" Airplane had always dreamed of becoming: strong, cool, doing as he pleased—just like how every little kid had dreamed of becoming Ultraman.

How could he just stand by and watch himself kill Ultraman with his own hands?!

Shang Qinghua bemoaned his dilemma for a while. After he finished, he had a perfectly shameless thought. It would be fine if he just didn't watch, right?

So, he turned his head and raised the stone up high...

Nope. He still couldn't do it.

Shang Qinghua chucked aside the cumbersome murder weapon with a plop. His eyes shone with excitement, and by now he was almost completely on top of Mobei-Jun.

I can't, I can't—the more I look, the more I feel this face is just too damn mesmerizing!

In truth, deep down, Bing-ge's fair and clean pretty-boy type didn't really suit the tastes of "Great Master" Airplane Flying Towards the Sky. He had only assigned this sort of configuration to the protagonist to meet his stallion hardware specifications. The art of growing stallions was grounded in science, and the research was clear: women preferred men who looked cultured, pretty, and even a bit soft and feminine.

Protagonists couldn't avoid getting roasted; it was fair to say that Bing-ge had a fan every three steps and a hater every five. But Mobei-Jun wasn't the same. Supporting characters inevitably attracted a lot of love, and Mobei-Jun had practically never been hated on.

This character had been created entirely according to the author's own tastes. And because Mobei-Jun was secretly favored by that author, he had embodied Airplane Shooting Towards the Sky's scholarly aesthetic for the ideal fellow man. Don't ask why Luo Binghe wasn't the embodiment of his ideal man; Luo Binghe's use had primarily been to fulfill his desire to be a badass and get revenge, as well as his desire for wanton【 this section has been censored 】.

Even this young Mobei-Jun, who hadn't yet grown into himself, was unconditionally in line with the sixteen words that described the author's true aesthetic: "Eyes deep as night, nose straight and high, full of heroic spirit, icily arrogant beyond compare."

This was the beautiful man of his dreams!

The stony murder weapon rose and lowered, lowered and rose. For the first time in his transmigrated life, Shang Qinghua was faced with a difficult life choice.

Finally, he decided: Time to get a room!

He would go to an inn to get a room—no, to find somewhere to stay.

At present, though, he was in a field of dead bodies. Shang Qinghua hesitated a bit, then tipped that load of Qing Jing Peak's heavy, useless nuisance right off the cart the way he'd take out the trash. He hauled Mobei-Jun onto it, face-down, so as to conceal the face that made him lose control every time he looked at it.

For the time being, he couldn't return to Cang Qiong Mountain. No one there would realize anything was amiss too quickly. This trip was supposed to last seven days, and only two had passed.

To stand steadfast by this demonic young heir and protect him while he had been weakened by a sneak attack—what a wonderful opportunity to garner some goodwill. While comforting himself with this justification, Shang Qinghua huffed and puffed as he pushed that large flatbed cart toward the city.

To rent the room, Shang Qinghua spent the secret stash he had been saving these last few years. At this point, he was only an average, run-of-the-mill outer disciple, and he didn't have the authority to manage accounts or draw from the sect coffers. Renting a room already stretched the limits of his economic ability. So, as a matter of course, it was a single room. So, as a matter of course, there was only one bed. Who this bed belonged to was also a matter of course.

Of course it was for himself!

For a while, Shang Qinghua sprawled out on the bed like a dead starfish. After he had finished stretching out his muscles and bones, he crawled up and hauled Mobei-Jun onto it.

This was necessary. Mobei-Jun was already in a bad mood and quite the temper after being injured. If he awoke to find himself lying on the ground or scrunched into a chair, could Shang Qinghua expect to keep his life? There was no question that Mobei-Jun wouldn't stop to consider the truth of the situation before rewarding him with an icicle through the chest.

They had just passed by a medicine stand, and Shang Qinghua had bought a bit of such-and-such ointment. Although, given demons' unusually strong vitality, he could probably just toss him in the corner and ignore him, and no matter how large a hole had been poked into him, it would gradually close. However, since Shang Qinghua had decided to cling to those thighs, he knew he had to discard all reservations and display his sincerity. As a self-proclaimed "frank and honest reprobate," "Great Master" Airplane Shooting Towards the Sky looked down on hypocrites who kept up the aloof poser façade despite clearly wanting to cling to people's thighs.

He boldly scooped up a large lump of ointment and shoved it into the hole above Mobei-Jun's kidney until it was more or less closed, then flipped him over, arranging his hands palms-together in a Sleeping Beauty pose. After spending some time admiring this perfect face, which he had modeled after his mind's-eye ideal, he pillowed his head on his arms and fell asleep on the outer edge of the bed.

The summer night was stiflingly hot. Even with the window open, not a wisp of cool breeze flowed in. After tossing and turning for half the night, Shang Qinghua had finally managed to doze off when someone suddenly shoved him to the ground with a kick to the rear.

Shang Qinghua was nearly scared to death. Scrabbling, he fled beneath the table and turned his head in a panic. Mobei-Jun sat straight up on the bed, eyes shining with blue light like an overcharged battery about to explode.

Shang Qinghua had thought up his lines long ago. He beat his chest and stomped his feet, saying with deep expression, "My king, you're finally awake—"

Mobei-Jun was unmoved, looking at him coldly.

"Do you remember who I am?"

Mobei-Jun didn't respond.

Shang Qinghua felt not a bit of embarrassment. Delightedly entertaining the possibility of amnesia, he barreled onward. "We met on a little road just a moment ago. I said I would follow you for the rest of my life, my king, as close as—"

Mobei-Jun cut him off. "Why were you hugging me just now?"

"...as a little padded jacket..." Shang Qinghua started. "What did you say? I did what just now?"

"You were hugging me."

A sudden realization, thunder from a clear sky.

Sleeping in this damn heat was like being baked in a furnace, and Mobei-Jun's body temperature just happened to be cold. In a muddled state of sleep, Shang Qinghua had subconsciously moved toward the cooler side of the bed, and the closer he got, the cooler and more comfortable he'd become. No wonder he had dreamed of a giant popsicle around which he'd happily wrapped his four limbs like an octopus as he licked and cried happy tears.

Shang Qinghua carefully peeked at Mobei-Jun's face and neck. Seeing no unusual shine of moisture upon them, he couldn't resist letting out a thankful prayer. "Your body was ice-cold," he said cautiously. "I was afraid you weren't going to make it, so I was holding you."

At this, Mobei-Jun scoffed. "Fool. This is my natural state; the colder my body is, the better my condition. I'm not a human, for whom cold means the onset of death."

Shang Qinghua carefully measured Mobei-Jun's every word and expression. Seeing him relax a bit, a smile soon spread across his face. Just when he was about to slither out from under the table like a snake crawling up the stick used to strike it, Mobei-Jun suddenly recovered his ice-cold demeanor.

"Go on. Try moving another inch."

Shang Qinghua was instantly scared stiff. He pathetically clung to the table leg, curled into a ball under the table like a hamster.

"What do you want?" asked Mobei-Jun.

"I don't really want anything," Shang Qinghua said shamelessly. "I just want to follow you for the rest of my life."

Mobei-Jun acted as if he hadn't heard. "You're an An Ding Peak outer disciple."

Shang Qinghua kept feeling that whenever anyone stressed these three words "An Ding Peak," they carried an undertone of prejudice. For fear that Mobei-Jun would deem him useless and do away with him forthwith, he stuck out his head. "My king, listen to me—I'm young, so I have opportunities to rise in status—"

"Get back!"

Shang Qinghua hurriedly retreated to safety.

Satisfied with this distance, Mobei-Jun said, "The assistance you lent me, was it for 'opportunities to rise in status'?"

As proud and arrogant as expected. He hadn't used "save," a verb that would have implied being the weaker party in the situation, but rather "assist," which implied it had been merely support.

Shang Qinghua chuckled, playing dumb. If he said no, the credibility rating of his response would be less than three percent. But if he said yes... Mobei-Jun rather looked down upon such spineless reprobates. This was the reason Mobei-Jun hadn't thought twice about killing the original flavor Shang Qinghua, because he had never planned on letting him live in the first place. How could Shang Qinghua shamelessly admit that he had done it just to grind friendship XP?

Fortunately, Mobei-Jun had already come to a conclusion, and he slapped the label of "Greedy for Life, Afraid of Death, Slippery Bootlicker, Sect Sellout" right onto Shang Qinghua. He didn't need him to respond before letting out a cold snort, and he lay down once more.

Shang Qinghua waited for a long time, not moving another step. Had he received a concession for the time being? Or...had Mobei-Jun fainted again?!

In the end, Shang Qinghua didn't dare to rashly approach and remained crouched under the table, making do for the rest of the night.

After struggling with himself for half the night, as soon as he woke the next morning, Shang Qinghua officially began a busy day of being ordered left and right.

By noon, Shang Qinghua had worked hard without complaint, running up and down the stairs more than twenty times and changing the water in the bathtub seven or eight.

This water was to help Mobei-Jun heal his wounds. Soaking in water was the best option for this ice-powered great lord, after all. But a perfectly good tub of warm water didn't last an hour before he turned it into icy slush. Shang Qinghua huddled in the corner, chewing on some rations he had with him while watching Mobei-Jun undress, nursing both extreme envy toward and extreme admiration for the figure and abs he had longed for in his dreams.

As he watched, he suddenly realized Mobei-Jun had stopped undressing and was staring at him, an unhappy look on his face.

Shang Qinghua chewed a couple of times, hurriedly swallowing a few extra bites, just in case Mobei-Jun suddenly demanded he hand over his rations.

"You're very fishy," Mobei-Jun said.

"Not fishy," Shang Qinghua said hurriedly. "This one is sweet."

He didn't have the chance to eat more than a couple bites before a few strips of black shadow hit him full in the face.

So, Shang Qinghua couldn't stand around fishily anymore, as he had to go wash his newly claimed master's clothes.

Indeed, this young demonic heir had only brought one change of clothes, and now it was full of holes and blood and sweat. How could he wear them any longer? Obviously they had to be sewn and mended and washed and dried.

Low-fantasy xianxia worlds doggedly adhered to these kinds of unromantic, dismal, and disgusting principles of realism!

Shang Qinghua swore that if he ever had the opportunity to change back into "Great Master" Airplane Shooting Towards the Sky, his next book would be high-fantasy xuanhuan of the sort where wild plot bunnies ran rampant and science was fed to the dogs. Characters would weave clouds into garments and trim the moon into a belt, and all manual labor would be resolved with the twitch of a pinky finger. There would never again be a need for dismal existences like those of An Ding Peak's disciples!

Shang Qinghua considerately patched the hole in Mobei-Jun's clothes that had once covered his kidney, wrung them dry, and hung them up in the room. He felt he had made a very good show of himself that day. So, that night, with the confidence of the ignorant, he thickened his face and crawled toward the bed. But before he got close, history repeated itself and he was again kicked off.

He sat on the ground, tears in his eyes and voice trembling. "My king, you won't let me on the bed. What if during the night you get cold, thirsty, hungry, or want to turn over... What then?"

Mobei-Jun lifted an eyebrow. "Easily seen to."

So, he ordered Shang Qinghua to find a length of cord. One end was tied to his finger, while the other was tied to Shang Qinghua's...

Finger?

In your dreams. It was tied to his neck, nothing more.

Shang Qinghua lay on the ground like a corpse. *The fuck,* he thought to himself. *Dogs have it better than I do...*

The only comforting thought he could scrounge up was that at least Mobei-Jun wasn't some sort of pervert; the other end of the cord could've been tied to his [beep–]. That treatment would have been truly inhumane.

Shang Qinghua spent only four days suffering such hardship, but he honestly felt the days dragging by like years. Even his nights were an unceasing nightmare.

On the final day, in the middle of the night, Shang Qinghua was sound asleep as he once again dreamed.

This time he dreamed he was still in the real world, crying and weeping at a computer screen. Beside him was a fiendishly large man holding a thorny cucumber shaped like a rather hairy lower leg. He was fiercely thrashing Airplane Shooting Towards the Sky's face, and as he thrashed, he roared, "Everything you write is unhinged trash!"

Airplane Shooting Towards the Sky dodged the cucumber like his life depended on it as he strove to explain himself. "It's been so long since I've updated. Cucumber-bro, don't be like this!"

"Then hurry and update!" With this, Peerless Cucumber tied a corded loop around his neck.

Submerged in great suffering, Shang Qinghua fought to wake up only to find the cord still tightening around his neck. Following it with his gaze, he found Mobei-Jun lying on the bed, mechanically pulling on the cord tied to his hand.

"My king, what do you require?" Shang Qinghua asked lifelessly.

Only after asking a couple more times did he discover that Mobei-Jun wasn't tormenting him on purpose. He was profoundly passed out and was merely tossing and turning in extreme discomfort while unconsciously yanking on the thing in his hand to try to find relief. As the unfortunate soul around whose neck the other end of the cord was tied, Shang Qinghua's eyeballs were nearly squeezed out of his head under the force of the pulls.

Mobei-Jun creased his brow, restlessly flipping back and forth. Shang Qinghua quietly tiptoed to his bedside. When he saw the shallow beads of sweat seeping from Mobei-Jun's smooth forehead and felt the faint heat radiating from his clothes, he understood.

The wound on Mobei-Jun's back looked just like a little cut, not anything alarming, but in truth, the situation was a bit serious.

It was just that he was stubbornly trying to ride it out and had refused to admit it. In addition, it went without saying that the ice demons hated hot weather more than anything. It was the height of summer, and the wound was possibly becoming something similar to inflamed, or even beginning to fester.

His kidney was healing so slowly—did he need some sort of medicine to strengthen it a bit?!

The Mobei clan needed the cold. If they didn't have cold temperatures, they just had to make their own. Shang Qinghua muttered a, "His sleeping posture is really so fucking bad," then accepted his fate and went out. Unhindered by the annoyance he earned for knocking on doors in the middle of the night, he asked for two leaf fans, a basin of water, and two clean towels. He returned and wiped Mobei-Jun down, then placed a wet towel on his forehead. Taking up one leaf fan in his left hand and the other in his right, he fanned like his life depended on it.

He fanned and yawned incessantly, fanning until his eyes were bleary. Half-dreaming and half-awake, he seemed to see Mobei-Jun's eyes open. Icy-blue pupils were bright and cold under the moonlight, like a pair of magnificent and eerie chrysoberyls.

This scene was profoundly frightening. Shang Qinghua shuddered and opened his eyes wide to take a better look, but Mobei-Jun's were clearly shut tight.

Once Shang Qinghua awakened, he realized there was a major problem.

During the night, he had become dizzy from the heat. As he waved and waved those leaf fans, he had managed to topple over on the bed and fallen asleep.

Too close, too close!

Thankfully, Mobei-Jun was still asleep—if he'd woken, he might well have kicked Shang Qinghua's brains clear out of his head.

Shang Qinghua hurriedly jumped off the bed and lay down in the corner of territory he had claimed for himself on the floor by the headboard.

After a while, the bedframe began to creak lightly, and Mobei-Jun finally sat up. Shang Qinghua hissed to himself; that had been too close. If he had woken up even a little later, he'd have been turned into a blood splatter on the spot.

The next day, having obtained King Mobei's gracious permission, Shang Qinghua was finally able to see the light again, and he went out on the street for a stroll.

Well, actually, he had clung to Mobei-Jun's thighs and wailed, "My king, I'm out of rations. My cultivation level isn't so high that I can eat when I want and abstain when I don't like you can. If you don't let me go out to buy food, I'll starve to death and my corpse will stink up your room..."

He bought a bowl of thin congee to drink from a shop on a street corner. The congee was clear as water. When he looked down and glimpsed his own reflection, he beheld a chrysanthemum battered by the rain—a trampled mien, wan and sallow.

Just as Shang Qinghua was wallowing in his wretched misery, he suddenly heard someone call him "shidi" from behind. He turned to see some five young men exuding immortal auras, their sleeves and hems fluttering in the breeze as they shouldered longswords and walked solemnly toward him.

Comrades! His comrades from Cang Qiong Mountain Sect!

Right, seven days had passed, so they had organized a group to come find him!

Shang Qinghua was moved to tears. Reaching out a trembling hand, he called, "Shixiong—Wei-shixiong!"

A reserved smile graced the face of the leading youth. Two swords hung at his waist, one long, one short, and his sleeves billowed as if filled with a cool breeze. It was Wan Jian Peak's Wei Qingwei. When he saw Shang Qinghua rush out to greet him, he raised a hand to meet him, moved. "X-shidi, you... What happened to you? How have you so completely transformed as to reach such a state in the few days since we last met—you don't even look human!"

Shang Qinghua choked down a wave of hot tears, then awkwardly said, "That's probably because I'm not X-shixiong."

Sure, he had become a bit skinnier because he wasn't eating well, but what was with that "don't even look human" remark? Moreover, Shang Qinghua had been to Wan Jian Peak's sword trials terrace at least three times to polish swords for Wei-shixiong and his buddies, and every time they'd wanted him to sweep their rooms while he was at it, *and* to make them food, *and* to also feed their pangolins—how could they have already forgotten his face?!

"Can't you see I'm making a joke?" Wei Qingwei asked. "What, is it not funny? Oh, right, Shang-shidi, why are you all alone? Where are the others? Why did you delay your return? Did something happen?"

"Uh, Wei-shixiong, you really need to work on your jokes. As for the others... The others..."

This attack had been too sudden, and Shang Qinghua couldn't make up a seamless alibi on such short notice. So he just swayed a couple of times, his face deathly pale, then fell to the ground with a plop.

As he looked like he couldn't hold up much longer, no one would be suspicious if he pretended to faint.

While he was playing dead, he felt Wei Qingwei crouch down and poke his face a couple of times.

The others said, "Shixiong, he fainted. What should we do?"

"What else can we do?" Wei Qingwei asked, still poking. "Let's drag him back first and figure it out after."

At Qiong Ding Peak, rows and rows of dead bodies were arranged outside the main hall. Other than Shang Qinghua, every An Ding Peak outer disciple who had been sent to retrieve goods that day lay in repose, down to the last.

Shang Qinghua knelt in front of the bodies, tears falling to the ground. There was no way around it; it was hard to get by in this cultivation world. Someone like him, with mediocre innate ability, really couldn't make it without well-developed tear glands. If he hadn't had those, he wouldn't be able to put on this act of "a sorrow so heartbroken, it stilled the tongue" in front of the peak lords.

After the peak lords finished questioning him, they went into the hall to discuss, the atmosphere serious and solemn. Shang Qinghua suddenly heard the tinkling of sword tassel pendants, and a youth wearing Qing Jing Peak's uniform slowly approached him.

This youth had snowy-fair skin, slender brows and eyes, pale lips, and a somewhat harsh appearance. His black hair was neatly tied behind his head with a light-green ribbon, and a sword was held in his arms. It was precisely that inauspicious star, that heartless ghoul, that certain, uh, eccentric fellow from Qing Jing Peak, *Proud Immortal Demon Way*'s scum villain par excellence of the next generation: Shen Qingqiu.

Once Shen Qingqiu finished examining the bodies, he asked carelessly, "Did that demon ask you to bring back some message, or perhaps some object?"

Shang Qinghua started, shocked that Shen Qingqiu had actually chosen to grace him with unsolicited words. "No?"

Shen Qingqiu had a habit of raising his chin, so he was often looking down his nose at others. Every time they spoke, Shang Qinghua felt like Shen Qingqiu was sneering at him. Granted, the sneering didn't really matter; he was pretty used to it...

"Then that's strange," Shen Qingqiu said, his expression like a smile, yet not. "All the others died. If you don't have some message to bring to us, why would you of all people be the only survivor?"

Shang Qinghua blinked his eyes, tears once again streaming down his face. "This... That is..."

This time, Shen Qingqiu smiled for real. "Shang-shidi. Exactly how did you escape unscathed to return to Cang Qiong Mountain?"

Shang Qinghua absolutely could not afford to give a careless response to this question.

The Shen Qingqiu of this world functioned in accordance with his original settings. He wasn't like those low-IQ, paper-thin cannon fodder villains, and he was under no circumstances easy to deceive. If Shang Qinghua blew his cover and got reported, his clandestine second career would be over before it even began.

So, he played dumb and laughed awkwardly for thirty seconds. Suddenly, the lightbulb in his head lit up and he instantly began to stammer, "That is... It might be because..."

Because he hadn't for a second hesitated to kneel?

Because he'd yelled "My king!" with volume and sincerity?

Because he'd brazenly abandoned all dignity?

Shen Qingqiu waited patiently and, for his trouble, received a fit of gut-wrenching coughs from his target. Shang Qinghua coughed until tears poured from his eyes. Shen Qingqiu backed up a step, a shade of disgust on his face.

Everyone has a weakness—just you see who I'll summon to deal with you!

Sure enough, after five seconds of this, Yue Qingyuan's voice came from behind them.

"Qingqiu-shidi, in the first place, the behavior of the demon race has no logic to speak of, and moreover, Shang-shidi only just managed to escape a terrible catastrophe. Even if there are questions to ask, why not wait until he recovers a bit?"

And he appears! The god-tier summon, do-gooder, and future sect leader: Yue Qingyuan enters the battlefield!

Shang Qinghua silently began to count.

Shen Qingqiu raised his hand. "Fine, fine. Since you find my words so unpleasant to hear, I won't say any more of them. Yue-shixiong, as you please."

One hit.

"Our shidi from An Ding Peak descended the mountain to help handle affairs for Qing Jing Peak. Why must Shidi be so reluctant to grant him even a bit of sympathy?" asked Yue Qingyuan. "Shang-shidi, why is your coughing growing worse? Do you need me to call Qian Cao Peak's Mu-shidi to take a look at you?"

Two hits.

Shang Qinghua shook his head at Yue Qingyuan, shedding tears of gratitude. He continued to count.

Shen Qingqiu sneered. "The twelve peaks all oversee their own duties, and each has their own expertise. An Ding Peak is supposed to do this sort of thing in the first place; why must Yue-shixiong speak like they've been wronged in some way? As if An Ding Peak is the only one with things to do in Cang Qiong Mountain. Besides, don't tell me Shixiong believes they really do work hard without complaint. You think they don't curse us out behind our backs every day?"

Three hits.

Yue Qingyuan's expression was unerringly patient from beginning to end. He was just about to respond when Shen Qingqiu cut him off.

"Stop. Thank you for your instruction, Yue-shixiong. Qingqiu will continue to listen in the future. I'm going."

Four hits. Combo!

Shang Qinghua knew in his bones that if these two struck up a conversation, they would inevitably part on bad terms by the fifth exchange.

After Shen Qingqiu walked away, carrying Xiu Ya, Yue Qingyuan finally turned around. "Shang-shidi, you've suffered a scare."

"No, no, no..." Shang Qinghua said hurriedly.

Compared to the exhaustion and exploitation he'd suffered these past few days, a little scare was nothing at all.

But all things had a silver lining. After this incident, perhaps because the old An Ding Peak Lord wanted to console Shang Qinghua or whatever, he was promoted to an official inner disciple.

Shang Qinghua sang happily the whole way, returning to the large common dormitory to pack up his things before arriving at An Ding Peak's highest-level dormitory, the Leisure House, to report for duty.

That's right, you didn't read that wrong. On An Ding Peak, the disciples who ran around here and there all their lives like exploited servant girls lived in a dormitory called the "Leisure House."

Leisure, my ass! "Great Master" Airplane Shooting Towards the Sky swore he hadn't come up with this name with any satirical intent, but nowadays every time he saw those words, he was overcome by the incredible malice of this world.

Shang Qinghua found his own small room. Exhausted in both body and soul, he persevered and laid out his bedding, then turned around to pour himself a cup of water. But as soon as he turned back, there was another person lying on his bed.

In an utter cliché, the new teacup he had just received from the steward's office dropped from his hands right onto his foot. His legs softened, nearly sending him falling onto his rear. "My king."

Mobei-Jun turned to face him. He was expressionless, but his voice was cold as ice. "You'll follow me for the rest of your life, hm?"

Shang Qinghua was going to cry in fear.

Mobei-Jun had even followed him back here. He'd never thought... No, strictly speaking it wasn't like he'd *never* thought about it.

After all, Mobei-Jun had a special ability: "Mysterious Phantom: Come and Go Like a Shadow." Shang Qinghua had thought it up in the first place so Mobei-Jun could help Bing-ge slaughter and pillage, and so he could move under the cover of darkness anywhere and at anytime.

Shang Qinghua proceeded to babble nonstop. "My king, allow me to explain. That day, as soon as I went outside, I just wanted to drink some congee and come back, but who could have known that fate was messing with me—I ran into a familiar shixiong. I was afraid he'd ask too many questions and I'd let something slip, and that he'd take people to look for you, my king, and pick a fight with you, which wouldn't have been good. In addition, your injuries weren't causing you serious trouble anymore, so I thought it through from different angles and decided that for my mission, I had to endure disgrace and follow them back here, from where, if I saw an opportunity, I would—"

The hand Mobei-Jun was using to prop up his temple seemed to have gotten tired, and he switched to the other. "They told you to return, and you just followed them back."

"What else could I have done?" Shang Qinghua asked, aggrieved. "Refused to submit on pain of death? Show my hand and fight? That wouldn't do. Aside from the fact that I can't defeat them, the important thing is that I still have to be an undercover agent for you, my king, so how could I ruin my reputation with Cang Qiong Mountain now?"

In the midst of this wildfire burst of enthusiasm, he struck while the iron was hot. "A report for my king: I've already become an inner disciple. Doesn't that demonstrate ample drive to succeed? Doesn't that show I have a lot of potential?"

Kissing up. He was kissing up as hard as he could.

However, no matter how much it looked like he was kissing up on the surface, "Great Master" Airplane Shooting Towards the Sky's inner heart was as placid as a spring day. He had always firmly believed:

1: There's gold when a real man kneels (yes, in that order);[6]

2: A real man doesn't cry for no reason—but if he doesn't cry at times like this, then when will he?!

6 A corruption of the saying "Below a man's knees, there is gold," meaning that a man's subordination is as rare and valuable as gold. Shang Qinghua's alteration implies profit in subordination.

These two major life principles told him that in times of great need, kissing up a bit wasn't anything remarkable. If you thought about it another way, Mobei-Jun was a character Shang Qinghua had created, and as the author, Mobei-Jun was like his own son. For a father to concede a bit to his own son, to show a bit of love—that clearly couldn't be called anything strange. What was that saying? "Children are the debts parents owe from their previous lives..."[7]

Ping-ping, pang-pang.

Shang Qinghua suffered another good beating and thereafter hugged his knees, crouching in his chair, where he adeptly fooled himself into taking this as a pyrrhic victory.

After stretching his muscles and joints, Mobei-Jun lay back down on the bed, where he sprawled out and turned his back to Shang Qinghua. He spoke in a sleepy voice, neither loud nor soft: "We'll continue tomorrow."

Shang Qinghua was struck silent.

Continue?!

He had an urge to scream and shout, to call down the entirety of Cang Qiong Mountain to accompany him to his death.

Of course, the reason an urge was an urge was because it could usually be checked, and because it shouldn't actually be carried out.

Not even removing his boots, Mobei-Jun lay upon Shang Qinghua's brand-new, not-once-slept-on bed. Shang Qinghua's heart was as desolate as a winter wasteland.

"My king, this is Cang Qiong Mountain."

A highly lethal pillow flew over and struck Shang Qinghua, making him grimace in pain.

---

7 *A reference to the superstition that if you are indebted to someone in this life or a prior one, they may be reincarnated as your child to collect on what you owe.*

Shang Qinghua picked up the pillow. He attempted tact. "My king, that is my bed."

Mobei-Jun stuck up a finger and waved it at him. Cool and aloof, he said one word: "Mine."

Understood.

Because Shang Qinghua's whole person belonged to Mobei-Jun, his things also belonged to Mobei-Jun. Naturally, this included his bed.

Did the reverse also stand? At this kind of time, that one saying applied but with a twist: What's yours is mine, what's mine is also mine.

Shang Qinghua rolled off the chair with a huff and silently went to pick up the broken pieces of teacup at his feet. He began to hum a little tune as he did, "You're on the bed and I'm on the ground, / I get radish husks and you eat meat by the pound..." while tidying his new room.

At least a single pillow had been kindly bestowed upon him. Before, he hadn't even had that.

Know how to be content with your situation and you'll always be happy. He cuddled his pillow; it was finally time to retire after a long day of service.

Three days later, Shang Qinghua was as hardworking as a happy little honeybee. Mobei-Jun had slept in the Leisure House for those three days, then disappeared without a word.

Only with this had Shang Qinghua fully realized just how unscientifically god-tier the cheat he'd given Mobei-Jun was: Three. Days. In three days, there had been no warning bell, no suspicion, no nothing! Not a single person had found out that a demon had strutted all the way up to live on An Ding Peak and ordered about a future elite (logistics) disciple as his own beast of burden!

Like a freed serf singing in joy, Shang Qinghua floated about at full energy for a while, right up until he received his next mission from the old An Ding Peak Lord.

An Ding Peak's missions were invariably day-to-day miscellany, differing only in whether you battled through logistics or struggled on the front lines. But it was inevitably alarming to be in close proximity with dangerous organisms.

For example, rushing in to deliver blood-replenishing talismans and pills to Bai Zhan Peak when they were in the thick of battle with resentful spirits was a cruel and frightful type of mission no matter how you looked at it.

At least Mobei-Jun was a capable protector.

Shang Qinghua thought Mobei-Jun had already tossed him to the back of his mind. But on several later occasions when he ended up in hot water, he would be fished up in passing by some strange creature that was clearly demonic in appearance, and he was thusly able to remain intact.

This really counted as "stick close to me, and I'll protect you," didn't it?

Shang Qinghua couldn't help but conclude that clinging to thighs and whatever was both quite useful and quite necessary. If it weren't, he never would have survived this far!

— PART 3 —

ONE DAY, Shang Qinghua's concise Great System delivered a new command: *Become the An Ding Peak head disciple within three years.*

He'd already run missions into the outside world and made a good showing under Mobei-Jun's "care," but if he wanted to become head disciple, he would also have to pay more than a little attention to affairs within Cang Qiong Mountain itself.

As everyone knew, all the cannon-fodder supporting cast in *Proud Immortal Demon Way* only had an IQ of 40. Therefore, the so-called "palace intrigue" was pretty much all at this level:

So, the old An Ding Peak Lord already had a head disciple, let's call him A. A was outstanding to the max (where outstanding meant being a master of serving tea, changing water, washing clothes, and folding blankets, and that he was considered a dab hand at the housekeeping services center). Some days, the old peak lord requested that A make twelve delicious flatcakes and send one to each peak. All Shang Qinghua needed to do at such a time was stealthily scatter a ton of salt or sugar on every flatcake that A had meticulously made in order to render them flat-out unpalatable. Repeat the above process three times. And okay! Now the old peak lord has finally lost all hope in his former senior disciple!

Think about it. If you can't even make a good flatcake, what can you possibly do?

Now all Shang Qinghua needed to do was display his expert culinary skills a couple of times, and he could successfully ascend!

This was called: If you don't have enough IQ, make up for it with stupid plot twists. If you can't do the best, then be the worst.

If the plot is so imbecilic that readers roast it like crazy, that's also kind of a success!

In *Proud Immortal Demon Way*, these types of plots were too numerous to count. The way in which readers flocked together all year round to roast them could have been said to be one of the great spectacles of the Zhongdian comments section. And the fiercest roaster of all was none other than Peerless Cucumber.

As Shang Qinghua thought about this, he couldn't help but feel bit of nostalgia for those comments section companions, and for that one dear friend in particular.

He truly missed the force behind those inexhaustible howls that ran along the lines of: "Airplane Shooting Towards the Sky, it's exactly because you have these kinds of ideas that you're only a third-rate stallion novel writer!"

However, as the An Ding Peak head disciple, his troubles only increased. For example, in his time as an outer disciple, he never would have had the chance to descend the mountain on a quest with Shen Qingqiu and Liu Qingge.

How many fucking lives of disastrous karma must he have lived to draw this super special prize?!

Cang Qiong Mountain placed a high emphasis on maintaining kinship between peers. It was common for a handful of head disciples to group up and sally out on side quests every now and again. On this one, the division of labor between the three of them was clear. Liu Qingge was the thug hired to be the vanguard, while Shen Qingqiu was in the center, in charge of feigning civility and deploying sneak attacks and finishing blows, as well as waving his fan and being a poser (but don't let anyone know he said that.)

And Shang Qinghua? Naturally he was the one in charge of driving the carriage, making inn reservations, carrying luggage, and managing both the trip's income and expenses. Logistics, you know?

If only he had been let off so easily; that would've been great.

"They say that at night, if you stick your head over the edge of the well and look into its mouth, you'll see your reflection within, looking up as it smiles faintly and beckons. Out of nowhere, it drags people in and drowns them. Sometimes you'll even see your dead relatives..." Shang Qinghua coughed. "Shen-shixiong, Liu-shidi, can you...can you let me finish first?"

He put the scroll down.

Shen Qingqiu whisked a book out from his sleeve. He could turn on his poser act anytime and anywhere, sitting or standing. At present, he was leaning on the trunk of an old banyan tree in the shade, putting his magnificent scholarly essence on full display. Meanwhile, Liu Qingge had already gone to stand by the mouth of the well and stuck his head over the edge to look inside.

Liu Qingge wanted to wrap things up as fast as possible to avoid having to interact with Shen Qingqiu at any point during the trip, and Shen Qingqiu wanted to let Liu Qingge finish doing all the hard work and get lost as fast as possible. Neither one cared to burden himself with the other's presence; each had their own considerations; and neither was listening to Shang Qinghua's careful explanation of the mission.

Liu Qingge looked back up. "It didn't."

Shang Qinghua understood. Liu Qingge meant, *My reflection didn't smile faintly and beckon to me.* He spread his hands. "Well... How about we have Shen-shixiong go over and try?"

Shen Qingqiu stowed away his book, swapping it for a folding fan. He strolled over to the side of the well. "Please step aside."

Liu Qingge had already "stepped aside" a good dozen paces. Shen Qingqiu carelessly took a look into the well, but this also seemed to yield no results.

Shang Qinghua flipped through the scroll, paper rustling. "That's so strange, this clearly said..."

The unfortunate thing was, no matter how hard he rustled the paper, he couldn't drown out the sound of Shen Qingqiu's malicious question. "We've both tried. Isn't it your turn?"

Sure enough, in this world, even the monsters bullied the weak and feared the strong. When the other two had looked, they hadn't seen a damn thing, but when it was Shang Qinghua's turn, he clearly saw his own reflection coquettishly wave its hand.

Without another word, Liu Qingge smacked his sword's hilt. In a powerful arc, Cheng Luan flew from its sheath and rushed into the well.

After a moment of silence, the tranquil surface of the water began to churn and bubble. Shang Qinghua scrupulously took one step back, then another, retreating a safe distance away—only to hear a burst of ghastly wailing before a giant, wispy blob of spirits spewed out of the well and shot into the sky.

Liu Qingge smashed apart the clump of women's heads that were chasing and biting at him. "Get back!"

Usually, once the fighting started, any An Ding Peak disciples not in charge of replenishing supplies were supposed to scram as far away as possible and hang back at a safe location. Unfortunately, Shang Qinghua had miscalculated and didn't scram far enough. All his means of egress were blocked by the resentful spirits, which had taken the form of a white haze. Now that things had come to this, he could only bust out his special ability. His eyes rolled back in his head and he collapsed on the spot.

Playing dead was a time-tested technique!

In the chaos of battle, Liu Qingge and Shen Qingqiu accidentally pressed their backs together, and their faces simultaneously contorted with looks of revulsion. Shen Qingqiu had already shot out a spiritual blast, which brushed by Liu Qingge's shoulder as it passed. Liu Qingge, angered, immediately retaliated with a blow.

Great. The entirety of their combat forces were now ignoring the enemy in order to fight amongst themselves.

"Are you blind?" Shen Qingqiu yelled. "What are you hitting?!"

Liu Qingge wasn't any more polite. "Who hit first? Who went blind first?!"

Shang Qinghua lay on the ground, eyes still rolled back. He had clearly seen when, moments ago, a faint white shadow peeked out from behind Liu Qingge. Shen Qingqiu's attack had passed Liu Qingge's shoulder to disperse it.

As he watched, the blows his peers rained down on each other grew fiercer and fiercer, their eyes going red with bloodlust. Forgetting to play dead, he sat up and called weakly, "You guys, don't fight. Liu-shidi, you misunderstood; in fact, Shen-shixiong was just—"

Shen Qingqiu flung out his hand, and several deep, deep cracks were smashed into the wall by Shang Qinghua's head. Dust and pebbles streamed down.

"If you're going to die, then die completely," Shen Qingqiu said icily. "Don't change your mind halfway."

Without another word, Shang Qinghua collapsed and went back to contentedly playing dead.

At last, they sealed away the well creature and all the resentful spirits it had collected in a retrieval vessel, not missing a single one. Shang Qinghua led over the cart and horse. Without sparing them a single glance, Liu Qingge took off down a different road.

Shang Qinghua said hurriedly, "Liu-shidi, where are you going?"

Liu Qingge snorted. "I will not journey alongside a backstabbing colleague."

Shen Qingqiu clapped his hands and smiled. "How wonderful. For my part, I don't care to journey alongside someone who's all brawn, no brains. Shang-shidi, let's go."

He grasped Shang Qinghua's shoulder, and Shang Qinghua squeaked an agreement through teeth clenched in pain. Finally struggling free of Shen Qingqiu's evil clutches, he caught up with Liu Qingge to caution him. "Liu-shidi, Shixiong has a word of advice to offer. Don't cultivate by yourself all the time; it's easy to fall into a qi deviation."

Liu Qingge still hadn't responded when on the other road, Shen Qingqiu used the base of his fan to rap on the rails of the cart. Shang Qinghua hurried back.

The whole way home, he watched Shen Qingqiu closely while driving the cart.

Shen Qingqiu was leaning on the side of the carriage reading a book, but under Shang Qinghua's stare, his expression grew darker and darker. He narrowed his eyes. "What are you staring at me for?"

"Shen-shixiong, I...really wasn't going to say anything," Shang Qinghua said timidly. "But since you've asked me so sincerely, then... You're holding your book upside down."

In a split second, Shen Qingqiu's face reddened. He abruptly rose and drew his sword.

"No, no, no, no, no, no—*don't do anything rash*!"

Shen Qingqiu had the thinnest face! If you tore down his pretenses right in front of him, he would remember you for a lifetime. Shang Qinghua was already regretting the quip. But if a person like Shen Qingqiu—who had perfected the art of poserhood—was holding his book upside down, he really had to be incensed.

That sounded about right. He had gone to all that trouble to do a good thing, but the result hadn't met his expectations. But if that was the problem, then he should just go and explain himself to Liu Qingge—just admit he was trying to help him out! But Shen Qingqiu wouldn't do it.

If you won't do it, just let me help you explain, thought Shang Qinghua. But Shen Qingqiu wouldn't compromise his own pride. Maybe he was too embarrassed. *People really shouldn't twist themselves into knots—that's just self-torture.*

Shen Qingqiu stared at him with a vicious gaze, and cold sweat flowed down Shang Qinghua's back.

After a while, Shen Qingqiu finally sat back down and sheathed his sword. With great effort, he composed himself, then said with a superficial smile, "Shang Qinghua, shut up. All right?"

Shang Qinghua's heart itched ferociously. He raised a hand. "Can I say one more thing?"

Shen Qingqiu rubbed his temple with his right hand, then lifted his chin to indicate permission to speak.

Shang Qinghua looked at him with an earnest gaze, then spoke the most meaningful and heartfelt string of words he had spoken since an electric current had shocked him into *Proud Immortal Demon Way*:

"If, in the future, you see someone fall into a qi deviation, don't panic, and don't rush up rashly thinking you can save them.

You must stay calm and call for help; don't try to do it yourself. If you don't, you'll definitely be more of a hindrance than anything, and you'll make a big mess, and you'll abandon yourself to despair from there on. You'll never be free of it for the rest of your life—even jumping into the Yellow River won't wash you clean!"

Shen Qingqiu was mystified. "If someone else fell into qi deviation, what would that have to do with me? Why would I panic? Why would I want to help?"

Shang Qinghua's face was the very definition of *I knew you'd say that*. "Either way, just make sure you remember."

Once Shang Qinghua became the peak lord, he at long last no longer needed to bow and scrape to anyone.

A busy life was still a busy life, but at least he had been promoted from "exploited servant girl" to "head of internal affairs"; this totally counted as rapid progress in long steps.

Apparently, that particular person on Qing Jing Peak whom no one could afford to offend had fallen ill. After he recovered, a secret meeting was held on Qiong Ding Peak.

In the side hall of Qiong Ding Peak, ten of the twelve peak lords were present and accounted for.

"Do you feel that Qingqiu-shidi...has been very odd these past few days?" Yue Qingyuan asked, completely focused on the topic.

Several peak lords agreed.

"More than just odd," said Liu Qingge in a solemn tone.

"He's practically a whole different person," muttered Qi Qingqi.

Just then, Shang Qinghua stepped into the side hall, worn and weary from travel. Over the past few years, Qian Cao Peak's Dragon-Bone Cantaloupe seeds had been selling quite well outside the sect, and he had already spent several months rushing about on sales trips. He had been dragged into this mysterious meeting as soon as he got back, and he still didn't quite understand the situation. He rubbed his hands together. "About that, I haven't seen Shen-shixiong for a few days. Could everyone please elaborate? How exactly has he been odd?"

"He had a calm and harmonious conversation with me for a whole two hours," said Yue Qingyuan.

Shang Qinghua was both speechless and terrified. "Aiyah, my god! How odd! That really is very odd!"

Ordinarily speaking, the bridge between these two was impassably burned. Without rebuilding the bridge, there was absolutely no chance of harmonious developments. Thus far, the T-Minus Five Sentences Until They Part on Terrible Terms rule had held true as baseline normal. A whole two hours' worth of a calm and harmonious exchange—this was more than a fantastical level of progress.

"In the Ling Xi Caves, he...helped me," said Liu Qingge.

Shang Qinghua finally remembered. Right, by now, Shen Qingqiu should already have "helped" Liu Qingge to his death. So how could Liu Qingge still be hanging about, sitting here to attend a meeting?!

Was it possible that the warning Shang Qinghua had given Shen Qingqiu after defeating the well creature had actually made an impact?

The other peak lords continued to list Shen Qingqiu's every behavioral oddity over the last few days. "Sustaining injury while beating back an impetuous demoness" this, "stepping forward to protect his disciples and showing care and concern" that... Shang Qinghua's face began to twitch.

He thought it over back and forth, but no matter how he looked at it, this kind of altruistic self-sacrificing character behavior was seriously OOC!

Unable to resist, he said, "Wait. He...couldn't have been possessed, could he? Wei-shixiong, how is your sword trials terrace? Did he visit?"

At the sword trials terrace of Wei Qingwei's Wan Jian Peak, there was a mystical sword known as Hong Jing, which no person had ever been able to draw. But if something like a resentful soul or evil spirit were to approach the blade, it unsheathed of its own accord. If Shen Qingqiu really had been possessed by some impure creature, as long as he approached the sword trials terrace, Hong Jing would emphatically sound the alarm.

However, Wei Qingwei said, "He went three times and tried to draw it every one, and there was absolutely no sign of movement."

"There is no demonic energy in his body," Yue Qingyuan said slowly. "I could detect no signs that he has been possessed."

Qi Qingqi spread her hands. "It doesn't make any sense for him to be possessed. Possession at least involves some sort of goal. But he hasn't been doing anything; he's even more idle than before."

After the discussion session, they remained unable to reach a decision.

In the end, Mu Qingfang said, "It's not necessarily a case of possession. In my opinion, perhaps Shen-shixiong's old problem has reappeared."

All the peak lords looked at each other.

What this "old problem" was didn't need to be said aloud; everyone understood.

Shen Qingqiu, as a person, was ambitious and aggressive, proud and arrogant. This wasn't the first time he'd tried to force instant success. Maybe he had gone off to cultivate in secret again and had ended up falling into a qi deviation.

Mu Qingfang continued his analysis. "I have heard of quite a few such cases. When a person is hit on the head with a large rock, or if they perhaps suffer a violent shock, sometimes they lose a few of their memories of the past. So, it's not necessarily impossible for someone to fall into a qi deviation and forget their past, thus leading to their temperament to undergo major changes."

"Then is it possible to recover?" Yue Qingyuan asked.

Qi Qingqi wrinkled her nose. "Zhangmen-shixiong, do you actually hope he'll remember and recover his previous...character and conduct?"

Yue Qingyuan started. "Me? I cannot say." When he continued, it was earnestly, "Even though the way he is now is overall very good as well... If he *can* remember, it will be for the better."

"Before, he never offered a proper greeting when he met Zhangmen-shixiong or his fellow sect members," one of the other peak lords said in confusion. "He never visited us at our homes, and when he spoke, it was all needles concealed in silk floss, full of biting sarcasm—what was good about that? The way he is now is quite an improvement."

Yue Qingyuan smiled faintly, but he did not speak.

"The last time I went to write his prescription for Without a Cure, I examined him," Mu Qingfang said awkwardly. "There were no significant symptoms, so it would be difficult to know where to begin. I'm afraid we can only let nature take its course."

Having reached the verdict, "The Qing Jing Peak Lord has lost his memory; celebrate and spread the joyful news," the meeting adjourned.

After this meeting concluded, Shang Qinghua felt he was very much obligated to investigate these strange happenings (in passing, while delivering Qing Jing Peak's funds).

But before Shang Qinghua started his investigation, he went to Bai Zhan Peak.

Normally speaking, in terms of seniority, Qing Jing Peak was ranked second in Cang Qiong Mountain and Bai Zhan Peak was ranked seventh. After making his deliveries to the first-ranked Qiong Ding Peak, his next stop should have been Qing Jing. But on the one hand, Shen Qingqiu was too hard to please, and Shang Qinghua had to rack his brains every time he went to figure out how not to offend him. On the other hand, Bai Zhan Peak loved fighting, so Shang Qinghua felt safer giving them their funds first.

Safer how? Mm, it was precisely the sense of safety a small shop-owner felt when handing his protection fee to the local gang boss...

The one who greeted him was Liu Qingge's shidi, Ji Jue, who was as enthusiastic as always. The two exchanged some small talk, and after the handover was complete, Ji Jue said, "Shang-shixiong, take care, I'm returning to the training grounds."

When Shang Qinghua realized that Ji Jue seemed reluctant to see him leave, he said, "Liu-shidi has been staying at Bai Zhan Peak more often lately. Has any shidi had a sudden increase in cultivation?"

Liu Qingge spent all his time in the outside world looking for people to fight. No one on Bai Zhan Peak was a match for him, and he typically only came back once a month at most. Whenever Bai Zhan Peak's disciples and juniors flocked to Qian Cao Peak to seek treatment, that meant he had just returned. But lately, Qian Cao Peak's doorsteps had nearly been trampled flat by those great lords from Bai Zhan Peak, and the medicinal peak's funds were getting light.

Mu Qingfang had started to ask Shang Qinghua for loans every few days, which Shang Qinghua found strange. He couldn't help but wonder, had an extraordinary genius who could stand up to Liu Qingge appeared on Bai Zhan Peak? So, he asked.

Ji Jue drooped in gloom. "It's not our peak. It's Shen Qingqiu."

Shang Qinghua hadn't expected any earth-shattering news, so he just smiled and nodded. "Oh, Shen Qingqiu, ah... Shen Qingqiu?!"

As Shang Qinghua digested the enormous amount of information contained in those two words, he was almost ascended out of shock on the spot.

Shen Qingqiu? At Bai Zhan Peak? At the Bai Zhan training grounds, no less? Doing what? Getting a one-sided beatdown from Liu Qingge? No, given his skill in drawing aggro, it was probably a group beatdown—but what if it became fatal? *He's an important scum villain, you know! If he gets beaten to death, who's going to torment Bing-ge?!*

"Shang-shixiong, what's that look in your eye?!" Ji Jue asked after a silence. "Don't look at me like that—we didn't kill anyone! Shen Qingqiu is still alive, and no one's done anything to him! You should be asking what *he* did to *us*!"

So, Shang Qinghua jogged with Ji Jue all the way to the training grounds.

On the high basalt platform, Liu Qingge and Shen Qingqiu were in actual fact merely crossing swords in an orderly match.

Liu Qingge's movements were much slower than usual. Rather than calling it crossing swords, you might as well have called it feeding his opponent training strikes. The space between his brows was still rather smooth, and it emanated none of his typical homicidal tendencies.

Just then, Shen Qingqiu's sword struck air. He knitted his brows, and his left hand twitched.

Shang Qinghua's heart suddenly stretched taut. He glanced at Ji Jue out of the corner of his eye and saw that his expression also twitched, like he had an urge to shout out loud.

The two glanced at each other in a flash of wordless understanding.

Ji Jue, his heart still palpitating, said in a low voice, "I always feel like Shen Qingqiu is about to deploy a concealed weapon dipped in poison or something."

Shang Qinghua expressed his deep agreement. "Heroes think alike!"

It looked like Ji-shidi understood this character very thoroughly. Exactly what he expected from the fellow who had once picked a fight with Shen Qingqiu at a brothel; they were old enemies who had both soundly lost the faces of two whole peaks...

Shen Qingqiu drew back Xiu Ya and stopped to think. For one, he didn't let out a laugh cold like rustling wind, and for two, he didn't look askance at anyone. If one looked at him now, one would see a mild brow and peaceful gaze that still carried a modest air of elegant nobility.

Soon after, Shen Qingqiu said, "I don't understand."

Liu Qingge flicked a swift and fierce flourish with his sword. "Don't understand what?"

A disciple next to Ji Jue muttered, "Heavens, he doesn't understand again."

"I...I can't take it anymore..." another disciple said quietly. "My stomach feels bad, I'm going back..."

"Shidi, wait for me, me too..." Ji Jue said hurriedly.

His shidi pushed him back. "Stay! Didn't you just get back?!"

On the platform, Shen Qingqiu said, "Just then, in those few moves, if I blocked your sword with my right hand and let loose a spiritual blast with my left, finding an opportunity to strike your stomach, I would have had a chance of winning."

"Not possible," Liu Qingge scoffed.

"Most possible," Shen Qingqiu persisted.

"If you could have won, why didn't you try it?"

"Isn't this just sparring?" Shen Qingqiu said, aloof. "Attacking in earnest would be out of line."

Liu Qingge didn't bother to reply. Instead, he yelled into the crowd below the platform. "You, get up here!"

The person he selected ascended the platform with an expression like the hero Yi Shui, grimly prepared to stare death in the face. Using the method Shen Qingqiu had suggested, they traded a few blows with Liu Qingge—before getting blown straight off the platform by Cheng Luan.

Liu Qingge sheathed his sword and turned to Shen Qingqiu. "See? It wouldn't work."

Shen Qingqiu snapped open his fan and waved it in front of his chest. "I see," he said, all smiles. "Liu-shidi's reflexes are too fast. It wouldn't work after all."

"Every time he says 'I don't understand,' Liu-shixiong grabs someone to demonstrate *until* he understands..." Ji Jue quietly complained to Shang Qinghua.

No wonder the injuries at Bai Zhan Peak had only increased over the past few days, while Qian Cao Peak's front courtyard was as busy as a marketplace.

Shang Qinghua had only one thought in response to this: that Shen Qingqiu had to be doing this on purpose!

After he descended the platform, Liu Qingge continued to train (read: beat up) the Bai Zhan Peak disciples. Shen Qingqiu and Shang Qinghua exchanged greetings, then walked down the mountain together. Just as they were about to exit through the gate, Ji Jue caught up to them, carrying two sacks, which he gave to Shen Qingqiu and Shang Qinghua.

Shang Qinghua didn't understand, so he undid the tie to take a look. Inside, he saw two balls of bloody, hairy things nestled together. "And this is..."

"Liu-shixiong caught these short-haired beasts," Ji Jue said, expression stiff. "Apparently, they taste very good. Shixiong, please take them back to your own peaks to cook them as you please."

Short-haired beast? What short-haired beast? Did I really ever create this creature? Is it edible? Are you sure?!

It looked like Shen Qingqiu was also highly suspicious of the creature's edibility. "Thanks for your trouble..."

"Shixiong said: This is a gift in return for the tea leaves Qing Jing Peak recently sent," Ji Jue recited woodenly.

Tea leaves? Shen Qingqiu had given Liu Qingge tea leaves?! What was this? Were they exchanging presents?! Internally, Shang Qinghua yelled, *Holy shit!* while externally, he kept a smile on his face. "You mean to say that this is all thanks to Shen-shixiong's generosity. What sort of high-quality tea leaves were these?"

"They were harvested from the tea fields of my senior disciple Ming Fan's family," Shen Qingqiu said affably. "As for whether they're high-quality, won't Shang-shidi know if he comes for tea at Qing Jing Peak?"

Shang Qinghua thickened his face, shameless. "Then I have Liu-shixiong's generosity to thank as well."

So, each carrying a sack, talking about this and that, they walked toward Qing Jing Peak.

As soon as they passed the mountain gates, serene wind caressed their faces and faint birdsong chittered away. It was an atmosphere entirely distinct from that of the outer world. Together they walked over a soft layer of green bamboo leaves that covered the ground and found themselves feeling several times more refreshed.

For some reason, Shen Qingqiu's mood was quite good. He didn't look the least bit like he had just lost to Liu Qingge. He even offered an idle bit of praise: "Liu-shidi's swordmanship is truly quite something."

Shang Qinghua couldn't resist reminding him, "Shen-shixiong you… How many times did you lose?"

Shen Qingqiu thought it over. "Hm? Mm, you're asking about this morning? It was only seven or eight times."

Then how are you this calm?!

Shouldn't you be gnashing your teeth in fury, tears staining your face like raindrops on a flower petals (ahem)—a cuckoo crying blood as you whip around to go back into seclusion for three months, swearing to duel again?

Don't you know you're being OOC? Can't you show a bit more dedication to your role?!

Shen Qingqiu bashfully tapped the handle of his fan on his nape. "There's nothing you can do about losing to the Bai Zhan Peak Lord. It would be more accurate to say that winning would be the unusual outcome."

Shang Qinghua had no words. He felt there was no way to communicate with this guy.

He's lost his memory. He definitely fell into a qi deviation and lost his memory. If this Shen Qingqiu and Liu Qingge were playing out a scene of a friendly senior and his respectful junior, full of harmonious fraternal love between fellow sect members—oh, heavens, maybe in a few days, Shen Qingqiu and Luo Binghe would be striking up flirtatious banter!

The second after this frightful vision flashed through Shang Qinghua's mind, a white shadow darted toward them, and something sticky and clingy suddenly threw itself into Shen Qingqiu's arms. That soft little lump called out, "Shizun!"

Shen Qingqiu was nearly knocked on his back. He swayed, then grabbed on to a thick bamboo stalk and finally managed to regain his footing. He noticed Shang Qinghua detachedly observing the scene, expressionless.

You couldn't fault Shang Qinghua for his frozen expression. At the sight of that little wee little lady-killer, with his two arms encircling Shen Qingqiu's waist like a steel hoop, the name "Bing-ge" had nearly escaped his mouth!

Shen Qingqiu stiffly waved his fan with one hand, embarrassed. "If you're going to call to me, then just call; don't drag your voice out like that. Throwing yourself at people every day—and while your shishu is here!—what manner of decorum is this?"

Luo Binghe slowly removed his hands and stood straight. He obediently said, "Shang-shishu," then, "after this disciple finished morning lessons, he waited here for Shizun to return. I forgot myself in a moment of excitement..."

"Great Master" Airplane Shooting Towards the Sky's heart nearly crumbled.

Luo Binghe switched to hugging Shen Qingqiu's arm. "Shizun, why were you out for so long?"

"There were a lot of people today."

As Shang Qinghua took in Shen Qingqiu's leisurely and contented smile, he couldn't resist guessing how many times the Qing Jing Peak Lord "hadn't understood" earlier, and how many times he'd had Liu Qingge "demonstrate" for him.

Luo Binghe automatically took the sack out of Shen Qingqiu's hands. "Next time, can I go too?"

"That depends on your progress in swordplay," Shen Qingqiu said casually. "There's some sort of monster in the sack; your Liu-shishu said it's edible. See if you can clean off the hair and figure out how to cook it."

You've made Bing-ge into a kitchen girl—only the female protagonists are allowed to eat the male protagonist's cooking! Can't you stay in your place? Ah, forget it. Shang Qinghua didn't have the energy.

"Oh." Luo Binghe happily agreed. As he shook the sack, the thing inside suddenly began to struggle. "Shizun, it's still alive!"

By the time they arrived at the drawing room of the Bamboo House, Shen Qingqiu's flock of disciples had surrounded that mysterious creature and were taking turns poking the sack. With each poke, that short-haired beast let out a plaintive cry, and yet they were delighted each time, clicking their tongues in wonder.

"Shizun, it really is still alive!"

"What do we do if it's still alive? Do we still kill and eat it?"

"Let's not. It's so pitiful..."

Shang Qinghua forced himself to ignore this flock of young disciples sitting all over the ground and lowered his head to drink his tea, his heart twitching.

He remembered the last time he'd come, every disciple had worn a face full of great bitterness and deep resentment. They'd stood like pines or sat like clocks, each with an old text in hand, reciting wherever they went like they were chanting curses, quoting chapter and verse when they spoke, a musical cadence to their voices. When he looked at them today... Was this still that renowned Qing Jing Peak that produced countless poser youths full of literary airs?

This place had become a daycare center for ADHD children.

"If it's still alive, then keep it as a pet," said Shen Qingqiu.

"Let's eat it—let's just eat it," Ming Fan hurriedly retorted. "We've never kept one before; we don't know how much it needs to eat, and changing its water and taking it out for walks and whatnot will be awfully troublesome..."

Ning Yingying pouted. "That's enough. If we keep it, it definitely won't be *you* taking care of it—Shizun would obviously give it to A-Luo." She lifted her head and asked, "Shizun, where did you get this strange thing?"

"The Bai Zhan Peak Lord gave it to me. A return gift for the tea."

At this, Ning Yingying whined, "Shizun, I don't like Bai Zhan Peak. They're so annoying... Last time they used their superior sword skills to bully A-Luo; they were chasing and beating him..."

Shang Qinghua thought this quite normal. Bai Zhan Peak's uniform malice toward Luo Binghe was entirely natural. It was the sort of instinctive reaction single-celled organisms had toward traces of concealed evil. This wasn't throwing shade at Bai Zhan Peak; Shang Qinghua was a fan of theirs, for his part.

After enumerating their shortcomings, Ning Yingying put forth her request: "Shizun, you have to help us teach them a good lesson!"

"Puh—" Shen Qingqiu choked once, turned toward Shang Qinghua, and smiled politely as he coughed. "These children, what are they on about? There ought to be harmony and familial affection within the sect. How could I 'teach them a good lesson' for such a reason?"

Shang Qinghua repeatedly stated his agreement, returning the same forced smile and drinking tea like his life depended on it.

Miss Yingying, ah, your Shizun doesn't need to make a move; Liu Qingge has already taught them quite a cruel lesson. In fact, Shen Qingqiu is in charge of "harmony and familial affection," and Liu Qingge is in charge of "teaching them a good lesson." This right here is the true nature of a hypocrite!

Shang Qinghua was deeply comforted by this. Even after going through a qi deviation and losing his memory, sure enough, Shen Qingqiu was still his treacherous old self!

Luo Binghe had gone to fetch tea leaves, and at this moment, he entered the drawing room to present them to Shang Qinghua.

"Come, Shidi, we have been indebted to An Ding Peak's care for a long time now..." said Shen Qingqiu.

But one kid on the floor was still unwilling to back down. "Shizun, you have to avenge A-Luo!" Ning Yingying said, impassioned.

Shen Qingqiu was at the end of his patience. "Yingying, go play outside."

"You mustn't avenge me or whatever else," Luo Binghe said hastily. "It's just that this disciple's skill is inferior to theirs, and he lost face for Shizun and Qing Jing Peak."

"Your foundation is just a bit lacking, and you can't expect to catch up to them straightaway," Shen Qingqiu said, offering words of comfort. "As long as you remain diligent, given some time, you will assuredly surpass them."

Ming Fan scoffed. "It would take a hundred years for *him* to surpass Bai Zhan Peak."

Ning Yingying flew into a temper. "If you look down on Qing

Jing Peak and A-Luo that much, why don't you just go to Bai Zhan Peak and see if they'll take you?!"

Shen Qingqiu put his head in his hands. "Didn't I tell you to go outside and play? Why are you still here? Binghe, get them outside quick; don't make a circus of yourselves in here."

"All right, Shizun. But, as for this thing, are we eating or keeping it...?"

Shang Qinghua was struck dumb. He was choking down so much that his heart was about to stop.

This scene featuring Shen Qingqiu as the ever-attentive teacher and Luo Binghe as the clingiest hanger-on—what the hell was this?!

Don't fucking tell me Shen Qingqiu really did go to Bai Zhan Peak and mess with people just to avenge Luo Binghe!

This benevolent father and filial son act—no, no, no, it was more like "lifting one's tray to eyebrow level"—no, no, no, "treating each other as honored guests"![8] This was even more fantastical than Shen Qingqiu and Liu Qingge's harmonious spar. If things kept going on like this, maybe there really would be a day when they exchanged flirtatious banter. Pah, if that day really came, he'd eat three kilos of shit!

After "Great Master" Airplane finished swearing, he had a rare moment of careful thought. He had never quite used classical idioms properly, and he had hauled out his limited supply to describe Liu Mingyan's beauty. The ones he used with the highest frequency were "soft bosoms trembling" and "as delicate as the finest gossamer." To use "treating each other as honored guests" *was* correct here, right? Hm, if he looked at the literal meaning, then yes, it was correct!

8 *"Lifting the tray to eyebrow level" when delivering a meal refers to deep respect between spouses. "Treating each other as honored guests" also refers to mutual respect between spouses.*

At that moment, the "Great Master" Airplane Shooting Towards the Sky assiduously struggling to recover from this episode had not yet realized that the scum villain Shen Qingqiu had already been replaced by that unmatched hater, Peerless Cucumber.

To think that in days of yore, when this guy's rants had grown excessively ferocious, Airplane had sometimes casually cursed him, maliciously praying that no matter how peerless his cucumber was, he would never get a chance to use it for the rest of his life. Who could have expected that in some manner of speaking, this curse had been fulfilled?

These days, Bing-ge's mood was especially bad.

Shang Qinghua could understand. As the stallion protagonist who, in the original work, could fuck his way across the continent solo, he had now captured and imprisoned Shen Qingqiu, and...

Yup, just imprisoned him. Imprisoned him and nothing else.

Could you believe it?! He was the original author, and even he didn't dare believe it!

If he could still control the current Bing-ge with his pen, guided by the principle of "satisfying the protagonist is satisfying the readers," he would absolutely have let Luo Binghe defile Shen Qingqiu hundreds of times—yeah, *hundreds* of times, over and over like skewering a kebab. (This definitely had nothing to do with his personal grievances against Peerless Cucumber. Definitely not.) No props, position, or location would ever be repeated. Things would get easier once it was skewered, mind you, and of course feelings would develop during the skewering...

In comparison, the current Bing-ge's life was the dull and arduous sort, in which he might go three years without knowing the taste of meat. Shang Qinghua couldn't help but feel sorry for his dear son.

So, no brainless idiot would dare go up to Luo Binghe and be a nuisance at this kind of time.

In the assembly hall of the underground palace, everyone hurried about on their own business. Sha Hualing was sewing together that giant net of immortal-binding cables that Shen Qingqiu had torn apart as she stole looks at Luo Binghe, sometimes biting her lip in dissatisfaction. Mobei-Jun was taking a nap at the west end of the hall, eyes closed. Shang Qinghua bounced his leg, idle to the point of agitation.

He really didn't have anything to do, and he hadn't wanted to come to the assembly hall either. But this was demon territory. If he didn't stay within arm's reach of Mobei-Jun, who could say if he wouldn't be swallowed whole by some manner of bizarre creature?

Just when he was about to crawl over to Mobei-Jun and risk a beating to request that his king find somewhere with a less tense atmosphere to nap, Luo Binghe suddenly said one word.

"If..."

Every demon in the hall perked up their ears.

"If you hold unique feelings for a certain person, how can you make them understand your intentions?" Luo Binghe asked.

Poor Ice-brother! He was totally like a terminal patient desperately turning to any doctor he could find!

Even though his question was veiled, how couldn't they all tell that he was looking for romantic advice?

Moreover, he was actually trying to have a serious discussion about this sort of thing in front of his subordinates. *Sure enough,*

people (demons) just shouldn't fall in love, thought Shang Qinghua. *Because as soon as they do, their IQ drops like a stone.*

Obviously, no one dared to tear down Luo Binghe's facade and expose him directly, but this question was really very...unsuited to the demonic approach. After a long moment, not a single person had answered.

In fact, the answer was so simple that any normal human could have given it to you. If you liked someone, you should just tell them. Unfortunately, there was not a single "normal" person on the scene—and aside from Shang Qinghua, there also were no "humans" either.

Mobei-Jun thought about it. With the paths his mind was given to take, there was no telling how he had interpreted "unique" feelings. "Beat them up three times a day?"

Luo Binghe made a *stop* gesture with one hand and said wisely, "You don't need to answer."

Of everyone present, the only one who had a natural advantage due to their gender, and who therefore might be able to field this sort of question, was Sha Hualing. So, the others all swept their gazes toward her.

With *WTF? Why should I provide this sort of advice to the man I want to take for myself?* written all over her face, the finely shaped lips and brows of the Sha-meimei who had been extremely popular in the original work twitched several times. Finally, still spasming, she let out a dry, "Why doesn't my lord ask Senior Meng Mo?"

"I've already asked," said Luo Binghe.

No one knew better what sort of shit answer Meng Mo had given than Shang Qinghua. That guy was the same as Shang Qinghua—he was clearly of the "just do them first" persuasion!

Shang Qinghua broke and let out a chuckle.

Sha Hualing had been brooding, her chest full of repressed emotions with nowhere to vent them. Latching on to his break, she erupted. "You dare! Who are you to sneak into the assembly hall and make a disturbance while my lord is discussing important matters?!"

That kind of question...couldn't be called important matters, could it? And he had only let out one sound; how did that count as a "disturbance"?

As this wasn't the first time Sha Hualing had picked on him, Shang Qinghua was adept at meeting her with indifference. He kept himself planted in his seat, pretending he was nothing more than empty air. As expected, Mobei-Jun was unconcerned.

Sha Hualing saw that no one was paying attention to her and indignantly wrung her long fingernails. "My lord, Mobei-Jun brings him everywhere every day without the least bit of discretion—and even brings him to the assembly hall! What is the meaning of this?"

Luo Binghe was also unconcerned. "You see him every day; are you not used to him yet?"

Sha Hualing was going to faint.

But this was the first time in months that Bing-ge had expressed an opinion on Shang Qinghua's existence! Immediately, Shang Qinghua started up an ecstatic internal chant of, *My son noticed me, he noticed me, ha ha ha ha!*

What he didn't expect was Luo Binghe taking a look at him and saying, "Since you laughed, does that mean you have something to say?"

Shang Qinghua was at a loss for words.

Sha Hualing let out a "Ha!" followed by, "Well asked, my lord. Since he is so familiar with Shen—with humans, he must have some remarkable and clever insight. All of us would do well to listen with respectful attention."

Shang Qinghua turned back to look at Mobei-Jun, who was sitting behind him. Surprise, surprise, he had no intention of helping him out of this situation.

So, Shang Qinghua braced himself and said decisively, "Well... of course I have something to say! The secret lies in two words: 'Be clingy'! As they say, 'A fierce woman fears a clingy man; a brave hero fears a pampered lady.' As long as your skills are up to par, you can grind an iron bar into a needle. Even if he's as straight as an embroidery needle, you can still bend him into a paper clip!"

"What's with this 'straight' and 'bent'?" Sha Hualing asked. "Don't speak the Human Realm's dialect. My lord, I think he's simply acting enigmatic on purpose!"

But Luo Binghe was unreservedly immersed in Shang Qinghua's account. "I'm still not clingy enough?" he muttered. "Still?"

Shang Qinghua babbled nonstop. "Clinginess is the main tactic, but aside from this absolute truth, there's another terribly important angle you must consider. Gentlemen must understand that women's love comes from admiration, and men's from a desire to protect. The matter of women we will not discuss for now; I am convinced no woman could resist being subdued by my lord's peerless and godly strength, his elegant manner that defies the heavens, and his sincere affection, so we will reserve ourselves to the other case. If you—ah, no, my lord—if my lord wants a man to understand his true intentions, and furthermore, to respond in kind, then what ought my lord do? It's quite simple. No man doesn't wish for a weak, lovable, and docile partner. And what do I mean by lovable? Lovable means some person or thing that can evoke a heart's tenderest affections, so a partner must unquestionably be most obedient, most..."

Bullshit and flattery flowed forth in equal measure, and the crowd in the hall peered at Luo Binghe, seated high above them. His face was gloomy, his pupils glowing red, and a murderous aura surged beneath the surface, painting a most vivid picture of untouchability (a.k.a. discontent). The distance between him and the words "weak, cute, docile, and obedient" was practically a bottomless chasm.

Sha Hualing couldn't resist letting out a scoff.

Shang Qinghua hurriedly shut his mouth.

Luo Binghe rubbed his temple. "Continue."

Having been given official approval, Shang Qinghua continued to explain. "I'll take Shen Qingqiu as an example," he said, brimming with ill intent. "This guy, you know, he's a straight man... Oh, what does 'straight man' mean? Well, a straight man is a normal man—obviously I'm not saying you aren't normal, my lord. Rather, he very much values his dignity as a master and teacher. And teachers, they all like students who do as they're told, so if you want him to like you, the first step would be to listen to him and be good..."

The hall full of demons and beasts was practically scared stiff by his brazenness.

"Impudence!" Sha Hualing snapped. "You mean to have my lord p-p-pretend to be piteous and obediently *listen* to him? My lord is the grand ruler of the Demon Realm—how could he do such a shameless thing?!"

That's right, that's precisely what I mean! Sha-sha, turn around and take a look at the thoughtful expression on your lord's face. Does he look like he thinks this sort of thing is shameless?

Impassioned and vehement, his mouth running like a torrent from the heavens down to earth, Shang Qinghua concluded his twenty-minute-long romantic consultation. Sha Hualing had already throttled him to death with her eyes ten million times, and as soon as Luo Binghe left, Shang Qinghua hurriedly moved over to Mobei-Jun's side, pressing close to seek protection.

Mobei-Jun looked askance at him. "So, if you want to be liked by a man, the best method is to act pathetic?"

Shang Qinghua thought about it. "In theory, that would be correct."

Mobei-Jun reached out his hand.

Thinking he was about to be beaten up again, Shang Qinghua hurriedly put his hands over his head. But the pain he expected never arrived. Mobei-Jun only lightly tapped him on the top of his head.

Afterward, seemingly in a bit of a good mood, he got up and started walking out of the assembly hall.

Though Shang Qinghua was confused, he couldn't handle Sha Hualing staring at him from the side, her fiery gaze like that of a tiger eyeing its prey, so he hurried to catch up, taking three steps for every two.

— PART 4 —

IN THE END, it was still a whole ruckus.

As Shang Qinghua had planned in his outline, Mai Gu Ridge exploded into a mass of flying sand and countless pieces of rubble, with roiling smoke and clouds of billowing dust.

Moreover, he performed a heroic feat on the way and saved Mobei-Jun, who didn't know how to fly.

When he grabbed that hand of Mobei-Jun's in midair, Shang Qinghua could clearly see the astonished disbelief in his eyes. Understandable. Mobei-Jun undoubtedly held the firm belief that Shang Qinghua hung by his side solely to protect his own pathetic little life, and the human's sole uses were, at most: flattery, boasting about him, and a target for venting his anger or whatnot. And, if they ever met any real danger, Shang Qinghua would definitely be the first to run to save his own ass. To be honest, Shang Qinghua himself had also held this firm belief. He dared say he was even more astonished, even more disbelieving than Mobei-Jun.

Ever since then, perhaps because he had earned merit protecting his master and had performed well, his wages, material benefits, treatment, and so forth had all improved, and he was also permitted to return to Cang Qiong Mountain and visit his old home.

Yue Qingyuan, that great philanthropist, let all bygones be bygones and even permitted him to return to An Ding Peak, as well as to continue holding the title of peak lord. These past few days in the Leisure House, Shang Qinghua had, for the first time, truly been leisurely—to the point of agitation.

After munching on half a kilogram of melon seeds, he suddenly realized that the System hadn't made a peep in quite a while. For once, Shang Qinghua took the initiative to poke it.

The System gave him an earth-shattering response: 【 Objective completed. Downloading Return Home function. 】

Shang Qinghua was speechless.

After a moment, he began to furiously shake the System's (nonexistent) shoulders. "Objective completed?! Return Home function?!

What Return Home function?! Is it the one I'm thinking of? Huh? O Great System, this is the first time you've said so many words—can you say a few more?! I'm begging you, quick!"

【 Basic completion of Proud Immortal Demon Way's original outline achieved (slight deviation in romance plotline); objective complete. Retrieving function to return to original world; download complete. Activate Return Home sequence? 】

Basic completion of the original outline? That he agreed with. All the holes that needed to be filled had been filled. But this "slight deviation of romance plot" wasn't quite right. Bing-ge was now fully gay; how could you say that was a "slight deviation"? Ah, fine, fine, in fact, in his original outline, Bing-ge hadn't even had a romance plotline; he had been doomed to fade away, alone and unaging forever. If you insisted on adding a romance plotline, all right, that was whatever, so putting aside all the System's rambling...this meant he could return to his original world?!

Tears streamed down Shang Qinghua's face.

He hadn't written in so long. He reminisced about his Airplane Shooting Towards the Sky account, with its fans and haters equally matched, reminisced about that crowd of trolls in the comments section, reminisced about the rich benefactors who'd given him tips, reminisced about that laptop he had used since his first year of university, eternally crashing and screwing him over, and the giant video files on the hard drive of—you understand. And then there was the spectacular pile of boxes and boxes of instant noodles behind his swivel chair, the newest flavor of which he hadn't yet gotten the chance to taste even after buying it at wholesale price.

A dialogue box popped up from the System.

【 Function download complete. Activate? 】

Two differently colored buttons followed.

【 Yes 】【 Maybe Next Time 】

Shang Qinghua had a powerful urge to press the red button on the left.

But something stopped his hand.

As it happened, he didn't really have any family on the other side.

His parents had divorced early, each going their separate ways, and they had both made all-new families for themselves long ago. He occasionally got together with them for a meal, but no matter which side it was, he regularly felt that his presence was extremely obtrusive. As he politely picked up food and politely gave them subservient smiles, the meals would be even more formal than they would have been if he were eating with real strangers.

Even though his father was his legal guardian, when they weren't face-to-face, they didn't have contact other than a few phone calls on the new year and holidays, or when his father asked him if he needed money. Sometimes, his father would even forget to ask that, but Shang Qinghua never reminded him. No matter where he was, or who he was talking to, all he did was smile that familiar subservient smile.

He was an adult, after all. His parents still had to pay his university tuition, but it was up to him to find ways to pay for the rest of his expenses.

It was when he was thinking of such ways that he happened to register for an account on Zhongdian and began to write.

At the beginning, it was purely to vent, and he wrote whatever and however he wanted. Though the stories were unbearably shitty, and even struggled to get monetized, he did manage to get good reviews from a niche crowd.

At one point, it suddenly occurred to him to change his style and see if he could rescue his subscription numbers, which had dipped so low that the website editors had long since lost interest in asking after them. Thus arrived the instant hit, *Proud Immortal Demon Way*.

Airplane Shooting Towards the Sky had achieved supreme enlightenment; he had found his "way."

The more he wrote, the more of a shut-in he became, and the more of a shut-in he became, the more he wrote. As a classic worthless otaku, the people with whom he had the best relationships and got along with most were all on the internet, oceans and seas apart. He basically didn't have any friends like Mobei-Jun, and it would likely be very hard to find any again in the future.

Wait.

Mobei-Jun? A friend?

Since when had he started seeing Mobei-Jun as a "friend"?!

Shang Qinghua scared himself with the thought, and he hurriedly grabbed another sack of Qian Cao Peak's specially produced Dragon-Bone Cantaloupe seeds and binged another half of it to push down his fright. Then he went to sleep.

When Mobei-Jun dragged him off An Ding Peak to the northern border of the Demon Realm, blankets and all, he had just finished his melon seeds and was dreaming, mouth full of salt. He dreamed he was devouring those promised kilos of shit. He was frozen awake.

Mobei-Jun tossed him to the ground, straight into the knife-like snowy winds of the northern border. His silhouette and expression were more severe than ever.

Though Mobei-Jun was quite cool—*very* cool—Shang Qinghua was already too frozen to have any time to spare on enjoying his coolness. His tongue started icing over as soon as he opened his mouth to grovel, so he obediently shut his lips and started to crawl upright while shivering, wrapped in his blankets.

An icy fortress rose from the ground ahead. Mobei-Jun set off toward it without a word, and Shang Qinghua hurried to follow.

The fortress doors, laid from blocks of ice, rumbled open and closed. They met not a single person all the way down the long, deep flight of stairs, until they approached a sleeping chamber, where a few guards and demon maids stood, not daring to make a sound.

Shang Qinghua peeked at Mobei-Jun's face. Though he was as haughty and aloof as usual, he looked somewhat more solemn than was typical. He couldn't resist the urge to ask, "Um, my king, how long will we be standing here?"

Mobei-Jun didn't move his head, but his eyes turned toward Shang Qinghua. "Seven days."

Shang Qinghua was nearly knocked flat by this information.

Ah, whatever, whatever. He was very possibly right about to return home to continue shooting his airplane. He figured he might as well use these seven days to properly bid his farewells. After all, once he returned, there would be no one to beat him up all the time or order him around like a beast of burden to wash clothes, fold blankets, serve tea, and carry water.

After standing there for a while, he felt colder and colder.

The Mobei clan's territory really wasn't suited for humans. Shang Qinghua jumped up and down in place to avoid being frozen alive into an ice statue. Mobei-Jun looked at him, a smile seeming to flash through his eyes. He reached out and pinched one of Shang Qinghua's fingers. "Quiet."

It was like all the chill in his body was sucked away via this one point of contact. Shang Qinghua felt that the cold was still cold, but it was no longer intolerable. He couldn't help but feel increasingly rueful about their upcoming separation, and somewhat loath to give this guy up.

Come to think of it, even though Mobei-Jun had a bit of a bad temper, was a bit bad at life skills, was a bit pampered and spoiled, and liked to beat people up a bit too much, he wasn't too bad to Shang Qinghua.

Especially at this point! His benefits weren't bad, and his salary wasn't bad either. Though the beatings remained a common occurrence, only Mobei-Jun was allowed to beat him up—no one else was permitted to lay a finger on him. In addition, recently, Mobei-Jun hadn't beaten him up very much at all.

Shang Qinghua was growing concerned about his twisted standards as to what constituted a fortunate lifestyle.

What would happen if he really returned home and Mobei-Jun suddenly wanted to find someone to beat up, but Shang Qinghua was nowhere to be found? When he thought about that happenstance, he felt a pang of sorrow, like the melancholy of an actor leaving after a play was complete, all the props in place but the people long gone.

Suddenly, a bone-deep chill returned to his body.

"Return where?" Mobei-Jun said icily.

Shang Qinghua finally realized that in his sorrow, he had actually spoken his internal dialogue out loud verbatim. Now was the real time to be "sorrowful"!

Mobei-Jun's fingers tightened like he was about to snap Shang Qinghua's index finger in half. "Now you're saying you want to leave?"

Shang Qinghua's face pinched in pain. "No, no, not right now!"

"Not right now?" Mobei-Jun pressed. "What is it you always say to me?"

I'll follow my king for the rest of my life. He had said this phrase countless times. But he'd thought no one was taking it seriously!

After a stretch of silence, Mobei-Jun said, "If you want to leave, then leave right now. You don't need to wait seven days."

Shang Qinghua started. "My king, if I really leave, from this point forth, we'll never see each other again."

Mobei-Jun looked at him with the gaze of someone peering at an ant from nine million feet above it. "What makes you think I would care about that?"

Although over the years, Shang Qinghua had trained his face to be impervious to sword or spear, these words made his expression pinch. He still wanted to explain a bit, but the situation had played out beyond his expectations.

"Get out."

His body suddenly flew backward, and he crashed into an ice wall, which was as solid as steel. The stab of pain only numbed his back for a moment before it spread through his guts.

Mobei-Jun didn't even lift a hand, didn't even spare a glance in his direction. Shang Qinghua's throat rapidly filled with a gush of warm, rusty-flavored liquid.

Mobei-Jun beating him up was nearly a daily occurrence, and he often told him to "get out"; Shang Qinghua should have been used to it. But at no other time had he been subjected to such an intense fury and loathing.

Like countless times before, he crawled up from the ground, silently wiped away the blood at the side of his mouth, and gave Mobei-Jun's back a subservient smile that no one could see.

After standing there for a while, he tried to speak again, but Mobei-Jun impatiently snarled, "Get out of here!"

So, Shang Qinghua hurriedly got out.

Honestly speaking, though no one could have known what he was thinking in the privacy of his mind, he still felt a bit embarrassed—specifically about that fleeting thought from before, concerning "Mobei-Jun" and "a friend."

Shang Qinghua trudged up the stairs. The guards and demon maids he had seen earlier had been driven away, and they ran even faster than him, darting out of the ice fortress like a swarm of bees. The chill remained the same, but the situation as he left was completely different from how it had been on his arrival.

At this time, a slanted silhouette approached, coming down the stairs. Shang Qinghua turned his head, gaze briefly flitting across a pair of peach-blossom eyes full of frosty light.

Though this pair of eyes didn't land on him, they sent Shang Qinghua into a fit of shudders, his heels gluing themselves to the steps.

Then, furtively, he turned around and followed.

Once the guards had been sent out of the underground ice fortress, it had been emptied of all demons. Mobei-Jun doubtless thought Shang Qinghua had obediently "gotten out" and thus didn't expect him to turn back. So, by the time Shang Qinghua returned to the hall in front of that sleeping chamber, he had not yet been discovered. He stopped there and shimmied up a pillar so giant it could be encircled by three people, onto the ceiling rafters, and found a spot from which he definitely wouldn't be seen, where he sat down.

However, though he definitely couldn't be seen by the people below him, he couldn't see them either.

"What are you doing here?" Mobei-Jun asked in his cold and placid voice; he sounded like he was forcibly suppressing his anger.

The next voice was that of an unfamiliar young man, who spoke with a smile in his tone. "My nephew is ascending to the throne; I came for a cup of celebratory wine. Is there something unacceptable about that?"

Mobei-Jun didn't answer the question. He snorted once and replied only after a long pause. "What celebratory wine is there to drink?"

"After these seven days, you'll be the real Mobei-Jun," said the other voice. "Isn't that something worth celebrating?"

Shang Qinghua knew both who this was and which plot arc—delayed, after the original plot had been thrown into disarray—was now unfolding.

Oh, shit. Mobei-Jun's in trouble.

This uninvited guest was Mobei-Jun's uncle, Linguang-Jun.

And the one who lay in the sleeping chambers ahead was, without a doubt, the father whom Mobei-Jun had seen only a handful of times since his birth—his body, that was.

According to the original outline, after the reigning head of each generation of the Mobei clan died, they passed seven-tenths of their martial aspect to their next-generation successor. Mobei-Jun was at an extremely critical juncture.

But, as Shang Qinghua had written in the original work, Linguang-Jun was using this precise occasion, the most critical and final day on which Mobei-Jun was digesting the martial aspect, to launch a sneak attack. Because Mobei-Jun had been lawfully determined to be first in the line of succession, Linguang-Jun had no claim to the martial aspect, and stealing it outright would have been useless. Illegal was illegal; the ancestral lines wouldn't acknowledge him. However, if Mobei-Jun died *after* he officially ascended to the throne, Linguang-Jun would be the only remaining descendant of the Mobei bloodline. So when that scheduled time came, the recipient of this seven-tenths of martial aspect couldn't just kick back and relax.

In the original work, Bing-ge was by Mobei-Jun's side during this, acting the part of the wolf in sheep's clothing and lending him a hand along the way—then undercutting the Mobei clan after Mobei-Jun ascended to the throne, as was only to be expected. But now Bing-ge had hared off to shamelessly torment his shizun. Come on, how could he have the time to bother with this? So the person Mobei-Jun had brought to help him was Shang Qinghua's useless-ass self!

Shang Qinghua despairingly pulled his own hair. *My king, you—you, you, you—what did you bring me for?! I can't lift a hand, I can't carry your burden. How am I qualified to protect you? For this sort of life-and-death situation, you should obviously find a trusted confidant—your most impressive ally! So what if you had no more hope of scraping Bing-ge off his shizun than you did of scraping burnt caramel off a pan, at least you could borrow a few thousand black-armored generals from him! No matter how desperate you are, you can't call on me other than to make tea, carry water, wash clothes, and fold blankets! Exactly which of my other skills aren't amateur at best?!*

Without the aid of the inextinguishable halo and plot armor Shang Qinghua had personally bestowed upon the male protagonist, at that fatal moment in seven days, Mobei-Jun would...

"You didn't bring a single person for this important occasion?" asked Linguang-Jun.

Mobei-Jun was silent before he coolly replied, "I didn't."

Linguang-Jun tittered. "You did, didn't you? I saw. When I arrived, I encountered someone walking out. It was that—that

An Ding Peak Lord who's said to follow you. How did he anger you? He'd been beaten into such a state. And here I'd heard those rumors that had me thinking your temper had changed for the better."

For a long time, no one spoke.

"Your uncle was only asking. Why are you looking at me with such an antagonistic expression?" Linguang-Jun's voice was all smiles again.

"I want you to leave," Mobei-Jun said bluntly.

"You're hurting this demon's feelings. Unfortunately, our clan has no rule to prevent others from observing the succession ceremony. What's more, I am your father's younger brother. If not for you, the one standing here today waiting for their inheritance would certainly be me."

Mobei-Jun seemed to know he wouldn't be able to drive Linguang-Jun away, and he said no more on the topic.

Linguang-Jun, on the other hand, was immensely pleased with himself; he didn't check his mirth in the slightest. "Ah, you've grown up, and you're going to be a lord now. You really have changed. You were much cuter when you were young."

At these familiar lines, Shang Qinghua anxiously wiped the sweat from his forehead, feeling a bit ashamed that he had written such a shameless character. This uncle even had the face to bring up Mobei-Jun's childhood!

Mobei-Jun had lost his mother very young, and the person to whom he had most closely stuck in his youth was precisely this youngest uncle, who wasn't much older than him. However, because of some conflicts and emotional disputes between the older generation of brothers, Linguang-Jun hadn't quite been able to begin liking this nephew of his.

One time, when the other demons weren't paying attention, Linguang-Jun had coaxed this obedient little nephew out the gate and thrown him into the Human Realm. He'd let a mob of cultivator thugs give chase to the little demon, who hadn't understood a thing and lost his head out of fear, falling every few steps as he fled. Those thugs had frantically hunted him down for days and days.

At the time, developmentally speaking, Mobei-Jun had been roughly equivalent to a human four-year-old child. If, after about ten days, his dad hadn't suddenly realized that his son hadn't been following his younger brother around for quite some time, and hadn't casually made a few inquiries, Mobei-Jun might have been locked up in the Huan Hua Palace Water Prison until he simply died of fright. To a demon of that age, being surrounded by a shouting crowd of humans was like a being surrounded by flesh-eating, blood-drinking monsters. Imagine a human four-year-old child getting captured and imprisoned in a nest of demons—their reaction would be about the same.

The former Mobei-Jun's head was as empty as a basin, where the "basin" was that of the Sichuan Basin. Either way, his son was stolen back in the end, more scared than hurt, and certainly not dead, so he didn't really pay the incident much mind. He scolded his brother a bit, then told them to keep "getting along well" in the future.

After Mobei-Jun was retrieved, messy-haired and dirty-faced, he never again spoke to his formerly favorite uncle. As his age increased, he grew more and more severe, until he was, in the end, unwilling to speak to anyone, and held a deep abhorrence for any kind of betrayal.

As Shang Qinghua mentally reviewed the melodramatic backstory of the aloof young lord he had fabricated, he also did some self-reflection. He mainly reflected on whether the demon race's cold and apathetic nature, which he had himself established, had been too inhumane. Secondly, he reflected on why he hadn't just added in a worldbuilding line like "No idle witnesses are permitted to be present at the succession ceremony—not even direct relations." If only he'd done that, Mobei-Jun wouldn't have to be keeping watch beside his father's body and waiting for the time of inheritance, unable to leave, but without good reason to drive away Linguang-Jun.

Reflecting on one hand while trembling with fear on the other, Shang Qinghua passed seven whole days until, finally, the last arrived.

After the seven days of observance, it was time for Mobei-Jun to officially inherit the martial aspect. He had very wisely yet to move and begin the transfer.

However, he would need to begin sooner or later.

"What is it?" asked Linguang-Jun. "Why do you hesitate?"

Because you're standing right there!

"Could it be...you're afraid I'll strike you unawares?" Linguang-Jun asked. "How could I? I am your uncle, after all. Mobei, you have to hurry. If you don't start now, you'll miss the opportunity. There won't be another chance to salvage it—you don't need me to remind you of that, do you?"

If he didn't begin immediately, the martial aspect would naturally dissipate, like a giant inheritance drifting away on the wind. But if he did begin immediately, Linguang-Jun would still be standing there like a tiger watching its prey, unquestionably harboring ill intent. Mobei-Jun's current situation afforded neither room to advance nor room to retreat.

Everything was playing out like it had in the original—it was just that they were down an Invincible Bing-ge and up a Useless-ass Hua-di.

In the end, Mobei-Jun let out a cold laugh.

Shang Qinghua gritted his teeth and, braving the possibility of being discovered by a demon and losing his neck as a reward, stuck out his head. Just then, a ball of blue light flew out of the sleeping chamber and enveloped Mobei-Jun—but practically in the same instant, Linguang-Jun suddenly played his hand!

Already on guard, Mobei-Jun spared a hand to catch this treacherous strike. But as he was preoccupied and thus a bit distracted, he let a wisp of demonic energy slip into his palm. This wisp of foreign demonic energy darted about inside Mobei-Jun's body. Handling it would only split his attention further, and he couldn't risk growing careless.

Realizing his first strike had succeeded, Linguang-Jun was wild with joy, but before he had the time to advance another step, someone suddenly leapt out at him, dropping down from above.

"At first I wondered how there could be a guard here even after they were all sent away," Linguang-Jun said coldly. "Aren't you the one who left seven days ago? What, back to protect your master? You certainly didn't look this devoted."

It was fortunate that Shang Qinghua hadn't been able to see him at first, because as soon as he did, his legs went even weaker. Though Linguang-Jun was quite good-looking, it was that soft-but-treacherous type of good-looking. That pair of peach-blossom eyes flashed with frosty light like poisonous needles. When he smiled, he revealed a hint of ominously pale teeth—the kind that were especially suited to tearing through raw meat.

Shang Qinghua braced himself and stood in front of Mobei-Jun. "First, who said I came back to protect my master? Second, who told you he was my master?"

"Then why are you standing in my way right now?" Linguang-Jun asked.

"I'm kicking him while he's down!" Shang Qinghua said forcefully. As he continued running his mouth, he pointed a shaking hand at his own face. "Take a look: he beat me into this sorry state. This nephew of yours really has a temper!"

Behind him, Mobei-Jun spat out a mouthful of blood. It was one hundred percent a product of pure anger toward Shang Qinghua.

"In all these years, the ribs I've broken could build another Mai Gu Ridge, and I could drown myself in the blood I've coughed up," Shang Qinghua lamented. "Devoted? Toward this kind of person—this kind of demon? Who the fuck could be devoted? After how he's treated me, if I, Shang Qinghua, could suffer in silence and swallow my anger without retaliation, how could I call myself the An Ding Peak Lord?!"

As Shang Qinghua said this, he absolutely didn't dare turn back to see Mobei-Jun's expression. His back was about to freeze over!

Linguang-Jun laughed out loud. "Mobei, do you hear this? I actually feel bad for you—you're doomed to be sold out and betrayed. How can you command the Mobei clan like this? If we really let you succeed the throne, with your disposition, wouldn't our clan forever be on the edge of collapse? You should listen to your uncle; relax and hand the important matters to me. Why don't you just go?"

On the verge of achieving his cherished dream of many years, Linguang-Jun was in a magnanimous mood. He turned to Shang Qinghua and asked generously, "And how do you plan to kick him while he's down?"

With a chortle, Shang Qinghua activated a fire spell and flung it behind him.

A burst of sizzling heat hit Linguang-Jun directly in the face, and red light danced madly before his eyes. The icy Mobei clan loathed flame more than anything, especially *this* flame, which appeared not to be mundane fire, but a fire that Shang Qinghua had shamelessly asked Shen Qingqiu to make for him from a few grains of Black Sun Tinder. A few grains of fear were mixed in with Linguang-Jun's loathing. He swiftly retreated and covered his face, somewhat astonished.

I had no idea that the stupid and cowardly An Ding Peak Lord of rumor was actually such a ruthless character, he thought. *I heard that Mobei-Jun was quite good to him. Who would have imagined that this guy was silently enduring it all for so many years?*

And the moment he played his hand, he was so vicious—using immortal flame to burn Mobei-Jun alive! It won't be a simple death either; this fire would probably burn him straight to ashes. If Shang Qinghua had used this spell on Linguang-Jun at that moment, he would also be in quite the sorry state. He shuddered to think that the human might still have a few grains of that fearsome tinder. But whether he had them or not, Mobei-Jun had no hope of survival.

However, once Linguang-Jun was certain in his calculations and straightened his posture to look, he was instantly enraged.

Mobei-Jun hadn't been devoured by the raging inferno. Instead, he was shielded between clusters of flame. At that moment, Shang Qinghua hadn't thrown his handful of tinder onto Mobei-Jun's body, he had drawn a large circle of approximately ten square meters around him. The leaping and dancing Black Sun Immortal Fire encircled the two within.

Though Mobei-Jun couldn't exit the circle, neither could Linguang-Jun enter. If he attempted a long-distance attack, the fire

would melt his ice spells. When he examined it again, this didn't look like an attack spell at all, but rather—a protective circle!

As he realized that he had been tricked, Linguang-Jun's face darkened.

The vicious demonic energy that Linguang-Jun had slapped into Mobei-Jun was still running rampant through his entire body and causing him trouble. He had fallen to one knee, face alternating between green and white, unable to spare the effort to give anyone a single glance. Shang Qinghua circled him, flustered, but he couldn't assist.

At a distance, Linguang-Jun paced around the circle of Black Sun fire, sneering as he walked. "I misspoke earlier. You're far more than devoted; you're practically faithful to the core. You're willing to come back and throw away your life for this disappointing nephew of mine! But I wonder, how long can your circle last?"

These words jabbed Shang Qinghua right in the sore spot.

He had thrown all the tinder Shen Qingqiu had given him in one go, leaving not a single spare splinter. He squatted by Mobei-Jun's side to frantically, but rather uselessly, cheer him on. "My king, did you hear? He wants to kill me—your uncle wants to kill me! You have to digest it faster. I really don't know how long this circle will last!"

Suddenly, with a giant crack of splitting stone, icy dust and frost fluttered down from overhead. Shang Qinghua lost his footing, and he swayed a couple of times with the leaping flames. Only then did he see Linguang-Jun remove a hand from one of the pillars in the corridor.

"You thought that if you didn't come out, I'd have no way to get to you?" he asked.

He planned to collapse the ice fortress and either crush Mobei-Jun to death or bury him alive.

An ominous web of cracks snaked up the ice pillar. With Linguang-Jun's second strike about to hit, Shang Qinghua said hurriedly, "Coming, coming—I'm coming right now!"

So, like a long-suffering frog jumping into a deeper fryer, he slowly hopped out of the circle.

Once he was out, he had no hope of getting back in. Agile as a specter, Linguang-Jun grabbed him with one hand. "What's the use of you coming out alone? Withdraw the fire!"

In fact, Linguang-Jun was also a touch flustered. He didn't know how long it would take Mobei-Jun to suppress that bit of demonic energy. If he was able to do so before the Black Sun fire burned out *and* finished digesting that martial aspect, today's rebellion would be nothing more than a giant farce.

"I only know how to set fires, not put them out," said Shang Qinghua.

"Then make him come out!"

"Well… My lord, look at the state of him. Even if he wanted to, he couldn't move."

Linguang-Jun sneered, putting his hand on Shang Qinghua's solar plexus. "Then say," he said amicably, "if your heart were to start freezing over, would he have the sudden impulse to come out?"

"If that kind of thing can be broken through on 'sudden impulse,' I recommend my lord try having a 'sudden impulse' to see if he can do just tha—"

And then he couldn't get out another word.

Linguang-Jun quietly hummed an ice spell, his tune cheerful yet malicious. "Mobei, ah, your uncle really didn't expect you to have a dog who refused to betray you, even in these circumstances. Wouldn't it be a pity if you were to lose such a good hound?"

Near his heart grew a field of ice and snow.

Shang Qinghua, lips turning purple, raised his hand. "M-m-my lord."

"Speak."

"If you're going to...f-f-freeze my heart like this, I-I-I can't scream aloud. It doesn't s-s-sound miserable enough—you won't g-g-get the 'sudden impulse' that you want from him. I advise...advise you to hit me instead. I promise I'll do my best to scream, scream very miserably."

"Oh. But I'm very heavy-handed. If I can't control myself and beat you to death, what then?"

"I-I-It's no problem, I can take it. I'm used to it, after s-s-suffering your nephew's—"

Before he could finish speaking, Shang Qinghua personally experienced how heavy Linguang-Jun's hands could be.

He didn't use demonic energy, preferring to rely entirely on physical strength to attack. However, Shang Qinghua clearly heard the sound of his every broken rib, as well as the sound of his throat hissing like it was leaking air after spitting up too much blood.

As his back teeth started to faintly loosen, Shang Qinghua decided that, compared to his uncle and other demons, Mobei-Jun was goddamn fucking gentle, even amiable—practically a little angel.

The longer he dragged this out, the more Linguang-Jun's impatience inched toward fury. He stepped firmly on Shang Qinghua's back and wrenched up one of his arms, grinning savagely. "Didn't you promise you would try your best to 'scream, scream very miserably'? And yet your mouth is so secure that you haven't let out a single sound."

This position had some extremely bad associations for Shang Qinghua. He hurriedly spat out the bubble of warm blood held in his mouth and screamed with great sincerity.

Linguang-Jun hummed. "Not bad. It's a pity, but that's still not miserable enough. I'll help you out."

From Shang Qinghua's shoulder came the terrible pain of flesh and tendons ripping. He opened his mouth, letting fear drown him, but he found he couldn't make a single sound.

Yet this pain didn't develop into an unsalvageable outcome. Suddenly, the arm that had been yanked behind him drooped limply down.

A corner of a deep-blue robe flapped in front of him, its collar billowing with wind and snow.

Mobei-Jun had caught them off guard, diving out of the fire circle to land a palm squarely on Linguang-Jun's solar plexus.

After being waylaid by this strike, half of Linguang-Jun's chest collapsed, demonic energy streaming out of it like a giant hole had been punched through his whole body. His heart chilled. This youngster's prior ability and the power in that strike could not be spoken of in the same breath. The delay had been long enough; Mobei-Jun had absorbed all the martial aspect the Mobei clan had passed down over generations.

On top of that, he no longer feared the Black Sun Immortal Fire. He'd leapt straight through it!

Though Linguang-Jun was full of dissatisfied resentment, he was by this point likely no match for Mobei-Jun. He could only hurriedly use ice to seal his own wounds, transform into a stream of black wind, and steal out of the ice fortress.

Shang Qinghua, lying with his face pressed to the ground, didn't see any movement for a long while, and no one came to help him up. *Is he still mad?* he mourned internally. *No matter how you look at it, I was beaten to a pulp for you. And you're not even helping me up! This is just inexcusable!*

Then he heard a heavy slam.

Grimacing in pain, and with incomparable difficulty, Shang Qinghua turned over.

Mobei-Jun had collapsed too.

Two figures, fallen in different postures beside a raging circle of fire, lay quietly, quietly, collapsed like dead NPCs.

Shang Qinghua finally realized that Mobei-Jun most likely had, in fact, *not* finished absorbing his clan's martial aspect, nor had he suppressed Linguang-Jun's demonic energy. Moments ago, he really had been taken by "a sudden impulse" and fought with all his strength to scare Linguang-Jun away at the last moment. Now Mobei-Jun had exhausted his final ounce of energy, and had moreover been roasted to a crisp by the terrifying Black Sun Immortal Fire, so he... had collapsed like a dead NPC.

Though Mobei-Jun was lying straight and stiff on the ground, unable to move even a finger, his eyes were still forcefully glaring at Shang Qinghua.

Under that stare, Shang Qinghua was no longer able to continue lying there at ease. He could only open his mouth to say, "That is, my king, you, ah—don't struggle, just lie down and slowly absorb it. The combined power of lords accumulated over generations isn't the sort of thing you can swallow down in a single gulp."

That gaze didn't subside in the least. Shang Qinghua's heart pounded like he was being showered with a rain of needles. He finally managed to catch his breath and sit up, already trembling like a Parkinson's patient.

Now Mobei-Jun would finally have to listen to him. He took a deep breath. "Uh, my king, in fact, in the first place, I didn't want to leave at this sort of time. I really didn't know that it just so happened to be the key moment when you were about to succeed your father's position. Why didn't you tell me about it earlier, when it was something so important?"

Mobei-Jun used his expression to say: *Kneel down, cry, and admit you were wrong, and* then *I'll pardon you.*

The corner of Shang Qinghua's mouth twitched. "To tell the truth, you shouldn't have brought me," he continued. "I can't do anything at all. I can barely serve as a punching bag for you to beat up from time to time. You saw me just then—I was thrashed this badly and I only bought you a bit of time. But you seriously injured your uncle and he probably won't dare come back again. You're almost done digesting it, right? So I'll just...leave first."

Mobei-Jun's expression had eased a bit, but upon hearing this last sentence, cold light beamed from his eyes. "You're still leaving?! You dare!"

Having suddenly been bellowed at, and still hurting from head to toe, Shang Qinghua was overcome with rage. He slapped the ground and yelled, "What don't I dare?!"

As one would expect, this strike couldn't scare Mobei-Jun, and it only made his own shoulder and arm explode with pain while stars burst in his eyes. Either way, Mobei-Jun couldn't move a limb, and Shang Qinghua grew bold in his fury, pointing at him. "I'll tell you the truth, then! I've endured you for too long, you pampered, spoiled young master! You vile-tempered demonic second-gen!"

This was a monstrous degree of audacity. Mobei-Jun's face was full of disbelief.

But Shang Qinghua's many years of accumulated grievance continued to spew out in this moment with the power of an arcing rainbow: "You saw that I had a good temperament, that I was easy to push around, and also that my cultivation was lacking—so I was fun and satisfying to torment, right? You thought I was really this... this...ah?!

"What are you looking at? You gonna argue with that?! I'm your dad! Call me daddy! I was just indulging you! Go on and try this with someone else, huh? Bing-ge would beat you to death, and the original flavor Shen Qingqiu would shade you to death!

"No one likes getting beat up every day, and no one would actually be all cheery after getting beat up every day! I'm not actually a dog! Even with a dog, if you kicked it twice a day, given enough time, it'd learn not to bother with you anymore!"

Mobei-Jun said, "Do you want to die?"

Under the circumstances, the intimidation factor of these words had suffered a huge loss in value.

"I don't," said Shang Qinghua. "And not only do I dare leave, I dare do other things, would you believe it? This peak lord will, right here, right now, beat you back for every time you beat him before!"

"You!" Mobei-Jun said angrily.

"'You'? 'You' what? 'You dare' again? I'll tell you what, right now, I really do dare. Come at me!"

With this, Shang Qinghua rolled up his sleeves, eagerly shaking a fist in front of Mobei-Jun's ashen face. Cold blades shot from Mobei-Jun's gaze, but Shang Qinghua wasn't frightened in the slightest. His fist swung in a strike straight toward Mobei-Jun's head.

On instinct, Mobei-Jun averted his face, only to feel the skin of his cheek tighten.

It was a very unfamiliar feeling. A bit itchy, a little bit painful, but entirely not the expected strike.

Two of Shang Qinghua's fingers had pinched his cheek on one side and forcefully pulled. "How's that—does it hurt?!"

While pulling, he thought, *This is not what I was fucking thinking of doing!*

Beat him! Yeah, beat him while he can't move! Tugging on his face and letting him off with just that? No matter how you look at it, you'll be getting the short end of the stick!

But there was nothing to be done. Sure enough, Shang Qinghua still couldn't bring himself to beat that face.

Cheek being pulled as it was, Mobei-Jun's words were unclear, but he persisted to say, "You're done!"

Shang Qinghua cackled. "You have backbone! You can still threaten me in this state—Daddy admires you."

His other hand joined in, pinching the other side of Mobei-Jun's face. Sometimes he pulled those cheeks in opposite directions, sometimes he pressed them together. Mobei-Jun's formerly aloof and noble image was wrecked, utterly exterminated by his treacherous pair of hands. All through it, Shang Qinghua was repeating, "Does it hurt yet? Does it hurt?"

Mobei-Jun refused to yield his lofty air. But it was to no avail; things like physiological tears could not be suppressed by lofty airs alone, and in the end, his cheeks were pulled until tears emerged at the corners of his eyes.

"It hurts...? That's right!" Shang Qinghua released his claws. "When you were beating me all the time, it was at least ten times as painful as that! How does it feel getting tugged on? Spoiled!"

Mobei-Jun's face went white with fury at this contemptuous "Spoiled!" and his cheeks were covered in green and red fingerprints. It really was a sight to shock the eye and astonish the heart.

When it came down to it, Shang Qinghua was in truth a coward. He had just committed a crime of passion and had his bit of fun, but after the fact, he began to fear being sent to the crematorium—especially when Mobei-Jun's face had recovered its normal shape. His expression was truly...was truly...

Shang Qinghua's heart quailed at the mere sight of it. He hurriedly patted his hem, preparing to break into a run and leave. He had skidded a few large steps away at meteoric speed when Mobei-Jun shouted at his back.

"If you want to keep your legs, stay there and don't move!"

On reflex, Shang Qinghua obeyed the order. He didn't dare turn around. "My king, I really am leaving."

"Shut up! Come back!"

Shang Qinghua continued, unimpeded. "Even if you're angry, don't come looking for me. After I return, you absolutely won't be able to find me again, so don't spend energy on a useless effort. So, my king—bye, then."

Mobei-Jun was nearly roaring. "If you have the guts to leave, then never let me see you again!"

Shang Qinghua turned a deaf ear. After a few steps, he added one more line. "I was very happy to meet you. Really. You're even cooler than I imagined!"

At this moment, he was in high spirits, radiant with delight, and wearing precisely the same expression he had worn in the split second he first set pen to paper to describe this character's first appearance.

When he reflected on his true emotions and honest feelings toward the character under his pen, this really was embarrassing. Although with parting near at hand, embarrassment was but a fleeting thing.

Shang Qinghua just didn't understand. Where was his agreed upon "parting near at hand"?

Why was it that it had been a whole month since the System released the Return Home function, and yet he was still idling his life away in the world of *Proud Immortal Demon Way*?!

Every time he poked open the System and faced the red and green 【 Yes 】and【 Maybe Next Time 】, he consistently ended up spacing out—then clicked the button on the right and closed the interface.

Next Time on top of Next Time; just a whole bushel of Next Times.

Shang Qinghua blamed this on chronic procrastination. *All that is evil, thy name is procrastination!*

He didn't dare return to Cang Qiong Mountain for the time being; he didn't know if Mobei-Jun was angry enough to go to An Ding Peak to head him off. But half of his savings were stashed in a cave in An Ding Peak, and the other half was in Mobei-Jun's official residence on the northern border. So this past month, though Shang Qinghua looked at ease, he had actually been living frugally, dining on the wind and lodging under the open skies. If not for that bit of spiritual energy he still had to depend on, there wouldn't have been much difference between him and a common vagrant.

After wandering for nearly a month, he unexpectedly ran into a certain master-disciple pair while they were enjoying a leisurely scenic tour around the world.

After realizing who they were, Shang Qinghua couldn't resist rubbing his eyes. After half a minute, he finally confirmed that the young man in plain cotton clothes, still dignified of comportment while carrying a fishing rod and hefting a basket of fish, was Luo Binghe; and after another half a minute, he confirmed that the other, who persisted in putting on his poser act of refined immortal airs to the very end, even while carrying boxes of food to deliver his own meal, was Immortal Master Shen, Peak Lord Shen, Shen Qingqiu.

You're here doing this cheerful, romantic, cottagecore roleplay while you just left Mobei-Jun alone in the Demon Realm and made me force myself to step up! How tragic, my fate!

Grumbling to himself was one thing, but—how should he put it? Seeing these two still made him very happy.

Especially because he hadn't eaten a full meal for days.

Don't complain about an immortal cultivator like him still caring about things like eating a full meal—the comments section had roasted him enough. He wasn't from Ku Xing Peak; he didn't play around with inedia!

As their cottagecore life had been disturbed by someone for no good reason, Luo Binghe naturally had no good looks to bestow upon Shang Qinghua. On Shen Qingqiu's behalf, he wouldn't show it on his face, but when, after exchanging a few greetings, Shen Qingqiu told him to "go sit down inside," Bing-ge's expression still darkened.

These two had, quite sentimentally, built a small bamboo house in a location between jade waters and green mountains. The longer Shang Qinghua sat, the more he felt that these two really were quite well off. As he lounged on a rattan chair, he said, "The house isn't bad."

Shen Qingqiu waved his fan. "Why don't you consider who built it? Could it be bad?"

Shang Qinghua thickened his face, shameless. "Your days truly have been much more comfortable than mine. Would it be possible to let me catch a whiff of Cucumber-bro's fortune and enjoy a touch of this carefree life for a while?"

"It's most unfortunate, but you've come at a bad time. We were just about to eat."

"You're too kind. Arriving early can't beat arriving on time; I see I came at just the right one. I'll see how your food is." With that, he rose and walked to the door of what he suspected was the kitchen, where he lifted the curtain.

Luo Binghe, wearing a light black robe, his sleeves rolled high and expression severe, was currently silently...kneading dough.

He was all grim concentration, with two patches of white on his face and a bit of flour on his eyelashes, like what he was pinching and pulling in his hands wasn't a ball of dough, but a scroll containing his grand ambitions to unite all the realms!

No, no, no, no, no—

Shang Qinghua felt like his guts were splitting open in dismay. The protagonist he had created, the Bing-ge who emanated pure tyranny as he conquered the multitudes of stallion male protags—

He was kneading dough! Making noodles! Noodles, noodles, noodles (ad infinitum)...

This really was an indescribable fright!

Shang Qinghua silently retreated in defeat. He sat at the table and reached out to find a cup of tea to drink and drown that fright, but it was fished back by Shen Qingqiu.

"Mine."

Shang Qinghua's heart was still palpitating. "Do you have a second cup in this house? What's wrong with letting me use it?"

Shen Qingqiu pointed at the kitchen. "You well know that there isn't a second cup. So, it's also his."

Shang Qinghua was silent.

"You'd dare to use it? If you would, I'll give it to you."

Shang Qinghua's hands changed from pulling to pushing. "Your honor can have it all to himself; unfortunately, I cannot partake."

Bing-ge continued to cook while the two chatted about this and that.

After listening to Shang Qinghua relay the tale about the emergency at the Mobei clan ice fortress, Shen Qingqiu expressed his doubts. "Really? Just like that?"

"What reason would I have to trick you about this sort of thing?" Shang Qinghua asked. "And what do you mean 'just like that'? My dignity was at stake. Of course I couldn't stay any longer."

"That's not wrong, per se." Shen Qingqiu thought, then said, "But you never seemed like that sort of person."

"What sort of person?"

"The kind who would care all that much about dignity," Shen Qingqiu said amiably.

With the strength of Airplane Shooting Towards the Sky's resolve, the thickness of his face, and the tenacity of his vitality, he really hadn't seemed the sort to run after a single beating from Mobei-Jun. After all, he had endured all those years before; how could he have suddenly become weak and sensitive and been overcome with emotion?

"Cucumber-bro," Shang Qinghua said, embarrassed, "sure, I never hesitated to sell out my principles to get upvotes and tips, and I only incidentally became An Ding Peak Lord, but if you judge me for all that, you'd be the one in the wrong."

"Aren't those two things you've just cited quite compatible with the conduct I'm judging you for?"

"Aiyah, be a bit nicer to me—a bit gentler, okay? Cucumber-bro, tell me, when would it be best for me to return to the modern world?"

"You really want to return to the modern world?" Shen Qingqiu asked. "So shooting your airplane too often really is bad for your eyesight—you can't even see the crux of your own problems anymore. Wake up. You're just waiting for him to apologize, then scoop you back up and continue to lightly beat you three times a day."

Before they had finished chatting, the meal was served. Luo Binghe carried over two bowls of noodles.

White noodles and red broth, fresh and oily chopped green onion, and topped off with a pile of tender slices of meat—the presentation was unspeakably exquisite. But Shang Qinghua wouldn't get grabby. Without even needing Bing-ge to open his mouth and say it, Shang Qinghua required only a seemingly nonchalant glance to understand that there was no portion for him.

Shen Qingqiu sighed. "See, I told you it was a bad time."

After all, this was the food Bing-ge had made with his own hands; not just anyone had the right to eat it. Shang Qinghua didn't have anything to say, and he shrank to the corner of the table to pitifully watch the pair across from him split their chopsticks.

Later, when Shen Qingqiu finally couldn't stand to watch anymore, he put a piece of meat in Luo Binghe's bowl while holding back a smile and finally lent him some mercy. "Forget it; no more teasing. Your shishu has been pitiful enough recently. Don't bully him anymore."

Luo Binghe put that piece of meat in his mouth and said, without lifting his head, "There's more in the pot."

Shang Qinghua giddily went to the pot, shovel in hand.

As he held the noodles, he slurped until his eyes were brimming with hot tears. For the first time, he had the deep-seated feeling that the most reliable thing in this world was indeed the friendship of Peerless Cucumber, his comrade from the same hometown.

After he had mooched a meal of incomparably delicious noodles, Shang Qinghua was already pleased beyond his expectations, and it entirely did not occur to him to ask for lodging.

What a joke. He did *not* want to eavesdrop through Bing-ge's wall. The quality of the sleep he'd get was one thing, but whether Bing-ge would cut off his ears and boil them with tomorrow's noodles was entirely another.

Ugh, but look at the sort of godly days Shen Qingqiu's living, then look at the sort I am. Then again, constantly comparing yourself to others will drive you to an early grave... Really, though, this is preposterous. Clearly I'm the author; I'm this world's divine creator deity. Can't you all be a bit better to me?! Love your authors! Protecting authors is everyone's responsibility!

Shang Qinghua, savoring the lingering taste of the only bowl of noodles his son had ever made him while using a piece of grass to pick his teeth, walked down the small path between the mountains. He walked and walked, until his foot suddenly slid out from beneath him.

There was a ravine right next to the path, and Shang Qinghua had tossed his pitiful little sword who knew where long ago. If he fell down there, he wasn't flying back up. He burst out in a string of curses at himself. "How can you slip when you're just walking on the road? You're not some female manga protagonist who comes with the supreme talent of tripping on flat ground!"

But when he sat down to look, he found neither an obvious banana peel nor a small tree root, only a tiny puddle.

However, that puddle was frozen over. The short weeds all around it were also covered with a faint layer of frost.

Shang Qinghua frantically rolled and crawled over to the closest rock face, his back against it as he sought out a bit of security.

He had thought that spending too much time dilly-dallying and tempting death by not returning until Mobei-Jun came knocking was already the worst-case scenario. Then a certain person walked out from behind the craggy rocks and drooping vines, and Shang Qinghua finally discovered that things could be even worse.

"Well, well, look here. Who's this?" Linguang-Jun said.

Shang Qinghua laughed dryly. "Right! Who is this?"

Linguang-Jun patted the top of his head. "Mobei-Jun nearly overturned the whole northern border looking for you. You sure know how to hide, ah?"

"My lord is joking. Since when was I hiding..."

"Right? I was also wondering: What's there to hide from? You performed such a meritorious service at the ice fortress, last we met, but Mobei didn't even have the chance to reward you. I can't figure it out; why did you run to this nothing place in the middle of nowhere?"

"Oh, that was nothing, nothing!" Shang Qinghua repeatedly

waved his hands. "That was nothing to do with me. That was all Mobei-Jun relying on his own skill..."

Shang Qinghua was denying his role in fear that Linguang-Jun would assign him the greatest responsibility for his defeat at the ice fortress. But unexpectedly, upon hearing this Linguang-Jun's face suddenly changed, and his tone turned harsh. "Do you mean to say that without you, a lowly, shameless, treacherous Cang Qiong Mountain dog, to jump out and wreck all my good work halfway through, that damned youngster could have defeated me all by himself?!"

Yes is wrong; no is also wrong... Shang Qinghua bemoaned this injustice to the skies. "How could he! Mobei-Jun defeated you, my lord, only because he relied on a sneak attack!"

"Are you mocking me?"

Shang Qinghua couldn't immediately respond.

When he thought about it... Oh, right, the one who had performed the first sneak attack had clearly been Linguang-Jun himself. The wind had blown his piss right back to him—no matter what he said, it was wrong. After clinging to people's thighs with a subservient smile for decades, Shang Qinghua had at last encountered a character too difficult to flatter!

He shut his mouth, a mournful look on his face.

Linguang-Jun sneered. "That little Mobei certainly never could have imagined I would just casually run into the person he expended all his energy on finding to no avail. So, I must use you well..."

"My lord! If you want to catch me and use me to threaten Mobei-Jun, it's completely useless!" Shang Qinghua said hurriedly. "I'll tell you the truth about why I ran away. In fact, at the fortress, while he couldn't move, I couldn't resist beating him up... And you know that damn temper of his! With that kind of opportunity, it would be hard not to hit him, right? But after, there was nothing I could do; I was afraid he would retaliate, so I just...ran. He's probably only looking for me because he wants to beat me in return. I don't have a mote of value in his eyes. At most, I'm a convenient attendant and punching bag."

Linguang-Jun paused, then said impatiently, "Why are you telling me all this? Do I look like the type of demon who'd do such a shameless thing?"

It's hard to say, ah? You weren't exactly upstanding when you sneak attacked Mobei-Jun... Shang Qinghua said sincerely, "You don't."

"Then do I look like the type of demon to be that patient?"

"That, I don't know. Then, my lord, how do you want to 'use' me?"

"How will I 'use' you?" Linguang-Jun laughed. "By killing you to vent my anger. Was that so very hard to understand?"

Shang Qinghua froze. "That's not necessary. You'd just be wasting your resources! My lord, you can probably use me to threaten Mobei-Jun or whatever—what a pity it would be to simply kill me!"

"'I don't have a mote of value in his eyes. At most, I'm a convenient attendant and punching bag.' Who said that again?"

"Humans have a saying, 'Modesty is a virtu—'" Before he had finished the word "virtue," Shang Qinghua threw out his hand, yelling, "Behold my Black Sun Immortal Fire!"

Numerous balls of roiling red flame shot through the air. Frightened, Linguang-Jun darted aside to dodge. However, the flames extinguished the second they hit the ground. It clearly wasn't Black Sun Immortal Fire, which was impervious to wind or water—that bastard Shang Qinghua was just tricking him!

Linguang-Jun was enraged, new resentment fanning old hate. Casually brushing his hand over a dangling drop of dew on a drooping leaf, he aimed right at Shang Qinghua and attacked.

Shang Qinghua only felt a chill in his calf before his leg had been shot through by an ice bullet solidified by demonic energy. He couldn't have run even if he wanted, and he crashed to the ground with a thud.

Linguang-Jun lightly pushed one foot into the kneecap of Shang Qinghua's other leg and pressed down. "You're just like a cockroach—too good at running! I'll destroy your legs first. We'll see how you run then."

Shang Qinghua didn't have any of the integrity required to remain unyielding in the face of destruction, and his soul nearly fled in a fright. "My king!"

Speak of the king and he shall appear.

An ink-blue silhouette fluttered into view like a specter. Two balls of black qi collided with a crack.

Linguang-Jun clutched one of his legs, now broken at the knee, crazed with anger. "You brat—do you have to show up so promptly?! Can't you wait just a bit longer?! Can't you wait to arrive until I've already brought down my heel?!"

With a kick, Mobei-Jun broke his other knee, then said coldly, "I can't."

Linguang-Jun was quite strong-willed. Both his knees had been pulverized into powder, but he didn't scream. Instead, he cursed his nephew out all the more hysterically. "You really are the seed of your frozen-faced father! You could have been like anyone, but you had to be like *him*. Turtle and tortoise born in the same nest—he steals and so do you! He died early—so why can't you die early too?! Fuck..."

Mobei-Jun said, "Keep cursing and I'll send you on to keep him company."

Shang Qinghua stared, tongue-tied. Though he knew Linguang-Jun had always nursed a deep resentment toward his older brother, he'd never thought it would be deep enough to make him wholly lose his poise and shout abuses in the street...

Amidst Linguang-Jun's crazed curses, Mobei-Jun casually flipped his hand and tossed him into the ravine. Falling down the ravine like that might kill a human, but a demon certainly wouldn't die. Shang Qinghua didn't remind him to pull the grass up by its roots. This was Mobei-Jun's own uncle, and his father had doubtless told him that no matter what Linguang-Jun did, to be a bit indulgent with him.

In truth, Shang Qinghua didn't want to remind Mobei-Jun of anything at all; if he could let him forget Shang Qinghua's existence entirely, that would be even better...

Mobei-Jun withdrew his gaze from the bottom of the ravine. "Stop right there!"

Shang Qinghua, dragging a perforated calf, had been about to furtively slip away. He hadn't expected to be exposed until that shout, and he froze in place.

Even a pervert caught red-handed wouldn't have had as guilty a conscience. He listened to the sound of Mobei-Jun's footsteps treading across frost and cracking ice as he walked over, and he hurriedly covered his own face.

Mobei-Jun seemed to be in quite the temper today; he wasn't the least bit aloof. "What are you doing?!"

"Didn't you say 'never let me see you again'?" Shang Qinghua asked awkwardly. "There's no way for you not to see me now, so I'll just cover my face."

Mobei-Jun lifted his hand, and Shang Qinghua covered his head out of habit.

Silence.

Mobei-Jun separated his two arms and straightened them, at the end of his patience. "If you let me see you do this sort of thing again... you won't be keeping your hands!"

There was just a hint of teeth-gnashing fury in his tone. Shang Qinghua reflexively wanted to cover his head again, but he managed to choke it down for the sake of this pair of hands, which had toiled so heroically as they typed on his keyboard.

Struggling to hold it all in, he began to shake and shake. He shook until Mobei-Jun said, "Am I that frightening?"

"Uh, actually, not really!" said Shang Qinghua. "It's just that I always feel like you're going to knock me around a bit, my king. Before, ah, the hitting or kicking, it was whatever, but now that you've officially succeeded to the throne, your cultivation cannot be compared to what it once was. You could make raging waves beat the shore or send stones flying to pierce the clouds with a single strike; I'm afraid I couldn't endure even a few of your hits..."

"Shut up," said Mobei-Jun. "Follow me, come!"

Shang Qinghua threw caution to the wind and firmly threw himself on the stone wall like a lizard. "I won't come! No—I want to leave! I want to return to my old home."

"If I let you hit me back, *then* will you not go?" Mobei-Jun asked.

"Especially if I stay to let you beat me up three times every day, I might as well... What?!"

Hit him back...?

Let me hit him back...?

Mobei-Jun is willing to let me hit back...?

In order to stop me from leaving, Mobei-Jun is willing to let me hit back?

This staircase of words cycled through Shang Qinghua's thoroughly shocked brain again and again.

Mobei-Jun lifted his chin, stiff and unmoving, emitting a bold aura of *Hit me however you like; I won't retaliate.* Nevertheless, he kept sneakily glancing at Shang Qinghua out of the corner of his eye.

When Mobei-Jun didn't see him move even after a while, he seemed to suddenly grow happy. Although when he was happy, the only sign was that the tips of his eyebrows raised a touch higher. "You're not going to do it?" he asked. "Time's up. Fine, I won't let you hit me. Let's go."

Wait a minute, I didn't say I wouldn't do it! thought Shang Qinghua. *There was a time limit?*

Mobei-Jun, the tiny lift of his brow hiding that extremely covert hint of pleasure, dragged Shang Qinghua away and broke into a run.

Shang Qinghua thereupon began to wail. "Ow, fuck—that hurts, that hurts, that hurts! My king—you—take a look at me! Look at me, look at me!"

Mobei-Jun indeed looked at him, then looked at his bloody leg. After a moment of silence, he tried to carry Shang Qinghua on his shoulder.

Shang Qinghua howled like he was dying. "My king, spare me! My king, spare me! If you carry me like this the whole way, this leg of mine really will be ruined!"

"Then what should I do?" Mobei-Jun asked.

"What about...find me a doctor first?" Shang Qinghua suggested, eyes filled with tears.

With a click of the tongue, Mobei-Jun turned and left.

A gust of cold wind blew by the abandoned Shang Qinghua, dumbstruck like a wooden chicken. Had…Mobei-Jun decided he was too much trouble?

After some time, Mobei-Jun returned, and he was dragging a handcart stolen from who knew where. The wooden chicken finally became a living chicken.

The oh so mighty second-in-command of the demon race, noble and aloof chief of the icy Mobei clan, lowering his dignified self to drag a broken-down handcart that completely clashed with his image. This scene was…amazing!

With a chuckle, Shang Qinghua broke down again.

At the sight of the blue veins faintly popping on Mobei-Jun's forehead, he hurriedly knitted his brows and started crying out in pain. After he called to him a few times, Mobei-Jun scooped him up and settled him on top of the cart.

Though he was sitting on a crooked and broken-down handcart, stolen off the old horse in some farming family's courtyard—a cart that was probably only used to carry things like fodder, firewood, and slop buckets—Shang Qinghua still puffed up in self-satisfaction as he emanated a majestic aura. Those not in the know might even have thought he was a scholar who, after ten years of strenuous study, had achieved the status of Zhuangyuan, First in the Imperial Examinations, and been bequeathed a marriage match from the emperor himself, and that he was now out with a procession of drums and gongs to receive his bride.

This really was the karmic cycle. The first time he had seen Mobei-Jun, he had used a handcart just like this to ferry the unconscious demon to rent a room!

For proof, a poem: Thirty years the river flows east, / Thirty years the river flows west. / Back and forth the handcart goes, / Next year, it's my turn. Ha ha![9]

Filled with a breezy, immortal air, Shang Qinghua declared, "I want to eat noodles."

That bowl of noodles from Bing-ge really had been delicious, but it hadn't been enough. Bing-ge hadn't saved more than a couple strands for him, so it hadn't satisfied.

"Mm," said Mobei-Jun.

"*Pulled* noodles," said Shang Qinghua.

"Okay."

Having won an inch, Shang Qinghua asked for a mile. "You make them."

The handcart abruptly halted, and Mobei-Jun stopped in place.

A faint cold of unknown origin drifted over. Shang Qinghua was instantly terrified, and he contorted his face into a subservient expression. "I'll make them, I'll make them—of course I'll make them. I was just joking, eh heh heh."

Alas. Fantasy was so abundant, but reality was so wanting.

After a while, the handcart wheels slowly began to turn again. Mobei-Jun, in front, said without turning back, "I'll make them."

Silence.

What had he said? He said he'd make them? Who was this? Mobei-Jun. And he was going to do what? Make pulled noodles.

This Mobei-Jun, who was willing to let Shang Qinghua hit back and willing to make him noodles. Had the stars aligned? He was striking it rich today!

---

9 The first two lines are from an idiom first recorded in The Scholars, a Qing Dynasty satirical novel by Wu Jingzi, which describes the inconstancy of fate. The latter two lines are Shang Qinghua's own invention.

Shang Qinghua made a decision. He was going to take up his old profession again. The pen name Airplane Shooting Towards the Sky was going to rush boldly back into the fray!

But what should he write? Shang Qinghua slapped his thigh. As he'd heard it, Sleeping Willow Flower's eighty-one-percent discounted *Regret of Chunshan* was selling like hotcakes. Hm, then he'd just go with the flow and write! Though he himself was upright without compare, where there were readers, there was a market. And if there was a market, he dared to write. Airplane Shooting Towards the Sky was the *best* at going with the flow; he'd just write whatever was popular. You couldn't go wrong with that!

The first step would be to figure out a good title that would be well-received by the masses, such as *Secret Annals of Qing Jing Peak*, or *My Disciple Can't Be This Cute*, or *How Lovely, My Shizun*—or something like that. He'd have to mull it over. His prose wasn't as good as Sleeping Willow Flower's, but that was all right; Airplane Shooting Towards the Sky had never sold because of his writing style.

On top of that, Airplane Shooting Towards the Sky didn't like how Sleeping Willow Flower, the Three Holy Mothers, and the rest kept such a tight focus. They wrote all kinds of stories, but in the end they were only ever about Shen Qingqiu and Luo Binghe; their scope was way too narrow. In fact, as he saw it, it was entirely possible to be more daring and unbridled. For example, if you were calling it *Regret of Chunshan*, why limit yourself to one couple? With a beauty like Liu Qingge on hand, wasn't it just a pity not to write him? Yue Qingyuan was also a beautiful fellow of noble bearing, accomplished in business and perfect spouse material. As for Mu-shidi and Wei-shixiong, both were basically idols in the eyes of this world: if you wrote a free-for-all sex scene and threw them into an orgy, you wouldn't have to worry that no one would read it.

In short, as long as he was sufficiently explicit, depraved, and shameless, sooner or later he'd once again become a hegemon of this land's literati. He wouldn't even need to sell homemade soap to become a prosperous and dazzling entrepreneur!

Airplane Shooting Towards the Sky propped up his legs, the handcart creaking and swaying along on the bumpy mountain road. The evening sun descended in the west, and Mobei-Jun pulled him along, going in who knew what direction.

This story was riddled with landmines, a whole chaotic mess with grade school-level writing, and maybe the more serious readers would throw it down with a curse of "What dogshit is this?" But "Great Master" Airplane Shooting Towards the Sky was used to making excuses for his own fraudulent behavior. He could throw out a thousand "it's justs" to smooth things over. For example:

It's just reading a novel, it's like living your life. Just have a good time—why take it so seriously?

It's just a silly novel the author wrote for fun. Don't set your expectations too high, everyone, and please bear with me!

It's just a brainless satisfying read. Wake up—what did you expect to read?!

It's just...

It's just.

...It was just that he really, very much liked this story he'd written.

27

Deep Dream

AFTER LYING DOWN to sleep, Shen Qingqiu opened his eyes to find himself in a different place. This wasn't his first time experiencing such a situation, so he wasn't flustered; he knew that he must have again entered Luo Binghe's dream realm. After drifting about for a while, he lightly landed on the ground.

With every brush of his foot, he propelled himself forward, as if traveling on the wind and stepping upon willows. Resplendent jade and gold glittered all around him, the decor magnificent and extravagant—plus, one of the corridors looked incredibly familiar. This was one hundred percent Huan Hua Palace.

He walked down that corridor, and at the end found Huan Hua Palace's main palace and assembly hall. In the past, Luo Binghe himself would have been waiting for him within the dream realm for a while now, but this time, Shen Qingqiu didn't see him. That was strange.

There *was* someone in the assembly hall. When Shen Qingqiu looked at that back, he found it familiar too. When he looked again from up close, he found it quite strange.

"Mu-shidi?" he said, stunned.

The "Mu Qingfang" solemnly standing in the hall was an illusion born from Luo Binghe's memories, so naturally, he didn't hear Shen Qingqiu. This junior of his had always possessed a mild temper, but as Mu Qingfang stood in the center of the assembly hall, his expression was devoid of any goodwill.

Shen Qingqiu recalled what the jianghu rumors had said: that not long after he'd played dead and escaped, Luo Binghe had kidnapped Mu Qingfang to Huan Hua Palace and demanded that he "heal" Shen Qingqiu. This scene must have occurred during that period.

A black shadow passed soundlessly by him, and Luo Binghe's voice said, "Mu-xiansheng."

This Luo Binghe's eyes held no trace of Shen Qingqiu's reflection, and he was entirely unaware of Shen Qingqiu's presence. So, this also wasn't Luo Binghe's real self, but rather a memory.

Shen Qingqiu was a little puzzled. Had he drifted into a part of the dream realm that even the real Luo Binghe couldn't control?

Neither the way in which Luo Binghe addressed him nor his attitude could be considered disrespectful, so Mu Qingfang replied, "Your distinguished self addressed me as Mu-xiansheng. Does that mean you recognize yourself as belonging to Cang Qiong Mountain? Or do you not?"

"Does it matter how I recognize myself?" Luo Binghe asked.

"If you don't recognize yourself as such, then why do you still address Shen-shixiong as 'Shizun'? And if you do recognize yourself as such, you should call me 'Shishu.' Moreover, why did you harm Cang Qiong Mountain's disciples to forcibly bring me here?"

"I have asked Mu-xiansheng to come so that he may take a look at my shizun."

Mu Qingfang smiled. "Shen-shixiong self-detonated before everyone's eyes in Hua Yue City and perished, devoid of any spiritual energy. I'm afraid that at this point, even his corpse will have long since festered and decayed. This Mu already knows that there is no way to bring people back to life."

As Shen Qingqiu listened to this exchange of questions and answers, he broke out in a cold sweat.

Mu Qingfang's personality wasn't like that of Qi Qingqi or Liu Qingge, who couldn't tolerate the slightest offense and would explode at the smallest thing, but his replies in this moment weren't very pleasant. Though Shen Qingqiu knew that everything would turn out all right, he couldn't help tensing in fear for Mu Qingfang, afraid that he would infuriate Luo Binghe and bring some unnecessary suffering upon himself.

Luckily, Luo Binghe was unmoved. "I only ask that Mu-xiansheng take a look," he said coldly.

As he was now under Luo Binghe's control, Mu Qingfang could only allow a group of yellow-robed disciples to escort him to Huan Hua Pavilion.

The frigid air within Huan Hua Pavilion cut to the bone. As the two of them crossed over the threshold, one in the front and the other in the back, the great doors immediately shut behind them. Shen Qingqiu stole in right on their heels.

Luo Binghe lifted the gauzy curtain over the sitting platform, tying it back. Mu Qingfang bent over for his examination. Shen Qingqiu also wanted to head over for a look, but unfortunately, Mu Qingfang practically sprang upright straight away, dropping the curtain and blocking Shen Qingqiu's line of sight as his face twisted a little.

"What method did you use to preserve his body?" Mu Qingfang asked.

"Mu-xiansheng is the Qian Cao Peak Lord," Luo Binghe said

very lightly. "You know better than I how to preserve a fleshly body without destroying it."

After a long pause, Mu Qingfang's original attitude of indirect refusal to cooperate finally collapsed. "Forcefully channeling your spiritual energy into Shen-shixiong's corpse every day does barely anything—you just barely prevent his body's decay while consuming an enormous amount of spiritual power. Furthermore, the moment you stop for a single day, all of your prior efforts will go to waste. With all due respect, Shen-shixiong has already—"

"Qian Cao Peak's medical skills are the best in the world," Luo Binghe interrupted. "Moreover, Mu-xiansheng is a peak lord. You must know of some alternative."

"There is none," said Mu Qingfang.

Faced with this stubbornness, Luo Binghe's already thin patience finally wore out completely. "If there isn't a way, think of one!" he sneered. "Until Mu-xiansheng thinks of an alternative, he has no need to return to Cang Qiong Mountain!"

With a fierce wave of his sleeve, the great doors of Huan Hua Pavilion suddenly burst open, startling Mu Qingfang. Before he'd recovered, he'd been thrown out of the pavilion, and a group of yellow-robed disciples promptly surged forward to grab him, having been waiting all that while. Right after, the doors slammed shut.

A gust of cold wind blew through the pavilion. The candle fire within swayed, flickering between light and dark.

Suddenly, Luo Binghe called in his direction, "Shizun."

Shen Qingqiu's initial reaction was to startle.

He thought that the Luo Binghe in the memory had seen him. However, he soon realized that Luo Binghe was only calling to him for the sake of it. He held no expectations that someone would answer.

Only after standing in the entranceway for a while did Luo Binghe slowly walk toward Shen Qingqiu. He sat on the side of the platform and tied up the curtain anew, then stared at that body's face in a daze.

This daze lasted for a long period of time. Shen Qingqiu stood there with nothing to do, to the point that it became unbearable. He shifted his weight back and forth, then, unable to take it any longer, also went to the platform. As Luo Binghe stared at his corpse's face, Shen Qingqiu stared at Luo Binghe's. They stared and stared, until Luo Binghe reached out and slowly unfastened the sash of that corpse's robe.

The leg with which Shen Qingqiu was crouching suddenly buckled a little.

Words like, "the scene was too beautiful to behold," really didn't suit this moment, because the corpse upon the sitting platform... really didn't look that great. From the neck down, it was wholly mottled and discolored: livor mortis.

Luo Binghe removed his own outer robe. Then, like he was handling a large doll, he pulled the corpse into an embrace so that they were pressed skin to skin. If a stranger saw this, they would definitely either be frightened out of their wits or they would find the whole thing overwhelmingly disgusting, and a selection of nasty words would come to mind. But in reality, Luo Binghe only held the corpse. He didn't touch it in any improper sort of way.

Luo Binghe's jaw pressed against the dark crown of Shen Qingqiu's hair. One of his hands slid down the curve of his spine, gently caressing it. While he did so, he sent large amounts of spiritual energy into the body. The green-purple spots of liver mortis slowly faded, and the skin once again became a smooth snow-white.

This position and these movements both pulled gently at a string within Shen Qingqiu's heart.

He remembered. He'd once performed these exact movements for Luo Binghe.

It had been a night not long after Luo Binghe moved into the Bamboo House.

It was a winter night. A frigid wind wailed through the forests of Qing Jing Peak, the thousands of bamboo stalks rustling with the gusts.

Shen Qingqiu reclined upon his bed, not asleep but resting with his eyes closed. As he rested, from the small world on the other side of the screen there came a quiet, restrained creaking. It was as if the person there was tossing and turning, unable to fall asleep.

Then the sounds of restless shifting abruptly ceased, and someone lightly got off the bed, lifted the curtain, and exited the Bamboo House.

What was Luo Binghe doing, slipping outside in the middle of the night instead of sleeping? Shen Qingqiu didn't recall this period of the plot having an adventure that required sneaking outside during the wee hours of the morning. Curious, he also rose.

His cultivation was on a different level than Luo Binghe's, and his movements were both light and swift. Therefore, even once he'd circled around to come up behind Luo Binghe's back, his disciple completely failed to notice.

Luo Binghe hadn't gone very far either. He hadn't headed to some secret and mysterious location for an adventure. Rather, he simply stood in the backyard before he pulled up a small stool to sit on. The clothes on his upper body had already been removed; they now lay neatly folded upon his left thigh, while his right hand poured a small amount of something into his left palm, which he applied to his body. When he rubbed himself a couple times thereafter, soft gasping breaths escaped his mouth.

Beneath the moonlight, his youthful fifteen- or sixteen-year-old body wasn't frail, but it also wasn't strong: it was covered with belt after belt of purple bruises, and the faint fragrance of medicine and alcohol drifted over on the night wind.

"Luo Binghe," said Shen Qingqiu.

The person in question jumped in shock, springing up from the stool. The neatly folded shirt fell to the ground. "Shizun!" said Luo Binghe, astounded. "Why are you awake?"

Shen Qingqiu walked over to him. "This master wasn't sleeping."

"Did this disciple wake Shizun?" asked Luo Binghe. "I'm sorry! I came out because I didn't want to disturb Shizun's rest, but to think I still..."

So the child had been afraid that his tossing and turning would wake him. That was why he'd come out in the dead of night to apply a medical tincture to himself. The pain must have been truly overpowering.

"Where did these injuries come from?" asked Shen Qingqiu.

"They're not a problem!" said Luo Binghe. "It's just that recently, this disciple failed to properly conduct his cultivation training, so he needlessly ended up with more injuries than usual."

Shen Qingqiu looked closely at those injuries. "Bai Zhan Peak picked on you again, didn't they?"

Luo Binghe didn't want to say yes, but he was also unwilling to lie.

The more Shen Qingqiu regarded his silent appearance, the angrier he became. "What did this master teach you before?"

"If you can't beat them, run."

"And did you do that?"

"But... But if this disciple did that, wouldn't he lose a great deal of face for Qing Jing Peak?"

"Hitting people just because they feel like it—what's the difference between Bai Zhan Peak and the common thugs and bullies down the mountain? In all seriousness, exactly which of us has lost face? Is it Qing Jing Peak or Bai Zhan? This master is off to look for Liu Qingge this instant. There are three hundred and sixty-five days in a year; if he took just one of them to discipline his juniors, they wouldn't be so barbaric."

Luo Binghe grabbed him. "Shizun, you mustn't! If Shizun ends up quarreling with Liu-shishu again because of this disciple, then he...then he..." Unable to restrain Shen Qingqiu, his legs went limp. When Shen Qingqiu stopped, he quickly added, "Besides, these aren't all from my Bai Zhan Peak shidi. I injured myself more getting knocked around during cultivation training; that's why it looks so awful."

At the sight of his agitation, Shen Qingqiu let out a sigh. "When cultivating, one must proceed gradually and step-by-step, following the natural path. How can one force growth? As you are, it's as if you're uprooting sprouts to make them taller. If you end up damaging your base, won't you live a life full of regret?"

And one day, Shen Qingqiu would definitely think of some way to teach those Bai Zhan Peak brutes a lesson. He'd even use Liu Qingge to discipline them, so that they'd be unable to voice their objections.

The seventh-ranked peak dared to challenge the second-ranked? Had they no concept of seniority at all? How could he let this go!

"Yes," Luo Binghe murmured.

"You should head inside," said Shen Qingqiu.

Luo Binghe waved his hands back and forth. "No. I'll stay outside. If I go in, I'll disturb Shizun's rest."

Shen Qingqiu curled his finger, and the shirt on the ground flew into his hand. He shook it out and draped it over Luo Binghe's shoulders. "What rest? Now that this master has seen you, how can he allow you to stay alone outside while braving the cold wind?"

Once the two of them were back inside the Bamboo House, Luo Binghe wanted to return to his bed, but Shen Qingqiu took the medicine he was holding and gestured for him to get on the couch in his personal chamber.

Luo Binghe was pulled over to it, still stunned, and he remained so until Shen Qingqiu started to unfasten the sash he'd just retied. Then his entire face flushed red as he pulled his collar tightly shut and backed up several steps. "Shizun, what, what, what—what are you doing?!"

Shen Qingqiu shook the little bottle of medicine. "Applying medicine for you. I'll massage your bruises after."

"No need, I'll do it myself!" Luo Binghe flung himself forward, trying to grab the bottle, but Shen Qingqiu flipped his right hand over and grabbed his wrist. He pulled Luo Binghe's arm toward him and said expressionlessly, "Can you see the location of the bruises on your back?"

Luo Binghe shivered. "I'll…I'll just apply it everywhere!"

He still refused to give up on retaking the bottle. Normally, Luo Binghe was unfailingly submissive, gentle, and calm. This was the first time Shen Qingqiu had seen him with his ears so red that they seemed about to drip blood. He found it amusing, and he thought that it was probably because the child had grown up a little; thus he now felt that being beaten was shameful, and having his master apply medicine for him because of that was even more shameful.

Though Shen Qingqiu was secretly laughing in his heart, his face remained solemn. "Nonsense," he scolded him. "Qian Cao Peak always sends a set amount of medication every time. How can we let you waste it so?"

"I…I…"

Luo Binghe couldn't even manage to say "this disciple" anymore. Tears welled in his eyes as he held his shirt tightly closed over his chest, looking like he had completely lost his wits.

Shen Qingqiu grasped him by the shoulder to swivel him around. Then he swept off his shirt in one go before applying the liquid inside the little bottle to the wounds on his back.

Taken by surprise, Luo Binghe made a small sound: "Ack."

Shen Qingqiu swiftly lessened the force of his touch. "Was I pressing too hard?"

Luo Binghe shook his head violently.

"Then what are you crying out for? You're a big, strong man. Yet you can't withstand even this tiny bit of pain?"

Luo Binghe's voice was like a mosquito. "No, it's not pain…"

Putting aside his worries, Shen Qingqiu rubbed the wounds for a while, then attempted to send a slow stream of spiritual energy into Luo Binghe from his palm.

"Ah!" Luo Binghe cried out again.

Shen Qingqiu was confused. "How can you make such a fuss? You've entirely lost your sense of decorum. Can you claim to be a disciple of my Qing Jing Peak with such manners?"

"I...I... This disciple, this disciple is fine now that the medicine's been applied," Luo Binghe said in a quavering voice. "Shizun doesn't need to waste his energy."

Shen Qingqiu's right palm pressed seamlessly against the bare skin of Luo Binghe's back as it moved slowly. "Does this feel all right?"

Luo Binghe didn't speak. He seemed to be biting his lip.

Shen Qingqiu had one hand on his waist as he massaged, light and gentle, but internally, he was confused. Did it not feel good? That couldn't be. He hadn't misremembered the body's acupoints. And the level of spiritual energy ought to be just right. The bruises had faded by quite a bit as well, so why did Luo Binghe seem so agonized? It couldn't be... Was Shen Qingqiu one of those people who was all thumbs?!

He withdrew his hand, and Luo Binghe breathed a sigh of relief, his eyes bloodshot. He could never have predicted that in the next moment, he would be yanked into someone's arms and wholly enveloped in an embrace.

While holding Luo Binghe, Shen Qingqiu lay down on the couch.

Luo Binghe sounded like he was about to breathe his last. "Shizun... Shizun!"

Shen Qingqiu hadn't removed his inner robes, but there was only a thin layer between them as their heartbeats pounded against each other. There was greater contact area within an embrace, hence the amount of spiritual energy that could be transmitted was also greater.

"It wouldn't be fast enough to use only my palm," said Shen Qingqiu. "If we stay like this for a moment, once this master's meridians finish circulating a couple of times, your wounds will be about healed as well. It will be far more effective than any medicine."

Luo Binghe thrashed about in his arms like a little hedgehog. "Shizun! Shizun! I'm covered in medicine!"

The friction from his struggling incited a fire within Shen Qingqiu—an emotional fire. He gave Luo Binghe's behind a firm warning slap. "What are you squirming for?" he asked, manner dignified. *I'm treating you—be good!*

After that slap, which was neither light nor hard, Luo Binghe stiffened into a stick. A stick being roasted over an open flame, at that, long-suffering and tortured.

"Shizun...this isn't appropriate..." said the stick. "Let—let me go..."

"Luo Binghe, if you were Yingying, this master would obviously never do something like this, even if you weren't squirming about so much," said Shen Qingqiu. "But you aren't a young maiden. Are you afraid this master will eat you?"

At this, Luo Binghe indeed stopped squirming, though his point of focus had strayed. "Shizun is saying that he...he wouldn't do this to Ning-shijie?"

If the person injured that night had been Ning Yingying, even if you'd given Shen Qingqiu a hundred shots of courage, he would still never have dared to use this method of treatment. Unfortunately, he couldn't loudly proclaim his shining purity and perfect sincerity to the entire world. "Of course not," he said resolutely.

Then Luo Binghe said, "Then...if it weren't Ning-shijie, but another disciple who had been injured, would Shizun—would Shizun do this?"

Shen Qingqiu paused. "What nonsense is going through your head? Calm your mind and breathe."

The hedgehog in his arms finally settled down.

Satisfied, Shen Qingqiu picked the most comfortable position he could and hooked his chin over Luo Binghe's head. Freeing up one hand, he used it to trace his disciple's spine, gently stroking it over and over in a pacifying manner.

He didn't get to be comfortable for very long when holding Luo Binghe began to grow difficult. The youth was boiling hot, as if he'd just emerged from a steamer. The sweat from his upper body had practically soaked through Shen Qingqiu's inner robe.

Shen Qingqiu was astounded. Surely the spiritual energy he'd sent Luo Binghe hadn't managed to give him a fever!

He was about to yank Luo Binghe's face up to study his complexion, but what he got was a handful of fine sweat, slick and slippery. The body within his embrace suddenly began to thrash with all its might. Like a great white fish out of water, Luo Binghe slid out of his arms and fell off the bamboo couch with a crash.

It didn't stop there. What followed was a terrible-sounding clang—then a bang!

Luo Binghe had kicked over the stool and knocked his head into the screen. Then, like he'd gone mad, he crawled and rolled to his feet, and rushed out of the Bamboo House.

At the end of that whole spectacle, Shen Qingqiu was left frozen stiff on the couch. For a while he sat there in utter bewilderment before he finally defrosted, jumping off the couch and chasing after him. "Luo Binghe?!"

Luo Binghe had already sprinted several meters ahead. As he ran, he yelled, "I'm sorry, Shizun!"

Shen Qingqiu's expression was dark with dismay. "What are you sorry for? Get back here already!"

On the night wind came a distant, teary voice. "I can't! Shizun, I can't see you right now! Don't come near me—absolutely don't come near!"

What on earth had possessed him?!

Logically, Shen Qingqiu's cultivation outstripped Luo Binghe's by quite a bit, and he was categorically faster as well, but whether due to an adrenaline rush on Luo Binghe's part or some other factor, he simply couldn't catch up.

The two of them dashed along the roads while shouting at each other. Within a few moments, the entirety of Qing Jing Peak had been jolted awake. Lamps everywhere lit up in twos and threes: a herd of disciples carrying lights flocked together in great numbers.

"Who's yelling so loudly this late at night, disturbing the tranquility of Qing Jing Peak?"

"That voice sounds like Shizun!"

"Nonsense! How could Shizun do something so uncouth—"

That last voice had yet to finish when Shen Qingqiu flew past them like a gust of wind, face expressionless. For a moment, everything was utterly silent.

Shen Qingqiu worried that with Luo Binghe's mindless running, he'd fail to watch his step and wind up falling off a cliff. He took a deep breath and yelled, "Ming Fan! Stop him! Stop Luo Binghe!"

Ming Fan had just thrown on an outer robe and was walking over with a lantern. He stared at the sight and gasped. That bastard Luo Binghe was sprinting away, full of terror, while Shizun chased after him, roiling with murderous intent—

This scene! Everything had finally returned to normal!

Ecstatic, he yelled, "Shizun! This disciple will assist you! We'll grab that brat and teach him a lesson! Come, my shidi, get him!"

While disciples rushed over from all directions, Shen Qingqiu finally caught up to the wild, runaway horse that was Luo Binghe. But before he could grab the kid by the collar and pick him up, Luo Binghe refused to submit and threw himself forward with all his might—

With a splash, water sprayed everywhere. Luo Binghe had hurled himself into a clear, tranquil pond on Qing Jing Peak.

With this action, he seemed to have hurled himself into clear-headedness. His entire body now soaked in cold water, he finally stopped moving.

"Calmed down yet?" asked Shen Qingqiu.

Luo Binghe ducked his head down hard, then raised both hands, covering his face with them.

Meanwhile, Ming Fan was so moved that tears were streaming down his face. A Luo Binghe drenched in cold water, shivering and looking like he'd been viciously beaten. A Shizun with his arms crossed, standing across from him with a chilly smile. Ah, such a warm, familiar scene—ah, such a nostalgic sight!

A group of disciples surrounded Luo Binghe while whispering to one another. Luo Binghe was still within the pool, silent with his hands over his face.

As a girl, Ning Yingying always needed more time to dress and comb her hair, so she arrived late. The moment she did, she was greeted with this sight and she blurted out in shock, "A-Luo! Why... why are you sitting in a pond? Who was bullying you this time? Shizun, what's happening here?"

Shen Qingqiu was silent before he said coldly, "This master also wishes to know exactly 'who' is at fault, and 'what' is going on."

Luo Binghe shook his head, face still covered. "No one's to blame. And nothing happened."

Shen Qingqiu stood at the edge of the pond for a while, then suddenly sighed. "Get up. What are you doing, still sitting in there?"

Luo Binghe continued to shake his head. "No, Shizun. I'll stay here. Just let me stay here for a while..."

It was winter and it was freezing. There might not have been snow, but if Luo Binghe was allowed to stay in the icy pond like this for a whole night... Did he want to die?

Shen Qingqiu lifted his hem, ready to enter the water and pull him out.

"Shizun, don't come in!" Luo Binghe said hastily. "The water is cold and dirty—don't get wet..."

Shen Qingqiu had already waded through the water to his side, crossing the distance of three steps in two. There he stared down at him severely.

Luo Binghe's head drooped even further. He didn't dare meet Shen Qingqiu's eyes and instead sank himself deeper into the water.

"Do you need this master to help you out too?" asked Shen Qingqiu.

Luo Binghe was silent, then said, "Shizun, I—just let me stay here by myself!"

Shen Qingqiu was at the end of his rope with this kid. He steadied himself, then suddenly turned to the Qing Jing Peak disciples who were watching them. "What are you looking at?" he asked sternly. "Disperse and return to your rooms. Go to sleep."

The group jostled back and forth, but still they loitered, unwilling to leave.

"You'll wake at three for morning classes," said Shen Qingqiu. "Anyone who's late will be copying scrolls a hundred times."

Three! But it was already past one in the morning! Copying scrolls—and a hundred times!

The moment these words left his mouth, the shore of the pond emptied of people like clouds swept away by the wind.

Once Shen Qingqiu was sure no one was watching, he turned around and stooped down, moving to lift Luo Binghe under his back and the crook of his knees.

Realizing what he wanted to do, Luo Binghe acted increasingly like a great white fish, hiding and splashing within the water. "Shizun! Shizun, don't do this—don't do this!"

Shen Qingqiu was sprayed with a face full of water; his robes were thoroughly drenched. He wiped at his face with a sleeve. "Haven't you kicked up enough nonsense tonight?"

When Luo Binghe no longer dared move, Shen Qingqiu steeled himself and lifted Luo Binghe up and into his arms.

A little heavy. Having muttered that in his heart, Shen Qingqiu carried Luo Binghe back in the direction of the Bamboo House.

Halfway there, Luo Binghe suddenly spoke from his arms with a pained expression: "Shizun, I...I'll return to the woodshed."

"Luo Binghe! Exactly what has gotten into you tonight?" Shen Qingqiu said severely. "Being all timid and evasive, even running away with all your might! An outsider who didn't know what was going on would imagine that this master had done something unforgivable to you!"

The Luo Binghe of that night had truly disgraced himself and destroyed his own reputation.

A dark past! That was one hundred percent Luo Binghe's dark past.

Later, Shen Qingqiu had at times recalled the incident and used it to tease Luo Binghe. But Luo Binghe wouldn't even blush; he'd truly grown up, and his face had grown thicker too.

"I was at the age when one is most susceptible to passions," he would explain. "The person I most admired had held me in his arms, and he both hugged and rubbed himself against me. Shizun, how could you ask me to keep myself under control? Having realized my feelings, I was unable to control my body's reactions, but I was afraid you'd notice. What could I have done other than make a fool of myself?"

When he recalled Luo Binghe saying those words, along with how his face had revealed some rarely seen hints of genuine shyness, Shen Qingqiu couldn't help but smile.

He smiled and smiled, but then he couldn't anymore.

He dared not think about how the Luo Binghe before him was feeling now, as he held Shen Qingqiu's body in his arms.

This dream realm, which Shen Qingqiu couldn't leave, was both drawn-out and monotonous, exactly how Luo Binghe's life at Huan Hua Palace had been.

Luo Binghe spent over half the hours of every day huddling inside the frigid Huan Hua Pavilion; he even brought all his documents inside to deal with them there.

Shen Qingqiu rarely got to see Luo Binghe working so seriously.

Most of the time, Luo Binghe's behavior in front of him was a little odd, like a lovesick young girl from head to toe. And when Luo Binghe was handling important demonic affairs, Shen Qingqiu consciously practiced avoidance, making sure not to disturb him. On the occasions he intruded, Luo Binghe immediately lost interest in his work, throwing aside the heaping mountain of documents upon his desk in favor of appealing to Shen Qingqiu as he acted all lovable and obedient. To think that it was only inside this dream realm that he could carefully observe what Luo Binghe was like when he was alone and diligently handling official business.

Shen Qingqiu took to sitting next to Luo Binghe's desk, where he would marvel as he stared at that quiet, serious side profile. Luo Binghe would slightly frown, reading ten lines at a glance, his brush strokes swift and accurate. The instructions he left were comprehensive yet concise, his ink sparingly used. In short, he worked with a level of gravitas that could scarce be believed.

He also kept up his old habit of cooking every day. Exquisite snacks in the morning, four side dishes with a soup at noon, and a bowl of congee in the evening. Snow-white rice, deep-green scallions, light-yellow shredded ginger. It was the same as the first bowl Luo Binghe had ever made for him. It would be poured inside a snowy porcelain dish, and once the drifting steam faded, Luo Binghe would personally arrange everything inside a lunchbox, which he would deliver to the pavilion.

Even without anyone to appreciate his efforts, he insisted on making everything just like how he had on Qing Jing Peak. It was as if he was waiting for the day Shen Qingqiu would suddenly awaken and open his eyes. That way, the food would be available straightaway and he wouldn't need to wait.

Sometimes, Luo Binghe would leave for half the day. Most of the time, it would be to address trouble on the demon side of things that no one else could handle, so Luo Binghe would have to personally deal with it himself.

He pretty much never got hurt; then one day, he hit the jackpot and came back bloody.

Luo Binghe walked through the doors at first, but then, as if he'd suddenly thought of something, he backed up a great many steps and removed his bloodstained outer robe. Expelling a little energy from his hand, he set it aflame, burning it away completely. Only after making sure that there was no blood on himself did he slowly approach the sitting platform.

His expression was the same as ever, and he said to the body on the platform, "Shizun, something came up and caused a delay. This disciple ended up returning late, so there won't be any congee."

Naturally, no one replied, which highlighted the way in which this situation was just a little...comical.

Shen Qingqiu felt a bit stuck, unable to either laugh or cry, but his heart twinged, a sour feeling within it. He replied, "It's fine that there isn't."

Over these days in the dream, he'd come into the habit of speaking to himself. Separated as they were by time and space, Luo Binghe couldn't hear him, and Shen Qingqiu couldn't touch him either, but in the end...he still wished to answer.

Luo Binghe silently stood there for a time, then said, "Never mind."

He turned around and left. After a while, he returned through the doors with a steaming hot bowl of congee. He placed it down on the desk in passing, then began slowly and methodically removing his clothing. "Liu Qingge rescued Mu Qingfang."

Shen Qingqiu made a sound of acknowledgment.

Luo Binghe continued talking to himself. "It's fine that he's been rescued. At any rate, Mu Qingfang only ever said, 'There's no way.' He's totally useless."

"How can you bad-mouth your shishu like that?" said Shen Qingqiu.

Luo Binghe removed his outer robe. Upon his chest was a wound that was slowly healing. Shen Qingqiu could tell at a glance that the gash had been caused by Liu Qingge's sword glare. Beneath this new wound was an old one, ever stubborn and resistant, unwilling to fade.

Luo Binghe lay down and rolled over, pulling that body into his arms. "In the past, when Bai Zhan Peak came and knocked me around, Shizun would always come up with a method to take revenge for me. When will Shizun do the same and exact revenge on Liu Qingge himself?"

Shen Qingqiu sat upon the sitting platform. "That's impossible; I can't defeat him."

"Shizun."

"Mm."

"Shizun, I can't hold on for much longer."

Shen Qingqiu didn't speak.

Luo Binghe smiled. "It's true. Shizun, if you don't wake up soon, I...I won't be able to hold on for much longer."

But Shen Qingqiu knew that he would hold on.

He would hold that ice-cold, lifeless corpse and hold on for almost two thousand more of these days and nights.

His heart ached with an overwhelming pain, so much so that it exploded within his chest. Shen Qingqiu saw a hand stretching forward, futilely trying to touch that stark-white face of Luo Binghe's.

He watched that hand as it trembled, unable to touch anything, then suddenly realized, with a shock, that it was his own.

"Shizun—Shizun?"

In his daze, Shen Qingqiu felt someone grasping his shoulder as they sat up. He drowsily opened his eyes.

Luo Binghe was inches from his face, nervously staring at him in concern. "Shizun, what's wrong?"

Shen Qingqiu had yet to recollect himself mentally; he stared at him blankly.

At the sight of this, Luo Binghe became increasingly anxious. The day before, he'd reached a critical point in his cultivation. That night, he'd shut off his consciousness and so had no opportunity to control his dream realm. After falling into a troubled sleep, he'd been shocked awake in the middle of the night. Next to him, Shen Qingqiu's brow had been tightly knit, his forehead dripping with sweat. Luo Binghe knew something was wrong. He realized he must have failed to restrain his powers and forced his shizun to be trapped in a nightmare.

He was terrified that Shen Qingqiu might have had an exceptionally terrifying dream because of him. "Shizun, what were you dreaming of just now?" he asked persistently. "Are you injured?"

"I..." Shen Qingqiu had stayed within that dream for too long, and his soul had yet to make it all the way back. As he looked at Luo Binghe's face, it seemed both real and yet not, and his vision wavered, at times blurred and at times clear. He didn't know what to say.

Luo Binghe became even more frantic, and he raised his voice. "Shizun! Say something!"

Suddenly, inspiration struck Shen Qingqiu. He blinked, then pulled Luo Binghe's face down and kissed him.

Luo Binghe was speechless.

Though he had no idea what was going on, the sudden kiss had made him intensely happy, and his eyes opened very wide. In the next moment, his hand pressed against the back of Shen Qingqiu's neck as he took the initiative to deepen the kiss.

Shen Qingqiu didn't stop there. After some rustling, he'd already unfastened Luo Binghe's sash and grabbed his hand, moving it inside his own open collar. He led it along the firm lines of his chest, all the way to his enthusiastically pounding heart.

At this point, Luo Binghe seemed a little shocked by the indulgence; he didn't dare to be too impatient or impulsive, and his movements became cautious.

However, during his moment of slight hesitation, Shen Qingqiu had flipped them over, pressing Luo Binghe beneath him as he roughly tore open his inner robes.

Luo Binghe's breathing was a little unsteady as he held Shen Qingqiu's waist, a faint flush dyeing his cheeks. "Shizun..." he stammered, "what's gotten into you tonight?"

Shen Qingqiu leaned down and said into his ear, "Tonight, I feel like...I like you a great deal."

In an instant, Luo Binghe's entire body went rigid from head to toe.

He abruptly sat up and trapped Shen Qingqiu within his arms. Lightly drawing a breath, he said, "Shizun, I...I might not be able to be gentle."

At the sound of the forced calm in his voice, Shen Qingqiu laughed. "You speak as if it doesn't hurt when you *are* gentle." Before Luo Binghe's face had the chance to change, Shen Qingqiu was reaching out with both hands. "I'll endure it gladly."

28

Return to Childhood

WHEN HE WOKE UP, Shen Qingqiu slowly turned over in bed, but he didn't find an arm locked around his waist as he usually did.

The light of dawn spilled in from beyond the window. He covered his eyes with the sleeve of his inner robe, but this single movement made his waist and back begin to ache and his arm feel weak. A faint, tearing pain came from a certain part of his lower half, accompanied by the strange sensation of some dried sticky liquid.

After last night's whole stretch of nonsense, waking up had come with a wave of consequences. Wondering why Luo Binghe hadn't woken at the crack of dawn to clean him up and make breakfast on the way, Shen Qingqiu rasped, "Binghe?"

No one responded. Even more confused, Shen Qingqiu forced his eyes open and looked down, only to find a small head with a curtain of soft black hair.

Shen Qingqiu was speechless.

The owner of this small head had a cute and pretty face with a natural flush on his pale and tender cheeks; a long, thick curtain of lush black eyelashes; tightly shut eyes; and pale pink lips. This person was also curled up in a ball like a little kitten by Shen Qingqiu's side, his head pillowed on his own arm.

Even though this person wasn't the same size, and even though he looked to be about five or six years old at the most, and even though...

There were no more "even thoughs." Even if he'd shrunk to another size, Shen Qingqiu could absolutely still recognize him at first glance—this was the face of the great male protagonist!

With a shudder, his voice jumped up an octave. "Luo Binghe!"

He was going to try pinching his own arm to see if he could pinch himself awake, but as soon as he sprang up, that ache in his lower half sent him collapsing stiffly back down. Still curled up in a little ball, Luo Binghe's lashes trembled, and he slowly drifted awake.

With a red mark across one half of his face from his own arm, he squinted at Shen Qingqiu's half-dressed form across the bed and reached for him in a *give me a hug* gesture. "Shizun..."

This voice was soft and squishy, so tender and sweet that it practically dripped. Accordingly, Luo Binghe froze as soon as he opened his mouth.

They gave each other a blank stare.

After a period of chaotic fumbling, they finally managed to sort out what exactly had happened.

Luo Binghe had been at a critical juncture in his cultivation lately. The common wisdom was that he should have been clearing his mind and keeping himself pure of base desires in order to prevent any mishaps from occurring. Yet the evening prior, he had lost control and rolled around with Shen Qingqiu all night, and finally—he'd suffered a qi deviation.

Shen Qingqiu didn't find this at all difficult to accept because this plotline had occurred in the original text of *Proud Immortal Demon Way*. Of course, Airplane Shooting Towards the Sky hadn't written that arc for cute fluff, but rather because the de-aged Luo Binghe had been able to openly strut into all sorts of locations an adult man couldn't enter. (Exactly what those locations were, one can imagine for oneself.) And such a little kid was way better at lowering young women's guards, so they could proceed to have intimate contact, and then, right when they least expected it—he'd win them over in a single blow!

This plotline had taken so long to show up that Shen Qingqiu had thought it had been skipped. He'd never expected that it had just been unable to occur on time.

Shen Qingqiu pressed a hand to his forehead. "How much of your martial aspect remains?"

"Not even a tenth." Luo Binghe had a stern expression written all over his youthful face. Not only did it fail to convey the severity of the situation, it was instead...extremely funny.

So, Shen Qingqiu, very uncharitably, began to laugh. After he was done laughing, he rearranged his face into a serious expression and said with a cough, "Just one-tenth? All right. Then we can't stay in the Demon Realm."

Luo Binghe had offended more than a few humans and demons both. At this sort of time, the obvious next move was to flee as far away as possible and hide as well as they could. Shen Qingqiu's first thought was, therefore, to grab chibi Luo Binghe and make a run for it ASAP.

Having made up his mind, he went to get up and get dressed—only for his face to twitch in pain again as soon as he straightened his back.

Every time before, after they finished, Luo Binghe had carried him into the hot springs while he was still deep asleep and helped him clean up. But now, Luo Binghe could at most cling to one of Shen Qingqiu's legs, much less haul him anywhere. Luo Binghe crouched down next to him, eyes huge and on the verge of tears.

Shen Qingqiu was silent for a moment, then comforted him, "Forget it, it's fine. I can do it myself."

In the deepest part in the middle of the natural hot springs Luo Binghe had dug in the underground palace, the water rose past Shen Qingqiu's chest. If he tossed chibi Luo Binghe into it, he'd immediately be submerged up to his head. So, Shen Qingqiu had to carefully sit down on the round stones along the edge while holding him, and even instructed him to sit tight so as not to slip.

He was about to start giving himself a cursory cleaning when he saw Luo Binghe straining to reach a nearby chunk of limestone to try to hand him the box of soap sitting there, but no matter how far he stretched, he fell short.

This scene reminded him of Luo Binghe crouched in a valley when he had first arrived at Cang Qiong Mountain to seek tutelage, a patched-up cloth bundle on his back as he assiduously dug holes. Shen Qingqiu looked at him for a while and couldn't resist pulling him into his arms. Expressionless, he began to squish and tug at Luo Binghe's face.

While subjected to this aggressive harassment, Luo Binghe inhaled a few gulps of water. His skin already had a faint flush from the warm steam, and with his struggles, his entire body practically turned pink. In a surge of emotion, Luo Binghe instinctively grabbed Shen Qingqiu's wrist and tried to shove him down against the limestone.

Though Shen Qingqiu considerately cooperated and let Luo Binghe "shove" him down, Luo Binghe's pretty little face went instantly dark.

With this body...even if he shoved Shen Qingqiu down a thousand—ten thousand—times, there would be no point! He couldn't do anything about it!

At the sight of Luo Binghe's face going from red to white to dark, Shen Qingqiu practically gave himself an internal injury from trying not to laugh. "You were so impetuous when tormenting this master last night; suffering the consequences today, are you?"

"Wasn't it Shizun who seduced this disciple first?" Luo Binghe cried out, betrayed.

This made Shen Qingqiu's face flare red as he internally gasped in shame. He righted his expression and quickly let go.

Caught off guard, Luo Binghe slipped into the water, disappearing in a stream of bubbles.

Shen Qingqiu's preferences being what they were, the first haven he thought of was naturally Cang Qiong Mountain. But Luo Binghe would rather have died than go back there.

That was about right. As of now, with Luo Binghe's martial aspect damaged, he'd definitely get hounded by onlookers if they went, and Liu Qingge would definitely be within that crowd.

So, Shen Qingqiu compromised and just brought him to the Human Realm.

As they say, the greatest form of solitude is solitude within a city. Thus they settled in an especially prosperous town. While Luo Binghe was repairing his martial aspect, they would take up residence there to pass the time. Shen Qingqiu soon got so bored that his bones began to itch, so he casually took up work at the largest academy in the city.

Naturally, Luo Binghe was unhappy with this. First of all, he disliked it when Shen Qingqiu took other disciples. Wasn't that throng of disciples on Qing Jing Peak enough for him? And now he was taking more?!

Second of all, he disliked it even more when people assumed he was Shen Qingqiu's son—especially because every time they got into bed at night, he was kissed and hugged, yet he couldn't do anything at all. He even had to listen to Shen Qingqiu teasingly call him "good boy" and "my little darling." More and more, he came to *hate* his own lack of ability.

When Shen Qingqiu returned from the academy one day, he saw that Luo Binghe had brought a stool to the doorway and was sitting there waiting for him, an aloof and unfathomable expression on his face.

If you swapped him with the adult version, this sight would naturally have made one shrink back in fear, trembling in their boots—but what about when he was the wrong size? All he did was make it irresistible to reach out with a pair of fingers to pinch his wee face. No matter the depths of refusal he summoned to his face, even the little chirping sparrows surrounding him couldn't stop building dirt castles all around his stool, one after another, as they occasionally tried to cajole him to join their games.

Said sparrows were the neighboring families' kids. Since the first day Luo Binghe and Shen Qingqiu moved in, the children had submitted to the male protagonist's charisma halo and clung to him like nothing else; he couldn't even chase them away. Fortunately, they were all afraid of Shen Qingqiu—every child was afraid of a teacher—so as soon as they saw him return, the flock scattered.

Thus Shen Qingqiu gracefully extended his fingers and moved to claim his usual pinch of Luo Binghe's cheeks.

Then a series of bright, crisp voices called "Shen-xiansheng!" from behind him, and a few graceful figures decked out in silver and gold walked into the courtyard uninvited.

Shen Qingqiu turned and saw that the newcomers were a few of the town's rather energetic married ladies. He gave them a nod, but before he could offer a greeting, the one in the lead strode up and caught his arm, whereupon she tried to drag him out and away.

"Shen-xiansheng, we've been looking for you all day! Come on, come on, come with me quick—the girl's going to go mad waiting!"

"Go where?" Luo Binghe snapped. "What girl?!"

Shen Qingqiu was also confused.

Lady A, startled by Luo Binghe's dark expression, fanned herself and let out a sound of surprise. "Such a little one, yet he's so scary when he talks. Whatever is the young master so angry about? Shen-xiansheng, is he mad at you?"

Lady B bustled over. "Here, here, come over here, Young Master. Jiejie has some candy for you; don't get in your daddy's way."

Luo Binghe ignored them and assumed a cold look. "Shiz...did you make any plans today?"

"This mas...I don't remember?"

Lady A tutted at him. "Shen-xiansheng, you know perfectly well, and you still ask. Do you have to make me say it clearly? Fine, fine. I have a niece in my family, an excellent and respectable girl. I thought you two would be a good match, so we arranged a banquet in the Cheng Xi Pavilion to let you get to know each other."

"And the girl from my family."

"And my cousin. My cousin too!"

It looked like everything happened fast in lively places. Shen Qingqiu hadn't been here very long, but all the residents of the city were already talking about how there was a new scholar in town, and not only was he well read and highly talented, polite and soft-spoken, he also had a handsome and elegant appearance and was very refreshing.

Of course, all of this was superficial! The most important thing was that he had to be rich, stinking rich! He'd thrown down the money for a respectable courtyard all at once—how could he have managed that if he wasn't rich? And he'd even come with a four- or five-year-old son, and what a pure and adorable child he was, already a handsome sprout at this age. He would certainly develop into an elegant and dignified gentleman in the future. How devastating! Anyone with an unmarried daughter of suitable age or a newborn daughter without an arranged betrothal would be raring to snag them. A match with either the elder or the younger—neither would be a bad deal!

Luo Binghe's face was green with rage. "He doesn't need matchmaking!"

His rightful partner wasn't dead yet!

Lady C strolled over, swaying her hips. "Little Young Master Shen, do you not want your dad to marry a new wife? Won't it be good to have a gentle, pretty new mom to take care of you?"

"That's right, that's right," Lady B added. "Shen-xiansheng, you can't spoil your son like this. I hear you even bring him with you to the academy, and he even sits on your lap? You don't have to take it from me, but if you pamper him this much, you won't raise him into a good man. My son, you see—"

At the sight of Luo Binghe on the verge of flattening this entire courtyard with a flick of his arm, Shen Qingqiu hurriedly picked him up and retreated. "This Shen accepts all of your good intentions. I do not plan on, um, restringing my qin, as it were. I have no one at home and a young son to look after, so please forgive me for my inability to accept your invitation."

"What is Shen-xiansheng saying?!" asked Lady A, who wore a large red peony pinned at her temple, as she spoke with a righteous vigor. "Men and women ought to get married when they come of age. And you have such a large residence—how can it go without a lady to attend the house? By what logic ought a person of such character and elegant demeanor be all alone with a single child? Not only will you be uncomfortable, it won't look good. People will talk!"

Lady A waved her round fan, brooking no resistance. "It's a date! Shen-xiansheng, you're coming with us right now. The little young master can stay home; someone will come to keep him company."

Luo Binghe sneered. "Just who do you think is going to leave?!"

Shen Qingqiu wasn't able to keep up with this savage charm for long. In consideration for the lives of his three eager matchmakers—and everyone else in town—he flung out a few talismans to render them unconscious, abandoned the residence he had bought not even a month ago, and fled.

The only place they could flee was back to Cang Qiong Mountain. Leading Luo Binghe by the hand, Shen Qingqiu started up the long mountain steps.

The man sweeping the stairs did his work as diligently and earnestly as he always had during his ten-some years. As Shen Qingqiu strolled up, their eyes met, and he gave the man a faint smile. Shen Qingqiu was about to greet him when the man looked at him, then at Luo Binghe holding his hand, and his face twitched.

All of a sudden, he tossed aside the broom that was as tall as he was and sprinted up the steps like his rear end was on fire. In a flash, he was hundreds of steps away, and in addition to shock, Shen Qingqiu felt a sense of pride. That was Cang Qiong Mountain for you—even the stair sweeper was a hidden master!

The stairway was lengthy, and before they had gone halfway up, Luo Binghe began to yawn. He was low on strength at present, so it was unavoidable that he grew tired easily. Shen Qingqiu picked him up. "Get some sleep."

Getting a read on a disciple's heart was like finding the proverbial needle in a haystack. Sometimes Luo Binghe was willing to be picked up, but sometimes his entire face would go red and he would struggle out of Shen Qingqiu's hold, preferring to walk himself. Now he was probably truly exhausted. He curled up in Shen Qingqiu's arms, shut his eyes for a while, and just like that, fell asleep.

Once he'd climbed the Heaven-Ascending Stairs, Shen Qingqiu sensed strange gazes directed at him as soon as he stepped into the main plaza, and he heard a surge of whispering from all around. The stair sweeper started down again, hugging his broom, and gave him an especially strange look on the way.

Shen Qingqiu walked up to Qing Jing Peak, holding Luo Binghe. At the doorway of the Bamboo House, all his disciples rushed over in a frenzy.

As soon as Ming Fan saw Luo Binghe curled up in Shen Qingqiu's arms, he looked as if he had been punched in the solar plexus or struck by lightning. While the others fought their way forward to look, he staggered back.

Ning Yingying shoved aside the people in front of her, stared at Luo Binghe deep asleep in Shen Qingqiu's arms, and covered her mouth. "He looks like A-Luo… He looks like A-Luo!"

Nonsense. If he didn't look like Luo Binghe, who else would he look like?

Ning Yingying grabbed Shen Qingqiu's sleeves in excitement. "Shizun, does he have a name? Did you name him yet?"

Shen Qingqiu was perplexed.

"If he doesn't have a name, I…can I give him one?"

What the hell.

Luo Binghe shifted restlessly in his arms and mumbled, "Loud."

Shen Qingqiu raised his folding fan threateningly in midair, then jerked it back and made a *shush* gesture.

Then the door of the Bamboo House came crashing down. Luo Binghe jerked and opened his eyes, startled awake.

Liu Qingge strode in like a flying meteor. Shen Qingqiu sent a death glare at the furtive-looking Ming Fan, shifted Luo Binghe behind him, and gave Liu Qingge a fake smile. "Liu-shidi, long time no see."

"What are you hiding for?" Liu Qingge snapped.

"Hiding what?" Shen Qingqiu replied. "I'm not hiding."

Luo Binghe planted a hand on Shen Qingqiu's chest. "There's no need to hide—I'm not afraid of him!"

Liu Qingge walked over and glared down at the challenge written all over Luo Binghe's little face. After a long time, he managed to stammer out, as if he was forcibly suppressing some emotion, "You—when did you…and Luo Binghe… When did you and he…"

"When did we…?"

When did they what? What had they done?

Liu Qingge seemed to find it difficult to speak, so Ming Fan cried out in his place, "When did you have a son with him? He's so big!"

Silence.

"Great Master" Liu! Airplane Shooting Towards the Sky didn't write a green Jinjiang mpreg novel!

After very impolitely blasting "Great Master" Liu off Qing Jing Peak, Shen Qingqiu still felt like he was numb from a particularly electric shock. "How can a man give birth to a child?"

Having been told the true sequence of events, Ning Yingying now knew that the child Shen Qingqiu had carried back wasn't his own baby. She was greatly disappointed, and she felt that her heart, full of passion and the fifty-some names she'd come up with, had gone to waste. "It was the stair sweeper gege who went around telling everyone," she said, pouting. "We all assumed it was true. Who could have thought A-Luo could also suffer a qi deviation?"

Stair sweeper, how talented. Not only are you fast, your galaxy brain-level delusions are also so unique! Shen Qingqiu will remember this.

"This disciple thought that when it came to the demon race, making a man give birth to a child wouldn't be outside the realm of possibility," Ming Fan said awkwardly.

Everyone vigorously nodded.

Shen Qingqiu suffered even further mental collapse as he attempted to argue for logic. "Even if I did, a kid wouldn't have grown this big in a few short months!"

"Who knows?" Ming Fan said. "We disciples thought that if it was that monster Luo Binghe's child, it wouldn't be impossible for a kid to be that big when even they were born."

Shen Qingqiu was speechless.

That night, Qing Jing Peak's long-abandoned mass book-copying punishments made a grand reappearance.

It was a rare occasion that Shen Qingqiu managed to make time to return to Cang Qiong Mountain while the twelve peak lords were all in one place. Naturally, they had to get together for a meeting or a meal.

It had been a long time since Shen Qingqiu had sat, doing his poser act, in the second chair of the rear hall of Qiong Ding Hall. He missed the sensation.

He nodded at and greeted the peak lords one by one, exchanging a series of "It's been a long times," "I hope you've been wells," and "Same to yous"; he snapped open his fan, face brimming with joy.

Yue Qingyuan's expression seemed to be a bit strange when he saw Shen Qingqiu, but he didn't say anything much. He just sat down at the head seat, smiled at him, and then placed a stack of files on the table. Shang Qinghua scurried up to collect and distribute them to everyone else.

Shen Qingqiu accepted the list from Shang Qinghua, but first gave him a cursory glance. There was no telling what Shang Qinghua had done to piss off Mobei-Jun this time, but the corner of his lip was swelling as he gave Shen Qingqiu a pathetic smile. Shen Qingqiu couldn't bear to look, so he shifted his gaze back to the file. The key points of discussion had already been marked in bold cinnabar red.

With the first glance, the sip of tea he had just drunk spewed out of his mouth.

First, aggressively restrict access to copies of Regret of Chunshan, Song of Bingqiu, *etc. Forbid the distribution of any edition on any occasion, whether public or private. Set a one-month deadline for copies to be turned over, after which anyone found to be in possession of or circulating copies will be severely punished. Punishment shall be increased by one level for illustrations.*

Second, because of numerous complaints, the relevant leadership of Bai Zhan Peak shall tighten their supervision. Inter-peak brawls are strictly prohibited.

Third, because of a small number of complaints, Qing Jing Peak shall take note of the time when practicing the qin; please avoid the noon break and night times.

Fourth, Xian Shu Peak requests permission to fortify and increase the height of their fences, and petitions for their fences to be electrified.

Fifth, Ku Xing Peak's numbers have dwindled over the years, and they request permission to increase their recruitment efforts. They petition for first rights to select new disciples the next time the mountain gates are opened.

Sixth, the peak lords must increase attention to education on each peak. Sect members must not fight publicly with Huan Hua Palace disciples while identified as Cang Qiong Mountain disciples.

Seventh, if demons are encountered while carrying out missions, do not rashly attack. Make sure to ascertain their lineage and affiliated division before deciding whether to fight.

Spitting out one's tea in front of everyone was extremely improper behavior, but Shen Qingqiu didn't need to worry about this failure of etiquette, because after reading the first item on the agenda, most of the other peak lords also spat out their tea. Given his surroundings, he didn't stand out very much.

The meeting room sank into an awkward confusion. Even if Shen Qingqiu fanned hard enough to raise the wind and waves, he failed to fan away the miasma.

By what great merit had *Regret of Chunshan* come to be first on the list? And what the hell was this new one, *Song of Bingqiu*?!

After the meeting concluded, Shen Qingqiu began to sulkily head toward Qing Jing Peak, but before he got very far, he realized quite a few of the peak lords were following him.

"Shidi and Shimei, I believe the way back to your peaks does not lie in this direction," Shen Qingqiu said amicably.

"That's because I wasn't going back to my peak in the first place," said Qi Qingqi.

Shen Qingqiu had known this hurdle was coming, but he still made a valiant attempt to clear it. "Why have you suddenly thought to come visit Qing Jing Peak? My Bamboo House is simple and crude; I am afraid I cannot provide ample hospitality."

"What are you playing dumb for? I know your Bamboo House is simple and crude—who wants to visit you? I'm obviously going to see that darling disciple you've hidden away."

Everyone in this crowd was eagerly plotting to gawk at Luo Binghe like he was some rare curiosity. Helpless, Shen Qingqiu said, "He'll be angry."

"You don't have to take it from me, Shen-shixiong, but how does a disciple like him dare to be angry with his shizun? Do you not discipline him properly?"

"That won't do. No matter what your relationship is now, you should keep up discipline where it's due."

"So what if he's angry? What's there to be afraid of? Luo Binghe's powers are less than a tenth of his usual. If we don't anger him now, when else can we?"

Because of his ascetic lifestyle, the Ku Xing Peak Lord had a fiery temperament, and he was impatient after having failed to acquire the selection priority he wanted. "Enough with this blathering—are you just afraid we'll empty out your stock of tea?! We're coming, we're coming."

Shen Qingqiu knew there was no escape, and his face darkened as he was dragged off toward Qing Jing Peak. *How do you guys know the situation so well? It's like you know it even better than me!*

He could maybe hold off one or two of them, but when several peak lords swarmed into the Bamboo House all at once, there was nothing he could do to stop them.

As soon as Qi Qingqi walked in the door, she lost it and let out a chuckle.

Luo Binghe was lying on the bed, deep asleep and tucked in tight, looking just as he had when Shen Qingqiu left. Shen Qingqiu gestured as if to say, *He's asleep; don't disturb him.*

Liu Qingge sent a glance inside and couldn't resist remarking, "Why does he look different from yesterday?"

Different? Shen Qingqiu turned, and sure enough, he was different. Luo Binghe seemed to have aged two years, and now looked to be about seven or eight.

"Admirable growth, admirable growth!" Wei Qingwei said quietly.

Qi Qingqi peered closely at him. "At this rate, he's going to grow out of those clothes soon."

Shen Qingqiu hadn't considered this issue. He pondered this, then realized that Luo Binghe's clothes truly hadn't fit so well that morning, and a chunk of his wrist was showing. "True indeed; I have been careless. I'll take him to buy a few more sets tomorrow."

"What do you mean buy?" Qi Qingqi asked. "Do you not know how to use what we have? Just go to Xian Shu Peak and ask a few jiejie and meimei to make some outfits for him."

At this, a few of the peak lords rather ungenerously began to chuckle. The vision of a crowd of sweet-smelling immortal ladies surrounding an aggrieved demon cut-sleeve and chirping in their birdlike voices was enough to give these peak lords, who had nothing better to do, a good laugh.

Seeing their glee at kicking Luo Binghe while he was down, Shen Qingqiu's heart began to hurt for the dregs of his disciple's dignity. "Don't overdo it, don't overdo it. Let's go and sit in the drawing room; don't stand around here staring at him. Stop laughing! Careful, you'll wake him up."

"You wouldn't let us look at him before, and you won't let us look at him now either? Shen-shixiong, you're such a killjoy."

"Give me some face."

"All right, then Shen-shixiong should come drink with us on Zui Xian Peak tonight."

"I still have to look after Luo Binghe..."

"You used to hole yourself up in here all the time, refusing to budge, then you got dragged around all over the place. You're finally back for once, so forget the kid! Let's get together. You need time for yourself—you can't just orbit around your disciple all day."

After Shen Qingqiu finally managed to shoo away his sect siblings and return to the Bamboo House, he felt as if his head had swelled a full size.

Luo Binghe was awake and sitting at his old desk. His legs weren't long enough to reach the ground and hung in midair, and next to him was a pile of documents even taller than he was. He held a brush dipped in red ink as he reviewed some lists and made notes.

Shen Qingqiu looked at him for a while, then walked in. "What are you doing?"

Luo Binghe looked up. "Shizun hasn't been back in a long time, and there was no one to organize the books. This disciple wanted to make a new catalog and put them in storage."

"Just get some rest. You don't have to take care of these things."

"But Shizun wasn't here, and I had nothing else to do. I thought I might as well just do it."

Shen Qingqiu sat down next to him, thought for a moment, then asked, "Are you so unhappy to be back at Qing Jing Peak?"

Luo Binghe gave him a faint smile. "What is Shizun saying? How could this disciple be unhappy?"

Shen Qingqiu slowly got up and went to head outside. But suddenly, he couldn't move his feet.

Luo Binghe had jumped down from the table and grabbed onto his legs. "You're right," he ground out through gritted teeth. "This disciple...is unhappy!"

"There you go. If you're unhappy, just say so. From now on, if you have something to say, don't shut it up inside your heart and stifle your feelings. If you really don't like Qing Jing Peak, we'll leave once you recover your original form. It's just that in your current state, you're unsuited to constant travel. If anything happens, Cang Qiong Mountain can at least protect you."

"I do like it! But the Qing Jing Peak I like is only Qing Jing Peak—it's not Cang Qiong Mountain. And aside from Shizun and myself, it has no other people."

But, Shen Qingqiu thought, *the Qing Jing Peak you like has never really existed, has it?*

Luo Binghe mumbled, "Shizun, is it true that being with me has made you lose a lot of opportunities to do things for yourself?"

Shen Qingqiu burst out laughing. "You put on quite a good act of being asleep. Your ears are sharp too. How much of your martial aspect have you recovered?"

"Shizun...the reason I didn't want to come back wasn't because I don't like this place. Rather...it's too easy for you to be stolen away here," he mumbled, depressed. "If I were my actual self, I'd have some confidence that I could steal you back, no matter what I had to do. But as my current self, I really feel like...I can't win against others."

Shen Qingqiu rapped the top of his head. "Who asked you to win? You don't need to steal me; Shizun will go with you himself."

The appearance of one's conversation partner was truly of utmost importance. If this were the adult version Luo Binghe, Shen Qingqiu wouldn't have said something so nauseatingly frank even if you held a knife to his throat. But since this was the mini-version who he could pick up in his arms, and who was also willing to cling to his legs and throw a tantrum to seek comfort, Shen Qingqiu was free of all psychological pressures.

Luo Binghe lifted his face and gave him an adoring gaze.

The flowers were in bloom and the moon was round, and at this fine hour, in this beautiful scene, a faint fragrance floated on the breeze, which set a perfect mood. Anyone's heart would race.

Luo Binghe's dewy eyes blazed brighter and brighter, and finally, unable to resist, he shoved Shen Qingqiu down on the bamboo couch and pounced. He sprawled out on Shen Qingqiu's chest as the two of them stared at each other.

"Um... You can...continue."

But even if they continued, he couldn't do any of the things he wanted to...

Shen Qingqiu's expression was full of a sympathy he couldn't manage to hide.

After a while, a howl of unbearable rage escaped from Luo Binghe's still youthfully tender throat.

29

Regret of Chunshan and Song of Bingqiu

"WAIT, WAIT, calm down first."

From his place nestled between Shen Qingqiu's legs, Luo Binghe shifted even farther forward. "But this disciple saw something very interesting today. I'm afraid I won't be able to calm down for the next few days. Shizun, what should I do?"

After resting for over a month at Cang Qiong Mountain, Luo Binghe had finally recovered his original form. Shen Qingqiu knew this day wouldn't end peacefully, but he still said with composure, "That's easy. What did you see? Bring it here and show this master so we can discuss it together. But before that, get in a more normal position so we can talk properly."

Luo Binghe nodded and ignored the last request entirely. "Okay, then I'll let Shizun see."

Slow and measured, he retrieved a thin little booklet from his lapels. The little booklet was illustrated in a flowery style, rather gaudy at first glance—not to mention familiar.

Shen Qingqiu was still pondering this familiarity when Luo Binghe flipped it open, straightened his back, and began to recite in a bright, clear voice.

"Once night fell, Luo Binghe lay on the bed, tossing and turning, unable to find slumber. He was used to passing out on the cold floor of the woodshed, and suddenly finding himself in a bed, he found it difficult to fall asleep—especially when the shizun he so longed for lay not far away, just on the other side of a single screen and a gauze canopy. The day's solicitous inquiries and attentive concern replayed before his eyes, fanning the fire in the pit of his stomach hotter and hotter, higher and higher..."

Shen Qingqiu was speechless.

Luo Binghe continued reading with a straight face. "Luo Binghe felt his way to the bed. Cloth rustled beneath his hands as he loosened the ties of Shen Qingqiu's inner robe, and when he reached beneath the layer of cloth, he found fine, smooth skin, and strong, supple muscle. Dazed and spellbound, he tore the waist sash in two..."

Shen Qingqiu cast a glance at the waist sash Luo Binghe had just ferociously torn open and tossed on the ground. Goosebumps rose all over his body. What was he supposed to say to this?!

Luo Binghe lowered the booklet, looked up, and said, in all seriousness, "It says here that this disciple lost his virginity the same night he moved out of the woodshed. In the flames of desire, lurid intentions bloomed. I snuck into the Bamboo House's inner room in the middle of the night under cover of darkness, and while shizun was in the grip of a nightmare, unable to move an inch, did such and such and so and so, amorous and tender, until the break of dawn."

What the fuck?! If I remember correctly, Luo Binghe was only fifteen back then! Utterly devoid of conscience! Perverse lunacy!

Luo Binghe continued as he flipped. "Though the Luo Binghe in this novel is more audacious than this disciple and dares to act more boldly, his feelings for Shizun aren't far from the truth."

"If you really 'dared to act' like that, this master couldn't guarantee he wouldn't take your life on the spot."

Luo Binghe leaned down and kissed Shen Qingqiu's earlobe. Warm breath spilled over the rim of his ear as he cajoled him. "Shizun, weren't you the one who said we would explore together? At least give it a second glance."

He didn't dare look. If that text burned out his eyes, there was no way to get them replaced!

Luo Binghe chuckled. "You won't look? Then allow this disciple to read it for you." Voice expressive, he went on.

"After Shizun lost his chastity to 'Luo Binghe' that night, he severely punished this rebellious disciple and intended to banish him from Cang Qiong Mountain Sect, but in the end, he couldn't bear to do it. He merely treated him coldly until the Immortal Alliance Conference was beset by sudden misfortune. Master and disciple were separated, several years passed, and when they reunited, 'Shen Qingqiu' finally fell into 'Luo Binghe's' clutches. Look here, Shizun, the Huan Hua Palace Water Prison chapter is really something else."

Shen Qingqiu couldn't compete with Luo Binghe's stubbornness, and he truly was a bit curious, so in a momentary slip of control, he snuck a glance out of the corner of his eye.

This single glance burned him to a perfect crisp.

Regret of Chunshan, Part 37: Flirtation in the Water Prison

SHEN QINGQIU shook his head, voice slurred as he spoke. "Luo…Binghe, you…let me go…"

Luo Binghe gripped the globes of his rear, kneaded them once, twice, then pulled them apart to expose the hole that had been ravaged countless times. "Shizun, now you're crying for me to let you go,"

he said with a wicked laugh. "Back then, did you ever think this day would come?"

Shen Qingqiu sobbed and sobbed. "It's too swollen… It won't fit…"

It was indeed very swollen, so much so that the sight was nearly unbearable. The ring of reddened flesh was so swollen that it nearly glowed, and it was shut tight, looking as if it would be most difficult to penetrate. Luo Binghe felt some sympathy for him, but he soon remembered how Shen Qingqiu had abandoned him, and his hatred rose yet again. Cold and merciless, he plunged inside once more, but before he got even halfway, he found further progress difficult, for while the inflamed entrance was warmer and slicker than usual, it was also narrower and tighter.

Tears rolled down Shen Qingqiu's face like raindrops on flower petals, his breath hitching in gasps, as pain blossomed along with the sudden and forceful intrusion of that cock. But his hands were tied, and even as he twisted and struggled in vain, he was unable to escape.

Shen Qingqiu couldn't speak. *Holy shit, what the motherfuck is this?!*

Who the fuck was this guy crying "like raindrops on flower petals"?! And who was Mr. Tall, Dark, and Deadly?!

The one who cried the most every time they got in bed was Luo Binghe, okay?!

He looked at the author's name: Sleeping Willow Flower. The name alone made him sound like some sort of scoundrel; he had to be the same sort of person as Airplane Shooting Towards the Sky.

After Luo Binghe finished reading, he said, "As for this disciple, he never could have forced you like this. If Shizun merely furrowed his brow, this disciple wouldn't have been able to continue. How could I let Shizun sob like this yet still not stop? The depiction here is a bit unrealistic."

Not only was it unrealistic... It was OOC. *Completely* OOC—OOC all the way off the map!

This fucking *Regret of Chunshan*! It was basically trashy RPF porn fanfic that was OOC to the heavens, yet it had somehow become so popular! No wonder he always heard girls say "the trashier a work, the more easily it becomes a niche hit"!

But that wasn't the main point... Shen Qingqiu cursed the author of this porn book and porn ballad to be unable to get it up for the rest of his life! Single dog! It'd serve him right to have to jerk it to the end of his days—to jerk it until he died, forever unable to find a wife!

"Why is Shizun's face going all red and white?" asked Luo Binghe. "The later parts are even more tempestuous and thrilling; they're worthy of both cheers and applause. In truth, I revered Shizun's body like a holy object in those five years and never dared to sully it in the slightest, but this is just a little booklet circulating in the streets. It can't hurt to read and laugh at such fantastical takes."

Shen Qingqiu eyed the title of this part: *Regret of Chunshan, Part 47: Five Years of Empty Waiting.*

His balls were going to shatter all over the ground.

No, no, no! This title! He wouldn't even get near enough to pass the gates into this brave new world! It didn't need to be this kinky, did it?!

But reality would prove that Shen Qingqiu had underestimated the depths the author of *Regret of Chunshan* was willing to plumb.

The candlelight flickered. Even if Shen Qingqiu was insensate, his brows were dark and his lips were red, his entire person dyed with a flush of spring.

Luo Binghe looped Shen Qingqiu's nerveless arms around his own neck before he went to kiss him, to make it look as if Shen Qingqiu had woken up and was hooking his arms around Luo Binghe's neck to return the kiss.

The curtains hung to the floor, swaying without a breeze. Amidst a desperate entanglement, tousled clothes rustled to the ground. Luo Binghe's low gasping breaths could be heard from behind the swaying gauze.

Shen Qingqiu splayed lifelessly on top of Luo Binghe, locked within Luo Binghe's embrace by the firm grip of his arms. The two pearls on his chest were sucked until they were swollen and scarlet red, like a pair of small ripe fruits. His rear was covered with green and purple handprints. The hole that had been fucked until it was a luscious red and still gently clasping the half-hard cock within it, a mess of liquid shining between his thighs.

Shen Qingqiu was going to cry.

This wasn't even "out of the question"! This was practically a challenge to basic values and the limits of morality!

And he'd heard mpreg novels were very popular on the Green JJ. *Heavens protect me, please don't let* Regret of Chunshan *have a pregnancy arc, too, thank you!*

As the pages flipped by, he would yet be struck by lightning from the heavens.

Regret of Chunshan, Part 55: Heavenly Demon's Nefarious Blood

THEY WERE PRESSED chest to chest. Luo Binghe could feel the tender, supple skin of the person in his arms; it was moist and glowing as they soaked in the mountain spring.

Without a word, he embraced Shen Qingqiu and leaned down to kiss him deeply, sometimes biting his lips and lightly tugging, sometimes plunging his tongue inside to brashly tangle with his.

Though Shen Qingqiu was unwilling, the heavenly demon's blood stirred within his stomach, and his entire body went weak. In addition, he was being kissed until he couldn't breathe, his chest rising up and down in uneven intervals, and as his nipples brushed against Luo Binghe's muscles, they slowly hardened. Without his notice, his legs had been pried open, and Luo Binghe plunged inside.

Though they had been entangled from dusk 'til dawn for a while now, and Shen Qingqiu had grown used to Luo Binghe's enormous length, this sudden intrusion was still extremely uncomfortable—especially as, when that fleshy member speared open his inner walls, warm spring water poured in along with it, and his entrance drank more than a little bit of liquid. The legs hanging from both sides of Luo Binghe's waist squeezed him tight, and his insides fluttered as well. Luo Binghe was only thrilled at how that little hole squeezed and sucked him in. Roughly kneading Shen Qingqiu's bottom to make him relax, he adjusted his position.

Not long afterward, Shen Qingqiu caught his breath and scolded him through his tears. "Get out!"

Luo Binghe smiled. "Shizun chides me so, but his body seems to disagree."

Shen Qingqiu clenched his teeth, unwilling to give in. "If you hadn't fed me that poison blood…how could I be so tormented by an ingrate like you…?"

Under the control of heavenly demon's blood, the only option left to him was to obediently spread his legs even further, relax his hole, and allow Luo Binghe to fuck him. His flesh seductively cradled Luo Binghe, lightly clinging to him. Shen Qingqiu's breaths came in gasps, on the brink of sobs, and after a particularly hard thrust, his lips drew tight, low whines seeping out from his nose. Luo Binghe had one arm under his bottom, keeping their hips tightly interlocked, as his other hand blithely smacked Shen Qingqiu's round, snow-white cheeks once with every thrust. Shen Qingqiu was overcome with humiliation.

Luo Binghe didn't let him rest for long after that round and carried him out of the spring. Once Shen Qingqiu left the water, his limbs and hole tightened, beset by the cold air. Luo Binghe set him down like a sacrifice on an altar, bare, on a nearby chunk of limestone. There he drew him into a interlocked embrace below the open sky.

The limestone was ice-cold, and Shen Qingqiu began to squirm as soon as he was set down. His skin was fair and pale, and after that vigorous round of lovemaking and the warmth of the spring, his entire body was flushed a bewitching pink. Black eyes painted like stars swelled with dewy ripples as their focus blurred, tired and drowsy, his spirit like dying embers. He turned his head, refusing to look straight at his traitorous disciple, Luo Binghe.

Luo Binghe slotted himself between his legs, slinging those pale calves over his shoulders, and sank his cock inside him, then began to thrust at an unhurried pace. Every inch of Shen Qingqiu's fleshy walls were stretched to the limit as they were scraped by that pillar. The creases at his entrance were stretched smooth.

Shen Qingqiu had nothing to say.

Drugging, non-con, force—what a marvelous buffet. This author was having a lot of fun, weren't they…

"Actually, I never imagined that heavenly demon's blood could be used in such a way," said Luo Binghe.

Shen Qingqiu was silent. After bearing witness to the depths of the original *Proud Immortal Demon Way*'s depravity, it wasn't as if he had never thought of it. He'd just never expected that one day, this usage would be applied to him.

"My eyes have been opened," said Shen Qingqiu.

Luo Binghe nodded. "My eyes have been opened." And he continued, "So, this disciple can't have had his eyes opened for nothing, can he?"

"Luo Binghe, even though this master has allowed you to… I never allowed you all this *variety*," Shen Qingqiu said in a warning tone.

Luo Binghe started. "Oh. This disciple understands."

He looked a bit disappointed, but he didn't push the issue. Now Shen Qingqiu was the one feeling uneasy.

Luo Binghe had never made any requests of him when it came to these matters. Because of his lackluster skill, he was always cautious in the extreme, and he even somewhat capitulated to Shen Qingqiu. Now he had finally acquired some instructional materials and found a bit of self-confidence, hoping to try them out together, only for Shen Qingqiu to toss a basin of cold water over his head...

Shen Qingqiu squirmed in his seat. After a while, he finally picked up his fan to cover his face and said with some reserve, "How do you want to do it?"

All at once, Luo Binghe came alive, like a flower blooming in the warmth of spring. Shen Qingqiu was inwardly pleased by this, and he told himself he might as well forsake his poor face and play along. They had already done it either way; what did he need face for?

Just to be safe, he forced himself to pick up *Regret of Chunshan* and flip through it rapidly even as a vein jumped in his forehead, but he didn't find any positions or techniques that seemed *too* illogical and so relaxed a little bit—

Only to turn around and see Luo Binghe walking toward him, all smiles as he earnestly held up an even thicker booklet. "Shizun, why are you looking at that one?"

Shen Qingqiu had no words. The cover of the booklet Luo Binghe was holding indicated it was the promising newcomer that held the honor of being a target of aggressive restriction alongside *Regret of Chunshan*: *Song of Bingqiu.* Its author was listed as: The Three Holy Mothers.

"This one has even more to teach, and is far more detailed," said Luo Binghe. "It doesn't take long to get the hang of putting it into practice either. This disciple brewed a jar of flower wine according to its instructions. Shall we see whether its effect is as described?"

Looks to me like it just has even lower depths to plumb!

Shen Qingqiu knew that under no circumstances was this jar of wine meant for drinking.

Wait a minute. The props were all prepared—had Luo Binghe just been putting on a pitiful act to mess with him?!

Luo Binghe pulled Shen Qingqiu's hips up, leaving his rear pointed high as his back arched into a limber curve, his back toward Luo Binghe.

This was the condition Shen Qingqiu had set for accepting his request: if Luo Binghe insisted on trying something from the book, he would do it from behind, or else Shen Qingqiu really wouldn't be able to hang on to his easily wounded dignity. Though Luo Binghe was eternally obsessed with "fucking Shizun face-to-face," he was impatient to put what he had learned into practice, and he had learned from this booklet that the person on the bottom could more easily feel pleasure if they did it from behind, so he happily agreed.

He picked up that jar of rare fine wine, pressed its long, skinny neck to the tight pink entrance on Shen Qingqiu's lower half, and slowly pushed it in.

The neck of the jar was tapered, so it entered easily, but the farther in it was pushed, the tighter his hole clung to it. The chilly wine poured in, and his insides clenched at the sensation. Shen Qingqiu grabbed the blankets beneath him, brow knitting together.

He could hear the gurgles of the wine as it poured into his intestines, and the swollen drooping sensation in his abdomen was more and more obvious. Shen Qingqiu couldn't help but say, "That's enough..."

Luo Binghe obediently stopped, but the mouth of the wine jar remained inserted inside him.

This wine was refreshing at first blush, but its delayed effects were strong. Soon, Shen Qingqiu's insides began to burn fiery-hot.

Unable to relieve himself of this painful itching sensation, he shifted his arms to crawl forward slightly.

This time, Luo Binghe didn't stop him. The mouth of the jar slid out of his entrance with a pop. Shen Qingqiu clenched before the wine could dribble out, and then...he didn't know what to do.

Letting wine pour out of his ass right in front of Luo Binghe would be far too humiliating. But he had only moved a bit and he already couldn't take it; he was afraid his hold would slip with even the slightest movement.

Luo Binghe draped himself over Shen Qingqiu, one hand playing with his pointed, pale red nipples as he gnawed on the smooth skin of his shoulder. His other arm lifted Shen Qingqiu's sore, weakened hips and lined up his cock. The hot, hard tip poked threateningly against his rear until it found that small hole and rubbed against it.

Looks like he really did learn a lot from that damned little booklet... Shen Qingqiu couldn't take this teasing. His hands twisted in the sheets beneath him and sweat rose all over his body.

As soon as his attention had wandered for a second, his clenched shut entrance was breached in one decisive thrust.

Shen Qingqiu immediately went limp from waist to legs. His arms also failed to support the weight of his upper body, and he sprawled over the bed. The only good thing was that with Luo Binghe's considerable size, his entrance had been entirely plugged. The wine was sealed securely inside Shen Qingqiu, unable to leak out. It still hurt having that thing thrust inside him all at once, but amidst the pain, something seemed to be different.

The wine lit his insides on fire, the feeling full and hot and wet. When Luo Binghe began to thrust, Shen Qingqiu couldn't stop the liquid from spilling out as his delicate flesh was pulled outward, dripping like flowing nectar. The wet sounds that came with each movement made his entire face flush with embarrassment. A tingling sensation alongside an ache spread from deep inside his lower belly. That spot inside him thirsted to be rammed roughly against, to be fucked raw until it itched, but that flared head only brushed against that patch of tender flesh. Shen Qingqiu's waist twisted in frustration, and he couldn't stop himself from pushing his hips back into the thrusts.

Luo Binghe missed none of his tiny movements. He paused, panted for breath, then continued joyfully. "Shizun? Does it feel good? Am I doing well?!"

He pistoned in and out, and more and more of the faint red translucent wine leaked out from the point of their union. Liquid splashed between Shen Qingqiu's fair thighs. Fine wine and his disciple's cock surged inside him, raising waves. Shen Qingqiu's knuckles went white as he clung to the blankets, and he clenched his eyes shut in anguish.

Luo Binghe wouldn't give up. "Does it feel good? Does it feel good or doesn't it?"

Shen Qingqiu mumbled something. Luo Binghe couldn't make it out, so he leaned down to hear him, sending that thing between his legs even deeper inside.

Shen Qingqiu's tailbone ached with the stretch. He gasped, "Face…face…"

The burn of the wine had made Shen Qingqiu red all over; as if his entire self had been steamed in liquor, even his breath took on a refreshing flavor. Luo Binghe was tempted to lean in and kiss him at an angle, tongue searching inside his mouth, and found that even his saliva carried the heady fragrance of wine.

"Shizun," he said, "do you want to see my face?"

Shen Qingqiu nodded near imperceptibly.

"You better be sure. It was on Shizun's request that we're doing it from behind. If you want to be face-to-face now... I'm afraid it won't be so easy to turn back."

His low, hoarse voice puffed warm breath into Shen Qingqiu's ear. Shen Qingqiu's head spun, and he dazedly clenched his hole.

Luo Binghe abruptly pulled out and roughly flipped him over into the powerless position of lying face-up.

A pink flush clouded Shen Qingqiu's pale cheeks. His eyes and the tip of his nose were especially red, and some tears hung from the ends of his eyelashes. Luo Binghe kissed each of them, one by one, the fingers of one hand tenderly circling the soft outer rim of his entrance as the other slid under his back to support him. He said lightly, "Shizun...look."

He guided Shen Qingqiu's chin. As soon as Shen Qingqiu looked down, he saw the mess of wine and fluids at the base of his fair thighs. Between two plump mounds of flesh, a flower seemed to have bloomed, its ring of petals swollen a little larger, leaving some of the entrance outturned as it twitched pitifully and dribbled white fluid.

Shen Qingqiu couldn't manage to speak, and he subconsciously lifted an arm to cover his eyes.

Luo Binghe gave him a few comforting kisses on his cheek, then thrust in again.

Again, it burned like fire. Luo Binghe let go of his back and Shen Qingqiu collapsed, black hair splayed everywhere across the bed, fingers powerlessly sinking into the taut muscles of Luo Binghe's back, his neck arched.

After another round of vigorous thrusts, the wine in Shen Qingqiu's belly had more or less entirely leaked out. The passage that had been thoroughly washed with strong wine was in an excellent state, warm and flexible, sensitive and amorous, but guarded, yearning to squeeze and cling to the outside invader with all its strength, yet afraid this thing would tear its thin walls. Wet sounds came from Shen Qingqiu's hole, and his legs locked tightly around Luo Binghe's waist, buttery-smooth inner thighs rubbing against his skin, toes curled, a drunken look on his face.

The fragrance of alcohol drifted through the air, going to their heads. Shen Qingqiu was truly...intoxicated.

But before he sank so deep as to lose consciousness, Luo Binghe woke him up. He put an arm beneath Shen Qingqiu's hips and stood up from the bed.

Shen Qingqiu sank down under his own weight. The cock inside him instantly pushed through layers of flesh and hit a spot extremely deep inside him. His heart was nearly thrust right up into his throat, like what was piercing him in that instant was a honed sword, and he began to squirm desperately. But at that moment, he was entirely suspended in midair, and however much he twisted, he could only further embed that invading object into his hole, making this traitorous disciple's length furiously grow in girth, stretching him until he felt about to retch.

But the scariest part was still to come. Luo Binghe began to walk.

This position sent Luo Binghe's cock extremely deep inside Shen Qingqiu. With every step, that thing didn't pull out, but rather vaguely jostled about inside him, the angle constantly changing, but always enjoying a massage from Shen Qingqiu's hole as it clenched and trembled. Moreover, in addition to being fucked so deep he felt he was going to retch, Shen Qingqiu became afraid he would fall.

He really couldn't take it anymore. He gasped out in fits and starts, "Wait, wait a minute... It's too deep... Bing...Binghe, put—put me down..."

Luo Binghe nibbled on his earlobe and mumbled through slightly heavy breaths, "Shizun...it's not deep enough... Still not enough..."

He had stuffed Shen Qingqiu's belly full! "How deep do you want...?" Shen Qingqiu groaned. "Where else are you trying to go?!"

Having had his fill of fucking him while standing, Luo Binghe pressed him down on the table. Shen Qingqiu's upper body was shoved down against the top of the table, his arms twisted behind his back as his legs trailed weakly to the floor.

The edge of the table fit into the crook of his pelvis, spread wide open, as Luo Binghe's hips crashed against his, the table shaking under their movements.

Shen Qingqiu's face was pressed to the table as that hardness moved in and out between his legs. He was already at his limit, trembling all the way from his hips to his toes, nearly unable to stand. But Luo Binghe was still holding those two pale mounds of flesh in his hands, pressing them together in the middle so he could experience the overwhelming pleasure of being squeezed by hole and ass all at once.

Shen Qingqiu felt more tormented than ever by the foreign object between his hips—not to mention how his bottom was being kneaded and slapped in a way that didn't hurt, but which was extremely humiliating. Not long afterward, Luo Binghe switched techniques again. He only pulled out a little bit each time, then thrust back in even harder as the flesh beneath his hands was squeezed out of shape with the force of his grip. Shen Qingqiu sprawled over the table, his center burning under this steady grind in a way that both hurt and itched. He felt on the verge of insanity but was locked in place, unable to move an inch, forced to take everything Luo Binghe gave him.

Luo Binghe truly deserved the title of star student. He could overwhelm someone simply by copying from the lesson materials!

Shen Qingqiu wanted to weep but couldn't find the tears, and he could only weakly whimper, "You...what exactly did you read...?"

30

Honeymoon

AFTER HARBORING the devil incarnate Luo Binghe for a dozen or so days, Qing Jing Peak's disciples finally couldn't take the harassment anymore and begged Shen Qingqiu to take the person in question and "lie low."

"Shizun, I hate Bai Zhan Peak," Ning Yingying whined. "Hate, hate, hate! They're such brutes! They've destroyed the mountain gates so many times already!"

"Shizun…I really didn't tell them this time! This disciple swears; you have to believe me!" Ming Fan complained tearfully. He nervously glanced at Luo Binghe. "Why not let Luo-shidi out to spar with them a few times? After beating them up enough times, they'll no longer dare to harass Qing Jing Peak!"

Luo Binghe was utterly unmoved. "Shizun and I barely have any time to discuss business. Where would I get the extra hours to spar with those wild monkeys?"

Shen Qingqiu demurely waved his fan, unspeaking.

To be fair, this so-called "discussing business" was more researching new dishes, cleaning the Bamboo House's cutlery and furniture, and coming to act cute and sweet with all those propositions, no matter the time and location…

Ming Fan sniveled tearfully as he wailed. "Shizun, do something!

An Ding Peak is no longer willing to come fix our gates. Every time this disciple has to descend and ascend the mountain, traveling several hundred kilometers and spending out of his own purse—"

His howling annoyed Shen Qingqiu to no end.

Ultimately, he finally and magnanimously did a great deed: accompanied by Ming Fan's overflowing gratitude and Ning Yingying's reluctance to see them go, the great master left Qing Jing Peak.

Hence, he was rather depressed.

Shit, what the hell was this?!

Shidi L— had condoned his subordinates' and minions' (ahem) attack on Shixiong S—'s gates, and he hadn't even provided any compensation afterward. Having suffered economic losses, Shixiong S— went to Shidi X—'s department to request an allocation of public funds, but Shidi X— refused to approve it.

Then Disciple M— not only demonstrated zero selfless spirit with regards to contributing to the collective funds, he even kicked his own master off the mountain.

Traitors, the lot of you!

That said, Luo Binghe looked very happy. As long as he could cling to Shen Qingqiu, anywhere they went was the same in his eyes. Plus, it was more in line with his desires to not have that group of eyesores hovering over them every day.

"Shizun, where shall we go next?" he said in delight, tugging on Shen Qingqiu's arm.

Shen Qingqiu glanced down at Luo Binghe's pose, at how he had encircled his arm with both of his own, and found it hard to look. He really was becoming more and more like a maiden.

They looked exactly like two "Mushroom-Picking Little Girls"[10] walking out the door, hand in hand. ╭(′▽`) ╭(′▽`)╯

Shen Qingqiu was blasted by his own man-made landmine. He asked in response, "Do you have anywhere that you'd like to go?"

Luo Binghe gave it some thought. "How about we go to places we've been to in the past and see how they've changed?"

Thereafter, the two arrived at the first stop following their eviction from Cang Qiong Mountain, Shuang Hu City.

Originally, Shen Qingqiu had intended to go by sword, which would have let them arrive within an incense time. But Luo Binghe seemed to have gotten some kind of idea in his head and insisted that they use a carriage.

Using one was fine; Shen Qingqiu didn't care either way. Who could have guessed that after they got on the carriage, Luo Binghe would use that shyly expectant expression (that he thought he was hiding well) to stare at him?

The carriage interior wasn't very large, so Shen Qingqiu had nowhere to run; he took that burning stare until his hair stood on end.

Are you asking for car sex? Don't even think about it! This master absolutely won't agree! You really are a traitor!

Luo Binghe stared at him for a long time, but when he saw no particular gestures from Shen Qingqiu, meaning they weren't of one heart, his head slowly drooped. He prodded his fingers together cutely. "Shizun...don't you remember?" he asked, a bit at a loss.

Shen Qingqiu realized then that, when it came to his everyday internal monologue, it basically always started with a beat of silence.

"Remember?" he asked. "Remember what?"

---

10 A Chinese nursery rhyme.

Luo Binghe was disappointed. "Back when the Qing Jing Peak disciples left the mountain together for a training experience, you let me ride with you..."

To think Luo Binghe remembered even such dusty old affairs with such clarity! Meanwhile, Shen Qingqiu had pretty much forgotten most of it.

Luo Binghe sighed. "So Shizun really didn't remember."

Faced with this contrast, Shen Qingqiu couldn't help but feel guilty. He waved his hand, letting Luo Binghe lean against him, then rubbed his cheek to pacify him. "Shizun only temporarily forgot. I'm sorry."

Having been pacified, Luo Binghe was satisfied, his lips curving upward. "Mm. Shizun's acts of kindness toward me far surpassed this moment. How could he remember each and every one?"

Pure silence.

Could you not head canon me as such a loving Holy Father!? I really had just forgotten! I can't live up to your divine expectations!

Shen Qingqiu and Luo Binghe wandered leisurely down the main road past Shuang Hu City's gates. Stalls crammed with eye-catching goods bordered them on either side. In the middle of it all, a gorgeous banner fluttered in the breeze.

Shen Qingqiu's gaze was drawn to the banner before it dropped to the face of the stall owner sitting beneath it. His smile, with its trademark "subtle, looking warm and elegant at first glance, but in truth cool and lofty" cast froze upon his lips.

Luo Binghe was far too sharp. "What's wrong, Shizun?" he instantly asked. "An acquaintance?"

Crowds thronged around the small table below the banner. It seemed to be a jianghu fortune-teller's stall. Behind the table sat a beautiful and sultry woman, radiating a thousand types of grace. With a toss of her fine hair and a lift of her lovely face, she met Shen Qingqiu's eyes from a distance—and promptly looked like she'd swallowed a kilogram of arsenic.

But then her gaze turned and landed on the face of Luo Binghe, who stood beside him. Her love for this specific type of man came first above all, and her eyes shone with a sudden bright light. So, she took the initiative to greet him: "I trust that the immortal master has been well!"

"It's been a while," said Shen Qingqiu. "The madam is even lovelier than she was when last we met."

This beautiful woman was Madam Meiyin.

She waved away the enamored male customers by her table, clearing out space for them while smiling delightedly. "The immortal master is radiant with happiness today. So? Did my words from our last meeting not all prove true?"

Though she was certainly talking to Shen Qingqiu, her eyes were turned in Luo Binghe's direction, and her flirtatious air was both enchanting and seductive, making clear her true intentions.

It had been a long time since Shen Qingqiu recalled the fortune Madam Meiyin had told for him way back when, but the keywords had been: younger; illustrious status; outstanding talent; first-class beauty; often together; deeply in love... Shen Qingqiu realized with a shock that every single one had been dead-on.

"This Shen deeply admires the madam's skill," he said. "However, it seems that back then, you forgot to tell me the most important thing."

She'd gone on and on, hyping it all up until it had practically been raining flowers, but she'd failed to say: "Shen Qingqiu, your fated partner is a fucking man!"

Luo Binghe blinked a little, then smiled. "Shizun, your relationship with this madam seems quite intimate."

Though he was smiling, at these words, Shen Qingqiu felt a toothache coming on.

When he thought about it, Luo Binghe and Madam Meiyin had originally been meant to be a pair of cheaters who engaged in countless one-night stands. But now they sat very properly opposite one another as they each talked past the other, and the atmosphere was supremely uncomfortable. Indeed, it made for an extremely unsettling picture.

Shen Qingqiu gave a hollow laugh. "It's not intimate. Not intimate at all. It has been many years since we met. I never thought we'd meet again in the jianghu, nor that the madam would have started this sort of business in Shuang Hu City."

Madam Meiyin humphed. "Isn't this all thanks to that cultivator who accompanied your distinguished self on your previous patronage?"

"Which cultivator?" Luo Binghe suddenly said.

Shen Qingqiu's smile froze a second time.

Madam Meiyin commenced angrily complaining. "Don't blame me for speaking badly behind his back, but when you came, we extended such a courteous invitation, and we treated neither of you immortal masters poorly. Yet he was truly incredible—collapsing half my cavern right off the bat and scaring away most of my sisters. The next few times we met, he wouldn't leave me even the slightest bit of face! I've lived for a long time, but I have *never* met such an unfeeling man, one who understands neither romance nor tenderness, who only runs about fighting and killing. Pah!"

Your name's been spat upon, Liu Qingge. You've actually been spat upon!

The kind of violent actions described could only be attributed to one person. Of course Luo Binghe understood, and he stared at Shen Qingqiu. "Shizun, was it Liu...-shishu? When did you leave Cang Qiong Mountain alone together?"

Shen Qingqiu saw the veins bulging in his forehead and coughed dryly. "That was...when you were absent."

Luo Binghe pinched his palm hard. "Shizun, could you give a concrete explanation to your disciple as to what exactly happened between you, Liu...-shishu, and this succubus, who's as beautiful as a flower?"

Coaxing Luo Binghe was already a piece of cake for Shen Qingqiu. The steps were:

First, calmly say, "Not as beautiful as you."

Then, before Madam Meiyin's spasming smile, promise, "Nothing happened, really."

If this doesn't work, repeat steps 1 and 2.

Madam Meiyin clearly thought the flames hadn't been fanned high enough. "I did throw some of our succubus's Mesmerizing Fragrance on that cultivator you were with before I left," she said from the side. "Though given his frigid nature, I doubt it was much of a problem."

A succubus's Mesmerizing Fragrance; the name alone told you everything. An aphrodisiac!

Luo Binghe's face was rapidly filled with rage. "'Nothing happened?'"

I swear to the heavens, really, nothing happened! I didn't even have to jerk him off!

Luo Binghe was both jealous and bitter. "This disciple was in the Endless Abyss cutting his way through thorns, while Shizun was surrounded with green hills and crystal waters and enjoying himself with other men...”

What the hell do you mean, “other men”—can't you use proper terms like “colleagues” or “sect siblings”?!

Shen Qingqiu waved his fan with incomparable integrity and humphed. “What do you mean by ‘enjoying himself’? In a desolate mountain full of frenzied monsters, one person kicks the other into a freezing watering hole and gives them pneumonia. What's there to envy in something like that?!”

“That's all?”

“That's all.”

Madam Meiyin chewed her nails. “What do you mean ‘watering hole’!” she said hatefully. “That was my beloved rose pool...”

Since they'd come to Shuang Hu City, naturally they needed to look for something to do. For example, they ought to at least eliminate some pests for the civilians.

After asking around, it turned out that Chen Manor was yet again experiencing strange incidents.

That one year, the wicked, vicious Skinner Demon had transformed into the old master's beloved concubine Die-er and hidden within his manor. After they'd killed her, the room in the wing where she'd once lived had been the site of continuous disturbances: every night there were wails and screams that sent all the residents into a panic. This had remained unresolved for years.

Councilor Chen was already approaching seventy years old; his hair was a snowy white, but his ambitions were the same as ever. Many years ago, for better or worse, the only lovely concubine clinging to him had been Die-er. But today, he had a girl on either side, and they made for a beautiful pair of matching wives. The Skinner Demon who lurked at his side in the past hadn't weakened his ardent passion for women in the slightest.

This old gentleman was already of advanced age, but his memory was by no means poor. When he saw Shen Qingqiu, he even loudly called out to him: "Immortal Master Shen."

Immortal Master Shen's lofty aloofness was the same as it had been last time around. He waited until Old Master Chen asked about the young master beside him, then finally tugged his lips up a little and said gently, "This is indeed my little disciple from back then."

Old Master Chen smiled. "No wonder he looked so familiar. Only after seeing this immortal master and his beloved disciple together did I realize how many years had passed."

The conventional exchange of greetings was naturally handed to Luo Binghe, who'd already assumed his former role as the little secretary who handled everything. Shen Qingqiu was happy to stand aside and shut his mouth, sliding into his badass poser act.

As he watched the Badass Darkened Demon Lord Luo Binghe work patiently, acting as sweet as a true apple of his eye, Shen Qingqiu inevitably began to float with happiness. It felt so *wonderful*; his gaze on Luo Binghe couldn't help but fill with more and more parental affection. Meanwhile, with every two lines Luo Binghe spoke, he looked over at Shen Qingqiu as well—and once his gaze shifted over, it was unable to leave. In this way, master and disciple spent a long period of time making eyes at each other before Shen Qingqiu suddenly and finally snapped out of it.

How immoral were they being?!

On their way to the room in question, Luo Binghe kept trying to hold his hand. Shen Qingqiu was 1) worried about outsiders, and

2) wanted to tease him, so he purposely refused to let him. The two of them skirted around each other, whipping out all sorts of tricks. If anyone from the cultivation world or Demon Realm had seen this master and disciple duo using their sect's techniques to play fight (flirt), until those arts were unrecognizable, they would definitely have coughed up three liters of blood.

As no one dared to approach the room that was rumored to be haunted, it was naturally very quiet and peaceful. The courtyard was the same courtyard as it had been when last they saw it. It hadn't changed at all, except for the considerable amount of yin energy. When he saw that, at last, there were no people around, Luo Binghe latched on to Shen Qingqiu without delay, rubbing against him as he held his waist from behind, his chin hooked over Shen Qingqiu's shoulder. He asked in a whisper, "Does Shizun remember this place?"

Of course he remembered. Wasn't this the place where he'd first turned on easy mode?!

All right, that was a joke. How could he not remember? This was the place where he'd screwed Luo Binghe over for the first time, and so terribly.

Back then, in order to preserve his own life, he'd almost let the Skinner Demon strike Luo Binghe on the head. It had been a rather unkind thing to do, and now that he'd recalled it, he even felt bad. He was too ashamed to think about it deeply.

When he didn't answer, Luo Binghe began to bitterly complain. "Shizun, you...you've really forgotten? This disciple is so anguished."

Ever since the two of them had begun fooling around (ahem), Luo Binghe hadn't been able to pass a single day without becoming anguished at least several dozen times. When Shen Qingqiu spoke a couple of words to other people, he'd become anguished; when Shen Qingqiu took two fewer bites, he'd become anguished; when Shen Qingqiu complained that the bathtub was too small and kicked him out, he'd again become anguished... His anguish was like snacking on broad beans—showed up with a snap, then disappeared with another snap.

But now that he was standing at the scene of his former crimes, Shen Qingqiu felt guilty and couldn't help but soften a little. His roast of "crazy demon" dissipated before it could be posted. He quickly reached up and patted Luo Binghe's cheek. "Don't be angry. Today, Shizun will grant you one request. But let's deal with the evil spirit here first."

Luo Binghe was delighted. "Really?"

"When has Shizun ever—" Shen Qingqiu was about to continue, but he shortly shut his mouth to avoid tragically embarrassing himself. Whether he finished with "lied to you" or "screwed you over," both would basically be slapping himself in the face.

"Since Shizun said so..." Luo Binghe pulled out length after length of red rope, his face flushed.

Hello, immortal-binding cable! Goodbye, immortal-binding cable!

When Luo Binghe saw Shen Qingqiu's look of sheer disbelief, he didn't force it. He just sighed, staring up at the sky. "For some reason," he said softly, "ever since the day this disciple safely escaped from the Skinner Demon, on many nights, he experienced strange dreams."

Uh, what do you mean by strange dreams? The kind of dream where you have to wash your underwear after waking up?

Shen Qingqiu had sinned! It turned out that he had even been the pubescent Luo Binghe's Sexual Awakening 101 instructor.

A person's object of sexual epiphany was very important. Even if it wasn't a mega-buxom older lady with all her flowing curves, it ought to at least be a slender, delicate younger girl with a demure personality. Luo Binghe's life was so unbelievably tragic that it was hard to sum up. The one who'd given him his sexual awakening had a goddamn hot dog… Shen Qingqiu wanted to bow to him while crying in sympathy.

But no matter how sympathetic, Shen Qingqiu would not give in. Though Luo Binghe's endless pestering and wheedling had ground away most of his integrity, every little bit he could retrieve counted.

Even more importantly, can we deal with official business first? There's a cloud of black fog gathering behind you. It's here! It's appeared!

Luo Binghe acted like he hadn't noticed a thing and continued giving voice to his anxieties. "Even now, this disciple is at times tormented by this dream."

If he'd said "in days past" it might have been believable, but a Luo Binghe who had mastered controlling dream realms being "tormented" by them? This lie was way too thick-faced and shameless—and said with all confidence, at that.

Shen Qingqiu put his hand on Xiu Ya and lightly chuckled. "So?"

Luo Binghe didn't even turn his head. "So, I…"

That black fog couldn't take it anymore. "&*% ¥ #@&-ers!" it snarled. "Are you both blind? Can't you see me?!"

This voice was very familiar—like that of a dear friend.

"Die-er?" asked Shen Qingqiu.

"Don't Die-er or Hua-er me—I'm *me*!" the black fog snapped. "I'm the Skinner Demon who once struck fear into this city!"

Shen Qingqiu was speechless.

Was this really that insignificant monster that he'd killed with a slap during a beginner-level quest? So the rumored vengeful spirit had been this guy all along. In both life and death, they didn't forget to harass the residents of this manor. What a work ethic!

The black fog forcefully spat out a mass of black smoke. Shen Qingqiu guessed that to them, this was the same as spitting out a mouthful of saliva.

"You two adulterers dare come to fool around before me, completely unaware of your impending death!" they snapped.

Luo Binghe furrowed his brow. "Shizun, should we just kill them, or capture them for later interrogation?"

Shen Qingqiu wanted to see just how stupid the black fog could get, so he raised his hand, signaling for Luo Binghe to stay still for now.

The black fog made a questioning sound, then drifted closer to Shen Qingqiu. "You look a bit familiar."

Of course I look familiar. The culprit who murdered you is standing right before your eyes, and all you can do is doubtfully say, "Ah, you look a bit familiar."

How many years had passed? It had to have been at least ten. So under the powerful influence of easy mode, Die-er's IQ hadn't increased in the slightest, and their memory had even declined quite a bit!

Shen Qingqiu coughed once and reminded them. "This Shen...is the Qing Jing Peak Lord."

A silence, and then the black fog exploded. "Shen Qingqiu! So it was you! Then who is he?!"

"You know him too," Shen Qingqiu said reluctantly. "He was also at the scene that time."

After the black fog thought for a long while, understanding suddenly dawned on them. "He's your little whelp of a disciple! Ha ha ha ha ha ha ha!"

Now that Die-er had finally remembered, they laughed madly without pause. "Shen Qingqiu, good and evil both receive their due; heaven enforces karma for all! To think you actually got...heh heh, by your own disciple! What an utter degenerate! Absolutely disgusting! I just knew that someone would come to exact heavenly justice!"

Shen Qingqiu had no words. *No, that's wrong. As a demon who's committed many evils and received its due retribution—which is to say dying in a single slap from someone exacting heavenly justice—a line like "good and evil both receive their dues; heaven enforces karma for all" doesn't really suit you, does it?*

As the black fog laughed and laughed, something strange happened. It was as if a great wind blew by, scattering a mass of smoke, and the black fog gradually dissipated. Only a final black wisp remained, and it was still sighing in satisfaction. "Retribution, retribution! Shen Qingqiu, you've finally met retribution. Serves you right—I can now die without regrets!"

Had they become a buddha? Ascended to heaven? Been exorcised? Their bar for dying without regrets was surely a bit too low...

And no matter how troublesome Luo Binghe was, it wasn't to the point that he could be called "retribution"!

The yin energy within the courtyard suddenly vanished.

"Shizun, shall we continue?" asked Luo Binghe.

Shen Qingqiu's lips twisted, and he looked at Luo Binghe, who was still clutching his handful of immortal-binding cables. At a loss for words, he said, "What do you want to continue?"

"Didn't Shizun say that he would grant me one request today? So, my request is to ask if Shizun would deign to cooperate a little and allow this disciple to...lightly tie him up with this immortal-binding cable, then stay bound for a while so that dream can come true and fulfill this disciple's years-long wish. Then this disciple can...die without regrets!"

Shen Qingqiu stared at them.

Though Die-er had already peacefully ascended to heaven via their own inexplicable sense of self-satisfaction, Shen Qingqiu felt like he couldn't return Xiu Ya to its sheath just yet.

He expressionlessly headed outside. Luo Binghe ran in front him, cutting him off. "Shizun, you promised."

Shen Qingqiu coldly pushed his hurt face out of the way.

"Shizun, how can you do this to me again?" Luo Binghe said accusingly.

What are you crying about? Even if you cry, it's no use. Don't embarrass us in front of outsiders!

Sure enough, when it came to this little beast, tender feelings and sympathy were fully unnecessary.

He took back his words. Luo Binghe really was karmic retribution!

31

100 Random Questions on Luo-Shen's Affinity

THE QUESTIONNAIRE interviewees: Luo Binghe x Shen Qingqiu.

The questionnaire interviewer: Airplane Shooting Towards the Sky.

The questionnaire provider: the System.

Airplane Shooting Towards the Sky's System had issued him a quest: an extremely bizarre questionnaire. He had no idea what the questionnaire was trying to ascertain. The further down he read, the more disturbing the questions became.

But no matter how disturbing it was, he had to farm some points, didn't he?!

After abandoning his dignity (what little remained in the first place) and pleading with Master Shen, Shen Qingqiu finally, reluctantly agreed to bring along that...disciple he'd raised for the purpose of completing this questionnaire.

Now presenting: Live updates from Airplane.

"Your names, please?" asked Shang Qinghua.

Having just sat down before hearing this question, Luo Binghe raised his eyebrow and said unhappily, "If you don't even know our names, why would you ask us anything?"

"Your ages?"

To tell the truth, Shen Qingqiu didn't really know the precise age of this body. He raised his head at Shang Qinghua. "Wouldn't you know better than I do?"

Shang Qinghua twirled the brush in his hand. He'd never thought about this question either, so he figured he might as well just say whatever. Therefore he randomly wrote a number down in a couple of strokes. "Your genders?"

Having received three idiotic questions right off the bat, Luo Binghe had already stopped bothering to answer.

Shen Qingqiu couldn't take it anymore either. "We've been recategorized into the Green JJ's danmei section—what do you think?"

Shang Qinghua silently drew a line through the next thirty or so similarly stupid questions, then started asking anew. "How is your personality?"

Shen Qingqiu thought for a while. "All right, probably. This Shen should be considered relatively easy to get along with."

"Don't know," said Luo Binghe.

"And what about your partner's personality?"

Shen Qingqiu began counting off traits. "Crybaby, maiden-hearted, lovesick, chuunibyou, and clingy."

A watery shimmer shone in Luo Binghe's eyes. Having been disparaged, he felt a little hurt, but he still obediently answered the question. "Naturally, Shizun's personality is the best. Gentle and strong and considerate."

Shen Qingqiu fell silent. Suddenly he felt a bit bad! *What is this?!*

He coughed dryly twice and changed his tune. "Actually, this child's personality isn't too bad. He has one good trait that is especially rare: he listens and does as he's asked. That's enough in itself."

A blush rose on Luo Binghe's cheeks.

"When did the two of you meet?" Shang Qinghua asked in a monotone. "And where?"

He already knew the answer to this question!

"The first time I met Shizun was right after I'd passed Cang Qiong Mountain's initiation trials..."

Shen Qingqiu was feeling ill at ease. At that time, Luo Binghe had met the original flavor, not him, and it wasn't a particularly wonderful memory either. He waved his fan. "Pass, pass!"

"What was your first impression of your partner?"

Luo Binghe continued to reminisce. "A lofty, untouchable immortal," he said buoyantly.

"A small bun," Shen Qingqiu said frankly. *And a handsome little sprout.*

"What do you like about your partner?"

"He listens to me well enough," Shen Qingqiu said kindly.

Luo Binghe smiled. "I like everything about Shizun."

"What do you hate?"

"Nothing," Luo Binghe said firmly.

Shen Qingqiu was a little moved by this resolute and decisive answer. So he reciprocated and also said, "Nothing."

Besides, if he really said he hated something and made Luo Binghe cry in front of someone else, that would be way too shameful...

"How do you address your partner?"

Finding this dull, Luo Binghe turned his head. "Shizun, these questions are ridiculous. Exactly what did we come here for?"

"Be good, Binghe," Shen Qingqiu said calmly. "It's just a formality. Think of it as saving your Shang-shishu's life."

"How do you want your partner to address you?"

Luo Binghe's face reddened.

This bashful reaction made an ominous premonition well up inside Shen Qingqiu. He waved his hand. "Pass! Pass, pass, pass!"

Having caught on to a possible point of interest, Shang Qinghua wheedled. "What do you mean 'pass'?! If you just 'pass, pass, pass' every single question, what's the point in even asking? Bing-ge...uh, Shizhi, go ahead and say it!"

Luo Binghe nervously glanced at Shen Qingqiu out of the corner of his eye and quietly said, "I'd like to be addressed in the way married couples normally address each other."

"Master Shen, did you hear that?" Shang Qinghua asked instantly. "Bing—ahem, Shizhi wants you to address him like you're married. Husband, hubby, honey, you choose one."

"You shut up," said Shen Qingqiu.

"If you were to compare your partner to an animal, what would they be?"

Without needing to think, Luo Binghe said, "A white crane."

"I can't think of an animal," said Shen Qingqiu. "But I do have a plant. A black lotus."

Luo Binghe didn't understand. "Shizun, do lotuses come in black too?"

"If you were giving your partner a present, what would you choose? And what present would you yourself like?"

"As long as Shizun says the word, I will give him anything he desires."

"I don't think there's anything I particularly want," Shen Qingqiu said honestly.

As a peak lord, there really didn't seem to be anything that was hard for him to get. When he thought about it, it really did feel like he was sitting on top of a mountain of gold and letting it go to waste.

"Then I want Shizun to ignore everyone else and stay by my side for three days."

Shang Qinghua licked the tip of his brush and muttered, "Why not just have him stay by your side for a lifetime?"

Luo Binghe shook his head. "Then Shizun would be unhappy."

At the sight of his dejected appearance, like that of a grumbling woman, Shang Qinghua was tongue-tied with shock.

Conversely, Shen Qingqiu was completely calm. "Silly child, you're thinking wild thoughts again. Why would this master be unhappy?"

"How far has your relationship progressed?"

"We've done all the things we should have, and some things we shouldn't," said Shen Qingqiu.

"Why are there things we shouldn't have done?" Luo Binghe asked, hurt. "Does Shizun feel that we shouldn't have...done it?"

"No. If we really shouldn't have done it, this master wouldn't have let you do it."

"Where was your first date?"

"Huan Hua Palace Water Prison," said Luo Binghe.

Shang Qinghua was silent.

Shen Qingqiu was equally silent.

Bing-ge, you call that a date?!

"What was the mood between you at the time?"

"Not very good," said Luo Binghe.

That wasn't something that could be described as merely "not very good"!

"Where do your dates often take place?"

Shen Qingqiu rested his chin on his hand. "The moment I open my eyes, I see him. And when I close my eyes, he's still the one I see in my dreams. Does that mean we're on dates all the time?"

"Does Shizun find it annoying?" Luo Binghe asked cautiously.

Shen Qingqiu rubbed his back. "No. You're just overthinking."

Shang Qinghua thought that dating Bing-ge—no, Bing-mei, sounded really fucking exhausting. It had only been a couple of questions, but Master Shen had already soothed him three times! This glass heart kept shattering and getting glued back together—exactly when would it end?!

Fucking annoying!

Shen Qingqiu is basically a kindergarten teacher who's taking care of a kid!

"Who was the first to confess?"

"Me," said Luo Binghe.

"Of course it was him," said Shen Qingqiu.

"What things does your partner do that make you feel helpless?"

Shen Qingqiu shrugged and said weakly, "Whenever he starts to cry, there's nothing I can do."

"Whenever Shizun gets mad, I'm unable to do anything."

Shang Qinghua hummed in acknowledgment, bouncing his leg. He wrote it down while roasting them in his heart: *They really are exactly like a kindergartner and his teacher!*

"When you're together, what makes your heart race the most?"

"When he pats my head and gives me instructions," Luo Binghe said earnestly.

"Uh, when he tearfully begs me for something," said Shen Qingqiu.

Luo Binghe went on, "And also when he scolds me, and hits me..."

He was acting awfully twitterpated, but Shen Qingqiu was already very used to this.

Shang Qinghua silently added a note beside Luo Binghe's name: *A hopeless masochist. Beyond cure.*

"Have you lied to your partner before? Are you good at lying?"

Right after asking this question, he confidently wrote the words "Big Fat Liar" after Luo Binghe's name.

"Yes," said Luo Binghe. "But never again!"

"Have you fought before? What kind of fights were they?"

Shen Qingqiu sighed. "We fought a lot, and terribly too. Thinking about it now, I don't know why we did. It could all have been avoided."

"Why do you keep asking these kinds of questions?" Luo Binghe asked angrily. "You're making Shizun unhappy for no reason."

Shang Qinghua shrugged. "My bad. How did you make up afterward?"

Shen Qingqiu waved his hand. "We boned to save the world!"

"Is your relationship publicly known or secret?"

"Have you ever heard the *Regret of Chunshan*?" Shen Qingqiu shot back.

The questions after that were on a free fall in terms of degeneracy.

Shang Qinghua cleared his throat. "Are you the top or the bottom?"

Luo Binghe was uncomprehending. "What does that mean?"

While Luo Binghe genuinely didn't understand, Shen Qingqiu pretended not to. He waved his fan. "Who knows what it means? Pass, pass, pass."

"How did you decide that?"

Shen Qingqiu thought for a bit. "I really don't know. Somehow it just happened that way. Probably because he looked pitiful?"

Luo Binghe was perplexed. "I still don't know what he's asking."

Shen Qingqiu patted the top of his head. "It's all right if you don't understand," he said earnestly. "You're not at a disadvantage in any way."

"Where did you have your first time?"

Shen Qingqiu was about to answer when Luo Binghe barged in. "Qing Jing Peak."

"Mai—"

Luo Binghe once again barged in. "Qing Jing Peak, the Bamboo House."

All right, he'll never acknowledge such a failure of a first time, Shen Qingqiu thought. *Let it be Qing Jing Peak. There's nothing worth arguing over; let him answer however he likes. I won't correct him anymore.*

"What were you feeling at that time?"

Shen Qingqiu was silent. If he were to be honest, it came down to three words: pain, pain, and more pain. But saying this in front of others would embarrass Luo Binghe far too much.

Depressed, Luo Binghe said, "Shizun was wonderful. But I was completely useless."

"The morning after your first night, what was the first thing you said?"

"Shizun, breakfast is ready."

"Don't say anything else until you put your clothes on first!"

"How many times do you do it in a month?"

Shen Qingqiu thought this was beyond ridiculous. "Who's bored enough to count something like that? Also, why have the questions been consistently moving in such a strange direction?"

"Roughly speaking, once every three days," Luo Binghe said seriously. "If Shizun is happy, sometimes he'll let me touch him after only two."

Shang Qinghua chewed on the brush shaft, jotting down the records while muttering, "This is unscientific... According to the way I wrote him, even if he did it from the beginning of the month all the way to the end without taking a break, it shouldn't be a problem." Then, "Under normal circumstances, where do you get intimate?"

"He has an obsession with the Bamboo House," said Shen Qingqiu.

Luo Binghe smiled brightly while nodding. "Mm."

"And where do you want to try 【beep—】 the most?

"If we're doing it anyway, what does it matter *where* we do it?" asked Shen Qingqiu.

"Bai Zhan Peak," Luo Binghe said evenly.

The room fell silent.

"The Bai Zhan Peak training grounds," Luo Binghe said calmly.

The fuck?! thought Shen Qingqiu.

Is it your life that you don't care about, or your face?! thought Shang Qinghua. "What sort of agreements do you have about 【beep–】ing?"

"If it hurts, he has to tell me," said Luo Binghe. "He absolutely has to!"

"No crying allowed!" said Shen Qingqiu.

"Say, have you guys misunderstood the implication behind the word 'agreement'?" asked Shang Qinghua.

"'If you can't have a person's heart, then you should at least have their body.' Do you approve or disapprove of this line of thinking?"

"That's a loser's—ahem, a degenerate's take on things," Shen Qingqiu said contemptuously.

"Without the heart, what use is the body?" Luo Binghe asked.

Shang Qinghua thought sadly about how under his pen, Luo Binghe had obviously been a peerless stallion who'd pursued only his desire to [beep–], and the number of women he'd r- [beep–] -ped had definitely been in the double digits...

He'd known that the Luo Binghe in this strange world had turned gay, but exactly how had he fallen, step-by-step, to this point?!

"If your partner was ra—*ahem*—ped by a thug, what would you do?" asked Shang Qinghua.

This question was way too surreal.

Shen Qingqiu was speechless for a long time until he said, "Who would be stupid enough to rape him?"

Even if you were trying to die, at least look for a better-looking way to do it!

Luo Binghe rolled up his sleeves, then said in a leisurely manner, "I'd turn them into human swine and throw them into the Endless Abyss. Then I'd think of some other methods by which to slowly punish and play with them for ten years before finally killing them."

"If a good friend said to you, 'I'm very lonely, so just for tonight, would you...' and asked to be intimate, would you agree?

"I don't have such shameless friends," Luo Binghe said indifferently. "I don't need friends."

Head lowered, Shen Qingqiu scraped at the tea leaves in his cup, then took a sip. "I also don't have such friends."

"Really?" Luo Binghe said doubtfully. "Liu...Liu-shishu wouldn't say that kind of thing?"

Tea sprayed all over the floor.

Shang Qinghua, who'd had his upper body sprayed with tea, had gone to change his clothes and returned, and now continued his questions. "Do you think you're good at sex? What about your partner?"

Shen Qingqiu let out a dry laugh. Luo Binghe looked on the verge of tears.

Shen Qingqiu saw his melancholic expression, miserable beyond words, and pity filled his heart. He turned back toward Shang Qinghua and said angrily, "Isn't it obvious that this is a sensitive topic? Pass!"

Shang Qinghua picked at his ear. "Okay, okay, it's all my bad. Are you interested in S&M?"

"What is that? Shizun, why are there more and more things I don't understand?"

"Oh. He's asking whether you like me hitting and scolding you, or if you would feel anything if I pricked you with a needle or burned you with a flame," said Shen Qingqiu.

Luo Binghe looked a little bashful, then said softly, "As long as it's Shizun, how could this disciple dislike it?"

Shang Qinghua understood. He picked up the pen and with a flourish, wrote: *Luo Binghe has great interest in S&M!*

"What's the most agonizing thing about sex?"

"He's too small," said Luo Binghe.

"He's too big," said Shen Qingqiu.

Shang Qinghua silently swore at this master and disciple, calling them shameless, then wrote with another flourish: *Go figure it out yourselves!*

"Has the bottom ever actively tried to seduce the top?"

Shen Qingqiu pointed at himself. "Me? Do I look like that kind of person?"

"It's hard to say. Because you also looked pretty straight..." Shang Qinghua murmured. "Where do you like being kissed?"

Luo Binghe said, "Forehead, fingers, lips, everywhere."

"Honestly...this child can't kiss," Shen Qingqiu said helplessly. "He only knows how to bite."

"What's the best way to please your partner during 【beep–】?"

"Praise him for improving?" said Shen Qingqiu.

"Not crying," said Luo Binghe.

Shang Qinghua's brush flew like the wind, and he absentmindedly added another line: *Master Shen's standards are* so *low.*

"What do you think about at those times?"

"Who issued this questionnaire?" said Shen Qingqiu. "Do they have any experience at all? At that kind of time your mind is utterly blank. What else can you think about?"

"Do you remove your own clothes, or does your partner help remove them for you?"

"If I let him do it, I wouldn't have many clothes left to wear," Shen Qingqiu said.

"Shizun, how can I control my strength at times like that?" Luo Binghe said defensively.

"How many times in one night?"

"How many times?" Shen Qingqiu asked. "No, I mean, do people really make a point to count that?"

Shang Qinghua turned the page, ready to keep asking—

But Luo Binghe had long since lost his patience and smiled coldly. "If you want to know that much, I'll count today, then tell Shang...-shishu later. That will do."

"The last question! Really, it's the last one! What do you most want to say to your partner?"

Master and disciple glanced at each other.

Shen Qingqiu waved his fan. "We're done here, Binghe. Let's go home and eat."

"Mm, all right," Luo Binghe said obediently.

He wrapped an arm around Shen Qingqiu's shoulder, then kicked open the door and left. A strong wind gusted into the room, blowing over the pile of questionnaire sheets Shang Qinghua had just completed until they had drifted all over the floor. Shang Qinghua's lips twitched uncontrollably. He squatted down and picked up a couple sheets, but after some time, he suddenly fell to his knees.

"Cucumber-bro, you scam artist—that's definitely not 'what you most want to say to your partner'! My quest... Master System, please don't deduct points so quickly! There's only one question that didn't get answered—ahhhhh! Cucumber-bro, you fucker!"

32
Wedding

SHEN QINGQIU WALKED for a few steps, waving his fan, before he discovered that the person who had been clinging so tightly to him this whole time hadn't come along. He turned around to see Luo Binghe standing in place, staring at something in a state of distraction.

Curious, Shen Qingqiu asked, "Binghe? What are you looking at?"

Only at this did Luo Binghe snap out of it. "Shizun, I..."

Shen Qingqiu was even more curious now. He walked back and looked in the same direction Luo Binghe was staring only to see a lively crowd gathered before a moderately sized residence as they surrounded a couple of crimson-clad newlyweds whose faces were obscured. At present, the rowdy gathering was moving into the courtyard.

The street was loud in the first place, so he hadn't noticed that a couple was holding a wedding right in front of them.

Two young maids were standing at the gates, handing out wedding candy from the baskets on their arms to passersby. In crisp voices, they called, "Spreading good fortune! Spreading good fortune!"

Shen Qingqiu's first thought was classic wet blanket. "Has this family been beset by some evil creature or ghost?"

But no matter how he looked, he couldn't find anything strange. Just as he was about to ask, he saw Luo Binghe walk over on his own. The young maids had never seen a handsome man of his caliber, and both were struck dumb as soon as they looked up, forgetting to even hand over their candy. Luo Binghe ended up taking it from their hands himself with serene poise.

After acquiring their wedding candy, Luo Binghe returned to Shen Qingqiu's side, satisfied. "Shizun, let's go."

Shen Qingqiu nodded.

The two of them walked for a while, shoulder to shoulder. Luo Binghe was still playing with those two round wedding candies wrapped in red paper, and he took another look back at that festively decorated residence with its streams of people flowing in and out. He still seemed to be thinking about something.

"Is there something up with that residence?" Shen Qingqiu asked.

Luo Binghe started. "What does Shizun mean by 'something up with it'?"

"If there was nothing up with it, why would you pay it so much attention? You don't even like candy."

A look of understanding came over Luo Binghe's face, and he smiled. "It's nothing; just sharing in the good fortune."

He was so earnest when he spoke that Shen Qingqiu couldn't help but smile. "This master doesn't recall you believing in such things. Have you never seen anyone get married before?"

"It's not that I haven't seen it, I just never imagined that sort of thing could have anything to do with myself."

"You never imagined marrying a girl in the future?"

Luo Binghe shook his head.

Shen Qingqiu felt this was rather unscientific. "Really? Not even a bit?"

No matter how you put it, Luo Binghe—the former Luo Binghe, that was—was the male protagonist of a stallion novel. How could he never have nursed any beautiful hopes of that kind? And, with Airplane Shooting Towards the Sky's shitty tendencies, his "beautiful hopes" would hardly have stopped at marrying a beautiful woman. They would have been more like marrying a three-digit number of beautiful women all at once, at minimum.

Of course, Shen Qingqiu knew the current Luo Binghe wouldn't do such a thing. But how could he never even have thought about it? How could he have thought that marriage had nothing to do with him?

Luo Binghe thought, then said, "I truly never imagined it before."

Shen Qingqiu noticed that *before*. "So you mean to say, you think such things have something to do with you now?" he teased.

Unexpectedly, this time Luo Binghe didn't reply.

After that incident, over the next few nights, Shen Qingqiu didn't know if it was just him, but Luo Binghe seemed to be especially energetic. Meanwhile, his own old waist, hips, and legs were suffering even more than usual.

They returned to Cang Qiong Mountain every two months to "visit the family." Because of this, no one was surprised whenever they showed up again. Instead, they enthusiastically surrounded them while munching on their Dragon-Bone Cantaloupe seeds.

"Eh? Who is this?" Qi Qingqi started. "Isn't this the Qing Jing Peak Lord? You're back again? A rare guest!"

"It is he," said Shen Qingqiu.

"Did you bring any local specialties from the Demon Realm? Aside from that one next to you."

Luo Binghe clearly grew from the Human Realm's soil; he shouldn't count as a demonic specialty either way, should he? Shen Qingqiu thought. "Even if I did, no one would want to eat them, so I didn't bring any."

Suddenly a young man walked over, dangling something in his hand.

Shen Qingqiu called out, "Liu-shidi, long time no see, I—what is this?!"

Liu Qingge expressionlessly caught the feebly gasping thing Shen Qingqiu had thrown back at him and tossed it back. "A short-haired beast," he said. "It's edible."

Shen Qingqiu chucked it at him again. "I'm not eating it! I still have the one you gave me years back—it's grown enormous, and it spends all day gnawing on the bamboo on Qing Jing Peak. I don't want another!"

The two of them tossed the short-haired beast back and forth as it shrieked in midair.

"Shen-shixiong, I think you should just take it," Wei Qingwei cut in. "If one of them is male and the other is female and you put them together, maybe they'll be drawn to each other and won't gnaw on the bamboo anymore."

"But what if they're both males?"

Silence.

In the past, when Liu Qingge walked over, Luo Binghe would have begun to emanate an icy aura and make all sorts of snide remarks, enmity on full display. But today he seemed to be in a bit of a daze, standing by Shen Qingqiu's side and not saying a word. Shen Qingqiu found this rather strange.

Not only did he find it strange, everyone else found it strange too. Whenever the sect siblings from Cang Qiong Mountain got together, the conversation never stopped, and any little remark could get played on forever. But today, their conversation was extremely short. They usually headed off to Zui Xian Peak to have a meal together, but seemingly because of Luo Binghe's strange aura, no one brought up doing so.

Before everyone scattered, Qi Qingqi dragged Shen Qingqiu to the side and asked, "What's up with your disciple?"

"What do you mean what's up?"

"Today, your disciple, hmm... Did you have an argument?"

"We didn't." Shen Qingqiu didn't show anything on his face, but his hand tightened around his fan.

"Oh, then that's good. But I feel like your disciple was so odd today. Like he was holding something in."

Shen Qingqiu felt it too.

When they returned to the Bamboo House, Luo Binghe was still in that strange state.

Shen Qingqiu had just sat down on the bamboo couch when a huge crash came from the doorway. He rushed around the screen only to see Luo Binghe sprawled on the floor, with Ming Fan, Ning Yingying, and the other disciples gaping at him in shock.

Shen Qingqiu went to help Luo Binghe up. "What happened?"

"It's noth—"

Before Luo Binghe could finish speaking, Ming Fan yelled, "Shizun, Luo Binghe tripped over the threshold!"

Shen Qingqiu had no words.

Luo Binghe glared at Ming Fan, and Ming Fan shrank back in fear.

"Be on your way," Shen Qingqiu said hurriedly. "Go prepare for morning reading tomorrow."

As he closed the door, Luo Binghe silently sat down next to the table.

Shen Qingqiu looked at the red spot where his forehead had smashed into the ground and sighed. "What's been up with you these past few days?"

Luo Binghe was still silent.

"Sit, and don't move; this master will get you a hot compress."

He turned to go to the water basin, but just when he had wrung out a strip of cloth, he heard another huge crash behind him. He startled and turned around only to find Luo Binghe sprawled on the floor again.

Confusion written on his face and worried that Luo Binghe was too dizzy to sit or stand, Shen Qingqiu rushed over. "Are you—"

But as soon as he reached him, Luo Binghe grabbed his arm. "Shizun, marry yourself to me, won't you?"

Shen Qingqiu's expression cracked, just a bit.

Having noticed how unusual Shen Qingqiu's expression was, Luo Binghe hurriedly said, "Shizun, if you don't want to marry yourself to me, I could also marry myself to you!"

When Shen Qingqiu didn't reply, Luo Binghe's voice went monotone, and he asked again, "Shizun, are you willing to...to..."—his Adam's apple trembled more and more, and his voice began to quiver as well— "...marry...me?"

Shen Qingqiu still didn't say anything.

Bit by bit, the fire in Luo Binghe's eyes dimmed. After a long time, he said in a hoarse voice, "If Shizun is unwilling, I... I..."

"Slow down," said Shen Qingqiu. "You..." He struggled for a while. "So, these past few days, you were acting so odd because...you wanted to ask me this?"

Luo Binghe stared at him, then carefully nodded twice.

Shen Qingqiu found the next few words difficult to get out of his mouth. "So you're...pro...pro...?"

Luo Binghe helped him finish. "This disciple is...proposing to Shizun."

Shen Qingqiu was speechless. He sat down at the table and buried his face in his right hand. He didn't know what he should say or do.

He should have found it absurd. Even though he and Luo Binghe had confirmed their relationship a long time ago, he had never imagined that Luo Binghe would actually... How should he put it? Propose to him.

Holy shit, he had *proposed* to him. This word was profoundly frightening when applied to a young man like him.

And who knew how many times Luo Binghe had practiced in private just to say these few words? Not to mention how he had been so nervous that he'd been completely strange and abnormal, unable to even talk—he'd tripped over the threshold just trying to walk inside. And he'd even stuttered!

But Shen Qingqiu didn't want to make fun of him at all, nor did he want to play hard to get.

Yup, Shen Qingqiu was terrified to realize that the scariest part was that he was actually—just a little bit—happy.

Luo Binghe was clearly still nervous. His throat bobbed up and down. When Shen Qingqiu removed his face from his hand, he took the chance to say, "Shizun, if you don't want to, you don't need to answer my question! You—if you don't answer, I'll still understand what you mean. Please don't say it out loud; it doesn't matter. If you think it's too much trouble, you can just ignore me. Just pretend I was making a joke, it's fine..."

Shen Qingqiu smacked him across the head with his fan, furious. "It's fine, my ass!"

Having been suddenly smacked by that fan, Luo Binghe touched his head and blinked, clearly not understanding why he had been hit.

This innocent expression made Shen Qingqiu nearly choke on anger. He had just begun to feel happy about it when this brat, in the next moment, said, *It's fine, you don't need to answer—just pretend I was making a joke*!

The last bit in particular sent Shen Qingqiu into a rage, and he lashed out to smack him with his fan again. "Is this anything to joke about?!"

Luo Binghe quietly took the hit and whimpered, "I was wrong..."

"Of course you were wrong! And this master was just about to say *yes*!"

"I—" Luo Binghe was halfway through apologizing when he started. "Shizun," he said carefully, "what was that?"

"Nothing at all," said Shen Qingqiu.

"Shizun!"

Shen Qingqiu sighed. He didn't say anything, but he motioned Luo Binghe to come closer.

As expected, Luo Binghe moved. Given his total familiarity with every movement of Shen Qingqiu's body, the mere sight of Shen Qingqiu motioning at him meant he didn't need a single verbal instruction to understand the intent. He obediently went to pour a cup of wine. Then Shen Qingqiu took the jar and poured himself a cup, after which he motioned Luo Binghe to take the other.

"Shizun, is this...?"

Shen Qingqiu picked up the cup he had poured himself and wound his arm around Luo Binghe's.

Luo Binghe's handsome face immediately began to glow with life.

His hand shook so much that he nearly dropped the cup, and his arm trembled to a frightening degree. With their arms crossed, Shen Qingqiu nearly spilled the wine in his own cup all over his chest.

"I, I, I thought... I thought..." Luo Binghe stammered out.

"You thought you would definitely be rejected, didn't you?" Shen Qingqiu said expressionlessly.

Luo Binghe had no reply to that.

"So you said you didn't want to hear the answer. Because you thought you would definitely be rejected."

A silence. "I was extremely anxious." Luo Binghe looked straight into Shen Qingqiu's eyes. "Shizun, that day, didn't you ask me if I truly hadn't imagined such things before? I really never did."

"You're allowed to imagine," Shen Qingqiu said.

There was nothing wrong with fantasizing. Was fantasizing illegal now? Besides, what about the chance that your fantasies could actually be realized?

"When I was young, I thought that no one could want a person like me," said Luo Binghe. "So I never imagined that anyone would be willing to have me."

"You're far off the mark..."

"Later on," Luo Binghe continued, "I had Shizun. You were clearly already by my side, but even so, I could never overcome my anxiety. I felt that you might leave me at any time. I didn't know what I should do; I wanted to become stronger, and I wanted to become better, but I still felt like it wasn't enough. I still...couldn't stop myself from being afraid."

Shen Qingqiu also looked straight into his eyes. After a while, he stroked Luo Binghe's head and sighed. "Oh, Binghe."

"I still don't know what I should do now."

"Then just do what you want to."

Four hours later, they sat across from each other on the bed, shedding their clothes.

Luo Binghe had been terribly stubborn about certain things. He had instantly pulled out two sets of bridegroom's robes from who knew where, begging and cajoling Shen Qingqiu to put them on and go through the full proceedings again with him, to bow to the heavens and earth, drink the crossed-cup wine, and retreat to the bridal chamber.

Shen Qingqiu found himself thinking: *Even if we put the wedding clothes on, won't we just take them off again later?*

He sort of wanted to laugh, but he let Luo Binghe do as he pleased.

He'd really never thought that Luo Binghe would be the traditional type, constantly dreaming about getting married. At the same time, while it made him want to laugh, he was also overcome with affection, and he began to take it seriously as he too got caught up in the mood.

Luo Binghe's own red clothes were half-off when he started staring at Shen Qingqiu and lost the ability to move.

"Binghe?" asked Shen Qingqiu. "What is it?"

"Shizun, you look really good in red," Luo Binghe said in an earnest tone.

Shen Qingqiu's skin was fair, and the red of the wedding robes cast a rosy tint on his face, adding an eye-catching splash to his usual appearance. And Luo Binghe's gaze as he drank him in was even more besotted than usual.

Shen Qingqiu started, then let out a light cough. Though Luo Binghe always talked like that, he was still rather embarrassed. He said reservedly, "You also look…very good in red."

Very good was barely sufficient to describe the effect. He didn't believe a single girl could look at such a handsome bridegroom and not cry and wail to marry him. He was about to compliment him further when he saw Luo Binghe bring out a sheet of snow-white silk and reverently spread it over the bed.

Shen Qingqiu felt an ominous premonition. "What are you doing?"

Luo Binghe blushed. "This disciple heard that this is the common rule for a newlywed couple's wedding night…"

Before he could finish, Shen Qingqiu felt goosebumps erupt all over his body. Any other rules or traditions were fine, but this tradition was way too strange when applied to him!

"Shizun, this disciple swears he won't really let you bleed!" Luo Binghe said hurriedly, red-faced. "I just wanted to go through every step of the ceremony like a real married couple…"

Shen Qingqiu blushed. "Let's just forget these kinds of superfluous formalities." He was just about to take away the white sheet when he saw Luo Binghe looking at him, on the verge of tears. He could never withstand Luo Binghe looking at him like that, and now he couldn't bear to do away with the sheet. After a long time, he helplessly forced out a few words. "But as you said, even if we lay it out, it won't be of any use…"

Luo Binghe looked hurt as he replied, "But without this essential item and this essential step, how can it count as a wedding night?"

A beat. "Fine, fine, fine. If you insist, just leave it."

Luo Binghe promptly hugged him and buried his head in the crook of Shen Qingqiu's shoulder. "Shizun, you're so good to this disciple."

Shen Qingqiu forced himself to stay calm. "I'm so-so..."

As he spoke, he felt one of the arms around him going in the wrong direction.

Luo Binghe efficiently stripped Shen Qingqiu until not a stitch remained upon him, leaving only the pair of snow-white calf-length socks on his feet.

Even though this master-disciple pair had done it countless times already, for a person like Shen Qingqiu, some matters of pride couldn't be entirely conquered no matter how many times it had been. When he looked at Luo Binghe looming over him, he felt faintly nervous. He tilted his head and closed his eyes, feeling one hand land on the inside of his thigh, trying to spread open his legs. He resisted a bit at first, but soon, he went along with it and spread them.

He felt a finger on his lips as Luo Binghe cajoled him, "Shizun..."

Shen Qingqiu opened his lips a crack, allowing Luo Binghe to put a finger in his mouth. He licked it with a light touch. Because his eyes were still closed, the sensation of that slender finger stirring around in the warm cavity of his mouth, playing with his tongue, was even clearer. One wasn't enough, and soon, a second finger was pushed in. As Luo Binghe took in Shen Qingqiu struggling to take his fingers deeper, wetting them more with his tongue, his eyes sparkled. He pulled them out and reached toward Shen Qingqiu's lower body.

After some ministrations, the tight, pale hole in the valley between Shen Qingqiu's thighs was dripping wet, looking incredibly soft to the touch. Luo Binghe laid himself over Shen Qingqiu, careful not to crush him. Shen Qingqiu felt a hard, hot, round head press against that most secret part of him, and his entrance opened around the front half of the tip of that ferocious member. He could even feel the forceful pumping of its arteries.

"Shizun..." Luo Binghe said in a low voice, "I'm going in."

Shen Qingqiu had kept his eyes closed the whole time, but he nodded slightly. Luo Binghe held his waist with both hands, then plunged forward.

Shen Qingqiu couldn't keep a groan of pain from escaping his throat, and he grabbed the arm Luo Binghe had locked around his waist.

Even if he had made his mental preparations and relaxed himself as much as he could, if it didn't fit, it didn't fit. Luo Binghe's cock wasn't even halfway in before it was caught in place.

The person beneath him was warm and soft within, but that ring of muscle at his entrance refused to cooperate, clamping down and keeping him from going deeper. Luo Binghe spared one hand to stroke up and down Shen Qingqiu's cock. Pleasure trailed through Shen Qingqiu with the attention, and when Luo Binghe felt him relax a little, leaving room to advance, he continued to push forward.

Being split open was extremely uncomfortable. Shen Qingqiu's back arched, unwittingly presenting the two pale bumps on his chest to Luo Binghe's face. Luo Binghe's hand wandered up to rub his nipples.

As a man, Shen Qingqiu didn't really like when someone played with that part of him, as it filled him with a strange feeling of humiliation. He went to push Luo Binghe away with a trembling hand, but then Luo Binghe leaned down, and a strangely wet and swollen sensation came from the right side of his chest. Shen Qingqiu's face flushed so red it practically looked like it could drip blood, and he hurriedly tried to push Luo Binghe's head away. But just as he started to panic and become distracted, Luo Binghe sank down again and buried himself entirely into that place between his legs.

Shen Qingqiu felt as if his entire body had been split in two by a blade of flesh, and pain exploded in his lower body.

The pain spread from Luo Binghe's excessively large cock, bulldozing through his insides as it advanced into his passage, making him feel as if a whole arm had been stuffed inside him. And that large, full head was like the fist on the end of that arm, nearly making him want to pass out on the spot. But as Luo Binghe adeptly brushed past a certain spot inside Shen Qingqiu, his cry of pain changed its tune. Luo Binghe held him by the waist and rammed against that spot. After several more rounds of this, his hole finally softened, along with the tightly clenched muscles of his rear.

As soon as he relaxed, that place on Shen Qingqiu's lower body became awfully sweet. His entrance was long and deep, warm and wet, and it could be plunged into all at once while it was powerless to resist. From Luo Binghe's angle, he could see how Shen Qingqiu looked beneath him just by glancing down. Shen Qingqiu's eyes were closed, brow faintly knitted, expression hovering between unbearable pain and unbearable pleasure. His thighs were spread, his long, smooth, and pencil-straight legs folded up to his chest, and his white socks were still properly snug on his feet.

The sight excited Luo Binghe beyond measure.

Shen Qingqiu's hands were clenched in the sheets, and he took every slam of Luo Binghe's cock inside him with gritted teeth, each one making him fear that his internal organs were getting rammed out of place. But there was nothing he could do but wrap his legs around Luo Binghe's waist and adjust his own rhythm, clenching and relaxing as he took Luo Binghe in and out. The soft flesh around his entrance burned with pain from the friction, and he hissed. "Binghe, gentler..."

He felt he had definitely still ended up bleeding.

Luo Binghe looked down, then froze. Sure enough, a dark red streak trailed down from the point of their joining and seeped onto the snow-white sheet, spreading in a bright patch of color like a fallen peach-blossom petal.

After a long time, Luo Binghe murmured, "Shizun, I'm sorry... I said I wouldn't actually let you bleed, but I still..."

Shen Qingqiu was getting fucked to death and back, and he had absolutely no strength to prop himself up and look at his lower half. Either way, he didn't need to look to know it would be a frightful sight. The worst part was how even as Luo Binghe apologized, the movements of his hips didn't slow in the slightest. His movements were so forceful that Shen Qingqiu slid up and down as his bottom both prickled and ached. "Don't...don't..."

"Don't what?"

"Don't call me Shizun..."

Getting called Shizun at this sort of time, when his ass was blossoming right in front of him, always made him feel like he had been rather too assiduous in his role as a mentor!

"If I can't call you Shizun, then what should I call you?"

Shen Qingqiu sobbed. "Anything you want... Anything... Slow down—*aah*... Binghe, slow down..."

Luo Binghe slid an arm around his waist and gave him another two hard thrusts, took a gasping breath, and said, "Okay, then... Shizun, if you also call me something different, I'll slow down!"

With his waist being lifted, Shen Qingqiu felt that enormous thing plunge even deeper inside him. "Call...you...what?"

Luo Binghe paused in his movements, still holding him, and said, extremely bashful and reserved, "I—it's our wedding night, Shizun. You tell me, what should you be calling me?"

Silence.

Help—me—ah!

Shen Qingqiu shook his head frantically.

Luo Binghe was still waiting in blissful anticipation. "Shizun, that's what I want you to call me, okay?"

To his disappointment, Shen Qingqiu clenched his jaw, refusing to open his mouth even as tears welled in the corners of his eyes.

At the sight of his resistance, Luo Binghe's eyes instantly filled with tears. "Shizun," he said in dismay, "we've already come this far, and you... Why will you still not..."

Luo Binghe sounded extremely distressed. Shen Qingqiu told himself he definitely wouldn't fall for this again. But Luo Binghe's tears were basically some kind of fantastical item that he could summon with a snap, and just like that, they began dripping down.

"Just once," said Luo Binghe. "If Shizun is unwilling, do it just this once. I'll remember, and I won't push you to do it ever again after today—is that still no good?"

Shen Qingqiu's face was showered in Luo Binghe's tears as that thing assaulted his insides, leaving him in practically unspeakable suffering.

When you're like this, how am I supposed to say no?

In the end, Shen Qingqiu decided to concede one more time. But there would definitely, absolutely not be a next one!

With difficulty, he sucked in a breath and struggled to say in a quiet voice, "Husband..."

Luo Binghe's eyes immediately lit up. "Shizun, what did you say?"

Shen Qingqiu repeated, "Hus..." The latter half of the word was as quiet as a mosquito's buzz, furtively swallowed as he switched to pleading. "Binghe, you... Slow down, would you...?"

But how could Luo Binghe let him get away with it just like that? "Shizun, a bit louder, I-I-I didn't hear you clearly!"

In a surge of passion, he got overly excited, and his movements became greater as well. After a few hard thrusts, Shen Qingqiu felt as if his organs were roiling in his stomach, and finally, he fully surrendered.

Shen Qingqiu's hands tugged helplessly at Luo Binghe's hair as he sobbed and cried out. "Husband, husband, I'm begging you, stop—I can't take it anymore... I really can't take it anymore..."

Before he could finish crying, Luo Binghe picked Shen Qingqiu up entirely and made him sit in his lap as he plunged to the deepest spot inside him, one arm under his rear and the other around his waist as he moved him up and down. In bliss, he called out, "Wife..."

Save—me—ah!

As soon as he heard this, Shen Qingqiu's entire body, including his hole, clenched tight in despair. "Holy fuck, shut up! Don't... don't call me things at random!"

But Luo Binghe didn't listen to a single one of his protests. He forced Shen Qingqiu up and down on his cock as he embraced him. "Shizun, you're the best..." he said quietly. "I always wanted you to call me that. Can you do it a few more times?"

A flow of warmth trailed down the back of his neck. Shen Qingqiu didn't need to look to know that Luo Binghe was sobbing again.

Shen Qingqiu truly had no defenses against him whatsoever.

Their limbs were intertwined, both of them sticky with hot sweat. Luo Binghe's waist and back shone with moisture, and Shen Qingqiu nearly couldn't hold on with his legs alone, so he hooked his arms around Luo Binghe's neck to stop himself from sliding down. This drew them even closer, until the space between them was practically nonexistent, and he left a smattering of passionate kisses on Luo Binghe's face in encouragement.

To Luo Binghe, his cooperation was like candy given to a child. His eyes lit up in joy, and his lower body worked with even more force. The solid, ridged, flared head ground back and forth in Shen Qingqiu's well-tormented hole, until he finally surrendered and entirely stopped trying to clench his jaw, letting out a cry of both pain and pleasure.

Luo Binghe loved this sound more than anything. He loved every sound Shen Qingqiu made. Before Shen Qingqiu consciousness faded completely, he still heard Luo Binghe whispering in his ear, "Shizun...call me that again..."

When he woke up the next morning, Shen Qingqiu's first thought was that he wanted to smash himself to death against that extremely well-developed short-haired beast on Qing Jing Peak.

He swore up and down that he'd lost his entire life's worth of face last night. He absolutely couldn't suffer another moment more embarrassing than that!

Luo Binghe lay beside him in high spirits. As soon as he saw that Shen Qingqiu was awake, he swooped in for a kiss. Shen Qingqiu suspected he hadn't slept at all, and that he'd stayed up staring at him the whole night. Pretending to be asleep would be pointless. He wanted to say something, but his throat was so hoarse that he only got out a few slurred sounds.

With that kiss, Luo Binghe seemed to have gotten everything he wanted. "Shizun, get some rest. I'll go make breakfast for you."

He was about to get up and get dressed when Shen Qingqiu mumbled out a few words.

"What is it?" Luo Binghe asked.

Shen Qingqiu's face was already very red, and with Luo Binghe's question, his flush became even more evident. He mumbled, "N-nothing."

Luo Binghe wanted to press him on it, but he controlled himself. "Then I'll go make breakfast."

He carefully covered Shen Qingqiu back up with the blanket, turned, and got off the bed, where he picked up the clothes on the ground and slowly put them on.

Shen Qingqiu sat on the bed, the clothes that Luo Binghe had pulled over him draped over his body, and stared at Luo Binghe's slender and handsome silhouette from behind. He stared at him for a long while, and suddenly, as if he'd been possessed, mumbled, "Husband?"

Luo Binghe's body froze. As if his entire person had been nailed to the spot, he turned around extremely slowly. "Shizun, what did you just call me?"

Shen Qingqiu's tongue tied itself in knots. Eh? He wanted to explain, but there was nothing to explain. "This, this master... Um, I, um, hmm..."

As they said, people shouldn't trigger death flags. He'd *just* said he couldn't embarrass himself any further in this lifetime, and then he'd gone and embarrassed himself more right away!

This time, Luo Binghe hadn't pushed him to the messy brink of passion, nor had his heart been softened by Luo Binghe's tears; there was no excuse. That was to say, he had simply, for some reason, wanted to try calling him that.

But afterward, he was so embarrassed that he practically wanted to dig himself a hole on the spot—or bash himself to death against a chunk of tofu.

In the end, Shen Qingqiu finally gave up on explaining himself and lay back down in defeat. Forcing himself to remain calm, he said, "This master is hungry."

Luo Binghe lay back down with him, smiling. "Shizun, I'm hungry too."

"If you're hungry, then go cook..."

But being a bit late to breakfast once in a while was no big deal.

【 System Update Complete. 】

The Scum Villain's Self-Saving System

- FIN -

英语读者们好！

谢谢你们陪同我一起经历了渣反的世界。希望你们有度过一段美好的时间。

期望能早日再见！

墨香铜臭

Hello, English readers!

Thank you for accompanying me on this journey through the world of *Scum Villain*. I hope you had a wonderful time. I hope we can meet again soon!

–Mo Xiang Tong Xiu

The Scum Villain's Self-Saving System
REN ZHA FANPAI ZIJIU XITONG
Character & Name Guide

Characters

The identity of certain characters may be a spoiler; use this guide with caution on your first read of the novel.

Note on the given name translations: Chinese characters may have many different readings. Each reading here is just one out of several possible readings presented for your reference and should not be considered a definitive translation.

MAIN CHARACTERS

Shen Yuan (Shen Qingqiu)

沈垣 SURNAME SHEN, "WALL"

TITLE: Peerless Cucumber (web handle)

RANK: *Proud Immortal Demon Way*'s Most Supportive Anti

Probably the most dedicated anti-fan of *Proud Immortal Demon Way*, Shen Yuan was baited by its cool monsters and charming protagonist to read millions and millions of words of the hit stallion novel, though he cussed out the author's sellout tendencies the whole way. After his untimely death during a fit of rage over the novel's ending, he was rewarded with a chance to enter the world of the story and fix it his own damn self.

Years after entering the novel and growing into his new life as Shen Qingqiu, he has finally managed to "fix" the novel and save himself, at least as far as the System is concerned. But in a story that's no longer merely a story, things don't just end with a "happily ever after" and a ride into the sunset. Between handling the fragility of a new relationship and all the obstacles that crop up along the way, one thing's for sure: by the time this ends, Shen Qingqiu's dignity will be shattered all over the floor.

Luo Binghe

洛冰河 SURNAME LUO FOR THE LUO RIVER, "ICY RIVER"

TITLE: Bing-mei

RANK: Lovesick, Chuunibyou, and Crybaby Protagonist

SWORD (PRIOR): Zheng Yang (正阳 / "Righteous sun")

SWORD (CURRENT): Xin Mo (心魔 / "Heart demon")

As the protagonist of *Proud Immortal Demon Way*, the original Luo Binghe rose from humble origins to reign as tyrant over the three realms, his innumerable harem at his beck and call. Perhaps betrayal was written into his fate, as even in this story, where the transmigrated Shen Qingqiu gave him three halcyon years of love and acknowledgment, he was still cast into the Endless Abyss by those same beloved hands.

But all that is in the past now. After all was said and done, Luo Binghe's beloved Shen Qingqiu has promised to follow wherever he goes. So everything should be better now...right? Well, as it turns out, years of insecurities and abandonment issues don't go away just like that. Now, however, Luo Binghe is no longer alone, and he has all the time in the world to settle into a new life by Shen Qingqiu's side.

CANG QIONG MOUNTAIN SECT MEMBERS

Shen Qingqiu (Shen Jiu)

沈清秋 SURNAME SHEN, "CLEAR AUTUMN"
沈九 SURNAME SHEN, "NINE"

TITLE: Xiu Ya Sword (修雅 / "Elegant and refined")
RANK: Peak Lord (Qing Jing Peak)

Shen Qingqiu, the refined and elegant peak lord of the peak of scholars, was also the scum villain who seemingly made it his life's mission to make Luo Binghe's life miserable in the original *Proud Immortal Demon Way*.

When the transmigrated Shen Qingqiu's fumbling around filled in some of his backstory, his cruel and resentful actions took on new meaning. But there's a limit to what a third party can uncover post-mortem, so for the first time, the eponymous scum villain himself takes the stage to say his piece.

Discerning eyes may notice that the "qiu" of Shen Qingqiu's name is the same character "qiu" as in Qiu Haitang and Qiu Jianluo's surname.

Yue Qingyuan

岳清源 SURNAME YUE, "CLEAR SOURCE"

TITLE: Xuan Su Sword (玄肃 / "Dark and solemn")
RANK: Sect Leader, Peak Lord (Qiong Ding Peak)

As sect leader of the foremost major cultivation sect, Yue Qingyuan normally lives up to his responsibilities as a levelheaded leader and respected authority. However, when it comes to his shidi and childhood friend Shen Qingqiu, things tend to get messy.

Though the transmigrated Shen Qingqiu managed to dig up quite a few hidden details regarding Yue Qingyuan's character and motivations, some truths remained buried. Only with a proper dive into his past and his troubled relationship with the original Shen Qingqiu can the final missing pieces come together.

Ning Yingying

宁婴婴 SURNAME NING, "INFANT"

RANK: Youngest Female Disciple (Qing Jing Peak)

Luo Binghe's shijie and childhood friend. In the original *Proud Immortal Demon Way*, she was the first maiden to promise herself to Luo Binghe after she helped him confront his inner demons. As the world evolves away from the constraints of the stallion genre, Ning Yingying has grown up into a fine young woman who cares deeply for her peak and her shizun, and she is more than capable of showing some spine in a crisis.

Ming Fan

明帆 SURNAME MING, "SAIL"

RANK: Most Senior Disciple (Qing Jing Peak)

One of Luo Binghe's tormentors in *Proud Immortal Demon Way*, Ming Fan was a loyal lackey and coconspirator to the original Shen Qingqiu. But aside from his worrying habits of antagonizing the protagonist, the transmigrated Shen Qingqiu finds him to be a promising young man who doesn't let his spoiled upbringing interfere with his respect for his master. Ming Fan helps keep the peak running while the actual peak lord is otherwise occupied, and he does his best to live up to his master's teachings.

Liu Qingge

柳清歌 SURNAME LIU, "CLEAR SONG"

RANK: Peak Lord (Bai Zhan Peak)

SWORD: Cheng Luan (乘鸾 / "Soaring phoenix")

Despite being a character who never made an official appearance in *Proud Immortal Demon Way*, Master Liu had a legion of fanboys for his legendarily unparalleled skill in battle. After the transmigrated Shen Qingqiu saved him from a lethal qi deviation, his opinion of his distasteful shixiong took a one-eighty, and he will now go to drastic lengths to fight for his shixiong's honor. What moving camaraderie between good martial brothers, right?

Ji Jue

季珏 SURNAME JI, "JOINED JADES"

RANK: Disciple (Bai Zhan Peak)

One of Liu Qingge's many shidi and Shen Qingqiu's many haters on Bai Zhan Peak. Unfortunately, more often than not, neither of these roles turn out well for him.

Mu Qingfang

木清芳 SURNAME MU, "CLEAR FRAGRANCE"

RANK: Peak Lord (Qian Cao Peak)

A master of the healing arts, who feels a sense of responsibility for the well-being of his sectmates. His skills continue to be instrumental in solving medical dilemmas large and small, though even the most skillful healer has their limits.

Qi Qingqi

齐清萋 SURNAME QI, "CLEAR AND LUSH"

RANK: Peak Lord (Xian Shu Peak)

A woman with a straightforward and fierce temperament; a sectmate with whom the transmigrated Shen Qingqiu gets along well in his new world. Though she won't hesitate to speak her mind, she cares deeply for her sect.

Liu Mingyan

柳溟烟 SURNAME LIU, "DRIZZLING MIST"

RANK: Disciple (Xian Shu Peak)

SWORD: Shui Se (水色 / "Color of water")

The number one true female lead of *Proud Immortal Demon Way* and younger sister of Liu Qingge. Because of her peerless beauty, Liu Mingyan typically wears a veil to hide her face. She never loses her courage and poise as she grows into her own, and as an adult, she has begun to go out on her own adventures of all kinds.

Shang Qinghua

尚清华 SURNAME SHANG, "CLEAR AND SPLENDID"

TITLE: Airplane Shooting Towards the Sky
(web handle, 向天打飞机/ "beating your airplane at the sky")

RANK: Peak Lord (An Ding Peak)

Overworked and underpaid, the Peak Lord of An Ding Peak takes on a thankless job as the head of the sect's "housekeeping" department. Shen Qingqiu's fellow transmigrator may be rather shifty and unreliable, but sometimes a friend from the same "hometown" is just what he needs.

For the first time, the original transmigrator Shang Qinghua gets to tell his own story—becoming Airplane, his reincarnation journey, and beyond—from his own point of view. And while Shang Qinghua's reputation as a hack author may be mostly earned, he would like everyone to know: he has aspirations too!

Wei Qingwei

魏清巍 SURNAME WEI, "CLEAR AND TOWERING"

RANK: Peak Lord (Wan Jian Peak)

A master swordsman and the overseer of Wan Jian Peak, where Cang Qiong Mountain disciples go to find their personal swords. Has a penchant for rather unfunny jokes.

DEMONS

> Many demons go by titles instead of personal names. Titles styled like XX-Jun are for high-ranking demon nobility, and some titles may be hereditary.

Mobei-Jun

漠北君 "DESERTED NORTH," TITLE -JUN

RANK: Demonic Second-Gen

Luo Binghe's eccentric sidekick and scion of the Mobei clan. A proud ice demon turned plot device for Luo Binghe's plot-dictated power-up arc as well as Shang Qinghua's demonic employer. However, there may be more to the origins of his character creation and background than initially meets the eye—and a certain author may well hold the answers.

Linguang-Jun

凛光君 **"FRIGID LIGHT," TITLE -JUN**

Mobei-Jun's paternal uncle. Ever since a certain incident involving Mobei-Jun's mother, Linguang-Jun has nursed a deep-seated grudge against both Mobei-Jun and his father. Bitter and shameless, his most inopportune reappearance could mean major headaches for both his nephew and "Great Master" Airplane.

Meng Mo

梦魔 **"DREAM DEMON"**

RANK: Luo Binghe's Teacher in Demonic Techniques

Once a legendary master of dream manipulation, Meng Mo is now Luo Binghe's underappreciated "Portable Grandfather." Oh, the things a teacher will suffer to pass on his techniques.

Tianlang-Jun

天琅君 **"HEAVEN'S GEMSTONE," TITLE -JUN**

RANK: Saintly Ruler (former)

Luo Binghe's birth father, a heavenly demon. His thirst for revenge finally appeased, at the end of the main story, he was recuperating at Zhao Hua Monastery. However, he too once lived in simpler times as the exalted, carefree, and human-loving pacifist ruler of the Demon Realm, his loyal nephew by his side. All that changed, of course, when he met the love of his life, Luo Binghe's mother Su Xiyan, and all the darkness lurking just behind her...

Zhuzhi-Lang

竹枝郎 **"BAMBOO BRANCH," TITLE -LANG**

RANK: Tianlang-Jun's Trusted Right Hand

Tianlang-Jun's nephew and subordinate, born to heavenly demon and snake demon parents. Though he perished in the final battle of Mai Gu Ridge, he faithfully served his uncle for many years prior. The origins of his profound capacity for devotion lie in the history he shared with Tianlang-Jun, a tale intimately intertwined with that of the doomed love affair of a particular demon lord and a certain cool and calculating cultivator.

Sha Hualing

纱华铃 "GAUZE," "SPLENDID BELL"

RANK: Demon Saintess

A crafty and vicious pure-blooded demon who is eager to earn Luo Binghe's favor. However, her current role as an overworked and underpaid employee seems something of a downgrade from her original counterpart's status as a tyrannical member of Luo Binghe's harem.

Luo Binghe

洛冰河 SURNAME LUO FOR THE LUO RIVER, "ICY RIVER"

TITLE: Bing-ge, Original Flavor

RANK: The Great Protagonist, Saintly Ruler

The great and illustrious protagonist of *Proud Immortal Demon Way* himself, in the flesh. After brutalizing Shen Qingqiu in the dream realm punishment scenario, he finally makes his epic debut in the Scum Villain-ized universe proper, thanks to a mishap with Xin Mo. How will this young man, who holds all of heaven and earth in his hands, react to the curious relationship between the alternate version of himself and his archnemesis, Shen Qingqiu?

OTHER SUPPORTING CHARACTERS

Old Palace Master

RANK: Palace Master (Huan Hua Palace)

The master of Luo Binghe's birth mother. He met a horrific death within the Holy Mausoleum, though thanks to his treachery, his shadow continues to hang over the story.

Su Xiyan

苏夕颜 SURNAME SU, "MOONFLOWER"

RANK: Former Head Disciple (Huan Hua Palace)

Luo Binghe's birth mother. A mysterious woman who was originally slated to succeed the Old Palace Master of Huan Hua Palace, but somehow became involved with Tianlang-Jun. Sometime around Tianlang-Jun's sealing, she was said to have left her sect due to her relations with a demon. Set a newborn Luo Binghe adrift on the Luo River, then shortly after passed away.

Qiu Haitang

秋海棠 SURNAME QIU, "CHINESE FLOWERING APPLE," FULL NAME TRANSLATES TO "BEGONIA"

RANK: Hall Master (some random sect), Young Mistress (Qiu family)

The once pampered daughter of the wealthy Qiu family. Originally the most powerful family within their city, they met their end in a brutal massacre many years ago at the hands of none other than her own fiancé, the original Shen Qingqiu. Despite her unfortunate end in the main story, she and her brother shaped an important period of the original Shen Qingqiu's life and character development.

Qiu Jianluo

秋剪罗 SURNAME QIU, "CUTTING A NET,"
FULL NAME IS AN ANAGRAM OF 剪秋罗, "RAGGED-ROBIN"

RANK: Young Patriarch (Qiu family)

The older brother of Qiu Haitang and the original Shen Qingqiu's childhood owner. Cruel, arrogant, and sadistic, his endless torment of Shen Jiu over the years finally drove the latter to snap and murder him—an incident that escalated into the infamous Qiu Massacre.

Madam Meiyin

魅音 SURNAME WU, "BEWITCHING VOICE"

RANK: Abbot (Zhao Hua Monastery)

A gorgeous, fortune-telling succubus with a fondness for beautiful, fair-faced pretty boys like Liu Qingge and Luo Binghe. Unscrupulous and dogged in matters of love, she was one of Luo Binghe's many partners in the original *Proud Immortal Demon Way*, though she never entered his harem. During a particularly disastrous encounter with Shen Qingqiu, she makes some interesting predictions about his future.

Locations

CANG QIONG MOUNTAIN

Cang Qiong Mountain Sect
苍穹山派 "BLUE HEAVENS" MOUNTAIN SECT

Located in the east, Cang Qiong Mountain Sect is the world's foremost major cultivation sect. The mountain has twelve peaks (branches) with their own specialties and traditions, each run by their own peak lord and united under the leadership of Qiong Ding Peak. The peaks are ranked in a hierarchy, with Qiong Ding Peak being the first peak and Qing Jing Peak being the second. Disciples of lower-ranked peaks call same-generation disciples of higher-ranked peaks Shixiong or Shijie regardless of their actual order of entry into the sect, though seniority within a given peak is still determined by order of entry.

Rainbow Bridges physically connect the peaks to allow easy travel. Disciples are separated into inner ("inside the gate") and outer ("outside the gate") rankings, with inner disciples being higher-ranked members of the sect.

Qiong Ding Peak
穹顶峰 "HEAVEN'S APEX" PEAK

The peak of the sect's leadership; the Peak Lord of Qiong Ding Peak is also the leader of the entire Cang Qiong Mountain Sect.

Qing Jing Peak
清静峰 "CLEAR AND TRANQUIL" PEAK

The peak of scholars, artists, and musicians.

An Ding Peak
安定峰 "STABLE AND SETTLED" PEAK

The peak in charge of sect logistics, including stock transportation and repair of damages.

Bai Zhan Peak
百战峰 "HUNDRED BATTLES" PEAK

The peak of martial artists.

Qian Cao Peak
千草峰 "THOUSAND GRASSES" PEAK

The peak of medicine and healing.

Xian Shu Peak
仙姝峰 "IMMORTAL BEAUTY" PEAK

An all-female peak.

Wan Jian Peak
萬剑峰 "TEN THOUSAND SWORDS" PEAK

The peak of sword masters.

Ku Xing Peak
苦行峰 "ASCETIC PRACTICE" PEAK

The peak of ascetic cultivation.

OTHER CULTIVATION SECTS

Huan Hua Palace

幻花宫 "ILLUSORY FLOWER" PALACE

Located in the south, Huan Hua Palace disciples practice a number of different cultivation schools but specialize in illusions, mazes, and concealment. They are the richest of the sects and provide the most funding to every Immortal Alliance Conference. The Water Prison located beneath their foundations is used to hold the most notorious criminals of the cultivation world before trial.

Tian Yi Temple

天一观 "UNITED WITH HEAVEN" TEMPLE

Located in the central plains, the priests of Tian Yi Temple practice Daoist cultivation.

Zhao Hua Monastery

昭华寺 "BRIGHT AND SPLENDID" MONASTERY

Located in the east, the monks of Zhao Hua Monastery practice Buddhist cultivation.

MISCELLANEOUS LOCATIONS

Bai Lu Forest

白露森林 "WHITE DEW" FOREST

A forest on the edge of Huan Hua Palace's territory where the Sun-Moon Dew Mushroom can be found. Located on Bai Lu Mountain, under which Tianlang-Jun was once sealed.

The Borderlands
边境之地

Areas where the barrier between the Human and Demon Realms is thin and it's possible to pass between them without crossing the Endless Abyss. Because this prompts frequent raids from the more opportunistic members of the demon race, the borderlands are sparsely settled by humans, with only a few garrisons of cultivators remaining as guards.

The Endless Abyss
无间深渊

The boundary between the Human and Demon Realms, the hellish location of Luo Binghe's multi-year training arc before he reemerges as the overpowered protagonist.

The Holy Mausoleum

A restricted area within the Demon Realm where supreme rulers are entombed after their deaths. Filled with traps and treacherous creatures to deter any would-be tomb raiders from making off with the treasures within.

Hua Yue City
花月城 "FLOWER MOON" CITY

A city near Huan Hua Palace, located in a prosperous and densely populated area of the central plains. The city in which Shen Qingqiu self-detonated after escaping Huan Hua Palace's Water Prison.

The Mobei Ice Fortress

冰堡 "ICE FORTRESS"

A forbidding fortress of ice where the Mobei clan's succession ceremony takes place.

Jin Lan City

金兰城 "GOLDEN ORCHID" CITY

Once a prosperous trade center at the intersection of two great rivers, Jin Lan City found itself suffering from a mysterious plague. Its name, "golden orchid," is often used as a metaphor for "sworn brotherhood."

Jue Di Gorge

绝地谷 "HOPELESS LAND" GORGE

A mountainous region with all sorts of treacherous terrain, perfect for adventure.

Mai Gu Ridge

埋骨岭 "BURIED BONE" RIDGE

An ominous mountain ridge within the Demon Realm that houses a complex network of caverns and is shaped menacingly like a skull. Numerous demonic creatures are said to make their home there.

The Underground Palace

地宫

Luo Binghe's home base in the Demon Realm. It contains a replica of Shen Qingqiu's Bamboo House from Qing Jing Peak.

Name Guide

NAMES, HONORIFICS, & TITLES

Courtesy Names

A courtesy name is given to an individual when they come of age. Traditionally, this was at the age of twenty during one's crowning ceremony, but it can also be presented when an elder or teacher deems the recipient worthy. Generally a male-only tradition, there is historical precedent for women adopting a courtesy name after marriage. Courtesy names were a tradition reserved for the upper class.

It was considered disrespectful for one's peers of the same generation to address someone by their birth name, especially in formal or written communication. Use of one's birth name was reserved for only elders, close friends, and spouses.

This practice is no longer used in modern China but is commonly seen in wuxia and xianxia media; as such, many characters have more than one name. Its implementation in novels is irregular and is often treated malleably for the sake of storytelling.

It was a tradition throughout some parts of Chinese history for all children of a family within a certain generation to have given names with the same first or last character. This "generation name" may be taken from a certain poem, with successive generations using successive characters from the poem. In *Scum Villain*, this tradition is used to give the peak lords their courtesy names, so all peak lords of Shen Qingqiu's generation have courtesy names starting with Qing.

Diminutives and Nicknames

XIAO-: A diminutive meaning "little." Always a prefix.

EXAMPLE: Xiao-shimei (the nickname Ming Fan uses for Ning Yingying)

DA-: A prefix meaning "eldest."

EXAMPLE: Da-shixiong (how Ning Yingying addresses Ming Fan)

-ER: A word for "son" or "child." Added to a name, it expresses affection. Similar to calling someone "Little" or "Sonny." Always a suffix.

EXAMPLE: Ling-er (how Sha Hualing refers to herself when she is trying to be cute)

A-: Friendly diminutive. Always a prefix. Usually for monosyllabic names, or one syllable out of a two-syllable name.

EXAMPLE: A-Luo (the nickname Ning Yingying uses for Luo Binghe)

-GE/-GEGE/ -DAGE: A word meaning "big brother." When added as a suffix, it becomes an affectionate address for any older male, with the -gege variant being cutesier and more often used by young girls. Meanwhile, -dage is more often used by men to address someone they revere deeply. As the term implies hierarchy, it always carries a connotation of respect, which can be exploited for sarcasm. Can also be used by itself to refer to one's true older brother.

EXAMPLE: Qi-ge (what a young Shen Jiu calls his childhood friend)

-DI: A word meaning "younger brother." Can achieve a juxtaposition effect with "-ge," though is an affectionate suffix by itself.

EXAMPLE: Hua-di (as Shang Qinghua sarcastically called himself)

-MEIZI: A very informal term for girls and women. Not recommended to use as a suffix in real life.
EXAMPLE: Sha-meizi (how Sha Hualing is known by her fans)

-JIE/-JIEJIE: Older sister or unrelated female friend. Either can be used as a suffix or on its own.

-MEI/-MEIMEI: Younger sister or unrelated female friend. Either can be used as a suffix or on its own.

Formal

-JUN: A suffix meaning "lord."

-XIANSHENG: A respectful suffix with several uses, including for someone with a great deal of expertise in their profession or a teacher.

-LAOSHI: Another respectful suffix, though more modern, used for teachers and instructors.
EXAMPLE: Shen-laoshi (Mo Xiang Tong Xiu's nickname for Shen Qingqiu)

Cultivation and Martial Arts

ZHANGMEN: Leader of a cultivation/martial arts sect.

SHIZUN: Teacher/master. For one's master in one's own sect. Gender neutral. Literal meaning is "honored/venerable master" and is a more respectful address.

SHIFU: Teacher/master. For one's master in one's own sect. Gender neutral. Mostly interchangeable with Shizun.

SHINIANG: The wife of a shifu/shizun.

SHIXIONG: Senior martial brother. For senior male members of one's own sect.

SHIJIE: Senior martial sister. For senior female members of one's own sect.

SHIDI: Junior martial brother. For junior male members of one's own sect.

SHIMEI: Junior martial sister. For junior female members of one's own sect.

SHISHU: The junior martial sibling of one's master. Can be male or female.

SHIBO: The senior martial sibling of one's master. Can be male or female.

SHIZHI: The disciple of one's martial sibling.

Pronunciation Guide

Mandarin Chinese is the official state language of China. It is a tonal language, so correct pronunciation is vital to being understood! As many readers may not be familiar with the use and sound of tonal marks, below is a very simplified guide on the pronunciation of select character names and terms from MXTX's series to help get you started.

More resources are available at **sevenseasdanmei.com**

Series Names

SCUM VILLAIN'S SELF-SAVING SYSTEM (RÉN ZHĀ FǍN PÀI ZÌ JIÙ XÌ TǑNG):
ren jaa faan pie zzh zioh she tone

GRANDMASTER OF DEMONIC CULTIVATION (MÓ DÀO ZǓ SHĪ):
mwuh dow zoo shrr

HEAVEN OFFICIAL'S BLESSING (TIĀN GUĀN CÌ FÚ):
tee-yan gwen tsz fuu

Character Names

SHĚN QĪNGQIŪ: Shhen Ching-cheeoh

LUÒ BĪNGHÉ: Loo-uh Bing-huhh

SHÀNG QĪNGHUÁ: Shung Ching-hoowa

MÒBĚI JŪN: Mo-bay-June

WÈI WÚXIÀN: Way Woo-shee-ahn

LÁN WÀNGJĪ: Lahn Wong-gee

XIÈ LIÁN: Shee-yay Lee-yan

HUĀ CHÉNG: Hoo-wah Cch-yung

XIǍO-: shee-ow
-ER: ahrr
A-: ah
GŌNGZǏ: gong-zzh
DÀOZHǍNG: dow-jon
-JŪN: june
DÌDÌ: dee-dee
GĒGĒ: guh-guh
JIĚJIĚ: gee-ay-gee-ay
MÈIMEI: may-may
-XIÓNG: shong

Terms

DĀNMĚI: dann-may
WǓXIÁ: woo-sheeah
XIĀNXIÁ: sheeyan-sheeah
QÌ: chee

General Consonants & Vowels

X: similar to English sh (**sh**eep)
Q: similar to English ch (**ch**arm)
C: similar to English ts (pan**ts**)
IU: yoh
UO: wuh
ZHI: jrr
CHI: chrr
SHI: shrr
RI: rrr
ZI: zzz
CI: tsz
SI: ssz
U: When u follows a y, j, q, or x, the sound is actually ü, pronounced like eee with your lips rounded like ooo. This applies for yu, yuan, jun, etc.

The Scum Villain's Self-Saving System
REN ZHA FANPAI
ZIJIU XITONG

Glossary

Glossary

While not required reading, this glossary is intended to offer further context to the many concepts and terms utilized throughout this novel and provide a starting point for learning more about the rich Chinese culture from which these stories were written.

China is home to dozens of cultures, and its history spans thousands of years. The provided definitions are not strictly universal across all these cultural groups, and this simplified overview is meant for new readers unfamiliar with the concepts. This glossary should not be considered a definitive source, especially for more complex ideas.

GENRES

Danmei

Danmei (耽美 / "indulgence in beauty") is a Chinese fiction genre focused on romanticized tales of love and attraction between men. It is analogous to the BL (boys' love) genre in Japanese media. The majority of well-known danmei writers are women writing for women, although all genders produce and enjoy the genre.

Wuxia

Wuxia (武侠 / "martial heroes") is one of the oldest Chinese literary genres and consists of tales of noble heroes fighting evil and injustice. It often follows martial artists, monks, or rogues, who live apart from the ruling government, which is often seen as useless or corrupt. These societal outcasts—both voluntary and not—settle disputes among themselves, adhering to their own moral codes over the governing law.

Characters in wuxia focus primarily on human concerns, such as political strife between factions and advancing their own personal sense of justice. True wuxia is low on magical or supernatural elements. To Western moviegoers, a well-known example is *Crouching Tiger, Hidden Dragon*.

Xianxia

Xianxia (仙侠 / "immortal heroes") is a genre related to wuxia that places more emphasis on the supernatural. Its characters often strive to become stronger, with the end goal of extending their life span or achieving immortality.

Xianxia heavily features Daoist themes, while cultivation and the pursuit of immortality are both genre requirements. If these are not the story's central focus, it is not xianxia. *The Scum Villain's Self-Saving System*, *Grandmaster of Demonic Cultivation*, and *Heaven Official's Blessing* are all considered part of both the danmei and xianxia genres.

Webnovels

Webnovels are novels serialized by chapter online, and the websites that host them are considered spaces for indie and amateur writers. Many novels, dramas, comics, and animated shows produced in China are based on popular webnovels.

Examples of popular webnovel websites in China include Jinjiang Literature City (jjwxc.net), Changpei Literature (gongzicp.com), and Qidian Chinese Net (qidian.com). While all of Mo Xiang Tong Xiu's existing works and the majority of best-known danmei are initially published via JJWXC, *Scum Villain*'s series-within-a-series, *Proud Immortal Demon Way*, was said to be published on a "Zhongdian Literature" website, which is likely intended as a parody of Qidian Chinese Net, known for hosting male-targeted novels.

Webnovels have become somewhat infamous for being extremely long as authors will often keep them going for as long as paying subscribers are there. Readers typically purchase these stories chapter-by-chapter, and a certain number of subscribers is often required to allow for monetization. Other factors affecting an author's earnings include word count which can lead to bloated chapters and run-on plots. While not all webnovels suffer from any of these things, it is something commonly expected due to the system within which they're published.

Like all forms of media, very passionate fanbases often arise for webnovels. While the majority of readers are respectful, there is often a more toxic side of the community that is exacerbated by the parasocial relationship that some readers develop with the author as they follow serialized webnovels. Authors will often suffer backlash from these fans for things such as a plot or character decision some don't agree with, events readers find too shocking (often referred to as landmines), writing outside their expected genres or tropes, openly disagreeing with another creator, abruptly pausing or ending a story, posting a chapter late, or even simply posting something on their social media accounts that their fans do not like. Fan toxicity can be a huge problem for web novel authors who are reliant on subscriber support to make a living. This abuse can follow them across platforms, and often the only way to escape it is to stay off public social media altogether, which is a decision often made by the most popular of writers.

In *Scum Villain,* Shen Yuan could be considered one of these toxic fans due to his scathing commentary against the author of *Proud Immortal Demon Way*. However, he did seem to stop at criticism toward the story itself and continued to pay for all the content he consumed, making him a lesser evil.

TERMINOLOGY

ARRAY: Area-of-effect magic circles. Anyone within the array falls under the effect of the array's associated spell(s).

BLOOD MITES: Called blood gu (血蛊) in the original text, these parasitic insectile creatures that Luo Binghe fashions from his own blood are reminiscent of a curse in traditional Chinese witchcraft. According to legend, gu are created by sealing poisonous animals (often insects) inside a container and letting them devour one another. The resulting gu must be ingested by a target, after which the gu can be controlled remotely to harm or kill the host.

BOWING: As is seen in other Asian cultures, standing bows are a traditional greeting and are also used when giving an apology. A deeper bow shows greater respect.

BUDDHISM: The central belief of Buddhism is that life is a cycle of suffering and rebirth, only to be escaped by reaching enlightenment (nirvana). Buddhists believe in karma, that a person's actions will influence their fortune in this life and future lives. The teachings of the Buddha are known as The Middle Way and emphasize a practice that is neither extreme asceticism nor extreme indulgence.

CHINESE CALENDAR: The Chinese calendar uses the *Tian Gan Di Zhi* (Heavenly Stems, Earthly Branches) system, rather than numbers, to mark the years. There are ten heavenly stems (original meanings lost) and twelve earthly branches (associated with the zodiac), each represented by a written character. Each stem and branch is associated with either yin or yang, and one of the elemental properties: wood, earth, fire, metal, and water. The stems and branches are combined in cyclical patterns to create a calendar where every unit of time is associated with certain attributes.

This is what a character is asking for when inquiring for the date/time of birth (生辰八字 / "eight characters of birth date/time"). Analyzing the stem/branch characters and their elemental associations was considered essential information in divination, fortune-telling, matchmaking, and even business deals.

CHRYSANTHEMUM: A flower that is a symbol of health and vitality. In sex scenes, specifically for two men, it's used as symbolism for their backdoor entrance.

CHUUNIBYOU: From Japanese, literally meaning "middle school second-year disease." Describes people who are "edgy" or have delusions of grandeur. Used as a loanword in Chinese.

CLINGING TO THIGHS: Similar to "riding someone's coattails" in English. It implies an element of sucking up to someone, though some characters aren't above literally clinging to another's thighs.

Colors:

WHITE: Death, mourning, purity. Used in funerals for both the deceased and mourners.

BLACK: Represents the Heavens and the dao.

RED: Happiness, good luck. Used for weddings.

YELLOW/GOLD: Wealth and prosperity, and often reserved for the emperor.

BLUE/GREEN (CYAN): Health, prosperity, and harmony.

PURPLE: Divinity and immortality, often associated with nobility.

CONCUBINES: In ancient China, it was common practice for a wealthy man to possess women as concubines in addition to his wife. They were expected to live with him and bear him children. Generally speaking, a greater number of concubines correlated to higher social status, hence a wealthy merchant might have two or three concubines, while an emperor might have tens or even a hundred.

CONFUCIANISM: Confucianism is a philosophy based on the teachings of Confucius. Its influence on all aspects of Chinese culture is incalculable. Confucius placed heavy importance on respect for one's elders and family, a concept broadly known as *xiao* (孝 / "filial piety"). The family structure is used in other contexts to urge similar behaviors, such as respect of a student toward a teacher, or people of a country toward their ruler.

CORES/GOLDEN CORES: The formation of a jindan (金丹 / "golden core") is a key step in any cultivator's journey to immortality. The Golden Core forms within the lower dantian, becoming an internal source of power for the cultivator. Golden Core formation is only accomplished after a great deal of intense training and qi cultivation.

Cultivators can detonate their Golden Core as a last-ditch move to take out a dangerous opponent, but this almost always kills the cultivator. A core's destruction or removal is permanent. In almost all instances, it cannot be re-cultivated. Its destruction also prevents the individual from ever being able to process or cultivate qi normally again.

COUGHING/SPITTING BLOOD: A way to show a character is ill, injured, or upset. Despite the very physical nature of the response, it does not necessarily mean that a character has been wounded; their body could simply be reacting to a very strong emotion. *(See also Seven Apertures/Qiqiao.)*

COURTESY NAMES: In addition to their birth name, an individual may receive a courtesy name when they come of age or on another special occasion. *(See Name Guide for more information.)*

CULTIVATORS/CULTIVATION: Cultivators are practitioners of spirituality and martial artis who seek to gain understanding of the will of the universe while attaining personal strength and extending their life span.

Cultivation is a long process marked by "stages." There are traditionally nine stages, but this is often simplified in fiction. Some common stages are noted below, though exact definitions of each stage may depend on the setting.

- ◇ Qi Condensation/Qi Refining (凝气/练气)
- ◇ Foundation Establishment (筑基)
- ◇ Core Formation/Golden Core (结丹/金丹)
- ◇ Nascent Soul (元婴)
- ◇ Deity Transformation (化神)
- ◇ Great Ascension (大乘)
- ◇ Heavenly Tribulation (渡劫)

CULTIVATION MANUAL: Cultivation manuals and sutras are common plot devices in xianxia/wuxia novels. They provide detailed instructions on a secret or advanced training technique and are sought out by those who wish to advance their cultivation levels.

CURRENCY: The currency system during most dynasties was based on the exchange of silver and gold coinage. Weight was also used to measure denominations of money. An example is "one liang of silver."

CUT-SLEEVE: A term for a gay man. Comes from a tale about an emperor's love for, and relationship with, a male politician. The emperor was called to the morning assembly, but his lover was asleep on his robe. Rather than wake him, the emperor cut off his own sleeve.

DANTIAN: *Dantian* (丹田 / "cinnabar field") refers to three regions in the body where qi is concentrated and refined. The Lower is located three finger widths below and two finger widths behind the navel. This is where a cultivator's golden core would be formed and is where the qi metabolism process begins and progresses upward. The Middle is located at the center of the chest, at level with the heart, while the Upper is located on the forehead, between the eyebrows.

DAOISM: Daoism is the philosophy of the *dao* (道 / "the way"). Following the dao involves coming into harmony with the natural order of the universe, which makes someone a "true human," safe from external harm and who can affect the world without intentional action. Cultivation is a concept based on Daoist superstitions.

DEMONS: A race of immensely powerful and innately supernatural beings. They are almost always aligned with evil.

DISCIPLES: Clan and sect members are known as disciples. Disciples live on sect grounds and have a strict hierarchy based on skill and seniority. They are divided into **Core**, **Inner**, and **Outer**

rankings, with Core being the highest. Higher-ranked disciples get better lodging and other resources.

When formally joining a sect or clan as a disciple or a student, the sect/clan becomes like the disciple's new family: teachers are parents and peers are siblings. Because of this, a betrayal or abandonment of one's sect/clan is considered a deep transgression of Confucian values of filial piety. This is also the origin of many of the honorifics and titles used for martial arts.

DRAGON: Great chimeric beasts who wield power over the weather. Chinese dragons differ from their Western counterparts as they are often benevolent, bestowing blessings and granting luck. They are associated with the Heavens, the Emperor, and yang energy.

DUAL CULTIVATION: A cultivation method done in pairs. It is seen as a means by which both parties can advance their skills or even cure illness or curses by combining their qi. It is often sexual in nature or an outright euphemism for sex.

FACE: *Mianzi* (面子), generally translated as "face", is an important concept in Chinese society. It is a metaphor for a person's reputation and can be extended to further descriptive metaphors. For example, "having face" refers to having a good reputation, and "losing face" refers to having one's reputation hurt. Meanwhile, "giving face" means deferring to someone else to help improve their reputation, while "not wanting face" implies that a person is acting so poorly or shamelessly that they clearly don't care about their reputation at all. "Thin face" refers to someone easily embarrassed or prone to offense at perceived slights. Conversely, "thick face" refers to someone not easily embarrassed and immune to insults.

FENG SHUI: *Feng shui* (風水 / "wind-water") is a Daoist practice centered around the philosophy of achieving spiritual accord between people, objects, and the universe at large. Practitioners usually focus on positioning and orientation, believing this can optimize the flow of qi in their environment. Having good feng shui means being in harmony with the natural order.

THE FIVE ELEMENTS: Also known as the *wuxing* (五行 / "Five Phases"). Rather than Western concepts of elemental magic, Chinese phases are more commonly used to describe the interactions and relationships between things. The phases can both beget and overcome each other.

- ◇ Wood (木 / mu)
- ◇ Fire (火 / huo)
- ◇ Earth (土 / tu)
- ◇ Metal (金 / jin)
- ◇ Water (水 / shui)

FOUNDATION ESTABLISHMENT: An early cultivation stage achieved after collecting a certain amount of qi.

THE FOUR SCHOLARLY ARTS: The four academic and artistic talents required of a scholarly gentleman in ancient China. The Four Scholarly Arts were: Qin (the zither instrument *guqin*), Qi (a strategy game also known as *weiqi* or *go*), Calligraphy, and Painting.

FUDANSHI: A term originating from Japan, *fudanshi* ("rotten men") are the male counterpart to *fujoshi* ("rotten women"). It's used to describe male fans of BL and BL-related media.

GOLDEN FINGER: A protagonist-exclusive overpowered ability or weapon. This can also refer to them being generally OP ("overpowered") and not a specific ability or physical item.

GUANYIN: Also known as a bodhisattva, this is a Buddhist term whose exact definition differs depending on the branch of Buddhism being discussed. Its original Sanskrit translates to "one whose goal is awakening." Depending on the branch of Buddhism, it can refer to (among other things) one who is on the path to becoming a buddha, or to one who has actually achieved enlightenment and has declined entry to nirvana in favor of returning to show others the way.

GUQIN: A seven-stringed zither, played by plucking with the fingers. Sometimes called a qin. It is fairly large and is meant to be laid flat on a surface or on one's lap while playing.

HAND SEALS: Refers to various hand and finger gestures used by cultivators to cast spells, or used while meditating. A cultivator may be able to control their sword remotely with a hand seal.

HUMAN STICK: An ancient Chinese torture and execution method where all four limbs are chopped off. The related "human swine" goes a step further: on top of losing their limbs, the victim has their face and scalp mutilated, is rendered mute and blind, then thrown into a pigsty or chamberpot.

IMMORTALS AND IMMORTALITY: Immortals have transcended mortality through cultivation. They possess long lives, are immune to illness and aging, and have various magical powers. The exact life span of immortals differs from story to story, and in some they only live for three to four hundred years.

IMMORTAL-BINDING ROPES OR CABLES: Ropes, nets, and other restraints enchanted to withstand the power of an immortal or god. They can only be cut by high-powered spiritual items or weapons and often limit the abilities of those trapped by them.

INCENSE TIME: A common way to tell time in ancient China, referring to how long it takes for a single incense stick to burn. Standardized incense sticks were manufactured and calibrated for specific time measurements: a half hour, an hour, a day, etc. These were available to people of all social classes. "One incense time" is roughly thirty minutes.

INEDIA: A common ability that allows an immortal to survive without mortal food or sleep by sustaining themselves on purer forms of energy based on Daoist fasting. Depending on the setting, immortals who have achieved inedia may be unable to tolerate mortal food, or they may be able to choose to eat when desired.

JADE: Jade is a culturally and spiritually important mineral in China. Its durability, beauty, and the ease with which it can be utilized for crafting both decorative and functional pieces alike has made it widely beloved since ancient times. The word might cause Westerners to think of green jade (the mineral jadeite), but Chinese texts are often referring to white jade (the mineral nephrite). This is the color referenced when a person's skin is described as "the color of jade."

JIANGHU: A staple of wuxia, the *jianghu* (江湖 / "rivers and lakes") describes an underground society of martial artists, monks, rogues, and artisans and merchants who settle disputes between themselves per their own moral codes.

JINJIANG: Also known as the "Green Jinjiang" or "Green JJ" due to the color of the site. At time of publication, MXTX's first three novels are serialized here, and it generally hosts content oriented toward female audiences.

KOWTOW: The *kowtow* (叩头 / "knock head") is an act of prostration where one kneels and bows low enough that their forehead touches the ground. A show of deep respect and reverence that can also be used to beg, plead, or show sincerity.

LILY: A flower considered a symbol of long-lasting love, making it a popular flower at weddings.

LOTUS: This flower symbolizes purity of the heart and mind, as lotuses rise untainted from the muddy waters they grow in. It also signifies the holy seat of the Buddha.

MERIDIANS: The means by which qi travels through the body, like a magical bloodstream. Medical and combat techniques that focus on redirecting, manipulating, or halting qi circulation focus on targeting the meridians at specific points on the body, known as acupoints. Techniques that can manipulate or block qi prevent a cultivator from using magical techniques until the qi block is lifted.

MOE: A Japanese term referring to cuteness or vulnerability in a character that evokes a protective feeling from the reader. Originally applied largely to female characters, the term has since seen expanded use.

NASCENT SOUL: A cultivation stage in which cultivators can project their souls outside their bodies and have them travel independently. This can allow them to survive the death of their physical body and advance to a higher state.

NIGHT PEARLS: Night pearls are a variety of rare fluorescent stones. Their fluorescence derives from rare trace elements in igneous rock or crystalized fluorite. A valued gem in China often used in fiction as natural, travel-sized sources of light that don't require fire or qi.

NPC: Shortened for "Non-Player Character". An individual in a game who is not controlled by a player and instead a background character intended to fill out and advance the story.

Numbers

TWO: Two (二 / "er") is considered a good number and is referenced in the common idiom "good things come in pairs." It is common practice to repeat characters in pairs for added effect.

THREE: Three (三 / "san") sounds like sheng (生 / "living") and also like san (散 / "separation").

FOUR: Four (四 / "si") sounds like si (死 / "death"). A very unlucky number.

SEVEN: Seven (七 / "qi") sounds like qi (齊 / "together"), making it a good number for love-related things. However, it also sounds like qi (欺 / "deception").

EIGHT: Eight (八 / "ba") sounds like fa (發 / "prosperity"), causing it to be considered a very lucky number.

NINE: Nine (九 / "jiu") is associated with matters surrounding the Emperor and Heaven, and is as such considered an auspicious number.

MXTX's work has subtle numerical theming around its love interests. In *Grandmaster of Demonic Cultivation*, her second book, Lan Wangji is frequently called Lan-er-gege ("second brother Lan") as a nickname by Wei Wuxian. In her third book, *Heaven Official's Blessing*, Hua Cheng is the third son of his family and gives the name San Lang ("third youth") when Xie Lian asks what to call him.

OTAKU: Anime fandom slang for individuals who are deeply obsessed with a specific niche hobby. Generically it refers to those fixated on anime.

PAPER TALISMANS: Strips of paper with incantations written on them, often done so with cinnabar ink or blood. They can serve as seals or be used as one-time spells. Distinct from talisman charms, which are powerful magical objects capable of subduing or killing monsters.

PEACHES: Peaches are associated with long life and immortality. For this reason, peaches and peach-shaped things are commonly eaten to celebrate birthdays. Peaches are also an ancient symbol of love between men, coming from a story where a duke took a bite from a very sweet peach and gave the rest of it to his lover to enjoy.

PEARLS: Pearls are associated with wisdom and prosperity. They are also connected to dragons; many depictions show them clutching a pearl or chasing after a pearl.

PEONY: Symbolizes wealth and power; was considered the emperor of flowers.

PHOENIX: *Fenghuang* (凤凰 / "phoenix"), a legendary chimeric bird said to only appear in times of peace and to flee when a ruler is corrupt. They are heavily associated with femininity, the Empress, and happy marriages.

PILLS AND ELIXIRS: Magic medicines that can heal wounds, improve cultivation, extend life, etc. In Chinese culture, these things are usually delivered in pill form. These pills are created in special kilns.

PINE TREE: A symbol of evergreen sentiment or everlasting affection.

QI: *Qi* (气) is the energy in all living things. There is both righteous qi and evil or poisonous qi.

Cultivators strive to cultivate qi by absorbing it from the natural world and refining it within themselves to improve their cultivation base. A cultivation base refers to the amount of qi a cultivator possesses or is able to possess. In xianxia, natural locations such as caves, mountains, or other secluded places with beautiful scenery are often rich in qi, and practicing there can allow a cultivator to make rapid progress in their cultivation.

Cultivators and other qi manipulators can utilize their life force in a variety of ways, including imbuing objects with it to transform them into lethal weapons or sending out blasts of energy to do powerful damage. Cultivators also refine their senses beyond normal human levels. For instance, they may cast out their spiritual sense to gain total awareness of everything in a region around them or to feel for potential danger.

QI CIRCULATION: The metabolic cycle of qi in the body, where it flows from the dantian to the meridians and back. This cycle purifies and refines qi, and good circulation is essential to cultivation. In xianxia, qi can be transferred from one person to another through physical contact and can heal someone who is wounded if the donor is trained in the art.

QI DEVIATION: A qi deviation (走火入魔 / "to catch fire and enter demonhood") occurs when one's cultivation base becomes unstable. Common causes include an unstable emotional state and/or strong negative emotions, practicing cultivation methods incorrectly, reckless use of forbidden or high-level arts, or succumbing to the influence of demons and evil spirits. When qi deviation arises from mental or emotional causes, the person is often said to have succumbed to their inner demons or "heart demons" (心魔).

Symptoms of qi deviation in fiction include panic, paranoia, sensory hallucinations, and death, whether by the qi deviation itself causing irreparable damage to the body or as a result of its symptoms such as leaping to one's death to escape a hallucination. Common treatments of qi deviation in fiction include relaxation (voluntary or forced by an external party), massage, meditation, or qi transfer from another individual.

QILIN: A one-horned chimera said to appear extremely rarely. Commonly associated with the birth or death of a great ruler or sage.

REALGAR: An orange-red mineral in crystal form also known as "ruby sulphur" or "ruby of arsenic." In traditional Chinese medicine, realgar is used as an antidote to poison, as well as to repel snakes and insects. Realgar wine—realgar powder mixed with baijiu or yellow wine—is traditionally consumed during the Dragon Boat Festival.

SECOND-GENERATION RICH KID: A child of a wealthy family who grows up with a large inheritance. "Second-generation" in this case refers to them being the younger generation (as opposed to their parents, who are the first generation) rather than immigrant status.

SECT: A cultivation sect is an organization of individuals united by their dedication to the practice of a particular method of cultivation or martial arts. A sect may have a signature style. Sects are led by a single leader, who is supported by senior sect members. They are not necessarily related by blood.

SEVEN APERTURES/QIQIAO: (七窍) The seven facial apertures: the two eyes, nose, mouth, tongue, and two ears. The essential qi of vital organs are said to connect to the seven apertures, and illness in the vital organs may cause symptoms there. People who are ill or seriously injured may be "bleeding from the seven apertures."

SHIDI, SHIXIONG, SHIZUN, ETC.: Chinese titles and terms used to indicate a person's role or rank in relation to the speaker. Because of the robust nature of this naming system, and a lack of nuance in translating many to English, the original titles have been maintained. *(See Name Guide for more information.)*

SPIRIT STONES: Small gems filled with qi that can be exchanged between cultivators as a form of currency. If so desired, the qi can be extracted for an extra energy boost.

STALLION NOVELS: A genre of fiction starring a male protagonist who has a harem full of women who fawn over him. Unlike many wish-fulfilment stories, the protagonist of a stallion novel is not the typical loser archetype and is more of an overpowered power fantasy. This genre is full of fanservice aimed at a heterosexual male audience, often focusing on the acquisition of a large harem over individual romantic plotlines with each wife.

The term itself is a comparison between the protagonist and a single male stud horse in a stable full of broodmares. *Proud Immortal Demon Way* is considered a prime example of a stallion novel.

SWORDS: A cultivator's sword is an important part of their cultivation practice. In many instances, swords are spiritually bound to their owner and may have been bestowed to them by their master, a family member, or obtained through a ritual. Cultivators in fiction are able to use their swords as transportation by standing atop the flat of the blade and riding it as it flies through the air. Skilled cultivators can summon their swords to fly into their hand, command the sword to fight on its own, or release energy attacks from the edge of the blade.

SWORD GLARE: *Jianguang* (剑光 / "sword light"), an energy attack released from a sword's edge.

SWORN BROTHERS/SISTERS/FAMILIES: In China, sworn brotherhood describes a binding social pact made by two or more unrelated individuals of the same gender. It can be entered into for social, political, and/or personal reasons and is not only limited to two participants; it can extend to an entire group. It was most common among men but was not unheard of among women or between people of different genders.

The participants treat members of each other's families as their own and assist them in the ways an extended family would: providing mutual support and aid, support in political alliances, etc.

Sworn siblinghood, where individuals will refer to themselves as brother or sister, is not to be confused with familial relations like blood siblings or adoption. It is sometimes used in Chinese media, particularly danmei, to imply romantic relationships that could otherwise be prone to censorship.

THE SYSTEM: A common trope in transmigration novels is the existence of a System that guides the character and provides them with objectives in exchange for benefits, often under the threat of consequences if they fail. The System may award points for completing objectives, which can then be exchanged for various items or boons. In *Scum Villain*, these are called B-points, originally named after the second sound in the phrase *zhuang bi* (装逼 / "to act badass/to play it cool/to show off").

THE THREE REALMS: Traditionally, the universe is divided into Three Realms: the **Heavenly Realm**, the **Mortal Realm**, and the **Ghost Realm**. The Heavenly Realm refers to the Heavens and Celestial Court, where gods reside and rule, the Mortal Realm refers to the human world, and the Ghost Realm refers to the realm of the dead. In *Scum Villain*, only the Mortal Realm is directly relevant, while the Demon Realm is a separate space where all demons and their ilk reside.

suite with the groom after the ceremony and is only removed by the groom himself. During the ceremony, the couple each cut off a lock of their own hair, then intertwine and tie the two locks together to symbolize their commitment.

WHUMP: Fandom slang for scenarios that result in a character enduring pain—emotional and/or physical—especially if the creator seems to have designed that scenario explicitly for that purpose.

WILLOW TREE: A symbol of lasting affection, friendship, and goodbyes. Also means "urging someone to stay," and "meeting under the willows." Can connote a rendezvous. Willows are synonymous with spring, which is considered the matchmaking season, and is thus synonymous with promiscuity. Willow imagery is also often used to describe lower-class women like singers and prostitutes.

YIN ENERGY AND YANG ENERGY: Yin and yang is a concept in Chinese philosophy that describes the complementary interdependence of opposite/contrary forces. It can be applied to all forms of change and differences. Yang represents the sun, masculinity, and the living, while yin represents the shadows, femininity, and the dead, including spirits and ghosts. In fiction, imbalances between them can do serious harm to the body or act as the driving force for malevolent spirits seeking to replenish themselves of whichever they lack.

ZHONGDIAN LITERATURE: Likely intended as a parody of Qidian Chinese Net, a webnovel site known for hosting male-targeted novels. *(See Genres > Webnovels for more information.)*

狂傲仙魔途